ISLE OF THE DEAD

Alex Connor is also known as Alexandra Connor, and has written a number of historical sagas under this name. She is an artist and lives in the UK.

The illustrations within this book are copies of Titian's paintings, the portrait of Angelico Vespucci the author's own.

Also by Alex Connor

The Rembrandt Secret
Legacy of Blood
Memory of Bones

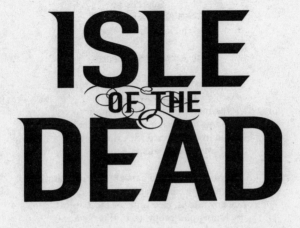

ISLE OF THE DEAD

ALEX CONNOR

10 9 8 7 6 5 4 3 2 1

Typeset by Ellipsis Digital Limited, Glasgow

Printed and bound in Great Britain by

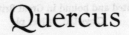

First published in Great Britain in 2013 by

Quercus
55 Baker Street
7th Floor, South Block
London
W1U 8EW

A CIP catalogue record for this book is available
from the British Library.

ISBN 978 0 85738 964 0 (PB)
ISBN 978 0 85738 965 7 (EBOOK)

TITIAN (SELF PORTRAIT)

PIETRO ARETINO (AFTER A PORTRAIT BY TITIAN)

ANGELICO VESPUCCI — THE SKIN HUNTER (IMAGE BY THE AUTHOR)

BOOK ONE

Thirty feet under the first supporting column of Grosvenor Bridge a savage tangle of birds were fighting, shaken on the shifting surface of the Thames, their beaks dipping and jabbing at each other to get closer to the package which had just been dropped there. Over the previous few minutes they had tried to rip open the plastic covering, but when they finally gained access to the insides they flew off, disappointed. Slowly but determinedly the tide finished off the birds' work and tugged aside the wrapping to expose the corner of a painting.

Incongruous under a sulky London sky, the painted face looked up as though surprised to find itself shuffled between the bridge supports; the merchant's vestments lapped by water as the painting headed towards a small launch vehicle. Then, buffeted by another early November wind, it spun on the current and was shunted away. Ten minutes later the portrait washed up on the slimy bank of the Thames where it was spotted by a tourist walking along the Embankment.

It was the first time the portrait of Angelico Vespucci had been seen in public for over four hundred years. As the painting was lifted out of the river, the varnished surface shimmered in the light, the eerie gaze of the sitter unblinking and oddly defiant. No one knew the history of the portrait, or of the man it portrayed.

No one knew that its discovery would result in brutal murder and the identification of a killer who had been active centuries earlier.

Prologue

Venice, 1555

I am afraid of water. Even though I was born with a caul on my head, which the old say is a protection from drowning. No one knows this, for people know little of me. That is my talent – to be invisible. Walking among people as unseen as the monsters under the Lagoon, the grasping weedy fingers lurking under bridges and the echo of drowned men, bleached and bloodless under the sea.

Winter has come quickly to Venice. Too soon, too cold, mists curling about the alleyways and the narrow bridges, figures looming up like ghouls as they go about their day. The atmosphere of the city has changed too. Long, fathomless nights and murky, unwholesome days lure in the city dwellers with the call of the bells from St Mark's. A darkness more profound than anyone can remember comes down on the city after dusk. Lamps struggle to make an impact, and they say more than fifty dogs have drowned, losing their bearings in the blackness.

Not only dogs are dying. Not long ago I saw a woman dragged up from the Lido, laid out for the passers-by to gawp at. She had been in the water a long while, caught up under one of the bridges, and was unrecognisable: her eyes blind opals, her tongue slimy, thick as a sea slug. Her throat was cut, the skin stripped from her torso and limbs.

At first it was thought that the tides had mutilated her, but later it was discovered that she had been flayed. Rumours began to circulate: the killer had been disturbed before he could finish his work, before he could strip the flesh from her face. People talked of a lunatic, come to the city from abroad. Others suggested it had to be someone with wealth and means, a man with room and time to mutilate a corpse. Still others blamed the whores. But everyone asked themselves the same question: where was the victim's skin? Where was the flayed hide?

Venice is waiting, dreading but expecting another victim. The courtesans talk of nothing else and stay away from the piazzas at night, while respectable women visit their priests and burn candles in the dying light.

1

London, the present day

Struggling to hold the package under her arm, Seraphina Morgan scrambled up the muddy bank of the Thames and on to the Embankment beyond. There she sat down, propping up the parcel she had just rescued beside her. She could see at once that the painting was old and that the frame was gilded and valuable, which made her wonder why the picture had found itself dumped, so ignominiously, in the Thames. Pulling back the brown wrapping, Seraphina realised that the picture had only been in the water for a little time. There was no damage – none that she could see anyway.

The afternoon was backing off, the sky glowering as Seraphina remembered the dealer, Gaspare Reni. In the past, Reni had been a showy, theatrical character, an Italian travelling extensively and buying copious amounts of Renaissance art for his private collectors. Once based in Venice, he had settled in London and prospered. But age had slowed him down, and as he entered his seventies the younger,

7

more ruthless dealers had usurped him. Gaspare Reni might still have his famous gallery in Kensington – previously a convent – but the money he had once found so easy to accumulate had all but disappeared and his rich lifestyle had become cramped and narrow.

Still staring at the painting, Seraphina made her decision. Tomorrow she would return to Venice and her American husband, Tom Morgan, but before she left London she would repay a favour. Many years earlier Gaspare Reni had bought some paintings from her parents, his intervention preventing the forced sale of their Venetian home. He had paid over the odds for the works, but later, when the dealer's own luck had stalled, he had refused any help in recompense. And the generosity he had extended so willingly to his friends had remained unpaid.

Until now. Now Seraphina Morgan – previously di Fattori – was hailing a taxi and setting off for Kensington. It was to be an act of kindness.

But instead it would unleash a bloodbath.

2

Huddled in front of the fire, Gaspare Reni held out his hands towards the heat, the room behind him deeply shadowed. A newspaper lay by his feet, and a plate with a half-eaten piece of toast on it. His head, once large and impressive, had shrunk with age, his bull neck as creased as a lace glove. Around the outer corners of his eyes wrinkles spread in semicircles, running towards the hairline like the tributaries of some slow, dun-coloured river.

Beside him sat a man in his thirties.

Nino Bergstrom, Gaspare's surrogate son. A man who had at one time been dangerously ill and, having no family or friends in London, had recovered in the dealer's home and been pressed to stay. A bond had grown between them, the usual roles reversed as the old man cared for his younger companion.

Long widowed, Gaspare had been more than willing to offer a temporary haven to a stricken acquaintance. Trading at the gallery had been slow, due to the recession and Gaspare's age, so his time was often empty, unfilled. Quiet days and perpetual nights had become irksome to the dealer, and it was with no small relief that he welcomed a companion.

'I was thinking about the time I first came here,' he said, turning to Nino. 'I bought the convent off the church – the paperwork! – and then opened it as a gallery. Took me over a year to get it all sorted out, and another six months to get a good enough collection to piss off every other dealer in London. I made a killing in those days – one of the real big hitters. But now . . . I've got old, haven't I?'

Nino glanced at the dealer. Sepia-toned, a Daguerreotype of a man.

'All gristle now,' Gaspare went on, pinching his arm. 'Gristle and bone.'

Nino shrugged. 'Maybe. But I'm the one with the white hair.'

It was true. Due to his illness, Nino's once black hair had lost its colour, and at the age of thirty-eight it was white as a snow goose. The effect was all the more striking against the peppercorn blackness of his eyes and provided a lasting reminder of that terrible time. Now fully restored, he had only to look in the mirror to recall the summer which had changed him. After collapsing on a film set in London, he had found himself under the care of Dr Steven Morrison, the world's foremost authority on neurological diseases. Morrison had lived up to his reputation, but Nino had faced a lengthy and expensive clamber back to health, which had all but obliterated his savings.

The long dry season of illness had turned a careless adventurer into a thoughtful onlooker. No more California for Nino Bergstrom; no more endless travelling. He was changed, shunted out of his old life and unsure of where to go next. It didn't help that he had no family and his closest friends were in California, USA. In London, where he had had the malign fortune to fall ill, Nino Bergstrom had no one.

Except for the old dealer, Gaspare Reni. Hearing of Nino's illness, the Italian had visited him in hospital and offered his home for as long as he needed to convalesce. The gesture had Nino dumbfounded. He had known Gaspare professionally for years, and had grown to like him, but his unconditional support had come as a blessing and a surprise. Too weak to protest, and certainly too frail to take care of himself, Nino had slid behind the protective and shielding walls of the imposing convent gallery. Fed by Gaspare and left to sleep, his recovery limped through the first week, but by the end of the second, Nino Bergstrom had climbed back to life. By the time the month was up, he was restored. Nothing about his build or face gave his illness away; only his hair did that, remaining defiantly white.

'Why don't you put the lights on?'

The old man shrugged. 'Expensive.'

'And the heating?'

'You know why,' he said, exasperated. 'I've told you over and over again. It's expensive.'

'And I've told you – over and over again – to let me pay rent while I'm here.'

'Pah!' Gaspare retorted, waving his hand impatiently. 'I don't want money! I like your company. And I like it dark. It's dramatic.'

'So's falling down a flight of stairs,' Nino replied, getting to his feet and flicking on the light switch.

The room was propelled into sudden view. Looming walls supported their skins of Turkish carpets, and a gaggle of oil paintings towered over the dour Spanish furniture and French commodes. Silverware, stacked piece upon blackened piece, leaned tipsily against blackamoor torchères and vulgar gilded screens. Tooled leather-backed books wheezed under the weight of ormolu clocks and obese cherubs, a suit of Japanese armour attempting a samurai pose by the door.

Looking up, Nino gazed at the painted ceiling, grown more yellow by the day, its caramel-coloured angels hovering above the mouldering room below.

'Christ, Gaspare, why you don't sort this mess out? Let me help you.'

'You're convalescing.'

'I'm fit again,' Nino replied. 'And anyway, I've got to start thinking about going back to work.'

'Too soon!'

Stiffly, the old man turned in his chair. He had liked having Nino around and was more than a little reluctant to let him leave. The refashioned convent, which had been admired and considered impressive in his younger days, was now too big for a single ageing man. The maintenance was a constant bleed to his wallet and gradually room after room had been cordoned off, space reduced as his years increased.

'You don't have to hurry to leave,' Gaspare went on. 'You used to like it here. You hired it more than once—'

'But it wasn't like this then, was it?'

He *had* hired the location for a Los Angeles film company and everyone had enthused about the place and used it several times. But that had been ten years earlier, before the damp had bloomed on some of the paintings, the dust turned sticky on the silver. Now the glamour was tarnished, ravaged by age and lack of funds.

'Why don't you sell up?'

Rising to his feet, Gaspare flicked off the light again, pitching them both back into candlelight.

'Sell it? Who'd buy?'

'Kensington's a prime location. This place could be worth a fortune.'

'Maybe I want to die here. Or maybe I should leave it to you? You're the closest I have to a family.'

He was being deliberately provoking: Nino's affection was not reliant on any inheritance.

'So why don't you sell some of your stuff?'

'*My stuff,*' Gaspare replied crisply, 'is important to me. I know every piece, and what it's worth.'

'Then let me pay the electricity bill—'

'You're broke, Nino. You know that, and I know that. Anyway, what's with all the electricity? I don't need to have the place lit up like a supermarket! I don't need to see it to know it's beautiful.'

Thoughtful, Nino studied the dealer. What he said was true: virtually all of Nino Bergstrom's money *had* gone. Not that he had ever saved that much in the first place. His life in Los Angeles, on the periphery of the movie business, had been well paid and Nino had spent extravagantly, expecting the largesse to continue. Hired to find film locations round the world, he had travelled from Australia to Sri Lanka, London to Tripoli, Hong Kong to Africa. His ease with people, and his skill at spotting unique locations, kept him in constant work. And the money rolled in. So did the parties – and the opportunities.

A brief, unhappy marriage had dented Nino's confidence, but an attractive man working in the film industry was never likely to be lonely for long. The clichés of glamour – sex, top-range cars and clothes bought from Rodeo Drive – became commonplace. It was difficult to appreciate plenty when it was readily available. And in the maelstrom of success prescience was for fools. Just as tomorrow was for the old.

And then Nino collapsed.

He had been scouting in London, on the Isle of Dogs, and a pain had gone off in his head like a car backfiring. Like a pistol shot. Like a window shattered by the impact of an extreme and violent blow. In the nanosecond the sound reverberated in his head Nino had stared ahead, looking for the source of the noise, then felt the muscles of his neck tighten with an involuntary spasm, his forehead engulfed by lacerating heat, his brain punctured and peeled by a dozen nails driven into his skull. His hands flew upwards, trying to protect his head, to hold together the breaking, bleeding mass.

He remembered falling ... but nothing else, until he woke up in hospital and Gaspare Reni was sitting by his bed ...

The memory was interrupted by the sound of the doorbell ringing in the gallery below.

Surprised, Gaspare glanced over at his companion, his expression questioning. They had few visitors in the day, none at night.

'Who the hell's that?' he said, moving over to the intercom, his voice brusque as he spoke. 'Who's there?'

In the street outside, Seraphina paused, momentarily taken aback. 'Mr Reni? It's Seraphina Morgan.' Knowing that her married name would mean nothing to him, she added, 'I used to be Seraphina di Fattori—'

'Di Fattori?'

'You knew my parents in Venice.'

Smiling, Gaspare buzzed her in, moving out into the hallway to greet her. Under the sullen gaze of a low-wattage light she seemed surprisingly young, holding a package tightly in her arms. Unused to the dim candlelight, Seraphina allowed herself to be guided into the sitting room and led over to a round table, Gaspare reluctantly turning on the chandelier suspended above them.

As it blazed into life, Seraphina blinked, laying her package down and turning to the dealer.

'So you remember me?'

He nodded, studying her. 'I do. You were always pretty.'

'You were always charming,' she countered, her Italian accent pronounced. 'My mother used to say you could flatter a saint into an indiscretion.'

'How is she?'

'Older, but well enough ... My father had a stroke. He's making progress, but it's slow.'

'I'm sorry to hear that,' Gaspare said, his tone genuine. 'Give them my regards and tell them I think of them often. And how are you?'

'Married. To an American. I came to London to do some research on gene therapy—'

'A scientist in the family?'

'Not all of us are cultured,' she said in a mocking tone.

Gaspare gestured for Nino to approach. The introduction was light-hearted. 'This is my closest friend, my borrowed son, Nino Bergstrom.' He grimaced. 'Italian mother, Swedish father, hence the name. What can you do? Nino's a location finder—'

'A what?'

'I find locations for movies. Or rather I *used* to.' Uncomfortable, Nino moved the conversation away from himself and gestured to the package on the table. 'What's that?'

'A painting—'

'*A painting?*' Gaspare echoed, curious.

Smiling, Seraphina looked at each of the men in turn. 'Can I take off my coat? It's a bit wet,' she explained, draping it over the back of a chair and glancing at Gaspare. 'You see, I've been splashing about in the river.'

Amused, Gaspare teased her.

'I haven't seen you for years, and that was in Venice. And now you just arrive out of the blue with a picture. A *wet* picture.'

Intrigued, he unwrapped the package and then caught his breath. What he was looking at was notorious – and priceless.

3

Ginza, Tokyo

For years afterwards Jobo Kido would remember the moment when the call came through. Having just lost out at an auction in New York, he had returned home to a disagreeable wife and a problem with the alarm system at his gallery. An unexpected heatwave had added to his discomfort and, exasperated, he had retired to his office and locked the door. When the phone rang he had been tempted to ignore it, but then snatched it up before his secretary could answer.

The man's voice that came over the line was elegant, verging on cultured. For a moment Jobo had thought he was English, then realised that the caller was, in fact, an American with a Boston accent.

'Mr Kido, I have something of interest to tell you.'

The same old line, Jobo thought; always the same few words intended to elicit curiosity and hopefully a sale. Disgruntled, he turned up the air conditioning in the office, his voice impatient.

18

'What are you trying to sell me?'

'I have nothing to sell,' the man replied coolly. 'I'm merely passing on information which I think will be of value to you. Are you still interested in adding to your private pieces?'

Hesitating, Jobo thought about his personal collection. The collection which was not shown in the gallery or at his private abode, but housed in an undisclosed location, several miles away. The pieces in this 'unique' collection had been acquired over the years from many – and disparate – sources, and while their existence was not a secret it was not generally known outside the art world.

It had begun when he was a child, taken by his school on a trip to London. But the Tower of London, Buckingham Palace and even Madame Tussauds had not cast their usual spell and instead Jobo had been fascinated by the exhibits in the Hunterian Museum. His curiosity had been caught by the images collected there. Mementos of cruelty had become mixed in his mind with Japanese legends of the samurai and Ronin. Jobo wasn't interested in torture so much as the depictions of the criminals themselves. Some obsession with their physiognomy captivated him and led to a lifetime fascination with the essence of evil. His question was always the same: could evil be read in a face? It was the same question Shakespeare had asked. The same question phrenologists and reconstructors had pursued for years.

The same unanswered, elusive question.

'Mr Kido, are you still there?'

'Who am I talking to?'

'My name's irrelevant. My information is all that matters,' the man replied. 'Have you heard of Angelico Vespucci?'

The name fired its malignant arrow down the phone line. 'Yes, I've heard of him. He was known as The Skin Hunter.'

'And Titian painted his portrait.'

'He did,' Jobo replied cautiously, 'but the painting went missing soon after it was completed—'

'What if I were to tell you that it's just surfaced . . .'

Jobo could feel his skin prickle with excitement.

'. . . and that the infamous portrait of a killer is now in London?' The man paused to let the information work its magic. 'There will be dealers who won't handle it. The piece has a dark reputation, after all, but it would be a wonderful addition to your personal collection.'

Jobo tried to swallow. 'Do you have it?'

'No, but I know where it is.'

'Is it coming up in a sale?'

'Who knows?'

'London?'

'Maybe.'

'Is it a private seller?' Jobo pressed the man hurriedly. 'Are you working as a broker?'

'All I can tell you is that the portrait of Angelico Vespucci has re-emerged. And if you want it, I would suggest you start putting out some feelers now, before another collector beats you to it.'

Before Jobo Kido could answer, the line went dead.

Light-headed, he put down the phone and slumped into the chair behind his desk. Outside he could see the unnatural blue of the Japanese sky, the hustle of buildings yammering upwards to the risen sun. The painting was in London, the caller had said. *London*, Jobo thought to himself. Was it worth a trip to England? Perhaps not until he knew more. But how could he find out more? The caller had left no contact details; perhaps he wouldn't ring again. Perhaps *another* dealer would get the prize . . . No, Jobo thought, calming himself, the man knew he had a ready buyer in Jobo Kido. Knew he would pay handsomely for the portrait.

An unsettling thought followed. What if the caller had contacted another dealer? Or several other dealers? Perhaps he was trying to drum up interest and, by extension, value? Everyone in the art world knew that competition dictated the price paid. Perhaps the planting of interest in several ears, and several countries, would ensure a more lucrative sale. To his surprise Jobo found himself sweating, even though the air conditioning was turned on full. He felt a morbid sense of anxiety, a panicky fear that he might lose. That something he would prize more than any other man might elude him.

Only five minutes earlier Angelico Vespucci had been little more than a footnote in Jobo Kido's mind. An intangible mirage, a half-remembered story he had heard many years earlier. But now this remarkable, feared work, this image of evil, had re-emerged. Melodramatically, mysteriously.

21

Like a vampire it had come back to life and, like a vampire, it had the capacity to haunt him.

Thoughtful, Jobo unlocked his safe and picked up a creased leather pouch. He gazed at it for a moment and then shook out a key. It was the only one in his possession. There *was* a copy, but that was in his bank, to prevent his wife, son or business colleagues gaining access. Holding the key against his cheek, Jobo thought of his private collection.

Outside, Tokyo might be unreal, greasy with heat, leaves falling from autumnal trees even as the temperature hit ninety degrees. At home, his wife might sulk, and at the gallery the burglar alarm might trip again at dawn – but what did it matter to him? All he could focus on was the thought of the Vespucci portrait.

Found again.

In London.

For now.

Soon in Japan. Soon his.

Smiling to himself, Jobo imagined where he would place the painting in his collection. He had no fear of its reputation. Superstition was only for the gullible. What interested him was not the crimes, but the sitter. He longed to see what The Skin Hunter had really looked like. Yearned to own Titian's magnificent portrait of the man who had murdered and mutilated four women. Ached to study the features of Angelico Vespucci and test them against other, later killers. To see if there was some likeness in evil, some repetition of feature or expression.

Jobo Kido had no fear of Angelico Vespucci. That would come later.

4

Kensington, London

'I found it in the Thames,' Seraphina said, glancing back at the painting. 'Well, not quite found. Actually, it was washed up by the Embankment – and I took it.' She shrugged, looking at Gaspare. 'I suppose it was a terrible thing to do, almost like stealing – but I thought I should bring it to you. After all, you're a dealer. You, of all people, would know what to do with it.' She winked mischievously. 'Besides, it might be valuable and make you a fortune.'

In the burning overhead light the portrait, released from its covering, glowed malignantly, the man's face arresting, his eyes as brilliant and merciless as a water snake's.

'It *is* a Titian,' Gaspare said quietly. 'I know this painting. Or rather, I know *of* it.'

'It is valuable?' Seraphina asked.

'*In*valuable.'

As Gaspare turned to examine the wrapping, Nino stared at the portrait. His left hand moved towards the brass plate

24

underneath and he wiped away the grime, revealing the name *Angelico Vespucci*.

'It says the sitter was Angelico—'

'Vespucci,' Gaspare finished.

Seraphina's eyebrows rose. 'You know who he was?'

'Yes. I'm afraid I do,' Gaspare replied, turning back to her. 'Did you see someone drop the painting in the river?'

'No. As I said, it washed up on the bank.'

'There's no writing on the wrappings,' Gaspare continued irritably, tossing the brown paper aside. 'No name, no address – nothing. So it wasn't sent from anywhere. Or delivered. Which means that it must have been dumped deliberately. And anonymously.' He studied the picture for several minutes, then turned to Nino. 'It's by Titian all right. Even without his signature, you can tell. The brushstroke, the flesh tones, the glazes, and that red colouring in Vespucci's cloak. Magnificent.' He touched the back of the canvas. 'And this painting wasn't in the Thames for long. There's no real, lasting damage, nothing that won't dry out gradually over a few hours ... Someone expected it to be found.'

'*Expected it?*' Seraphina echoed. 'How?'

'They relied on the tide.' Nino turned to her. 'Someone who knows the city and the river would know the ebb and flow of the Thames – that it would soon be washed up.'

'But how could they know *I'd* pick it up?'

'Oh, they didn't know that,' Nino continued. 'But they knew there would be plenty of people about. Tourists, office workers. And if one of those didn't pick it up, there are scavengers

25

along the Thames on the lookout for booty every time the tide goes out. Whoever threw this in the river knew it wouldn't be there for long. The question is, *why* . . .' He glanced over at Gaspare, but the dealer said nothing. 'Why wouldn't they just take it to Bond Street? Or an auction house? It's not complicated – you can just walk in off the street and get a valuation or a sale.' He kept staring at Gaspare. 'You said it was valuable.'

'*In*valuable,' the old man corrected him.

'So a lot of dealers would want it?'

'Some would. Some would do anything to be rid of it.'

Surprised, Nino stared at the dealer. 'I don't understand.'

'During his life, the sitter – Angelico Vespucci – was known as The Skin Hunter.'

Seraphina took in a breath. 'What?'

'It was never proved, but it was believed that he killed his wife. And then three other women in Venice. He murdered them, then flayed them and took their skins. Which were never found.' He shrugged. 'If you're someone with a taste for the macabre – and let's face it, people buy Nazi memorabilia all the time – then you'd want this portrait. It's unique, in its own twisted way. Some people would long to own the likeness of a killer. It's scandalous, sensational, corrupt.' He voice was bitter. 'Who wouldn't want the equivalent of Jack the Ripper on their wall?'

'I'm sorry . . .' Seraphina stammered. ' . . . I should never have brought it here.'

Clicking his tongue, Gaspare touched the back of her hand.

He could feel the coolness of her skin and a faint tremor. 'Are you cold?'

She nodded and the old man reached for a throw and placed it around her shoulders.

'Perhaps,' Seraphina whispered, 'we should get rid of it. After all, who would know? Only the three of us have seen it. If we say nothing, no one else will find out. Perhaps it would be better to throw back into the Thames?'

Taken aback, Nino glanced at her, then looked at Gaspare. He could see that the old man was trying to cover his agitation, but his face had taken on a sickly pallor.

'It's too late, Seraphina. It's been found now. And we can't destroy it.'

'*Why not?*'

'Because it was painted by Titian. One of the world's greatest artists. The painting is famous – infamous. It's been written about, studied through engravings, dreamed about, *feared* for centuries. Despite the character of the sitter I couldn't destroy it – or condone such an action.' Gaspare turned back to the portrait, thinking aloud. 'It was Titian's closest friend, Pietro Aretino, who organised the commission in October 1555. At that time Angelico Vespucci was a wealthy merchant with a beautiful wife, an ambitious man who had made a fortune from trade. With his enormous wealth he could afford to hire Titian.'

'And Titian agreed to do it?'

Gaspare glanced back at Nino, shrugging.

'Why not? When the portrait was begun, Angelico Vespucci

27

was just one more wealthy patron. The painting took months to complete, throughout the bitter Venetian winter of 1555. In November, Vespucci's wife was found murdered, so badly disfigured that she was unrecognisable. He was suspected of being her killer.'

'*Why* would he kill her?' Seraphina interrupted. 'For what reason?'

'She was unfaithful,' Gaspare replied, 'and he couldn't bear it.'

'So why wasn't he punished?'

'Suspicion fell on someone else and Vespucci was allowed to continue with his normal life. He had always been a close friend of Aretino's and his notoriety deepened their bond. Then, over the period of November, December and January, three other women were killed and skinned – all during the time the portrait was being painted.'

Blowing out his cheeks, Nino looked at the old man.

'Three other women killed in the same way? How could they *not* think Vespucci was guilty?'

'Like I say, they had another suspect.'

'Who?'

'I don't know. That's the part of the story no one knows.'

'What about the skins?' Nino pressed him. 'You said Vespucci was called The Skin Hunter, so what did he do with them? Anyone going to enough trouble to flay his victims would have a reason.'

Seraphina's voice was hardly more than a whisper. 'Don't killers keep trophies?'

'Some do. Serial killers anyway ... Perhaps Vespucci held on to the skins. Maybe he would have wanted to enjoy them, relive the killings.' Nino turned back to Gaspare. 'Were the skins ever found?'

The old man shook his head.

'No. If Vespucci kept them, he hid them so carefully they were never discovered ... They say that after the fourth murder he went insane. But he was sane enough to go about his business, and sane enough to escape capture. Sane enough to let another man take the blame. When the portrait was finished it was exhibited in the church where Vespucci had always worshipped. Two days later the church was destroyed by fire, but the painting survived.'

Silent, the three of them stared at the portrait on the table, Seraphina pulling the throw around her body as though to protect herself, Nino's eyes fixed on the unreadable gaze of the sitter. The collection of artefacts and curios which surrounded them seemed suddenly to shrink into insignificance, the caramel cherubs lifting their painted feet higher from the image below. The picture's malevolence curled around the bookshelves, slid under chairs and tables, smeared the flyblown mirrors, and hung its cobweb malice on the chandelier above.

After a pause, Gaspare continued. 'Absurd stories started to circulate. That the portrait could turn bass metal into gold; that it could take a woman's virtue and make men sterile. That a rival could pray to the image to have his competitor die and it would happen. The evil worshipped the portrait; the virtuous feared it. It was said that one woman looked on it and gave birth to a deformed child.'

Shivering, Seraphina moved over to the fire. 'What happened to Angelico Vespucci?'

'He disappeared. Nothing was ever found of him. No body. Nothing . . . The portrait was all that was left of him.'

Fascinated, Nino stared at the painted face: the long nose with its narrow nostrils, the breadth of forehead, the unremarkable mouth. And then he gazed at the eyes: slightly bulbous, watchful, gazing intently into the London room as once they had gazed into Titian's studio.

'So this is a portrait of a serial killer?'

'Yes. The first of its kind,' Gaspare agreed. 'Soon after it was completed, it disappeared. Some people presumed it had been hidden. But no one knew where—'

'Why wasn't it destroyed?' Seraphina interrupted. 'Surely someone should have burnt it?'

'I've told you – it's a masterpiece. The likeness of a monster, immortalised by a genius. No one would destroy that. But maybe they would hide it . . . The connoisseurs and historians only knew of the original through old engravings – Titian had made no copy. And so, gradually, everyone forgot about Vespucci. In time *The Skin Hunter* sank into oblivion and became little more than a myth. Forgotten – even in Venice. Only a few in the art world remembered.'

A moment passed. Nino was the first to speak.

'What are you going to do with it? Sell it?'

'*Sell it?*' Gaspare repeated. 'Yes, I could sell it and make a fortune. I could trade it, pass it on to a dozen collectors. We could – all three of us – become rich. But at what cost?' His tone darkened. 'This portrait is the art world's *Macbeth*. For centuries no one mentioned it, for fear of bad luck. No one talked of Angelico Vespucci, or his victims. No one mentioned *The Skin Hunter*.' He turned his back on the image. 'I can't sell it. I can only hide it. Put it out of harm's way. Make sure it's never seen again . . .' He stared at both of them intently. 'The three of us must make an agreement, here and now, never to speak of this to anyone. Never to mention that the painting has been found.'

'You can't expect—'

At once, Gaspare cut her off. 'Seraphina, go home to Venice and forget everything that's happened here—'

'But—'

'*Listen to me!*' the old man shouted. 'I'm trying to protect you. Both of you.' He turned to Nino. 'What I said to Seraphina applies to you also. Forget you ever saw this portrait. It's dangerous—'

'*Dangerous?*' Nino countered, studying Gaspare Reni. He had never seen the dealer unnerved before. Full of bluster, many times. Overambitious and charming, often. But afraid, never. And he wondered about the story, about how a black rumour could prey on an old man's mind.

'It's just a painting. What can a painting do?'

'I don't know, but I fear it,' Gaspare admitted. 'And I have good reason. You see, it was said that if the portrait of Angelico Vespucci ever emerged, so would the man.'

Venice, 1555

From where I am sitting I can see the painter, Titian, and walking beside him that most bestial of men, Pietro Aretino. He is pompous with his fame, thinks Destiny suckles him. All of Venice reads his work, licentious, vicious and immoral, but clever. He whores with the courtesans and eats until his girth hangs over the tops of his legs, his cloaks cut wide to cover him. And yet the artist loves him. Loves him like a dog with a history of malice, which is fed nonetheless.

They say Aretino attacked his mother and was forced to flee his birthplace. They say he was exiled from Rome for scurrilous libels and sordid writings. They say the Kings of France and England cosset him to quieten his pen. They say Aretino has many women in Venice. And more boys. And still the painter loves him.

Titian is growing a longer beard now, which suits his features. Wealthy, sleek but not cruel, he raises his hand in greeting to someone out of my line of sight. Aretino laughs with the painter then blunders off, his feet flat from the burden they carry, his hair cotton white at the crown.

Aretino does not know me. Would not have noticed me once over the years, though I have watched him avidly. His arrogance would dismiss me out of hand, his ambition would count me worthless. While he parades his talents, I hone mine. For it is a special talent to go unnoticed. An art to pass unseen, to be a watching, listening shadow. A vengeful, unexpected shade.

I have seen the influence Aretino has on the painter. I have watched the genius Titian take this cancer to his breast. He lets the writer speak and plead for him, flatter and cajole his patrons, travel overseas as his ambassador. And – he would have the world believe – Aretino does it all for nothing. In the name of friendship.

I know otherwise . . .

He will never realise how I await the opportunity to strike.

I know his weakness. For all his bombast, he looks to Titian as a cripple to a cross. The painter is his Saviour. His apologist. His ally. His womb of gold, his entrée to the elite, and the one true friend he will come to betray.

But for now Aretino has no premonitions. He has no intimation of his downfall, nor presentiment of doom. He walks likes a man loved and protected and never sees the shadow always one step behind him.

5

Venice

The tour guide was wondering why anyone, even a tourist, would want to visit Venice at the beginning of November. He certainly wouldn't be coming back; he'd stick to working the London tours instead. Fuck Italy . . . Pulling the hood of the plastic raincoat over his head, he felt the seeping damp curling around the boat, the sick bobbing of the tide drubbing his insides. He would, he promised himself, get a brandy as soon as he had finished the last lap of the tour. Not that the passengers on the launch could see that much anyway. The high tide had brought in the sea mist and only brief glimpses of Venetian landmarks flickered intermittently in front of them, like a Victorian light box manned by a drunk.

Lurching over to one side of the launch, the guide righted himself and reached for his microphone again. Swallowing a queasy reflex, he started to talk.

'Ladies and gentlemen, if you look to your right you can see St Mark's.' He peered blankly into the mist and the passengers struggled to see anything. 'Here are the famous lions of St Mark's Square, and the famous . . .'

His lips were moving automatically, going through the drill he had perfected. He could do it in his sleep, he had told his wife; the patter was second nature now, he had said it so often. In fact, he admitted, he could peel off yards of tourist information without engaging his brain at all . . . You should see them lapping it all up, he said to her. Thinking they're cultured . . . Cultured, my arse! They all piled back to the cruise ship quick enough afterwards, hustling their way to the 24-hour bars.

' . . . and if you look in the distance – I'm afraid, ladies and gentlemen, you'll have to take my word for it today – you can see the Lazzaretto Vecchio, the island where they used to put the plague victims. Recently they've dug up over two thousand bodies . . .' A thrill went round the boat. ' . . . About five hundred people a day used to die in Lazzaretto Vecchio. The Venetian chronicler Benedetti wrote, *"Workers collected the dead and threw them in the graves all day . . . Often the dying ones were taken for dead and thrown on the piled corpses."'* The guide paused automatically, to add some extra emphasis. *'"Manotti – literally vultures – were hired sextons who carried the dead from the streets to the massive graves. By night, however, the manotti broke into homes, threatening to haul the healthy to the lazzaretto if their demands were not satisfied."'*

'My God!' someone said in a hushed whisper as the launch made its choppy progress, the guide continuing his patter.

'Of course the Venetian courtesans were famed for their beauty and their learning. Titian – the great painter – immortalised many of them, including Veronica Franco. But although she had been a great beauty and a favourite of the nobility, she died in poverty.'

He paused again. Hell fire, the guide thought, it was getting even colder, and the mist was turning into a fog. He felt a momentary pity for the honeymoon couple on board. Then, watching them giggling, he reckoned that even a swamping fog could hardly put them off their stroke. Oh, what he'd do to be back in London, in bed with his wife. Their honeymoon had been a belter . . .

'Titian's beautiful models were famed for their colouring, hence Titian hair.' He continued, then paused, waited for the nods of agreement, the sharing of a well-known fact. 'But what most people don't know is that at the time it was fashionable for women to wear—'

A sharp knock against the side of the launch made the vessel shudder and the guide grabbed the side of a seat to steady himself.

'Jesus!' a passenger said. 'What the hell was that?'

'Looks like a package or something,' another remarked, as the guide moved over to the side and looked down into the deep water.

Grasping the handrail, he leaned out. What was going on now? he thought irritably. Bloody hell, not trouble with the boat again? . . . The mist was obscuring his view, then – for an instant – it lessened and he strained forward to

36

look deeper into the water. But he could see nothing. No debris, no dead birds, no wreckage and certainly nothing big enough to cause the boat to shudder. Leaning a little further out, he looked again, almost losing his grip as a bulky object suddenly lurched upwards with the current. Shaken, the guide stared, transfixed, as it turned slowly in the murky water just as the mist cleared. Then the woman's body was momentarily illuminated in a spit of sunlight. Her skinned face glowered like a mad angel from the water, her body flayed from the neck down.

Seraphina Morgan – once Seraphina di Fattori – had been killed only a hundred yards from the apartment she had shared with her husband. She had died within the echo of the bells from St Mark's, and within sight of Angelico Vespucci's old home.

6

Grand Central Library, New York

Between Lexington and Third Avenue stands the New York Grand Central Library, as doughty and solid as a battleship. Through its corridors, stairways, reading rooms and storage, thousands of students, reluctant school kids, lecturers and professors have passed. Some have returned; others remember the building as they would school: to be avoided at all costs. But for many the New York Grand Central Library is comforting and endlessly fascinating, the lure of the books a sop to the hustle of the world outside, the pages a balm to the troubled mind.

Seated on his own at one of the smaller tables was Reginald Oscar Theodore Jones, known to all in the art world as Triumph Jones. The sobriquet would suggest a man of some hubris, in keeping with his ridiculously victorious reputation, but the keeper of the nickname was, in fact, a reserved, middle-aged, six-foot-tall African–American. Slender as a reed, bald as a sheet of glass, his face lean and intelligent,

Triumph Jones was, at that moment, hunkered over the book he was studying intently. The loud crashing of a library cart against one of the nearby tables did not force an irritated look or a curt remark. His whole attention was fixed on the page to the extent that he jumped when touched lightly on the shoulder.

'I guessed you'd be here,' the woman said, ignoring Triumph as he put his finger to his lips in the universal sign for silence. Sliding into the seat beside him, she dropped her voice to a whisper. 'I suppose you've heard?'

'About what?' His voice was slow, suggesting a certain sluggishness of thought. Many a dealer had been caught out, taking him for a fool. Although they only ever did so once.

'You know what I mean – the Vespucci painting.'

Leaning back in his seat, Triumph studied the woman sitting next to him: Farina Ahmadi, wife of the reclusive Abdul Alim, a retired millionaire based in Turkey. Alim's acquisition of a collection of Italian Renaissance art had been sudden, purchased greedily over the last ten years by his ultra-competitive and striking wife. Having borne her husband two sons, Farina had then turned her restless mind to business, and her Louboutins had clicked their way through the galleries and auction rooms of London, New York, Tokyo, Sydney and Paris. Still in her thirties, her energy, ruthlessness, taste and money had made her a formidable opponent, and her acolytes made sure that Farina Ahmadi was the first to hear about anything that could increase the Alim Collection.

39

'So?' she asked, her dark eyes holding Triumph's gaze. '*Have* you heard about the Vespucci painting?'

He took a long moment to consider the question, then shook his head. 'No.'

'*No?* Is that it?' she asked, dropping her voice again. Her impatience amused him. 'Don't you want to know what's going on?'

'I'll hear in time.'

Her expression hardened. 'Speaking of time, maybe I'm wasting mine,' she snapped, pulling the book he was reading towards her. Curious, she read the title. '*Hieronymus Bosch and the Power of Religion.*' She looked back at him. 'Is there a Bosch up for sale?'

'I was just reading.'

'You don't just read, Triumph, you research,' she said firmly, crossing her legs and smiling.

Farina knew the power of her smile; it had a contagious quality to it. People couldn't help smiling back and that always made haggling harder. For them, at least. When she had first come on to the art scene she too had been fooled by Triumph's demeanour, but time had made her canny and she now admired the elongated, elegant man who was watching her with a look of practised composure.

'I know you're dying to hear, so I'll tell you. The notorious portrait of Angelico Vespucci was found in London two days ago. It was in the River Thames.' She paused, but Triumph said nothing. 'Gaspare Reni has it . . .'

Nodding, he let her continue.

' . . . *Gaspare Reni!* Of all people,' Farina went on. 'I mean, he's just not in the top league any more. He's a busted flush, too old, and with no contacts—'

'Yet he has the painting.'

She leaned towards Triumph, one hand brushing his arm. 'I rang him, of course. But he denied having it.'

Sighing, Triumph turned back to his book. Farina slammed it shut in front of him. '*For God's sake, it's the Titian portrait!*'

'I know who painted Angelico Vespucci,' Triumph replied, reopening the book and regaining his place, 'but that painting disappeared long ago. It was destroyed – it must have been, or it would have come on to the market before.' His voice slowed. 'And why – if it's genuine – would it turn up in London? Did you say in the River . . . ?'

'*Thames.*'

'So it's ruined?'

'No!' she snapped, then dropped her voice and moved closer to Triumph. 'It was only in the water for a short time before it was spotted and taken to Gaspare Reni—'

'And how d'you know this?'

Farina smiled. 'I know everything that goes on in the art world, Triumph.'

'Everything?'

She couldn't tell if he was teasing her or mocking her. 'Implying that you know more?' Her hand gripped the sleeve of his two-thousand-dollar suit. 'Triumph, we both want this painting.'

'It's bad luck—'

'It's Titian,' she snorted. 'I want it for my husband. The copy was all well and good—'

He cut her off. 'You have a copy of the Vespucci portrait?'

'Yes, a good one. I commissioned it a couple of years ago from some painter on their uppers. They copied it from old engravings.' She changed tack. 'But if I could get the original for Abdul, that would be incredible.'

Expressionless, Triumph studied her. It was rumoured that she had made a pact with her husband, Abdul Alim. He liked privacy, she liked to socialise. He liked family, she liked to live like a single woman. And so, in return for her having given him two sturdy sons, they had come to an agreement. The father would support and raise the children, leaving the mother free to bolster the Alim Art Collection.

'Does your husband know that the painting's turned up?'

'No!' she said hurriedly. 'And I don't want him to. I just want to get it for him and see his face when I take it home. It would do wonders for the collection. Kick a few people in the crotch. It's infamous. Imagine the publicity—'

'Farina,' Triumph said evenly, 'why are you telling me about this? You know I'll beat you if I go after it. So why confide? It's foolish.' He looked back at his book. 'The painting must be a fake.'

'It's genuine!'

'Have you seen it?' Triumph asked, turning over a page and staring at a coloured illustration.

42

'I'm flying to London tonight to try and get a look at it,' Farina replied.

She couldn't understand why Triumph was being so cool. Did he already know about the Titian? God forbid he had already got to Gaspare Reni. Or worse, did Triumph know that the painting was a *fake*? Was he reeling her into a set-up?

'Are you the only dealer who knows about it?'

She nodded. 'Apart from you, I think so.'

'What about Jobo Kido?'

Farina's eyebrows rose. She had already worked out that the Japanese dealer would want the painting. She might long to place it in the Alim Collection, but by rights the portrait of a murderer would suit Kido more. His fascination with killers was legendary. Hadn't he recently bought a painting by the notorious Japanese cannibal Issei Sagawa – a picture few dealers would touch, let alone buy?

'I don't know if Kido's heard about the Titian,' Farina said at last. 'But he'll want it, I know that much.'

Triumph looked up from his book.

'If I remember correctly, Titian painted Angelico Vespucci over a period when four women were murdered and skinned.'

'Yes, yes!' Farina said impatiently. 'I know – he was called The Skin Hunter.'

'As I said before, the painting's bad luck—'

'Only to the dealers who don't manage to get it,' she replied smartly. 'There's no bad luck in business. You just have to see an opportunity and grab it. This painting's

43

notorious. Think of the number of people who'd pay to see it, to revel in *The Skin Hunter* out of ghoulish curiosity. Besides, I don't believe that paintings have any power of their own.' Smiling, she folded her arms. 'For God's sake, Triumph, this is the twenty-first century. They might have believed all kinds of superstitious crap in Titian's time, but not now.'

'Maybe.'

'Does its reputation put you off?'

'No.'

'I thought not,' she said crisply. 'Well, I want it too. But I can't get it without your help.'

Calmly, he smiled. 'Why would I help a rival?'

'You know Gaspare Reni; you used to deal with him. The Italian's old school, and he'll talk to you.'

'Ah, but maybe he won't want to sell the picture.'

'He's struggling,' she replied, leaning forward in her seat. 'He's old and he's got that great albatross of a gallery hanging round his neck. It must cost a fortune just to keep it open. Trust me, Gaspare Reni will sell – but not to me. We had a run-in a long time ago, and he won't let anything come to the Alim Collection if he can help it.'

'I *could* help you,' Triumph said after a prolonged pause, knowing that by assisting her he would be publicising the find and upping its value, 'but then we'd be competing for the same painting – which means you'd lose.'

'You can't win every time,' Farina challenged him. 'No one wins *every* time.'

44

7

Sunnyvale Rest Home, London

Finishing her shift, Sally Egan pulled a coat over her uniform and left by the back exit. Her door keys were in her pocket, her handbag slung over her left shoulder. She was thinking, with some pleasure, of the man she had slept with the previous week, Eddie Gilmore. They had been a bit drunk, but he had still managed to perform pretty well and afterwards he hadn't hustled her either. Instead he'd made her a sandwich and together they'd pulled the duvet around them and watched a DVD. For the first time in years she had felt comfortable and treasured. At nine they had made love again, with real affection, but at nine thirty Sally's alarm had gone off and, reluctantly, she had dressed and headed home.

She hadn't heard from him since.

Briskly pushing open the gate, Sally hurried up to the semi-detached house and opened the door. Immediately a woman came down the stairs, dressed in a nurse's uniform.

'Your dad's asleep.'

'How's he been?' Sally asked, taking off her coat and moving into the kitchen to put the kettle on. The woman followed her.

'A bit het up this afternoon. Asking for your mother, but he calmed down later.'

Pulling out a chair, Jean sat down. For the previous three years she had acted as a part-time carer for Sally's father, who was approaching the last stages of Alzheimer's. At times she wondered how Sally coped with her full-time job at the care home *and* a senile father. How did an attractive, intelligent woman in her thirties take to being an incessant carer? Didn't she ever get sick of emptying bedpans and listening to interminable stories from the past and long to escape? Weren't there moments of complete despair as she walked from the care home across the green to the semi where her father was fading, hour by hour?

A couple of times over the years Sally had confided that she had wanted to go to art school. She'd been talented, she said – top of her class. But her mother's early death and her father's already erratic behaviour had prevented her from leaving home, and the need for a proper wage had shattered any illusions of pursuing a painting career. So instead of studying Michelangelo, she had started work in a nearby care home for the elderly, shelving Rodin for Radio 4 and incontinence pads.

If there was any bitterness, Sally never showed it. And if Jean had been told about her being a bit the worse for wear in the local pub, who the hell could blame her? Even the rumours about Sally sleeping around she had shrugged off. You had to find comfort somewhere, Jean had told her husband, and that poor cow's got precious little else going in her life.

'So he's asleep now?' Sally asked, passing Jean a mug of tea. 'Maybe he'll sleep through.'

'You should get someone in at night—'

'Yeah, right!' Sally laughed. 'And how do I pay them? I can just about cover your wages.'

'You need more help.'

Shrugging, Sally sat down. 'You know something? I was talking to one of the residents at the home and she said that when she was forty she'd had her first child. Forty.' Sally gazed across the kitchen. 'I mean, that was old then, but she did it. And it made me think that I could still have a shot at it . . . That's if I ever meet anyone.'

'You're good-looking—'

'That's bugger all to do with it. It's not attracting men, it's getting to keep the right one,' Sally replied, changing the subject. 'Anyway, I was looking at Dad yesterday and he looked pretty good. You know, not so thin. Maybe he's putting on a bit of weight?'

'I don't think so, love.'

'Nah, maybe not. I'm just imagining things. I know he can't get better, I'm not kidding myself. I know he's dying.' She sipped her tea. 'I just wonder sometimes how long. I mean, I love him . . .'

47

'I know that.'

'. . . but I wonder how long it'll go on. Because you see, I don't have him. Not my father. I've got someone else who looks like my father. And I don't know who he is, and sometimes, at night, I think about it and wonder if I owe *this* man. You know what I mean? If my father doesn't know me, do I have to know *him*?' She shook her head. 'I know I do! I know I have to look after my father for as long as it takes. But I can't help thinking that every time he deteriorates, a bit of me does too, and I don't want to be dried out at forty.'

Hurriedly standing, Sally moved over to the washing machine and piled in some dirty clothes. With the light on in the kitchen and the blinds open, she could see her reflection in the window and the image of Jean behind her, and wondered about Eddie Gilmore. About whether he would ever ring.

It never occurred to her that as she studied her reflection in the window someone was also looking in at *her*. Someone who had watched her laughing, getting drunk, larking about in the pub. Someone who had seen her kissing Eddie Gilmore. Someone who had been about when she left home at seven in the early morning darkness. The same someone who had followed her home across the green that night.

That night, and every other night, for the past three days.

8

Gaspare Reni sat at the table, gazing out into the walled garden of his house. What had served him as an extraordinary home and gallery for over forty years had once been a convent for a silent order of nuns. In among the gloss and activity of the Royal Borough of Kensington and Chelsea, it had served as a reflective nucleus of a changing world. Wars, the deaths of monarchs and the scandals of empire had passed beyond its gates, while nuns in meditative silence made pleas to Heaven.

Minutes earlier Gaspare had received a phone call from the Countess di Fattori, telling him of the murder of her daughter, Seraphina. He had flinched at the words, thinking of the last sight he had had of her, walking out into the London street, her hand raised, illuminated in the lamplight. Her coat had dried by the time she had left. And she wasn't carrying any parcel. Not any more. She had left the painting with Gaspare.

He had thought that would be enough to save her. He had been wrong.

And now, here was her mother, an old friend of his, trying to make sense out of the insensible. 'Her body was—'

She spoke quickly, almost as though she thought he could catch her distress.

'—the skin was taken off her.'

No! thought Gaspare, taking in a breath. No.

'They skinned her.'

No.

'I don't know why . . .' The woman, the mother, paused. Her words came from another place inside her. Raw from the heart. 'When you saw her, was Seraphina worried about anything?'

What do I say? Gaspare wondered. Confess? Tell an old friend, a grieving mother, that her child had found a painting which had indirectly killed her? How could he tell her that? What difference would it make? Seraphina would still be dead, still in a Venetian morgue with the water lapping at the city's wooden supports underneath her. And even if he told her mother about the Titian, how would he explain? Talk to her of rumours, old stories long buried? Or maybe he should tell her of The Skin Hunter. Maybe comfort her with the memory of a man who had once terrorised Venice.

'Seraphina said she had visited you in London,' her mother continued. 'I know she enjoyed herself but she was glad to be home, glad to be back with her husband . . . I wondered if there was anything you had to tell me? Tell any of us? Is there anything, Gaspare?'

He said no.

Negative.

Nothing to tell.

He said no because there was nothing else he could say that would help or give any comfort. But when Gaspare had put down the phone, severed the frail, terrible connection to Venice, he stared out of the window at the walled garden and thought of the portrait he had hidden in the rafters, high above his head. Looking upwards, his gaze scanned the painted ceiling, his pulse quickening.

... It was said that if the portrait of Angelico Vespucci ever emerged, so would the man.

Hadn't he said those words? Repeated the old belief? Not knowing if he truly believed the superstition, but wary enough to accept the possibility? He had had two people to consider. Two young people. One of whom was now dead. Closing his eyes, Gaspare fought grief. If only Seraphina hadn't seen the painting, hadn't picked it up, hadn't brought it to him. If only she had been looking the other way, or the tide had been going out, not coming in.

'Gaspare?' He turned to see Nino approach. 'What is it?'

'Seraphina's dead.'

Shaken, Nino moved over to the old man and touched his shoulder. He had only met Seraphina once, but he had liked her. 'A car accident?'

'No.'

'So what happened?'

Gaspare turned slowly in his seat. Above his head the portrait was propped up against one of the roof's rafters, a blanket thrown over the canvas to protect – and cover – it.

51

'She was murdered—'

Nino stared at him. 'What?'

'They found her in the Lido   '

Nino could see from the old man's face that there was more to it. 'How did she die?'

'I suppose they'll have more details when the pathologist has examined her—'

'But you know, don't you? Tell me.'

'She was found murdered. Her body was flayed . . .' Gaspare said, turning away. 'I should have stopped her leaving. I should have done something.'

'How could you have known what would happen?'

'Because I knew *something* would!' Gaspare snapped. 'I knew as soon as I saw that painting of Angelico Vespucci. For centuries people believed that if the painting re-emerged, he would too.'

'That's nonsense!' Nino said shortly. 'Dead men don't resurrect themselves. It was a story, Gaspare, nothing but a story—'

'Yet Seraphina found the portrait and now she's dead.'

'But Vespucci didn't do it! Gaspare, someone killed Seraphina, but not someone – or something – supernatural. It's not possible . . . You know that, don't you?' He paused, wary. 'Where's the painting now?'

'I don't know.'

'Yes, you do,' Nino replied, looking around him. 'You could have hidden that bloody thing in this place and no one would find it for years.'

'I dumped it,' Gaspare said, the lie smooth.

'Where?'

'In a skip. On Kensington High Street,' Gaspare replied. 'I dumped it the night Seraphina came here. When I looked this morning, the skip had gone.'

'I don't believe you. You'd never have got rid of that Titian.' He poured two whiskies, passing one to Gaspare and then sitting down. 'Go on, drink it, then we'll talk about what we're going to do.'

Obediently, the dealer sipped his drink. His panic had subsided; in the face of Nino's logic the idea of Vespucci's resurrection seemed ridiculous. But then again, Seraphina *had* found the picture. And now she was dead.

'*Why* would someone kill her?' he asked Nino.

'A robbery gone bad?'

'Maybe ... But why was she killed like *that*?' Gaspare countered, finally glancing back at him. 'And why now, when the portrait's re-emerged?'

'Coincidence?'

'That she might have been followed from London and murdered in Venice after she had found a portrait of a man who had killed in exactly the same way?' Gaspare clicked his tongue. 'Coincidence, no. No, I don't believe it.'

'What else could it be?'

'I don't know,' Gaspare admitted. 'Maybe Seraphina told someone she'd found the portrait.'

'You told her not to.'

'She was a woman and women talk – they can't help it sometimes,' Gaspare said, taking another drink of the whisky.

'Seraphina had gone home to Venice. It would have been hard to put the story out of her mind in the city where Vespucci had once lived. Could *you* keep it a secret? I doubt she could. Seraphina's parents are cultured; it would have been fascinating for them. Perhaps she couldn't resist confiding ...' He paused, shaking his head, remembering the phone conversation. 'No, her mother knew nothing. She was asking me what *I* knew.'

'What about Seraphina's husband?' Nino queried. 'Wives talk to their husbands. She could have easily told him. Asked him to keep it a secret, but then he slipped up.'

'Maybe.'

'What does he do for a living?'

'I don't know.'

'She said he was American. Perhaps he talked about the portrait to a dealer back home and the dealer confronted Seraphina about it?'

'No, not a dealer,' Gaspare replied thoughtfully. 'A runner more like. There are hundreds of small-time crooks in the art world, all hustling each other and scrabbling after the latest rumour or find. They live off the scraps dealers throw them for tips or information. Italy, in particular, has a massive trade in art crime. Paintings change hands or are stolen to order and then exported all over the world. Only recently a member of the mob confessed that the famous Caravaggio in Palermo was taken by the Mafia in the seventies.'

'So someone *could* have challenged Seraphina – but she wouldn't tell them anything. Wouldn't admit to finding the portrait. Or tell them where it was.'

'And they killed her?'

'Maybe that part was an accident.'

'So why do that to her body?'

Nino finished his drink and shrugged. 'You're the art dealer, I'm just guessing. But if this was a film, what better way to bring the painting to the forefront of everyone's imagination than by copying the murder method of the infamous sitter?'

'What?'

'You've often said that to raise the interest and value of a picture you need publicity–'

'Not murder.'

'It wouldn't work for you or me, but for some it would. You said yourself, people collect sick stuff. And this portrait is a Titian. It could be that the murder was an accident and the killer made use of the Vespucci legend to reignite the story.'

Nino could see Gaspare shift in his seat, and pressed him. 'You still have it, don't you?'

'I–'

'Don't bother denying it, Gaspare, but think about it. Perhaps having the portrait puts *you* in danger.'

'I'm an old man. Why should I care what happens to me?'

'*I* care. I care about Seraphina too. She didn't deserve to die.' Nino paused, thinking. 'You should back off. You're too old. I need your brain – the brawn I can supply.'

Puzzled, the dealer stared at him. 'What the hell are you talking about?'

'I know about the painting *and* Vespucci – probably as much as anyone else does now. I speak three languages, including Italian. I've been all over the world, travel comes easy, and people talk to me. Let me try to find out what happened.'

Immediately, Gaspare put up his hands.

'Let the police handle it—'

'I'm not going to interfere with the Italian police. I just want to ask around a bit.'

'You've been seriously ill—'

'I'm fit now,' Nino persisted.

'It's dangerous.'

'Is it? Maybe so, maybe not. There might be no connection between Seraphina's death and the portrait. But if there is, we need to find out what.'

'Leave it to the experts—'

'*There are no experts in this!* It's about Seraphina, her death, a painting and Angelico Vespucci.' He put down his glass, turning to the dealer. 'I'm fit again and I need to work. You won't let me pay for my keep – or repay you for what you've done for me – so let me repay you this way.' He pulled his chair closer to the old man. 'I'm a quick learner, you know that. I'm used to dealing with people and I don't scare easily. That picture came *here*. You can't undo that. It came to you – and now Seraphina's dead. I want to know why.' He held the dealer's gaze. 'Tell me you don't want the same.'

Venice, 1555

There was a rumour that the plague was returning to Venice, but this time we were spared, the merchants and the rich leaving their palaces and strutting about the piazzas like cockerels spared the knife. There is a fashion here for the men: at night the cloth covering their genitals is transparent, and some hang bells and tie ribbons on their appendages.

Meanwhile the industrious Titian is working on his latest portrait: a sitter known to Aretino, as licentious a man as any in Venice. Angelico Vespucci. When the contract was first signed Vespucci was respected, known to the Church, a giver of alms, a man loved by his servants for his kindness. They say he was gentle. They say he was generous. They say he loved his wife as no man had ever loved a woman before. Such was the noble merchant Aretino brought to the studio of Titian. Such was the sitter whose likeness was drawn out in red chalk.

The plague never came to Venice. Some other sickness came in its stead. On the night of November 11th the corpse I had seen

57

dragged from the Lido was finally identified as Larissa Vespucci. When the news spilt over the city Venice talked of little else. And while her lover fled to Rome, she was buried in the Vespucci crypt on the Island of St Michael. Skinned like a fish, like a rabbit, a dog, like vermin. Skinned, relieved of the beauty she had over-used.

The following week I watched the loathsome Aretino passing by St Mark's. This time he was walking with Angelico Vespucci.

Everyone suspects Vespucci of the murder of his wife. Everyone talks of it. But Vespucci is a wealthy man with clever friends. He slides into his pew on a Sunday at the Basilica di Santa Maria Gloriosa dei Frari, and clasps his hands together, looking upwards to the painting of the Assumption of the Virgin, his bulbous eyes catching the glance of no other.

Every week Vespucci slides himself and his wavering reputation to the studio of Titian. I have seen him enter, and wondered what the artist thinks of this sitter. Wondered if, as he draws in the line of brow or slant of cheek, he suspects that he is painting the likeness of a killer.

9

New York

Knowing that most of the important dealers would attend the auction in New York, it wasn't a complete surprise when Farina spotted Jobo Kido in the lounge at the Four Seasons. Assuming her famous smile, she moved over to him, Jobo leaping to his feet and nodding as she approached.

'Jobo! Lovely to see you.'

'And you, Farina. I expect I will see many familiar faces at the auction,' he replied, ushering her to a seat next to his. 'Would you like some tea? Or a drink perhaps?'

She shook her head, eager to dispense with the pleasantries and get down to business. Important as the upcoming sale was, there was little of interest to Jobo Kido. So perhaps his trip to the USA had been for another reason? Perhaps he hoped that being among his peers he might hear the latest gossip? From the instant Farina had heard of the Titian she had suspected Jobo knew of it. It was too macabre, too peculiar to his taste, to pass unnoticed by the dealer. Jobo had many connections in London – surely one of them would have told him about the notorious find?

'I was expecting to see you in New York,' she said blithely. 'Although it's not a great sale. Not the kind of pieces you usually go for.'

'Maybe it's time to expand my interests.'

'Or catch up?'

His eyes were steady. 'On what, Farina?'

'Any rumours, gossip.'

'About what?'

She waved her hand around in the air. 'Anything. Nothing. Who knows?'

You do, Jobo thought to himself. You've heard about the Titian, and you're trying to pump me for information. His gaze rested for an instant on the table in front of them, then he looked back to her.

'I think you're having a little game with me, Farina.'

'Never,' she replied, smiling enigmatically.

'So you've heard nothing of interest lately?'

'About what?'

'A painting?'

'I didn't think it would be about a second-hand Ford, Jobo,' she replied smartly. 'Why don't you ask me straight out?'

'Ask you what?'

'What you want to know!' she snapped impatiently.

He was too wily to be caught out. 'I really don't know what you're talking about.'

'Fine,' she replied, rising to her feet. 'Good to see you again, Jobo. No doubt we'll bump into each other at the auction.'

No doubt we will, Jobo Kido thought, watching as she moved across the hotel lobby. His instincts told him what she wouldn't – Farina Ahmadi knew about the Titian. Which meant that she would want it for her husband, using her money as a grappling hook to haul Angelico Vespucci to a new home in Turkey.

The hell she was, Jobo thought. If anyone was going to get the Titian, he was.

Leaning back in his seat, the dealer scanned the foyer, nodding to several people he knew and ordering some tea. From such a vantage point he could see who was arriving and should – by the end of the afternoon – know who was in New York for the sale. Of course there were easier, more discreet ways to find out, but Jobo wanted to be seen. Wanted everyone to know that he was in town. And in the running.

What he didn't realise was that he too was being watched. By a tall African-American who was – at that moment – talking to Gaspare Reni on his mobile.

'How are you?' Triumph asked pleasantly. 'Keeping well, I hope?'

Across the Atlantic Gaspare grimaced. So Triumph Jones was going to be the first, was he? And how many more dealers would be calling him in the days to come? How many people who had ignored him for a decade would suddenly remember his phone number? Gaspare had hoped that no one would have heard about the Titian. Had *prayed* it would stay a secret, hidden in his gallery's eaves. But as soon as Gaspare heard from Triumph he knew the news was out.

'I keep busy,' Gaspare replied, answering the American's question. 'And you?'

'Very busy. Look, Gaspare, I won't lie to you – I've a reason for making this call.' He tone was all lazy indifference. 'I've heard about a painting. The Titian portrait of Angelico Vespucci.'

'What about it?'

'I heard that it's in your possession.'

Some thought Gaspare Reni was past his best. In many ways, he was. Slower, certainly. Not as ruthless, as energetic as he had once been. But Gaspare had lost nothing of his basic cunning. And that, allied to the news of Seraphina's murder, made him wily.

'I admit I *had* the picture—'

'*Had it?*' Triumph echoed. 'You don't have it any more?'

Pausing, Gaspare pretended to be confused. 'It was ... it has a terrible reputation ... I was ...oh, maybe I acted without thinking.'

'What are you talking about?'

'I destroyed it.'

There was silence on the phone connection from London to New York. A thumping, disabling silence as Triumph took a moment to rally.

'I don't believe you,' he said at last. 'Gaspare, old friend, you don't need to lie to me. We can keep all this between ourselves. I certainly don't want anyone else to know about the Titian—'

'That painting was evil.'

The voice was slow. Soothing. 'It's a picture, nothing more. Remember Shakespeare? *It is the eye of childhood that fears a painted devil* ... It's just a portrait—'

'Of a killer.'

Calmly, Triumph glanced down from the mezzanine into the foyer below, where Jobo Kido was sipping his tea.

'Gaspare, I know you. And I know that you couldn't destroy a masterpiece.'

'You don't know me at all, Triumph. We've bumped into each other over the years, competed for lots, but you were climbing to the top when I was winding down. You know nothing of me. We had no shared friends, nor interests. If you hadn't wanted to know about this bloody portrait I'd never have heard from you. So don't insult me, don't treat me like an old fool.' His tone was contemptuous. 'When I tell you I got rid of that painting, I'm telling you the truth. *I destroyed it.*'

'But why would you?' the American asked, his usual composure wavering. '*How could you?*'

'Have you heard about Seraphina Morgan?'

'Who?'

'She used to be Seraphina di Fattori. She was a daughter of a customer of mine, a friend. It was Seraphina who found the Titian and brought it to me.'

63

'Where did she find it?'

'You don't know?'

'How would I know?' Triumph countered. 'I was only told that you had the work, nothing else.'

'She found it washed up by the Thames,' Gaspare continued. 'She brought the Titian to me and then returned to Venice. Where she was murdered two days ago.'

There was a long, uncomfortable silence between the men, Triumph so shocked that it took him a while to recover.

'*Murdered?*'

'Yes. In exactly the same way Angelico Vespucci killed his victims centuries ago.' Gaspare paused, exasperated. 'And you're asking me why I destroyed that painting? It would have been madness to keep it—'

'But what's the connection between a sixteenth-century portrait and Seraphina di Fattori's death?'

'That's what I'd like to know,' Gaspare replied curtly. 'Look, it's pointless talking any more. It's over. I destroyed the painting—'

'You can't have!'

'But I did.'

'*How* did you destroy it?'

'I burnt it. In the furnace in the basement.' The old dealer had rehearsed his speech repeatedly, until it was wholly convincing. 'I watched it until there was nothing left but ash. *There is no portrait of Angelico Vespucci.* Titian painted one, that's true, but it no longer exists. And thank God for it.'

10

'He's lying! He must be!' Farina snapped, walking into Triumph's gallery and marching into his office. Slamming the door behind her, she carried on. 'I tell you, the old bastard's lying!'

'I don't think so,' Triumph replied, gazing out of the window into the New York street twenty-seven floors below. 'I think he was telling the truth—'

'For a clever man, you can be fucking stupid!' she hissed. 'What better way to put all the dealers off the scent than by saying the Titian no longer exists?'

'It wasn't just the painting,' Triumph replied, his tone slow, measured. 'Apparently there was a murder after it was found—'

'So what?

He looked back at her. 'It was the daughter of an old friend of Gaspare Reni's—'

'Again, so what?'

'She was killed in exactly the same way as Angelico

Vespucci killed his victims,' Triumph replied. 'What if there's a connection?'

'What the hell are you talking about?' Farina demanded, surprised.

Triumph Jones, successful and sleek as a water vole, sounded unusually subdued, pausing between words. 'It's such a coincidence.'

'That a girl was killed in Venice?'

'She was skinned.'

'Skinned, fried, diced, roasted on a spit – so what? The portrait's all I care about, not some girl.' Farina leaned towards Triumph, dismissing his unease. 'Gaspare Reni is lying. He still has that portrait – I can feel it, I know it. We have to get it off him.'

The American wasn't listening to her, just repeating a name to himself. '*Di Fattori . . . di Fattori . . .*'

'What?'

Rising to his feet, Triumph walked over to a row of book-shelves. Taking a moment to scan the titles, he finally pulled down a battered, unbound volume. Carefully turning the pages, he began to read:

Angelico Vespucci, known as The Skin Hunter, was believed to have murdered his wife, and then killed and flayed three other female victims.

He paused, turning over several pages before he began to read aloud again.

One of the victims of The Skin Hunter was the Contessa di Fattori.

'I knew that name was familiar to me,' he said, closing the book. 'What if the murdered girl was related to the Contessa?'

Farina was exasperated. 'What has this to do with anything?'

He slammed the book down on his desk and leaned towards her.

'Doesn't it seem – even to you, my dear – something of a coincidence that the painting turns up, and then the descendant of one of the sitter's victims gets killed?' Triumph regained his seat behind the desk, pointing to the volume. 'You see that? It's over four hundred years old. Vespucci was notorious in his time, but virtually everything written about him disappeared, just as he did. It was pure chance that I came across that book in Berlin.'

'So?'

'It's one of the few references to Vespucci that still exists.'

She shrugged, irritated. 'I'm not following.'

'Doesn't it seem a little strange that everyone apparently forgot about such a notorious killer?'

'Maybe, maybe not.'

'That everyone was so afraid of the Vespucci legend that they tried to wipe him from history?'

She shrugged again. 'I'm not interested in coincidences, spooky goings-on, or any of that fucking rubbish. So Vespucci was a murderer – so what? Maybe his wife deserved to get skinned. God knows she wouldn't be the only one to get fleeced in this business.' Her expression was callous as she rose to her feet. 'I want the portrait for my husband and I know Gaspare Reni still has it. You give up on it if you want to, Triumph, but I'm not convinced. That painting's out there – and I'm going to get it.'

11

Venice

As good as his word, Nino left London, making for Venice, the place of Seraphina's murder and the home of Angelico Vespucci. Gaspare had prepared the way for him, but when Nino visited the di Fattori home, he found Seraphina's parents remote. It wasn't just the shock of their daughter's murder, but the details of her death that had felled them.

Subdued, Nino Bergstrom left their home and moved out into the murky November afternoon. It seemed as though he carried their grief with him, the echoing stillness of their house a reminder of a loved one having gone. All around them there were pictures of Seraphina. From babyhood to the full power of her adult beauty, each photographic image underlining the waste and cruelty of a stolen life.

Automatically reaching into his pocket, Nino reminded himself that he no longer smoked. This time Nino Bergstrom wasn't dealing with ego, but grief. He wasn't having to be charming, but sympathetic. There was no director to mollify, no location to secure. It was all different. *He* was different.

Crossing a humped bridge, Nino dipped his head under an arch, then moved into a narrow alleyway, checking the address he had been given – 176, Via Mazzerotti, a house tucked between two others, its door knocker in the shape of a Medusa's head. Beside the knocker were several pieces of faded paper, with names on them, the third being *Morgan, Tom and Seraphina.*

Pushing the buzzer, Nino waited, hearing footsteps approaching, a voice coming over the intercom.

'Who's there?'

'Nino Bergstrom.'

'Oh, yes . . .' the man said, opening the door and letting Nino enter.

The hall was vaulted, several suitcases piled on top of one another, a florid opera poster hanging over an ornate iron table. Without a word, Tom Morgan beckoned Nino to follow him into the main room. Low chamber music was playing, a photograph of Seraphina stood on the mantelpiece, and an orchid lay dying on a paint-cracked windowsill. Then, as the rain began outside, Tom flicked on some lamps.

'Seraphina's parents asked me to talk to you,' he said easily enough, although he was jumpy and Nino could just catch a faint scent of marijuana in the room. Fair-haired, over six feet in height, Tom Morgan was dressed in jeans and an open-necked shirt. But his feet were bare – surprising on a cold afternoon.

'So, what d'you want to know?'

'I'm so sorry about your wife—'

'*Sorry*,' Tom repeated, as though the word was an insult, 'sorry . . . yeah, I'm sorry too. I saw her, you see, in the morgue. The Venetians aren't very good with death. Apparently I wasn't supposed to see her body, but there was a mix-up . . .' He rubbed his eyes as though he could erase the memory. 'She was . . . Christ, it was terrible. She was everything to me. And then the fucking police asked me all those questions, making me feel like a suspect.' He turned to Nino, suddenly angry. 'Who are you really?'

'I'm asking questions about Seraphina's death.'

'And her parents hired you?'

'No.'

'So who did?' Tom countered, walking over to a cabinet and taking out a joint. He lit it and inhaled, smoke juddering from his lips, his manner veering between confusion and hostility.

'I'm working for an old friend of Seraphina's.'

'Who?'

'Gaspare Reni.'

'Never heard of him,' Tom replied, sitting down and flinging one arm along the back of the sofa. 'I know all Seraphina's friends, and I've never heard of him.'

'Gaspare's an art dealer. I met Seraphina through him. He knew her parents well,' Nino replied. 'Seraphina knew him when she was a girl, although he wasn't a close friend—'

71

'So why's he so interested in her death?' Tom put his head on one side. 'If my wife only knew this dealer when she was younger, why does her death matter so much to him?'

The hostility caught Nino off guard. 'Gaspare took Seraphina's death hard. He sent me over here to find out if there's anything which might lead us to her killer.'

Without being invited, Nino sat down. The action surprised Tom Morgan as he inhaled again on the joint, his narrow fingers shaking. Was it guilt? Nino wondered. Was he involved in his wife's death? Or just jumpy after seeing her body? Looking away, Tom closed his eyes, and Nino took the chance to study his surroundings. Although it wasn't situated in the most expensive area of the city, the apartment was sumptuous, well furnished with antiques and the ubiquitous modern additions of TV and computer.

Obviously Tom Morgan was successful.

'What do you do for a living?'

'Interior designer.'

'But Seraphina was a scientist?'

'Yeah,' Tom replied, 'scientists *can* marry artists.'

'So you think of yourself as an artist?'

'What the fuck!' Tom snapped, putting down his joint and leaning towards Nino. 'Look, I'm only talking to you because Seraphina's parents asked me to. It's a favour to them. But I don't *have* to answer your questions – the police have asked me plenty already.'

There was a sullen pause, Tom leaning back in the sofa

72

and crossing his legs. His expression was unreadable. At times belligerent, at times emotional – it was, Nino thought, like trying to talk to a firework.

'Did you know Seraphina?'

'Yes,' Nino replied. 'I only met her once, but I liked her.'

'Where did you meet her?'

'In London.'

'And this Gaspare Reni, is he based in London?'

'Yes.'

Recrossing his legs, Tom blinked several times, then inhaled deeply. 'Seraphina was visiting London on a short trip. She'd been there before with her parents and with me. She wanted to see the sights.'

'On her own?'

Again, the tilt of the head. 'Well, go on, ask.'

'Ask what?'

'What you've been trying to fucking ask ever since you came in. Were we happy? Was our marriage a good one? Did I have girlfriends? Did Seraphina have a lover?' He blew out his cheeks. 'Have I missed anything out? That's the usual list, isn't it? The police have already gone over it with me a number of times.'

'I'm not your enemy,' Nino said quietly. 'I'm only trying to find out what happened.'

'Seraphina was killed, that's what happened.'

'All right,' Nino said, his tone hardening, 'I'll be blunt. Did you have a good marriage?'

'Yes.'

'Did you have other women?'

'No.'

'Did Seraphina have another man?'

He smiled oddly, shrugging his shoulders. 'No.'

'Were you happy?'

Without answering, Tom stood up and moved over to his dead wife's photograph. Picking it up, he traced her face with the tip of his forefinger, pressing it firmly into the glass as if he wanted to break through to the image beneath.

'We met, fell in love, and got married. My company sent me here to work, and Seraphina was thrilled. After all, it was her birthplace; she loved Venice, knew so much about it.' He put the picture down and pushed his hands deep into his pockets. 'For the first six months it was heaven – I couldn't believe I could be so happy. My first marriage was shit—'

'You were married before?'

'Yeah, and before you ask, my ex-wife isn't dead. She went off with someone else.' His tone was abrasive. 'Then, when Seraphina and I moved here, things got even better.'

'So you didn't always live in this apartment?'

'No, she didn't like the one we first lived in, so we moved. Anything to make the little woman happy, hey?' He walked over to Nino. 'Are you married?'

'No.'

'I wondered, what with you being prematurely grey and all.' He smiled at his own joke, turning to look out of the window. 'Why was Seraphina visiting this Gaspare Reni?'

Lying wasn't difficult. 'She was just looking up an old friend.'

'She didn't tell me about it. Seraphina told me about everything else she did in London, but she didn't mention you or Gaspare Reni. So maybe,' he said, his tone challenging, 'I should be suspicious of *you*. Maybe I should be asking *you* questions. Like why was she visiting Gaspare Reni?'

'Just a social visit.'

'Nothing else?'

'No.'

'So my wife visited a man she hadn't seen for years, just to say hello?'

'That's right.'

Pausing, Tom Morgan stared down at his bare feet. With his left foot he traced out the pattern in the carpet, his hands still in his pockets. Silent, Nino watched him. Did he know about the painting? Despite Gaspare's warning, *had* Seraphina told her husband about it? And had he told someone else? He was an interior designer – a Titian portrait would have fascinated him. And it would have been very profitable if he'd been able to sell it. Perhaps Tom Morgan had been angry, wanting his wife to get the painting off Gaspare Reni so he could sell it on to one of his wealthy customers. Perhaps they had fallen out over it. Fought over it.

'How's your business doing?' Nino asked suddenly.

'Fine. How's yours?'

'This place,' Nino said, looking around, 'must cost a lot to maintain. Do you rent it or own it?'

'Rent it. We still own the other apartment.'

'You owned the one you moved from?'

'Yeah.'

Nino didn't know why he asked the question, it just came out. 'Why did you move from the other flat?'

'It had bad vibes ...' Tom said, laughing and regaining his seat. He rummaged around in the ashtray for the stub of his joint and relit what was left. 'Seraphina found out there'd been a murder there. It was supposed to have happened centuries ago. But then, I reckon every apartment in this city has a past. The place is so old, it must be littered with murders.' He paused, remembering his dead wife. 'Seraphina's just one more, isn't she? Just one more victim.' His left hand waved idly in the air. 'The police tell me that I can't leave Venice. But I didn't have anything to do with my wife's death. I loved Seraphina, I couldn't have hurt her. Her parents know that. They *must* know that.' He turned to Nino anxiously. 'Do they suspect me?'

'No.'

'Do you?'

'Should I?' Nino countered. 'I mean, if what you've told me is true, you were both happy. In love, in a new apartment. Why would you kill her? And in such a brutal way?'

'I couldn't!' he snapped. 'I couldn't do that to anyone ... Only a madman could have done that.'

'Just one more thing,' Nino said, following a hunch. 'Did you ever find out the name of the person who was killed in your old apartment?'

'Some woman,' Tom said dismissively. 'Is it important?'

'Maybe.'

Sighing, he concentrated, then glanced back at Nino. 'Claudia Moroni. I remembered it because of the painter Moroni.'

The name meant nothing to Nino, but he made a mental note of it anyway. He had hoped to draw out more information from Tom Morgan, and was disappointed. He had longed for a slip-up, a giveaway word, but it seemed that Morgan had nothing to give away. Or nothing to hide.

'Why would you do it?'

'*What?*'

'Kill your wife.'

'*I didn't!*' he snapped. 'I loved Seraphina – I love her even more now.'

'Now?'

'She was pregnant,' he said sadly. 'Seraphina was going to have my child.'

12

It was two thirty the following afternoon when Gaspare Reni heard the knocking coming from below. The gallery was closed, but apparently the visitor was either unable to read the sign or unable to take no for an answer. Puzzled, he waited for the knocking to end, but it continued, persistent and unsettling. He had always insisted that customers or dealers make appointments in advance, so that he would know who to expect. After all, he was getting old and the gallery was crammed with expensive pieces. Who knew who might walk in off the street?

Irritated, Gaspare moved to the window and looked down to the pavement below. From his vantage point, he could see the top of a man's head illuminated in the winter lamplight and ducked back when the figure looked up. But it was too late, he had been spotted. And the knocking began again.

Reluctantly, he moved down the stairs. Then, checking that the chain was on, Gaspare opened the front door.

'We're closed!'

'Mr Reni,' the figure said, trying to push against the door as Gaspare pushed back, 'perhaps we could talk?'

Anxious, the dealer put all his weight against the door and slammed it shut. Relocking it, he leaned against the wood, breathing heavily. But the man outside wasn't going anywhere.

'That's hardly polite,' he said. 'I only want to talk to you. About the painting.'

'Go away!' Gaspare snapped, unsettled. 'Or you can ring me for an appointment—'

'Where did you put it, Mr Reni?' the voice continued. 'In a bank? In safe storage? No, you're old school, aren't you? I think it's still with you in your gallery . . .'

Gaspare could feel his heart pounding as the man continued to talk.

'Hidden where? In the cellar? There are windows down there, Mr Reni, easy enough to break in. Or is the Titian in the attic?' A soft laugh. 'Simple to enter from the roof, wouldn't you say? Anyone could do it. Could creep in and surprise you. You wouldn't like that. To come across a thief. Why, they might attack you. Even kill you.' He paused, taunting the old man. 'You have such a big gallery, haven't you? So many rooms, so many windows, so many ways to get in.'

'*Go away!*'

'Why risk yourself for a picture, Mr Reni? Even a Titian?'

Stumbling away from the door, Gaspare hurried into the nearest room and grabbed the phone, dialling 999. He could

79

hear it ring out, then there was silence. The line had been cut. Alarmed, he dropped the phone, backing against the wall as he heard footsteps outside the front door. Someone was rattling the handle, shaking it vigorously, the brass knocker vibrating madly against the wood.

His heart seemed to be filling his chest, blood fizzing in his ears, as he thought of the hidden painting. His hands groped at his collar, loosening it as he gulped at the air. The voice called out to him again.

'You're on your own, Mr Reni. No one else there, is there? You're on your own. One old man. You haven't a chance. Just hand the painting over and I'll go away. Just give it up, before things get nasty . . . I know you can hear me, so let's get this sorted out.'

There was a pause.

'Mr Reni, don't be stupid . . .'

Another pause.

'Think about it.'

Again, a pause.

'This isn't over. I'll come back.'

Then there was silence.

Tensing, Gaspare listened as the footsteps walked away. Barely breathing, he heard them fade, then relaxed, slumping on to the sofa. Sweat was running down his face, his hands shaking as he leaned back against the cushions. How did anyone know that he had the Titian? How had anyone found out that it was in his possession? Had Seraphina talked before her death? Had Triumph? No, Gaspare thought desperately, he had told the American that the portrait had been destroyed. So who else knew? *Had Nino given him away?*

No, not Nino. He would never have put him in danger.

Still trying to slow down his breathing, Gaspare realised the danger he was in. The man had been right: he *was* alone and defenceless, and the capacious gallery was an easy target. If his tormenter had cut the phone line, he would certainly have disabled the burglar alarm ... Gaspare listened, but there wasn't a sound coming from outside the door. The man had gone. He had delivered his threat and gone.

In the semi-darkness Gaspare felt his heart rate finally settle, and a few minutes later he was recovered enough to move. Getting to his feet, the dealer moved into the back kitchen and locked the doors, turning to the stairs and then stopping dead.

There were footsteps overhead.

Whoever had been outside was now inside.

13

It took all of Gaspare's courage to mount the stairs. His heart hammering, he looked up the stairwell towards the noise above. Where was it coming from? The bedrooms? The attics? His hand gripping the banister rail, Gaspare Reni – seventy-eight years old, born in Milan, art dealer and historian – climbed the stairs. Composure replaced the earlier panic. Now he was enraged at being made to feel a victim in his own home. And determined that no one would get hold of the Titian.

Before Seraphina's death he might have tried to shrug off his fear, but her murder had confirmed it. The painting was dangerous. He couldn't allow it to leave his possession. People might mock the legend of Angelico Vespucci, but Gaspare believed it. He was old enough to be able to imagine possibilities he would have sneered at in his youth. Experienced and humble enough to fear what he didn't understand.

Holding the iron poker he had picked up from the grate downstairs, Gaspare rounded the bend on the landing and paused.

He listened.

There was the noise again.

Footsteps overhead.

From the attics.

Yes, the sound was coming from above. From the place where he had hidden the Titian. True to his word, the man had broken in and was now searching among the grimy eaves of the old convent roof.

Tightening his grip on the poker, Gaspare took the next flight. His steps were noiseless, but when he reached the bottom of the flight which led to the attic, the footsteps overhead suddenly stopped.

Holding his breath, Gaspare looked up.

There was a faint light showing at the head of the narrow attic steps, a torchlight flickering in the dimness. For an instant Gaspare paused and looked back, then, remembering that the phone line was cut, ascended the first stair. If he had wanted he could have left the house, run away, sought help. But Gaspare did what the intruder had never expected – he stayed.

And kept climbing.

One, two, three steps. Four, five, six. The light wasn't moving any longer – it was static, as though the intruder had put a torch down while they looked at something. Pushing back the door of the attic, Gaspare peered in. A man had his back towards him. He was squatting on his haunches in front of the Titian painting, the torch on a box beside him. He was so engrossed that he didn't hear the old man coming up behind him. So mesmerised by the image of Angelico Vespucci that he never felt the poker coming down on the back of his skull.

Venice, 1555

Angelico Vespucci is leaving now. Look, there he goes. And here runs
Aretino, off to meet his friend. They do much business. The bulk of
him seems all the more coarse for Vespucci's elegance, his bear's
arm slipped proprietorially through the merchant's. I imagine the
friendship will cost both of them more than either can afford. Certainly Titian will suffer. I know that, but it is beyond me to intervene.
I will, in time, but for now I watch, compelled to wait on tragedy.

We are deep in winter. The water is grey as a merle, the lamps
at the edge of the quay flickering nervously in the wind. From the
Jewish Quarter comes the muffled sound of singing, then the echo
of someone running. In these bitter days and nights there are always
running feet. They say the Devil has his workers out; that the wooden
piles which help keep Venice above the water are shaken nightly by
the kicking of their cloven hooves. They say the aborted foetuses of
a thousand courtesans are come back as vicious water sprites.

It may be true. We live in a city where men like Aretino and
Vespucci reign like potentates. Where a man might kill and mutilate

his wife and suffer nothing more than stares. And among the vulgar whispers there is always one question: where does Vespucci keep his precious hide? His own Bartholomew? Where does he lock away the skin that once he stroked and kissed? Is it dried out like the meat in the summer? Is it laid out, stiff and macabre, on what was once their marriage bed? Does he look at what once covered his dead wife and witch her back in his dreams?

14

Jerking awake in her chair, Jean stood up as Sally walked in. She was wavering on her feet, obviously drunk, her skirt creased, her make-up worn off. Once a month Jean babysat for Sally Egan's father, giving her a chance to go out. It was usually a Friday, and usually she came back slightly the worse for wear. But this Friday Sally was drunk, unable to focus, and Jean was out of patience.

'It's half past one in the morning!'

'Sssh!' Sally hushed her. 'You'll wake Dad up.'

'Fat lot you care about your father or you wouldn't be making all this noise coming in at this time!' Jean retorted. 'You said you'd be back at midnight. I had to ring my husband twice to let him know what was going on. It's not fair.'

Waving her hand impatiently, Sally slumped into a chair, her legs splayed out in front of her. Of course Eddie Gilmore hadn't rung. Of course not. She shouldn't have expected it. She'd been a mug, sleeping with him and thinking he gave a shit. And then she'd seen him in the pub and he'd blanked her. *Blanked her.* Christ, she hadn't known where to look . . .

And now here was Jean, moaning about having to call her husband. At least she *had* a bloody husband. At least she had someone who gave a fuck about where she was.

'You promised—'

'Oh, shut up!' Sally snapped, the booze making her aggressive, unlike herself. 'It's only once—'

'It's not once,' Jean countered. 'It's three times now. Three times I've had to wait for you to roll home. And always drunk.'

'*I'm not drunk!*' she hissed, running her hands through her matted hair. 'I just need to get out and have some fun. Christ, I'm entitled to that, aren't I?' Her voice turned into a wail, as she became increasingly maudlin. 'It's all the life I get. And some fucking life it is!'

Miserable, she rested her head on the arm of the chair. Jean sat down on the sofa beside her. She cared for Sally, always had, knowing the pressure she was under. But lately she was getting worried. It wasn't just the drinking – Sally wasn't taking the same care of her appearance and her usual good nature was foundering. It wasn't unusual – the strain of looking after a parent with Alzheimer's was hard for anyone. Especially alone.

But seeing her drunk again Jean's sympathy was becoming exhausted, anxiety getting the upper hand.

'You should look after yourself more.'

'Hah!'

'Walking home in this state. Why didn't you take a taxi?'

'They cost money!' Sally snapped, attempting to pull off

her jacket and giving up. Slumping back in the seat, she tried to focus on the woman in front of her. 'You don't know what it's like, living like this. I love my dad, but . . . You don't know what it's like.'

'You're drinking too much, love,' Jean said gently. 'That never helps anyone.'

'I only drink when I go out! God Almighty, maybe I should never go out again, sit in with my father day and night and accept the fact that I'll die single. Some dried-out old cow without a family of her own.' She leaned towards the other woman drunkenly. 'Would you like that, Jean? Is that how you see me ending up?'

'I'm not arguing with you—'

'*You are!*' Sally snapped back, staggering to her feet and fighting to keep her balance. 'You're like everyone else, trying to stop me having any fun. Well, I need a man, and I need sex, and I need it *however* I get it. Understand?'

Embarrassed, Jean walked to the door.

'I'll talk to you tomorrow, when you've sobered up,' she said firmly. 'Your father's asleep, so you don't have to worry about him—'

'*Worry about him!*'

'Get some coffee down you – you can't do anything the state you're in,' Jean replied, her tone disgusted. 'What if your dad wakes up and needs some help?'

'*What about me?*' Sally roared. 'Who worries about me?' Drunkenly she pushed Jean towards the door, shoving her out of the house. '*Go on, get out!* Get out! This is my house! I don't need you, I don't need anyone!'

'Sally—'

'Get out!' she repeated, slamming the door in Jean's face.

Furious, Jean walked to the end of the road and rang her husband on her mobile, waiting in the cold for him to pick her up. When he arrived three minutes later, Jean got into the car and told him – word for word – what had happened. And she said that she would never work for Sally Egan again.

And while they drove past the green and away from the Egan house, while Sally fell on to her bed and slid into a stupor, while poor Mr Egan dozed in his sedated sleep ... someone watched the house. The same someone who had been watching it for days. The someone who was now crossing the green and climbing over the fence, trying the back door.

Sally Egan was right about one thing. She died single. She died childless. And she died that night.

BOOK TWO

. . . Titian seemed to us a most reasonable person, pleasant and obliging . . . if you should acknowledge his talents and labours by the promotion of his son . . .

Gian Francesco Leoni, writing to Alessandro Farnese

15

St Bartholomew's Hospital, London

Running as fast as he could, Nino hurried across the road and entered the hospital. At Reception he was told that Mr Gaspare Reni had been admitted the previous night and that his condition was now stable. Relieved, Nino made his way up the back stairs to the fourth floor, moving on to the ward and spotting Gaspare.

The old dealer was lying on his back asleep, a bruise the size of a fist on his left temple.

'Excuse me, sir,' a nurse said, approaching Nino, 'you'll have to wait until visiting time.'

Ignoring the comment, Nino turned to her. 'How is he?'

'Who are you?'

'His son,' Nino lied. 'How is he?'

'Doing well. He had a lucky escape,' she replied. 'Your father had a bad fall – it could have been much more serious.'

So he wasn't the only one who was lying, Nino thought. Obviously Gaspare had given a sanitised version of events to the hospital, one that had no bearing on what he had told Nino over the phone.

Walking closer to the dealer's bedside, Nino stared at the old man. 'Is he going to be all right?'

'You'll have to ask the doctor—'

'Oh, for God's sake!' Nino snapped. 'Just tell me.'

'Your father should recover fully.'

Leaving them alone, the nurse walked off and Nino sat down beside Gaspare's bed. He ached to touch him but was afraid of waking the old man, and so he waited in silence, his hand lying half an inch from Gaspare's. Seeing him so vulnerable, Nino felt pity and an affection for his surrogate parent. When he had been ill, Gaspare had cared for him. Now it was Nino's turn.

'You look tired.'

Surprised, Nino saw that the old man's eyes had opened and he was looking directly at him.

'You told the hospital you had a fall—'

'Better that way,' Gaspare replied, smiling at his visitor. 'Thanks for coming back to London so quickly.'

'What the hell were you doing?'

'I thought I'd won,' Gaspare said wryly. 'I had an intruder and I went for him. I should have hit him harder. The poker only stunned him and he took it off me – and laid me out instead.' Touching the bruise on his face, he tried to shrug. 'I couldn't stop him.'

'Who was it?'

'I dunno. A man threatened me, then broke into the gallery.' There was a long pause. 'He got the Titian.'

'So what?' Nino said bluntly. 'He didn't get you. Why didn't you make a run for it? You should have got out of there.'

'*He got the painting!*' Gaspare repeated heatedly. 'That was the last thing I wanted to happen. I never wanted that picture out of my hands.' Wincing, he touched his temple. 'Seraphina was right – I should have destroyed it. I'll never forgive myself for that. What made me think I could protect it? Or keep it hidden? I should have burnt it.'

Trying to calm him, Nino took his hand. 'Forget it. It's gone. All that matters is that you're going to be OK.'

He nodded, unconvinced. 'What happened in Venice?'

'We can talk about that when you're better—'

'Dear God, Nino, I'm not a child! Tell me what happened. Did you find anything out?'

'I spoke to Tom Morgan, Seraphina's husband.'

'And? What was he like?'

'Jumpy. But then any man would be after what had happened. He said they'd been very happy. He said . . .' Nino paused, then went on, 'Seraphina was pregnant when she died.'

Gaspare closed his eyes for an instant, then reopened them, staring at the ceiling. Nino could see he was fighting back tears.

'D'you think he had anything to do with her death?'

'Honestly? I'm not sure. But I doubt it. He didn't seem very stable, but a killer? I wouldn't think so.' Nino paused, thinking back. 'And he didn't know about the painting. Or at least he wasn't about to admit it if he did.'

'So it was a wasted trip?'

'Not entirely. Tom Morgan did say something that stuck in my mind. Apparently Seraphina had insisted that they move from their previous apartment. When I asked why, he told me that a woman had been killed there a long time ago. She was called Claudia Moroni.'

Gaspare shrugged. 'The name means nothing to me.'

Pulling out a notebook, Nino balanced it on his knee and began to read. 'I went to look up the records and finally discovered that the house had been owned by her husband – Ludovico Moroni – back in the 1550s. It took some doing, but I then found out that Claudia Moroni had been killed and mutilated . . . It happened weeks after Larissa Vespucci had been murdered. You remember what you told me?'

Gaspare took in a slow breath. 'That four murders happened in the winter of 1555 to 1556, during the time that Titian was painting that bloody portrait. Did you find out who the other two victims were?'

'No. After that, I hit a brick wall. Suddenly no one wanted to talk to me, or even show me any old records.' He smiled grimly. 'It could just be that they didn't want some nosy foreigner poking around, but it seemed strange. Then I heard what had happened to you, and as I was leaving Venice I got message from a man called Johnny Ravenscourt. He said he'd like to talk to me.'

'About what?'

'I don't know yet. I'll call him later.' Nino leaned back in his chair. 'Shouldn't you rest?'

'I *am* tired,' Gaspare admitted, closing his eyes. 'Perhaps I'll doze for a few minutes.'

When the dealer had fallen asleep, Nino left the ward and moved into the corridor outside, where he asked to see the doctor. On being told that he would have to wait, he sat down and opened the evening paper someone had left on the seat next to him. On the front page was the headline :

CARE WORKER SKINNED

He stared at the words, rereading them, certain he was mistaken. But the article made it clear :

> Sally Egan, 34, a care worker who lived with her
> father, was stabbed and partially flayed last night.
> Her body was found by a paper boy this morning,
> displayed on the green of a London suburb.

It could have been any of a dozen murders, had it not been for the mention of the victim being skinned. Nino stared at the paper. Seraphina in Venice, Sally Egan in London. Two women killed in the same way, in the same week, after the Vespucci portrait had surfaced . . . There must be a connection, he thought, but what was it? What *could* the two women have in common?

Disturbed, he glanced down the corridor. The afternoon was failing, the great white orbs over his head giving off a sickly light. Finally, unable to wait another second, Nino moved out of the hospital into the car park. Hurriedly, he punched in Johnny Ravenscourt's mobile number. A moment later, a high-pitched voice came on the line.

'Hello?'

'Johnny Ravenscourt? This is Nino Bergstrom—'

'Oh, good, you called. Can we talk? I think we should, I really think we should. I heard that you'd been asking about The Skin Hunter, Angelico Vespucci. Well, I'm a criminologist writing a book about serial killers.' He laughed. 'I know what you're thinking – who isn't writing about serial killers? I should have got on with it a long time ago. I've been writing it for years. But you see, my book's about *old* serial killers. You know, not Ted Bundy and the like—'

'*Old* serial killers?'

'From past times. Like Vespucci,' Johnny replied. 'I did the usual suspects – Vlad the Impaler, Genghis Khan, even the more modern ones like Son of Sam, but then they were so boring, the stories so well known. And then I heard about Vespucci—'

'How'd you hear about him?'

'Goodness,' he replied, his tone amusingly camp. 'You are suspicious!'

'I'm just careful. You leave a message for me and I don't know anything about you. I don't even know how you heard about me.'

'People gossip,' Johnny replied. 'Venice gets very boring in the winter and strangers are always good copy. You came, apparently with a dashing head of white hair, and everyone noticed. Then you started asking questions about one of the city's least popular residents and it was reported back to me.'

'Why?'

'People know I used to be a dealer and that I'm interested in Vespucci, so naturally they told me about you.' He paused, affecting a hurt tone. 'We don't have to talk. I just thought—'

'No, I'd like to talk.'

'Good. Come and see me.'

'I can't. I'm back in London.'

'I'm back in London too,' Johnny replied, 'staying at my flat off South Molton Street. Number 234 – you'll see my name on the door. Shall we say around seven?'

'Fine,' Nino replied, glancing down the corridor and noticing a doctor approaching him. 'I have to go now—'

'When we meet, remind me to tell you about the Contessa di Fattori, will you?' Johnny went on, his tone unreadable. 'Now, there was a dangerous woman.'

16

After Nino had talked to Gaspare's doctor and been reassured that his 'father' would recover, he headed for South Molton Street. The evening was frenzied with the first of the early Christmas shoppers, traffic listless and heading for the West End, or Claridges in the next block. Buzzing the intercom marked *Johnny Ravenscourt*, Nino heard the door click open and climbed the stairs. As he approached Flat 3 he was greeted by two pug dogs barking shrilly at the door.

'Oh, do stop it!' Johnny said, shooing them to one side and waving for Nino to enter. 'Ignore them, they're just being silly.'

The effeminate voice that Nino had heard on the phone did not in any way prepare him for the strapping appearance of Johnny Ravenscourt. Tall and bulky, he had heavy Germanic features, dyed black hair and a slack mouth. As he busied himself chivvying his dogs, his colossal hands flapped like wounded birds.

Finally, he sat down on a Regency settee and looked over at Nino. 'So?'

'So,' Nino replied, bemused.

'You came to talk?' Johnny said, jumping to his feet again and pouring them both a gin and tonic. Smiling, he passed one to Nino and regained his seat. His nerves were obvious and surprising. 'How do we start?'

'*You* wanted to talk to *me*.'

'Oh yes,' Johnny replied, crossing his weighty legs and smoothing the crease on his trousers. 'About murder.'

'About Angelico Vespucci.'

Johnny sipped his drink, pausing for effect. 'Yes, Vespucci.'

'I couldn't find out much about him,' Nino went on. The room felt overheated and stuffy, the towering Italian furniture dwarfing its modest proportions. 'Is there anything I can read? Any books?'

'Mostly hearsay.'

'But?'

'You've guessed, haven't you?' Johnny said, getting up again and placing a thick sheaf of papers on the table in front of his guest. 'Those' he said, jabbing at them with a stubby forefinger, 'are all about The Skin Hunter.'

Wary, Nino looked at the notes. 'I'm very grateful – but why are you helping me?'

'I heard that you'd been hired to look into the death of Seraphina di Fattori. That's why. Are you being paid well?'

Hesitating, Nino paused. He had used up the last of his savings on the Venice trip and was beginning to wonder how he could continue his investigation without financial support. He could approach Gaspare, but the dealer had already done more than enough for him. Asking for a fee seemed like insulting Gaspare, who was mourning Seraphina and himself a victim of an attack.

'I could use some cash,' Nino admitted at last.

'Then it's yours,' Ravenscourt said, his tone indifferent, as befitted a wealthy man. 'I'll give you a retainer now and you let me know how much you need as you go along. Oh, and keep this between us, will you? I'd rather people didn't know of my interest.' He shifted in his seat, his figure bulky on the elegant sofa. 'Seraphina was my friend. She was very kind to me when I had a little . . . upset . . . with a gentleman in a bar. I mean, I'm gay.' He regarded Nino for a moment as though daring him to challenge the words. When he didn't, Johnny continued. 'Seraphina was a rare creature who didn't judge people. I find that a remarkable quality, don't you?' Before Nino had time to answer, Johnny hurried on. 'But I don't like her husband. I think Tom Morgan's a bad lot.'

'You think he had something to do with her death?'

'No, but I think he had a lot to do with her life,' Johnny replied enigmatically.

'I don't understand.'

'Seraphina went to London to get away from him. She loved him, but she needed a break. She was pregnant, you see, and worried about it.'

Nino made no show of having already known. 'Didn't she want the baby?'

102

'She did. Tom didn't.'

'Did they argue about it?'

'Constantly. Seraphina had been pregnant before, in their old apartment. She was never happy there, hated the place, but Tom wanted to stay there. Said it was impressive – but when Seraphina lost the baby she *insisted* they move. A little while later, she asked me to find out about the history of the old building.'

'Did you?'

'Yes. It had once belonged to the Moroni family. And – would you believe it? – Claudia Moroni was murdered. And partially skinned.' He waited for a response, but when Nino didn't give him one, he continued. 'I told Seraphina what I'd found out – and now I can't stop wondering about what happened to *her*. To die in the same way ... It can't be a coincidence. It just can't. And then you came to Venice and started asking questions and I knew that if I went to the police, they would brush me off. Laugh at any connection with the house, or Vespucci.'

'But you think there's one?'

'Mr Bergstrom, I'm not a fool,' Johnny replied curtly. 'Seraphina came back from her trip to London and she was upset. Really upset. I thought it was because of her hormones. You know, pregnant women get tearful about the slightest thing—'

'She didn't strike me as the tearful kind.'

'She wasn't usually, but she was scared.' He paused, looking back and remembering. 'Eventually she told me about the painting ...'

103

Nino blew out his cheeks.

' ... *I haven't told anyone else!*' Johnny said hurriedly. 'Seraphina made me promise and I've kept that promise. I know you met up in London. I know she found the Titian. And I know she's dead and I want to understand why.' He pushed the notes closer to Nino. 'Go on, read about him, about Vespucci. It's taken me nearly fourteen years to get all that information together. Cost me a lot of money too. I found out who and what he was, what he did, and what he tried to do to avoid punishment. I read about his cronies, his murders, and about the folklore which grew up around him.'

'Which was?'

'*When the portrait emerges, so will the man,*' Johnny laughed uncomfortably. 'Well, it's fantastic, of course! That's what I thought anyway. Until Seraphina, my friend, came back from London and told me that the portrait had turned up. And then I started to worry ...' He stroked one of his dogs, struggling to keep the emotion out of his voice. 'Somehow she had found out about her ancestor, the Contessa di Fattori. And the fact that she'd been murdered by Vespucci.'

'How did she find out?'

'I don't know who told her. Her parents maybe.'

Nino frowned. 'Why would they?'

'Seraphina could have talked about the Titian she'd found and they could have offered up the family connection.' He clicked his fingers impatiently. 'How do I know who told her! She just *knew*, that was all. It scared me—'

'Why?'

'I don't know,' Johnny replied. He looked at Nino, his gaze surprisingly intense, then glanced away. 'For the next two days I phoned her continually. We met up, went shopping. Ate out together. You see, I wanted to be with her, to watch out for her. Then, on Wednesday morning, she was found dead.' He paused, alert. 'What is it?'

Without answering, Nino took the newspaper out of his pocket and handed it over. Frowning, Johnny Ravenscourt read the headlines. A moment passed, then he pointed to his notes, lying on the table between them.

'I'm not a brave man, I think that's obvious. I'm a rich, spoilt old queen, with no taste for danger. But I loved Seraphina and I want to know who killed her.' He pushed the notes further towards Nino. 'Please take the help I offer you, Mr Bergstrom. In those papers is everything I know about Angelico Vespucci. Everything I think there *is* to know about The Skin Hunter.' His voice was insistent. 'Take them. You don't have to bring them back. I don't want them back. Just read them – and remember Seraphina.'

Nodding, Nino picked up the notes.

'I think this is just the beginning,' Johnny said, as he stared at the photograph of Sally Egan, 'so perhaps now is the time for you to start reading?'

Venice, 1555

Did I tell you I was afraid of water?

The tide is rising now, higher than it has ever done, over the steps behind the houses, lapping on to the stone floors, making lazy pools under tables, silk rugs floating like bladderwrack. And with it comes the mist. The Doge is ill; some say it is another omen, some intimation of disaster coming with the freezing tides.

Not that Aretino feels any trepidation. He has a new lover, a woman as amoral as he. The Contessa di Fattori. A whore all Venice knows. Her husband encourages her excesses, wills her to try new lusts. It is said he derives his pleasure from the recalling of it. She is tall, this di Fattori, hair red as a night fox, eyes eerily blue under the triumphant arches of her brows. Cosseted by her husband's wealth, she revels in her hedonism. Luxuries are imported for her, carpets from India, perfumes from France, and in her bedchamber there are flowers sent from Holland weekly, daring the winter tides.

Some say she is a witch. For all her power she may be so. Stealing her husband from his betrothed, she soon looked elsewhere. Walking

106

across the piazzas with her maid and blackamoor in tow, di Fattori is imperious, heading, unashamed, for low places, or one of the threatening tangle of back streets where she is expected. It is rumoured she will lie with Arabs or boys hardly above ten, her servants sleeping on the steps outside. Sometimes, at dawn, di Fattori can be seen returning home, with her head upright like a conqueror, smelling of sex.

It was inevitable that she should entrance Aretino and he is smitten, even knowing that she laughs at his gut and his poor manhood. Vicious and fascinating, di Fattori rattles the dice of her fate, not caring for the outcome. She is reckless, demanding, cruel. She is Aretino's true match.

They say all three writhe in a mutual bed, di Fattori demanding attention from the merchant when Aretino tires. And as this latest information came to the streets, December crawled in. It came with biting winds.

A body bumped up against the struts of a bridge, rolling and turning in the tide, and finally jammed itself against the stonework. A moment later, footsteps were heard running. Echoing, disembodied, they faded into the Venetian streets.

I heard that the woman was mutilated, her back skinned, but not the rest of her. This time the murderer had been disturbed, cheated of his enjoyment. The hunter had killed but had been denied his skin.

Let me set down the date for this record. It was 26th November 1555, and the second victim was the wife of a merchant. Her name, Claudia Moroni.

17

Ginza, Japan

The alarm had gone off again at two thirty in the morning. But Jobo Kido, preoccupied and unable to sleep, had been more than willing to leave his bed and drive to his company premises. Within a few moments he had turned off the alarm and then made himself a coffee in the staff quarters off the main gallery. His wife's constant bad temper had worn away at his feelings and when she had threatened to go and stay with her mother he had been ecstatic. With his son also away, the house would be his for a while. It would be peaceful, uninterrupted by shouting and slamming doors, a temporary haven he would relish. Of course Jobo wouldn't admit to enjoying his wife's absence, or she would be sure never to leave again. Instead he would affect a sadness at her leaving and relief at her return and hope further arguments would result in further hiatuses from her tirades.

Fully awake now, Jobo glanced at the clock – nearly 3 a.m. He wondered momentarily if he should go for a walk, but instead sat down at his computer. Seconds later he was looking at a reproduction of Titian's portrait of Angelico Vespucci . . .

What he wouldn't do to get that painting! Jobo thought. As for Farina Ahmadi trying to fob him off! Stupid woman, of course she knew about the Titian. He could tell just from looking into her sly little eyes that she was already imagining it on the walls of the Alim Collection.

He was disappointed at not having found out more in New York. Perhaps it had been too much to hope, but he had longed from some crumb of scandal to drop at his ready feet. And pumping Triumph Jones had been a tiring business. From his lofty height, the American had batted away Jobo's enquiries like a giant swatting summer wasps. It always irked Jobo that although he was taller than the average Japanese man he always felt diminutive around Triumph Jones. He had also noticed that every conversation they had was conducted with them standing up, the American giving Jobo a prolonged view of his impressive jawline.

But if Triumph Jones had the Titian he wasn't admitting it . . . Walking over to his safe, Jobo gave in to the temptation he had tried, feebly, to resist. It was the early hours of the morning – what better time to indulge himself? Fifteen minutes later he was letting himself into another building, double-locking the doors behind him and flicking on the lights.

The gallery was arranged in the normal way, but the exhibits presented a terrifying and disturbing vision. Portraits of known killers hung side by side with the work of John Wayne Gacy, the grotesque clown heads leering out in all their primary heat. And further along was a garish portrait of Jeffrey Dahmer, his stern gaze averted from the viewer, life size, the yellow pigments sour, the red the colour of a tomato, wrongly benign against the image of a killer. On the opposite wall, lit by a searching overhead portrait light, was a photograph of Albert Fish, the child killer and cannibal. And underneath were written his words:

I like children, they are tasty ...

Jobo's eyes moved down the line of monsters, lingering for a second on the drawings of Burke and Hare, the grave robbers, and beside them, a photograph of the dashing Victorian murderer Frederick Deeming, posing as Lord Dunn. The dealer's gaze rested on the next exhibit with a morose curiosity: Ed Gein, 1906–1984, murderer and grave robber from Wisconsin.

As ever, the monstrous nature of the sitters did not repel but rather intrigued Jobo. He was sure that there was a clue in their appearance, some insinuation of violence in the features. But although he had looked at his exhibits for many years the explanation continued to elude him. Every image was well known, studied minutely, the dealer's obsession increasing with every purchase, every image of a killer. But in among the photographs, pictures and drawings he knew something vital was missing for a notable collection. Skill.

His collection might display the skills of the killer, but not those of the artist.

The photographs Jobo had collected were press fodder – nothing remarkable, and certainly nothing to rival Titian's portrait of Angelico Vespucci. He stared at the images intently. It was true that his collection was impressive, but it lacked the definitive piece – a portrait of a famous killer, painted by a famous artist. He ached for the Titian. Staring at the display, Jobo mentally moved the resident images to make space for the Vespucci portrait. Owning a masterpiece would make his collection respectable; no longer to be sneered at but admired. After all, who could belittle a Titian?

Unfortunately the unknown caller had not got back in touch. Jobo had waited for a week for further contact, but there had been none, and he was getting impatient. Obviously the man had gone elsewhere and unless Jobo was careful he would find himself sidelined. He had two choices – he could either take a risk and wait for further developments, or set his own personal cat to put a flurry in the dovecotes.

Once decided, Jobo moved into the office at the back of the gallery and tapped out a number on the phone. His desire for the Titian had made him unusually reckless, determined to force action.

'Hello?'

Jobo's voice was all sweet concern. 'Triumph, is that you?'

111

'Jobo?' the American replied, drawing out the name like a piece of ribbon. 'What are you calling me for? It must be the middle of the night in Tokyo.'

'I couldn't sleep. And neither could you – if you knew what I do,' Jobo said enigmatically. 'I've just seen the Titian.'

There was a silence on the other end. 'Where?'

'Well, I've not actually *seen* it, I've just seen a photograph.' Jobo was making it up as he went along, trying to draw Triumph out and discover what he knew. 'Someone sent me a note in the mail.'

'Who?'

'I don't know. But it said that they'd also approached you about the portrait . . .' He paused, sly to a fault. When Triumph didn't respond, he threw the dice again . . . 'and Farina Ahmadi.'

'No one's been in touch with me, Jobo.'

Jobo didn't believe that for an instant. 'What about Farina?'

'She hasn't mentioned it.'

Jobo sighed expansively. 'Oh, that's all right then. I'm so glad I talked to you, Triumph. You know what I think, don't you? The painting's a hoax – someone's just trying to scam the dealers. Well, I'm not going to be taken in,' he said, his tone light. 'Sorry I disturbed you.'

For several minutes after they had concluded the call, Jobo sat in his office with the door open, gazing at his private gallery, his own personal assembly of freaks. He might have found out nothing, but he knew that his call would have immense repercussions. The American would realise that the news was out, and that it had travelled as far as Japan. There was no doubt that Triumph Jones had earned his sobriquet and his impressive cunning would ensure that he investigated any trail, even a false one.

What would happen next was anybody's guess, but the Titian was up for grabs and at least three dealers were after it. With such a coterie of egos nothing – not even Angelico Vespucci's portrait – could remain hidden for long.

18

At one time there had been some sort of order to Johnny Ravenscourt's notes, but as time went by the precise jottings had been replaced with slips of paper and reminders etched on the back of serviettes and empty cigarette packages. Old, barely decipherable newspaper cuttings were shuffled in among reproductions of Angelico Vespucci's portrait, along with contemporary engravings. In every one of them the same bulbous, heavy-lidded eyes gazed out, the eyes Nino remembered seeing the night Seraphina brought the portrait to Kensington. The eyes which had been covered by a blanket when the painting had been lodged, temporarily, in the eaves above the convent gallery.

Concerned for Gaspare's safety, Nino was pleased that the dealer had to stay in hospital for further tests. Nothing serious, the doctor reassured him – 'just to be on the safe side'. He didn't know how true the words were. Back at the Kensington gallery, Nino discovered where the thief had broken in and had the window repaired, changing the door locks as an added precaution.

But when he visited Gaspare in hospital that afternoon, Nino was unprepared for the dealer's refusal to involve the police.

'Keep them out of it!' he snapped. 'I don't want anyone to know about the painting. No one knows about the break-in – and no one will.'

'You were attacked—'

'*For the painting!*' Gaspare remonstrated. 'Now they've got it, why would they bother to come back? There's no danger for us.' He pointed to the newspaper which reported Sally Egan's death. 'We have other things to think about. That girl, for instance. Why was she killed in that way? Not another coincidence, surely. She must have some connection to the Titian portrait or Vespucci himself.'

Nino shrugged. 'Why? It's rare, but victims have been skinned before—'

Gaspare cut him off.

'But why would it happen *now*? Just when the painting of *The Skin Hunter*'s come to light? No. There's a connection, there has to be.' He looked around the private room, grateful that no one could overhear them. 'Did you talk to the Ravenscourt man?'

'Yes, I did, and he gave me his research, all his notes, everything he'd ever found out about Vespucci.'

'Really?' Gaspare replied, wary. 'What's in them?'

'I dunno, I haven't had a chance to read them yet. I'm going to look at them when I get back to the gallery.'

Picking up the newspaper, Gaspare read the headline again.

'First Seraphina, now this woman . . . You think they had something in common? I do. I'm sure something connects them.'

'Like Vespucci?'

Gaspare nodded thoughtfully. 'We need to go back to where it all began – in Venice. We need to know about Vespucci's victims. See if they had any connection to each other. Then we can see if they have any connection to Seraphina and Sally Egan.'

Nino paused, thinking back.

'You told me that Vespucci got away with the murders because there was another suspect—'

'But I don't know who. No one does.'

'Unless he's named in Johnny Ravenscourt's notes,' Nino suggested.

The old man leaned forward in his hospital bed, suddenly alert. 'Read them!' he said urgently. 'Read them!'

'And what do we do about the painting?'

'Forget about that for now! It's gone. It could well have been stolen to order – that's not unknown in the art world. It might be on its way to New York or Berlin as we speak. God knows how many dealers went after it—'

'But how would they *know* about it?'

'Seraphina?'

'She only told Johnny Ravenscourt.'

'And how many people did *he* tell?' Gaspare asked perceptively. 'What kind of a man is he?'

'Scared. He was very close to Seraphina.'

'D'you think he could have stolen the Titian?'

'No,' Nino said confidently. 'Johnny Ravenscourt isn't like that. He's no thug, just a rich man with time to indulge his interests. His obsession with The Skin Hunter came from his research into serial killers. The fact that there's a portrait in the mix means little to him – except for the legend that its emergence would bring back Vespucci.'

'He believes that?'

'Oh yes,' Nino said emphatically. 'He believes it – and it scares the shit out of him. I reckon the reason he gave me his notes was to get them off his hands. I'd say that Johnny Ravenscourt wants to put some distance between himself and his subject.'

'But Vespucci's victims were women—'

'That makes no difference – logic doesn't come into this. Johnny Ravenscourt's spooked. The moment he gave me his research I could see him relax. It was like watching a man jump over a gate to escape a charging bull.' Nino paused for an instant. 'His notes connected him to The Skin Hunter. By getting rid of them he severed that connection.'

'And?'

'I think he also believes that if the legend *is* true, Vespucci will come after me now, not him.'

117

19

There is a passageway from Kensington Church Street that leads through an archway to a scruffy path around the back of the church. Over the years the figure of Christ has hung in a shrine there, crucified and on view to the passing traffic. At times yobs have thrown paint over Him, others have laid flowers at His feet, and at Christmas tinsel is wound gently around the brutal crown of thorns. He has stood under the wind, under the snow, and hung His head when summer sun cracked His painted face. And He was still standing as Nino cut through the passageway, heading for the convent gallery.

Unlocking the back door and turning off the repaired alarm, Nino made himself a drink and then moved to the drawing room on the first floor. In Gaspare's absence he flicked on all the lights, spreading out Johnny Ravenscourt's notes on the table and sitting down. Above him loomed the caramel angels, the Japanese suit of armour on duty by the door, a globe – dented in the Horn of Africa – holding up a Turkish rug.

Painstakingly Nino began to sort out Johnny Ravenscourt's research. On his left he placed all the scraps of paper and hasty notes, on his right the photographs and reproductions, and in the centre he put the two notepads. He then started to read, choosing the journals first. Ravenscourt's handwriting was surprisingly small for a big man, but every word was readable.

Angelico Vespucci b. 1510 – not known where he died. Last heard of February, 1556. His list of victims is open to debate, but there are records in the chapel of the Mazzerotti church. (The priest was so difficult, I had to donate to the renovations before he would even talk to me and then he was evasive. No one wants to talk about Angelico Vespucci. They pretend he never existed, until you come along with proof or asking questions. He's like Venice's dirty little secret.) Anyway, their records list the deaths of Larissa Vespucci, Claudia Moroni . . .

Nino paused. *Claudia Moroni.* He knew about her. The woman who had once lived in the house where Seraphina had owned an apartment and lost her baby. Claudia Moroni, the second of The Skin's Hunter's victims . . . He scribbled down a note of his own, and continued to read.

The Moroni family were respectable, long established in Venice.* They were merchants, notable for the quality of their silks. Claudia Moroni came from a wealthy family and had one – or two, the accounts differ – sons, neither of whom survived infancy.

119

Apparently her brother came to live in the household soon after she was married.

Weirdly, when I visited the Moroni house I knew I'd been there before. It turned out to be Seraphina's first flat after she married Tom Morgan.

Nino scanned down the page to a note at the bottom.

*N.B. There is a painting of Claudia Moroni and her husband in the house.

Johnny Ravenscourt had pinned a photocopy of a portrait on to the page and Nino studied the couple depicted. The man was vulgarly handsome, the woman blonde, diffident, rather unremarkable except for the richness of her clothes. She certainly bore no resemblance to Seraphina, he thought, turning back to the notes.

I wanted to find out about the victims, but after spending two months searching for clues in 2008, I hit a brick wall. So I changed emphasis and looked at Angelico Vespucci himself.

Nino turned the page to find the familiar face looking up at him, in a variety of depictions of The Skin Hunter. As well as a copy of Titian's portrait, there were several reproductions of engravings and a sepia sketch. Curious, Nino studied it. The sketch was high quality, even he could see that. Vespucci was turned towards the artist, his expression extraordinary. He had the same unreadable, heavy-lidded eyes, but there was a tremor about the mouth, a look of unease which bordered on instability. The sketch seemed to catch the man in an unguarded moment, when his features could not fully contain his character.

It was chilling.

Vespucci's origins are unclear, Johnny's notes continued. *He seemed to come to Venice out of the ether. But he came with a great fortune around 1539, and was living on the Grand Canal by 1541, in a magnificent palazzo. Throwing extravagant parties, with the finest wines and foods imported, he became a popular figure. Generous and affable, he was well liked, but apparently he had a servant flogged publicly for serving bad oysters. Vespucci was very generous to the Church and worshipped at the San Salvatore, marrying Larissa Fiorsetti in 1546. (This much is in the records. After that it gets more difficult.) Nothing else is heard of him until 1549, when his daughter was born. His wife Larissa was, by all accounts, a great beauty. (See photos of contemporary paintings.)*

Nino paused, picking up the images of the glorious Larissa Vespucci. She *had* been an opulent beauty, full-fleshed, red-haired, her mouth tilting up at the corners. He could see at once why Angelico Vespucci would have fallen in love with her. And why he might well have been possessive. How could he not have been? She would have drawn attention anywhere. How difficult would that have been for a unpre-possessing man like Vespucci to endure?

121

Stretching his arms above his head, Nino yawned, then finished his coffee. Outside it was now fully dark and he drew the curtains, locking the doors front and back before returning to the notes.

The next mention of Vespucci is in 1555, when he is referred to by Pietro Aretino. Known as 'The Scourge of Kings', this heavyweight had considerable influence in Venice, his friendship with Titian alone making him a powerful figure in the city. What Titian liked about Aretino is anyone's guess; he was a crude man, but he was very productive in the promotion of the artist's work. He travelled abroad, spoke to kings and courtiers, and generally acted as Titian's agent. So it's not surprising when Aretino mentions that he has arranged for Titian to paint Angelico Vespucci's portrait.

Vespucci was respectable at this time. Larissa was still alive. (I had some difficulty accessing the records. There is mention of a boy dying and a girl surviving. All my efforts to trace any living descendants of Vespucci have come to nothing. Either there are none, or they changed their name to avoid scandal.) It was in October 1555 that the contract for the portrait was drawn up, the sittings to be commenced in November. See notebook 2.

Sighing, Nino reached for the second volume. The writing picked up immediately from where the first had left off, only this time the notes were different – short, without the conversational tone. It was as though Johnny Ravenscourt was trying to distance himself in his writing.

4th November 1555 – Larissa Vespucci found murdered and skinned.

Suspicion fell on Vespucci, but his protectors rallied round him. Larissa had been unfaithful.

Aretino stands up for Vespucci.

Titian continues painting the portrait.

November 26th 1555 – Claudia Moroni found murdered and skinned.

Venice in the worst winter for over a century. Fogs constant, temperatures below zero. The legend of The Skin Hunter begins.

Thoughtful, Nino put the portraits of Claudia Moroni and Larissa Vespucci side by side. There were no physical similarities between the two women, the unremarkable Claudia looking more like a housewife than an adulteress. Stretching across the table, Nino then placed the images of Seraphina and Sally Egan above the two murdered Venetian women. Again, no similarities, not obvious ones anyway. Disappointed, he frowned. Perhaps there wasn't a connection between a killer in the sixteenth century and another in the twenty-first century. Perhaps it was just coincidence.

And then again, perhaps it wasn't.

Taking a deep breath, Nino read on. Outside, it grew dark. In its shrine, the figure of Christ bent His head to the traffic, and as the lights changed on Kensington High Street a plane came in to land at Heathrow Airport. It carried one hundred and seventy-five passengers.

And one of them was a killer.

20

Six o'clock and the tide was in, nuzzling the Thames Embankment, as Triumph Jones sat on one of the benches overlooking the river. He had felt compelled to come to London, his guilt forcing his hand. Such vanity, he thought – how could he have had such vanity? His eyes closed momentarily, then opened again, stinging in the December wind. His ego had overridden his sense, his morals, and now the plan he had set in motion had spun out of control.

Leaning forward, he watched the river, remembering how, days earlier, he had taken a taxi and asked to be dropped off at Grosvenor Bridge. There he had paused, looking around and waiting. Finally he spotted a woman a little way off, and ducked behind one of the struts of the bridge to avoid being seen. He waited, certain that she was coming closer, then threw the portrait of Angelico Vespucci over the railings and into the ebbing tide. It hit the water with a hefty splash, the woman turning as Triumph watched.

He knew it had still been something of a gamble. What if there had been some alteration in the flow? Or some boat causing a wake that spun the Titian away from the bank? Or worse, what if it had remained in the water and been irrevocably damaged?

Still hiding, Triumph had seen the woman react. Surprised, she looked into the water, the Titian following a sudden push of tide and washing up on to the shingle. Relieved, Triumph had then seen the slight figure scramble down the grit towards it. Once she nearly lost her balance on the wet silt, but she recovered and, after looking carefully at the package, had picked it up.

Exhaling, Triumph had walked off in the opposite direction. His plan had been set in motion. Let the games begin . . .

Taking in a breath, he clasped his hands together, trying to stop them shaking. It had been a ploy to excite the interest of the art world, to push up the price of a notorious painting. A painting which had come his way via a thief in Madrid and a forger in San Francisco. A Titian everyone would be after. What better way to get a notorious work back on to the market than to have it found *by accident*? How much publicity could be generated by such a story?

Like many in the art world, Triumph had known about *The Skin Hunter* and was now relying on its gory reputation to start up a media scramble. Everyone knew that serial killers sold copy.

It hadn't mattered to Triumph who found the portrait or where it had ended up. The fact that it came to rest with Gaspare Reni was a bonus, unexpected but irrelevant. He had calculated that whoever found the Titian would sell to a gallery or put it in an auction – *where he would buy it*. It might cost him more, but after a little while he would sell it on and make an impressive profit while bolstering his own reputation at the same time.

Of course he had known that it could go another way. But if anyone tried to organise a sale illegally, Triumph would hear of that too. He hadn't earned his sobriquet by relying on the good nature of mankind. Over the years he had employed staff to run his gallery and his home, and hired a few others who lurked in the swamp of the art world, privy to unsavoury and dangerous secrets.

It should have been so simple.

And then Seraphina Morgan, aka Seraphina di Fattori, was murdered and flayed. The woman who had found the painting was dead – and the portrait was gone . . . Triumph hadn't believed what Gaspare Reni had told him. The old dealer would never have destroyed a Titian. What he *hadn't* expected was that Gaspare would keep it and hide it. Far from the portrait coming on to the market in a blast of notoriety, it had been concealed again.

Worse was to follow. Having set someone to watch Gaspare's gallery, his scrutiny had been too late. Gaspare Reni had already been admitted to hospital, after 'a fall'. It wasn't difficult to read the subtext. Somehow Triumph had been outwitted; before he could buy the Titian from Gaspare Reni the picture had been stolen. And worse, in a matter of days another woman had been killed. Another woman murdered in exactly the same manner as the first.

No one had to tell him that there was a connection.

For the first time in his life, Triumph Jones felt cursed. Everything he had wanted, he had achieved. The art world was becoming giddy with the leaking news of the Titian. How long before it was common knowledge? He had wanted that, but not what followed. How long before some hack made the front page by pairing the legend of The Skin Hunter with the deaths of Seraphina Morgan and Sally Egan?

And it was *his* fault. He'd built up the rumour, nourished the seed. There *had* been a killer called Angelico Vespucci, and a legend. Along with a shattering threat – *when the portrait emerges, so will the man*. That had been Triumph's plan, to utilise the fable when he had the cursed painting in his possession.

Ashamed, he thought back. God, he had hardly been able to believe his luck, that the infamous portrait should end up in his hands. But then greed had entered the equation. How could he ensure that the picture got on to the front pages, his coup publicised globally, adding another victory to his roll-call of triumphs? And so he resurrected a legend. Polished, embellished, refined, the tale taking its time to marinate, so that its revelation would be all the more news-worthy when the portrait came to light . . .

Shivering, Triumph wrapped his coat around him, still staring into the water. What had he done? *What had he called up?* The thought unnerved him. Of course Angelico Vespucci couldn't come back from the dead. It was absurd. And yet two women had been murdered by the same means The

Skin Hunter had employed over four hundred years earlier. So *something* had happened. Triumph's actions had triggered something

Unsettled, he grabbed at the comfort of a human villain. Maybe a killer copying The Skin Hunter? It was possible, Triumph thought, God knows, it was possible.

But it was still his fault. Two young women were dead. And his conscience floundered under the weight of their deaths.

21

Narita International Airport, Tokyo

Harriet Forbes came off the 18.06 flight from London irritable and tired. A bad journey hadn't improved her temper and the thought of having to check into her hotel and then return a list of phone calls depressed her. What, she asked herself, was the point of promoting yet another nail polish? What the shit did anyone need with another varnish? She waited for her luggage, tapping her foot impatiently, her short hair greasy, her face sullen with bad temper and lack of sleep.

Of course, if she had had the guts, she would have got out of PR years ago. But now she was forty-six, at the top of her game, and earning impressive amounts of money. Her friends were envious, coveting the first-class flights and the goodie bags dished out at every promotional event. Goodie bags worth more than a week's wage for most people. And all in the name of eyeshadows and lipsticks.

Harriet had grown bored with the lotions which had undergone intensive, ground-breaking scientific research and promised superb results. They never delivered, of course. But she promoted them because she was paid to. Paid to keep her own make up pristine, her urchin face and figure perfectly in tune with the fashion, her clothes following the messianic dictates of Dolce and Gabbana and Vivienne Westwood. She wore Rouge Noir on her nails, until it was commonplace, then switched to Jade. Her perfume depended on which launch she was attending, her scent in tune with whichever paymaster was signing off her expenses that week.

It was all so very chic. So very covetable. But all so very anodyne. As her friends had married, had children or divorced, Harriet had spun like a gadfly around the continents. She didn't see that she had aged until it was too late. She didn't notice that she was lonely until she realised it was three years since she had broken up with Arlene. And all that had been kept a secret, because a lesbian wasn't supposed to know about fashion and beauty. And because, if she was honest, Harriet didn't like being gay. The fact that she was attracted to women had been an embarrassment to her, only made acceptable when she entered a secure, long-term relationship with Arlene. But when that broke up, part of Harriet's self-image broke too. Suppressing her lesbian feelings, she found it easier to stay busy and deny herself any close relationship.

Reaching for her luggage, Harriet pulled the case off the carousel, moving away when she saw a man watching her. It was strange how much attention she received from men. It was ironic how many were attracted to her, never suspecting her inclinations . . . Sighing, she made for Customs, passed through and then paused, deciding she would go to the Ladies before she left the airport.

Entering the door marked with the Japanese symbol for toilet, Harriet walked in. Nodding to two uniformed cleaning women, she moved into a cubicle and relieved herself, taking a moment to straighten her clothes before she washed her hands. Her image in the mirror annoyed her and after fiddling with her hair for a few moments she lost patience. Then she found, to her amazement, that she was crying.

The sobs came deep and low as Harriet sat on her suitcase and clenched her fists. What had she done? Why had she wasted her life? Not taken enough time to think it out, to plan. She was meticulous, clever, practical in her work – why had she been so casual with her life? It was all so much waste. Days, weeks, months spent talking about foundation and primers, discussing the subtleties of colours which few customers would even notice. Why did it matter if the lipliner was taupe rather than bisque this year? It was all so fucking stupid, so small, so pointless. So undemanding.

Her hands clenched even tighter, nails scraping her palms. When she started she had had such ambition! A few years in fashion and beauty, then set up her own PR company and move on to health and lifestyle. She had imagined that she would then progress into interior design, investigating how a person's mood could be altered by a colour or a painting. Then, finally, she would enter the world of antiques. She had so much knowledge about art. Had, for a time, been fixed on the idea of working in an auction house. But in the end she had changed tack – and all her culture had been wasted. She had fallen for the almighty dollar, then the almighty yen.

Empty, Harriet stared at the tiled floor of the washroom, unable to find the energy to move. She despised herself. Despised turning her back on the woman she had been, to become an automaton circling the globe and chattering endlessly about mascara. In her twenties she would have cringed to see herself now, would never have believed that someone erudite enough to write about art would sell themselves out for cash.

But maybe it wasn't too late, she thought hopefully. She had put quite a bit of money aside. She could give up the beauty business and nurture her intelligence instead. It would be difficult – and financially tough – to make the switch, but anything was better than sitting in a Japanese toilet, trying to work up enough energy to get a cab to another dreary Hilton hotel.

Rising to her feet, Harriet lifted her case and slung her handbag over her right shoulder. She was tired, drained, but ready to step off the goodie train, stop the antidepressants, sleeping pills and amphetamines and get her mind clear. It wasn't too late, she told herself as she moved to leave the toilet cubicle.

But it was.

As the door opened Harriet felt a blow to her face which was so violent it knocked her backwards, splitting her nose and sending blood down her throat. Choking, she fell on to the tiled floor, cracking her head and falling into semi-consciousness. But she was still aware. Harriet Forbes lived long enough to see her attacker lock the door. Lived long enough to feel the knife tearing through her flesh and ripping into her organs. Lived long enough to feel – in her dying moments – her skin being severed, then torn from her breasts.

Venice, 1555

A banquet was held last evening in one of the palaces on Grand Canal, a little way from the Rialto and opposite the fish market. Pietro Aretino, defying the cold and the elements, invited the elite of Venice to attend, his pack of cohorts ready to greet the hardy who ventured out into the bitter night. As before, I watched him. As before, he saw nothing of me. Yet he seemed more callous than usual, his hair dyed black, his girth hardly encased in cloth of gold.

Beside him at the table sat Titian. Elegantly reserved, good-humoured and attentive to the ladies present, he wore his brilliance lightly and was all the more admirable for his humility. In a blatant effort to impress, a feast was served on solid silver plates, and when the diners finished, Aretino ordered the servants not to clear the plates but to throw them out of the window. Such is his wealth. His vulgarity amused those present, yet later, outside and beyond sight of the company, I saw the servants pulling in nets from the water, saving the silver dishes from the clutch of the outgoing tide.

Reserved, Titian remained in his seat while the bawdy Aretino danced with some of the most celebrated women in the city. Once or twice I saw the artist sketching in a little notepad he always carries with him, then applauding as the Contessa di Fattori rose to dance. The clock was striking the half hour after midnight when she excused herself from Aretino's grip and took another dancing partner, Angelico Vespucci.

He dances with perfection, but his vices tell on him, the dark lidded eyes puffy, his mouth a little slack as he moves in time to the music. His hands open and close like the mouths of drowning men, his palms unnaturally white. And as he moves in step with di Fattori the candles about them shuffle and belch their smoke.

And meanwhile Titian paints on.

22

The last person Nino expected to see as he entered Gaspare's hospital room was a tall, elegant black man, his expensive clothes marking him out immediately as wealthy. Impatiently, Gaspare beckoned for Nino to approach.

'This is Triumph Jones,' he said, turning back to the American. 'And this is my surrogate son, Nino Bergstrom. You can say anything in front of him – we've no secrets.'

Taken aback, Triumph regarded the handsome white-haired man, then glanced back at Gaspare.

'This is private.'

'Then you can bugger off!' Gaspare snapped. 'Talk in front of Nino, or go.'

Reluctantly, Triumph pulled one of the plastic chairs towards him and sat down, ignoring Nino as he stood at the foot of the old man's bed. Twice he cleared his throat, then ran his hand over his smooth, bald head. He voice was, as ever, languorously slow.

'I came to talk to you about the Titian painting. And

before you say a word, Gaspare,' he admonished him, 'I know you didn't destroy it. It was stolen.'

Nino raised his eyebrows. 'Did *you* steal it?'

'Do I look like a thief?'

'I don't know what a thief looks like,' Nino replied, not in the least cowed by the American's imperious manner. 'But if you didn't steal the painting, how d'you know it was taken?'

'I had someone watching Gaspare's gallery.'

Irritated, the old man threw back the bed clothes and sat up, tugging on his dressing gown. Walking over to the window, he opened it and stared out. 'I need some fresh air.' His tone was contemptuous as he looked back at Triumph. 'How dare you come here and tell me that you were watching my home!'

'It was for your own good—'

'*My own good!* You spied on me for my own good?' Gaspare echoed mockingly. 'So – did you see who took the Titian? Or is that too much to ask?'

'We were too late.'

'To see him? Or stop him?' Nino asked, moving closer to the American.

'We were too late to see him. I was told that an ambulance had taken you to hospital and that there was a broken window at the gallery. It was obvious what had happened. But I don't know who took the painting, or I'd tell you.'

'I doubt that,' Nino replied, as Gaspare slammed the window shut and leaned against the sill.

'Were you going to steal the Titian from me, Triumph?'

'No, I was going to buy it.'

Puzzled, Gaspare caught Nino's eye, then sat down at the foot of the bed.

'So what have you come here for? I don't have the painting any longer. And I don't see how I can help you. I'm a has-been, an old dealer with no clout. I understand why you contacted me after the Titian emerged, but why take the trouble to come to London to talk to me now?' Reaching for his glasses, he put them on, peering at the American. 'What are you up to? Or, more precisely, what have you done?'

'I need to talk to you alone,' Triumph repeated, glancing over at Nino. 'What I want to say is for your ears only.'

Gaspare shook his head. 'No, I want a witness to everything you say, Mr Jones. Because I don't trust you.' He looked the elegant American up and down. 'Why did the Titian suddenly turn up? It was missing for centuries – why did it just pop up out of thin air?'

'I don't know.'

'You'll have to do better than that,' Gaspare said, folding his arms, defiant in a dressing gown. 'You're famous, one of the biggest hitters in the art world. Notorious for your contacts. It didn't surprise me that you discovered I had the portrait, but now I'm wondering *how* I came to have it. I mean, it was very convenient that the picture was found. Very lucky, that. Or did you plan it?' He glanced over at his visitor. 'You look stressed, Triumph, like a man with something on his conscience.'

Playing for time, the American hesitated. If he had been alone with Gaspare Reni he would have confessed, sought some kind of absolution from the old man. But they weren't alone and he wasn't going to say anything which would implicate him.

It was Nino who broke the deadlock. Turning to Gaspare, he said, 'I'll leave you to it—'

'No, I want you to stay.'

'You won't find anything out if I stay here,' Nino replied, walking out.

It was several seconds before Triumph Jones spoke again. Several seconds in which he struggled with his conscience, wondering how much to conceal and how much to reveal. Should he confess to everything? Or try to minimise his deceit? But when he glanced over at Gaspare and saw the look of disdain on the old man's face, he was shamed into a full confession.

'I never meant for any of this to happen,' Triumph began, his head bowed. 'Someone came to me with the Titian portrait. I paid a reasonable sum – the man was no dealer and glad of what he got. I should have stopped then, but my ego didn't let me.' He wouldn't look up, didn't dare. 'I thought it would be amusing to hold back on it for a while, work up some real publicity for the painting. So I resurrected the story, the so-called legend – "*When the portrait emerges, so will the man.*"' It was bound to catch on.'

Gaspare's face was expressionless. 'And all this publicity would drive up the value of the work.'

139

Triumph paused, his voice catching. 'I didn't know Seraphina di Fattori would find it. I didn't know she would take it to you. You of all people! What was the chance of that?'

Gaspare shrugged. 'You said yourself, whoever found it would take it to a gallery or a dealer. Why's that so surprising? Anyway, the painting's gone. Stolen. You've lost. Is that what's eating away at you?'

'It's not that!' Triumph replied. 'Seraphina was killed in Venice. And now another woman's been killed in London. In *exactly* the same way as Vespucci killed his victims.'

'In the sixteenth century! You're not believing your own publicity now, are you? Dear me, Mr Jones, I wouldn't have thought you were the gullible type.' Gaspare's voice had a hard edge. 'I admit that I fell for it. But then again, I'm Italian – superstitious. I believe in legends. I was even a little afraid. You fooled me – well done. For a moment I thought that the Titian *could* summon up something, or someone, from the grave. It was a stroke of genius, Triumph, and you deserve your success. Your imagination and flair for publicity is second to none.' He clapped his hands sardonically, then paused. 'Unfortunately it's backfired, and it's going to cost you. Worse than that, it's already cost two women their lives.'

'You can't be sure of that—'

'You know I'm right,' Gaspare replied, cutting him off. 'There are some unstable people in this world. People who admire killers. People who read about them, write about them. Some even emulate them.'

Taking in a breath, Triumph looked at the dealer. 'Someone's copying Vespucci, aren't they?'

'How would I know? You created your own Frankenstein's monster – how can I predict what it will do? Maybe your greed made you meddle with a dangerous ghost. Maybe it just brought the *memory* of a killer back to life. But it tripped someone into action.'

The elegant American was sweating, his hands pressed together. 'How do we stop it?'

'It? Or him?' Gaspare queried. 'Why ask me? You started something. *You* did it. *You* live with it.'

And as Triumph Jones rose to his feet the news broke over the Internet that a woman had been killed in the lavatory of Tokyo Airport. She had been stripped, stabbed, and partially flayed.

BOOK THREE

. . . I am so fond of brothels, that the large amount of time I don't spend in them almost kills me . . .

Pietro Aretino

What really makes me marvel is that . . . [Titian] . . . fondles them, makes a to-do of kissing them, and entertains with a thousand juvenile pranks. Yet he never takes it further . . .

Pietro Aretino

23

Pausing as she applied her lipstick, Farina Ahmadi lost patience and threw it to one side. She couldn't remember where she had heard it – apart from on the news – but the name Sally Egan seemed familiar to her. She ran it over on her tongue . . . Egan, Sally Egan . . . but nothing came to her. Surely this murder victim – this care-home worker – hadn't been a client of hers? Farina paused, pressing her memory into service as she reached for the lipstick again. Had Sally Egan worked for her? No, Farina thought – she didn't even know the names of the cleaners, she left that to the house-keeper, so that couldn't be it. Maybe she had worked in the London gallery?

But the thought didn't gel. Farina filled in her lips with the coral gloss. Satisfied, she smiled at her own reflection, but the name wouldn't budge. How could she have known Sally Egan? A woman who worked in a care home wouldn't be working in an art gallery. After smoothing her eyebrows and fastening on her earrings, Farina finally remembered.

It had been several years earlier when she had been trying to mount an exhibition of famous portraits. Angelico Vespucci's image was at the top of her list, but Farina had only been able to get hold of engravings, and photographs of an old copy. A chance encounter with another dealer had brought Sally Egan into her sphere.

To all intents and purposes the Egan woman had been a talented artist, forced into menial work to pay the bills. So she had been more than pleased to do a competent oil copy of Titian's portrait of Angelico Vespucci. It wasn't supposed to deceive anyone, merely to be exhibited to show what the original had been like. Sally Egan had taken several months to complete it and when she had delivered it to the gallery, Farina had been impressed and paid her well, even promising that she might send other work her way ... Farina's smile dimmed, her pleasure at having remembered the woman overturned by the circumstances of Sally Egan's death.

Christ! Farina thought. She *was* the woman who'd been murdered and skinned. Like the woman in Venice before her ... For several moments Farina toyed with the idea that there might be some connection, jumping when the phone rang.

'Farina! a familiar voice greeted her. 'How are you?'

She rolled her eyes at Jobo's cloying tone. 'Well. And you?'

'Thriving. I take it your husband and sons are well also?'

'The whole fucking family is just peachy,' she replied. 'Get to the point.'

He was used to her manner, and carried on.

'Something incredible has just happened. Over here, in Tokyo,' he said, pausing to create the maximum effect. 'There's been a murder at the airport. Hardly that shocking usually, but there's something very odd about this one. The victim was stabbed and partially skinned.'

'So?'

'Well, it's the third, isn't it?'

'*The third?*'

'The third victim,' he said chillingly. 'First there was Seraphina di Fattori, then Sally Egan—'

Farina cut across him immediately. 'I was just thinking about what happened to her. How did you hear about her murder in Japan?'

'The internet. And besides, we have a bloodthirsty interest in such things.'

'You mean *you* do,' she retorted. 'I bet you've got a Google Alert out on violent murders. I wouldn't put it past you. God knows, you spend long enough drooling over those sick pictures of yours.' She doodled the women's names on a piece of paper, then paused. 'What's the name of the last victim? The one in the airport?'

'Harriet Forbes.'

Farina shrugged. 'Means nothing to me, but then again, why should it?'

'Well, we all knew – or knew *of* – Seraphina di Fattori, because her parents were collectors. I was just wondering if you knew the other victims.'

Hesitating, Farina took a moment to consider if it was in her best interests to admit that she had known Sally Egan.

Was it worth mentioning to the Japanese dealer? But then again, perhaps some shared confidence might strengthen their relationship? Make it more likely Jobo Kido could share information about the missing Titian?

'Oddly enough,' she began, 'I did know Sally Egan. Well, I didn't *know* her, I commissioned her. And you'll never guess what she did for me – she copied the Vespucci portrait.'

Her tone was light, but it rankled Jobo. '*She did what?*'

'Copied the Titian.'

'And now she's been murdered and skinned.'

Farina paused, uncomfortable. 'It could be a coincidence—'

'That she painted *The Skin Hunter* and was killed like that?' His voice rose. 'Don't be stupid, Farina, this is more than any coincidence. So, does the name Harriet Forbes ring any bells?'

'No! Why should it?'

'She didn't paint any Titian copies for you?'

Farina's tone was biting. 'No, she didn't. I've never heard of the woman.'

'The killer tried to skin her too—'

'*In Tokyo!*' she snapped. 'Seraphina di Fattori was killed in Venice, Sally Egan died in London, and your woman's been murdered in Tokyo. If it's the same killer, I hope he's collecting air miles.'

He ignored the sarcasm, deciding on his next tactic. Perhaps it was the ploy he should have used from the beginning, but now fate had played into his hands – and Jobo Kido was never a man to ignore good fortune.

'There have been three murders since the painting re-emerged. My God, it makes you think. I mean, I've always had a fascination with the dark side, but this is way beyond anything I've ever come across before. Perhaps the picture's really got some kind of power.'

'You think?'

'Maybe it *is* bad luck.'

She had already seen through the ruse.

'Bullshit, Jobo! You can't put me off it so easily. If the killings are connected, it's just some fucking lunatic copying Vespucci's methods. Could be they heard about the painting coming to light—'

'How?'

'Look on the internet, stupid. Since last night there's been a whole website devoted to Angelico Vespucci, the infamous Skin Hunter.'

'I haven't seen it!'

She carried on blithely. 'Anybody that interested would have heard about the painting. I bet some nutter's devoted their life to Vespucci and the re-discovery of the portrait's triggered him off.'

'To murder?'

'Why not?' she countered.

'By why?' Jobo persisted. 'What would be the reason? How would he pick his victims? And why them?'

'Goodness, Jobo,' she said snidely. 'I'd have thought that you of all people would have a theory. Of course you could

149

always ask your friends in your *private* gallery.' She laughed, knowing she was making him cringe. 'Have a word with them, why don't you? Or are you still hoping the Angelico Vespucci will end up side by side with all your other freaks?'

Breathing in, Jobo steadied himself before he spoke. 'You can laugh now, Farina, but I'll get that painting! It might take me a while, but I'll get it.'

'Really?' she countered, her tone amused. 'You'll have to kill me first.'

24

Within minutes of Triumph's departure, Gaspare had told Nino everything that had transpired. He listened expressionless, then whistled softly between his teeth.

'Mr Jones is too clever by half.'

Nodding, Gaspare climbed back into the hospital bed, pulling the blanket over him. He seemed chilled, taking off his glasses and laying them on the bedside table. To Nino's surprise there was a rosary he had never seen before, lying beside Gaspare's newspaper. The beads were spread out, the silver cross dangling over the edge of the table, swinging gently and throwing a sombre shadow on the wall behind.

'Are you all right?'

The dealer nodded. 'Just tired. Triumph Jones exhausted me. All that plotting, all that trouble, just to make himself even more important. And look what it cost him. He's now responsible for two murders.'

'*Three.*'

Expressionless, Gaspare stared at Nino. It was almost as though he had expected the words. That he had already heard them and absorbed the shock.

'Where?'

'Narita International airport, Tokyo,' Nino explained. 'A woman called Harriet Forbes was stabbed and partially skinned. It's all over the internet, and of course the police will start wondering if it's connected to Sally Egan over here. After all, Harriet Forbes was an Englishwoman – it's more than a little suspicious.' He paused, folding his arms. 'I think Triumph Jones is right about one thing – someone's copying The Skin Hunter.'

Reaching for his rosary, Gaspare fingered the beads. 'How far have you got with Johnny Ravenscourt's notes?'

'About halfway through.'

'Any help?'

'Yeah, they're giving me background information. But I'll know more when I've finished them.'

'Come across the scapegoat? The man who took the suspicion off Vespucci?'

'No, nothing on him,' Nino replied. 'Even Johnny Ravenscourt didn't uncover who he was.'

Not for the first time Nino wondered about Ravenscourt. If someone was copying The Skin Hunter, was it him? He had seemed benign – but was that an act? He certainly had the physical size to overpower and mutilate his victims. And the money and means to do so in private. Was he actually abetting and paying Nino *in order to keep close to him*?

152

Having put him on a retainer, Johnny Ravenscourt would want – *expect* – him to report back and fill him in with everything he knew. What if, instead of wanting to distance himself from the Vespucci business, Ravenscourt actually wanted to get closer?

'Talk to me.'

Nino looked up. 'Sorry, I was thinking. I want to find out everything about the victims, the three women who've been killed. I know about Seraphina, but nothing about the other two. I should talk to their families, their friends.'

'But not the police.'

'No,' Nino agreed. 'Not the police. They can do their own inquiries, and I'll do mine.'

Gaspare was reaching into his locker, rummaging for something. 'You'll need money. I'll write you a cheque.'

'I'm OK—'

'You can't be – you're broke. Let me help – you're doing this for me.' The old man paused, alerted as he saw the expression on Nino's face. 'What is it?'

'Johnny Ravenscourt's paid me a retainer—'

'*And you took it?*'

'Of course I took it!' Nino exclaimed. 'You haven't got money to throw around, Gaspare. I need travel money, expenses—'

'Not from him! You've just said he could be involved in the murders.'

'I know I did, but think about it. If I pull out now, refuse to take his money and work for him, it will look suspicious.

153

If Ravenscourt *is* guilty, I need him to trust me, not suspect me.'

Gaspare looked away, his tone edgy.

'I shouldn't have involved you in this. It was selfish of me – I didn't think it through. I just wanted to know what happened to Seraphina and I was pleased that you wanted to help.' He glanced back at Nino, his expression anxious. 'But it's getting too dangerous now. Three women are dead. And you're involved with Ravenscourt.'

'What about Tom Morgan?' Nino teased him, trying to break the tension. 'You haven't forgotten about him, have you?'

'Nino—'

'I called Morgan this morning. Strange man, hyped up, always on the defensive. Apparently he was questioned by the Venetian police again yesterday, but not held or charged. Interpol are involved, and the British police, but they couldn't hold Morgan.'

Despite himself, Gaspare's attention was caught. 'So he could have killed the women?'

'He's not supposed to leave the city, but as the police haven't taken his passport, yes, he *could* have killed them,' Nino said. 'But I've no idea where Johnny Ravenscourt was when Sally Egan and Harriet Forbes were murdered. He calls himself a spoilt old queen, and acts like one. But I've been thinking about that. What a perfect cover to fool everyone! He acts fearful, pets his dogs, talks in that high voice. No one would suspect him of violence – and remember, he has the money to travel as often, and as far, as he likes.'

'But why would he give you his research?'

'Maybe he wants an audience. The story's all over the news – maybe he's getting a vicarious pleasure from it. Maybe he wants to tempt fate, see if I can work it out.' Nino thought for a moment. 'Now I think about it, he came out of the blue and asked to talk to me. He said that he'd heard someone had hired me to investigate Seraphina's death, but he never explained *how* he knew about me. I didn't think about it at the time, but it's strange. After all, it's not my usual line of work, is it?'

'All the more reason why you should stop now,' Gaspare said, his thumb and forefinger closing over the crucifix. 'Maybe I've been wrong. Maybe the police should sort it out—'

'How can they?' Nino snapped. 'They don't know as much as we do. They certainly won't connect the painting with the women's deaths. Why should they?'

'But if they ask around—'

'You know the art world, Gaspare. They'll close ranks if they're questioned. No business on earth can hide a secret better, especially when there's money at stake. And who else would talk? Triumph Jones? Never – he's not going to admit his part in this publicly.'

Taking a breath, Gaspare watched him. He wondered fleetingly how different everything would have been if Nino Bergstrom had collapsed in France or New York. Wondered if the chance which had cemented their friendship might turn out to break them apart.

'Believe me,' Nino continued, 'the police will only ever get half the story. Let them carry on, but let me carry on too. I liked Seraphina and I want to pay you back for what you did for me.' He smiled, tapping his temple. 'My brain's active again, I feel fit. I can solve this, I know I can. Someone has to. Don't take this opportunity away from me, Gaspare. I need it.'

25

It was past seven when Louisa Forbes arrived at her sister's flat, standing in the doorway for a long moment before entering. She was pretending that Harriet was still alive, that at any moment her mobile would ring and she would start talking. But she knew this time was different, this time her sister wasn't phoning, or returning. She had been stopped in Tokyo, outside a toilet cubicle – killed within reach of a thousand people, within sight of a dozen cafés and bureaux de change. Only metres from the admirable Japanese plumbing, Harriet Forbes had died. And worse, she had been disfigured. It hadn't been enough that her clothes had been taken off her – the killer had wanted her skin too.

The thought made the hair stand up on the back of Louisa's neck. Who could have killed Harriet? That was the question the family were asking, the police were asking, and she was asking. Her sister had been a PR agent specialising in health and beauty, a freelancer dealing in nothing more provocative than lipgloss.

Walking into the flat, Louisa turned on the light and glanced around. The place was familiar, although she hadn't visited for several weeks after they had an argument about their parents. Louisa had loved her sister, but Harriet had been difficult to like at times, brusque, with a habit of dismissing other people's problems. Had she been a little callous with someone outside the family? Someone who took offence? A man perhaps? God knows, Harriet could attract any man – not that she was interested.

Many times over the years Louisa had expected her sister to confide in her about being gay. She had waited, not wanting to push the issue, but it had never been raised. Perhaps Harriet thought she had fooled her sister? Conned her into believing that she genuinely wasn't interested in getting married and having children, while all the time Louisa had known there had never been any chance of that. Why hadn't she talked to her? Hadn't she trusted her sister? Why live with a secret like that, as though it was something shameful?

Moving further into the flat, Louisa stared at the mess. Always running late, Harriet had left her home in a hurry and the kitchen still showed signs of her last breakfast, the cushions on the sofa in the sitting room scattered. She had drawn the blinds, but there was still a half-finished cup of coffee near the window where she had stood, waiting for her cab to arrive. Turning, Louisa remembered their last meeting in a wine bar. Harriet had been complaining about all the travelling she had to do, and Louisa had felt a flicker of jealousy. She was a bank manager – no exotic locations for her. Only a flat in Highgate and a husband working in IT.

But now the flat and the husband seemed precious. Louisa moved into her sister's bedroom and noticed the unmade bed and the laundry on a chair by the door. The family had been informed that the body would be held in Tokyo for forensic examination, after Harriet's father had flown over to identify her. It would be allowed home, but they didn't know when. And suddenly the thought of Harriet lying in some morgue, bloodless and mutilated, was too much for Louisa.

She sat down heavily, her hands trembling as she noticed her sister's laptop in the corner. Surprised that Harriet would have left it behind, she moved over and switched it on, waiting for the Microsoft welcome. And then the home page came up, with a photograph of her and her sister, arms around each other, smiling as though they had all the time in the world ...

In that instant Louisa knew that she had misjudged her sister, and failed her. Had been too jealous to make allowances, to see another point of view. Perhaps Harriet had envied *her*. After all, she was married and secure, able to express herself, not hiding any part of her character. It was obvious that their parents would never have been able to cope with Harriet being a lesbian, but Louisa could have. It wouldn't have made any difference to her. The shared confidence might even have brought them closer.

It was no use blaming Harriet for being secretive and dismissive. Perhaps she hadn't felt secure enough to confide? And now it was too late. Their parents were ageing, and Louisa felt a sudden and terrible grief for a sister who wouldn't be around when they were gone. For the loss of her, the shutting down of a shared past. For the companion she would never have again. For the blood link which some maniac had severed in a toilet in the middle of Tokyo airport.

Shaken, Louisa made a decision. She might have failed her sister in life, but she wouldn't repeat the mistake in death.

26

Staring at his computer screen, Jobo Kido remembered what
Farina, the bitch, had told him and typed into Google search
Angelico Vespucci – The Skin Hunter. Outside his office, he could
hear the new exhibition being arranged: a series of Japanese
lithographs. Not to his taste, but popular and always good
sellers. He jabbed his fingers on the SEARCH button impatiently, then watched as a website listing came up.

The Skin Hunter – Vespucci, 16th century, Venice

Good God, he thought, she was right. Pressing the entry,
he watched as an image of the glorious Grand Canal in
Venice came on to the screen.

It was like a normal picture postcard, until, suddenly, a
crude image of a body fell from the grand architecture and
plummeted into the water below, to the accompaniment of
Sting's 'Murder by Numbers'. Disgusted but curious, Jobo
pressed the ENTRY TO SITE sign and then watched as the
Venetian panorama closed down into a narrow, dark tunnel.

At the far end was an exit, a figure standing there. But just as Jobo saw it the figure rushed towards him, the screen filling with a splash of artificial blood.

'God!' he snapped, jumping in his seat.

Looking round to check that no one had been watching him, Jobo glanced back at the screen. What kind of a lunatic would build a site like this? he wondered, with a grudging admiration for its shock tactics. He scrolled down the table on the home page, clicking CONTACT, and waiting for a moment before the details were flashed on the screen.

You want to know about The Skin Hunter?
Join the Angelico Vespucci Admiration Society today – only $100.

As if! Jobo thought, returning to Google and checking if there were any other entries. There was just one, entitled *angelicovespucci.1555.com*

This site was altogether different. No cheap visuals, no crass music, just a very professional-looking biography of Vespucci, and a copy of an engraving of him. But, most importantly, across the top was written in copperplate:

ANGELICO VESPUCCI NEWS –
TITIAN'S FAMOUS PORTRAIT OF THE
KILLER HAS RE-EMERGED IN LONDON.

Immediately Jobo looked to see who had created the

site. But there was no name, only an email address –
avespucci-Venice.1555.

He typed a note:

I am interested in knowing more about this person. Can we
compare notes?

Then he sent the message.

Jobo waited. No reply. Five minutes later there was still
no reply. But when he came back into the office after an
hour, having attended to business in the gallery, there was
an email waiting for him.

Answer: *What do you want to know?*
Jobo wrote back: What can you tell me?
Answer: *You want to know about Vespucci? Or his victims?*
Jobo: Both.
Answer: *Who are you?*
Jobo: A fan.
Answer: *Where are you based?*
Jobo: Tokyo. You?
Answer: *I'm everywhere.*
Jobo: Can we talk?
Answer: *We _are_ talking.*
Jobo: How did you hear about the painting coming to light?
Answer: *Contacts.*
Jobo: Who has it?

Answer: *Wouldn't you like to know.*

Jobo: Do you know?

Answer: *I know everything about Angelico Vespucci. You've heard of the legend 'When the portrait emerges, so will the man' – well, he's back.*

Nonplussed, Jobo paused for a moment before continuing to type.

Jobo: Who were Vespucci's victims? I know about Larissa Vespucci and Claudia Moroni. Who were the others?

Answer: *Vespucci chose his victims with care. He picked them for a reason.*

Jobo: Don't you know who his other victims were? Rumour has it that he killed four women.

Answer: *Of course I know! After Claudia Moroni he killed Lena Arranti . . .*

This was news to Jobo, the first time he had heard of her.

Then he murdered the Contessa di Fattori.

Surprised, Jobo considered the name, then remembered the woman who had been killed in Venice weeks earlier – Seraphina Morgan, previously Seraphina di Fattori. A relative? Was the newly murdered woman a descendant of the Contessa? If so, there might be a genuine connection between the 16th and 21st centuries. Between two murderers five hundred years apart.

The realisation made him uncomfortable and he typed out his next words carefully.

Jobo: You said Vespucci chose the women for a reason. Why did he choose them? I know he killed his wife because she was unfaithful, but why the others?

Answer: *Why do you want to know so much?*

Jobo: I've told you, I'm a fan. You must be too, or you wouldn't have set up a website for Vespucci.

There was a long pause before the answer came back.

Answer: *I worship at the shrine of Angelico Vespucci. He was a rare man, his reputation has been abused. What he did he did for a reason, which will be made clear in time. His acts were deeds of great beauty. He made murder into an art form, poetic, brutal, sensual.*

Groaning, Jobo read the words and leaned back in his seat. The man was a lunatic. Some anonymous moron who had found his niche on the internet glorifying someone like Vespucci. A sick fantasist, getting a thrill from revelling in a murderer's grotesque actions. He could imagine some sweaty nobody in a sleazy flat, endlessly crouched over a computer, building up a fan base for a dead killer.

Irritated, Jobo wrote back: No one should glorify murder.

Answer: *So why are you asking all these questions? Or are you only interested in the painting?*

Jobo: Have you seen it?

Answer: *Of course.*

Alerted, Jobo leaned towards his computer screen, typing hurriedly.

Jobo: Where is it?

Answer: *I can't tell you that. But it's safe. He's safe.*

Jobo: Who's safe?

Answer: *Vespucci. I've told you, he's back – and he's killing again.*

The dealer held his breath, his hands shaking as he typed out the next words.

Jobo: What are you talking about?

Answer: *I'm talking about Seraphina di Fattori, Sally Egan and Harriet Forbes. Shall we chat again tomorrow, Mr Kido?*

And with that, he broke the connection.

Sweating, Jobo wiped his forehead. The stranger had used his name! But how the hell did he know who he was? Had he given himself away? Or was the man enough of a computer geek to track his email address? Jesus, Jobo thought, alarmed, he was really out of his depth ... Unnerved, he walked over to the window. Opening it, he breathed in the humid Tokyo air, but it seemed thick and tasted of tar. The absurd heatwave was glowering over the autumn trees, making their branches calligraphic symbols against the burning sky. And as he wiped his palms the first few drops of rain began outside. Then they stopped, drying on the bleached pavement below.

In the past, Jobo Kido's fascination with murderers had only ever gone so far. It was true he wanted the Titian, but his admiration for evil had always been from a distance. At close quarters, it was terrifying. How did the man on the website know about the killings? And how had he connected them to Angelico Vespucci?

Jobo tried to calm himself. The murders had been in the news, on the internet – anyone could have found out about them. A fanatic could easily have made a connection with Vespucci. The present-day killer had skinned his victims, so had Vespucci. Some unbalanced mind could easily have paired the acts.

Some unbalanced mind could just as easily have committed them.

Uneasy, Jobo moved back to his seat. He thought fleetingly of Farina Ahmadi and wondered if he should call her, but dismissed the notion. She would just mock him. And if she didn't, would the news tip her off, help her find the portrait? Likewise Triumph Jones ... Jobo flicked over the pages in his diary, trying to engage his thoughts on anything that wasn't Vespucci. But it didn't work. He had no interest in lithographs any more – all his concentration was on the exchange he had just had over the internet.

Did the man really know where the Titian was? And if

so, could Jobo somehow bypass his rivals to get it? The thought excited him. What risk wasn't worth the chance of securing the portrait? He paced the room restlessly, knowing that, like last night, he wouldn't sleep. Instead he would be waiting for his next website conversation.

A conversation with a freak. Or a killer.

27

St Bartholomew's Hospital, London

Having developed a chest infection, Gaspare Reni was kept in hospital, and Nino stayed at the convent gallery. He had tried to contact Sally Egan's family, but had been told that her only living relative – her father – had Alzheimer's and had been admitted to a nursing home. Further enquiries led him to Jean Netherton, who had helped to care for Mr Egan, and Nino had left her a message to get in touch with him.

In the meantime, he continued reading through the Ravenscourt notes. His research had been meticulous, thorough, dozens of little additions in the margin giving away his contacts.

Visit the Victoria and Albert, for painting . . . Check British Library for Joseph Hardone's book, Diary of The Grand Tour, Volume 2.

And on page 56 of the second notebook, he had written – *Sir Harold Greyly, Courtford Hall, Little Havensham, Norfolk. (Check him out for more information on Claudia Moroni.)*

Apparently the lead had not been followed up, because there was no further reference to Harold Greyly. Instead, Johnny Ravenscourt had looked into the life and times of the Contessa di Fattori.

When they were not directly referring to Vespucci, his notes had resumed their usual jaunty tone:

The Contessa di Fattori was beautiful by all accounts. Red-haired and striking. Allegedly Titian's model for 'Danae with a Nurse', she was immoral and debauched. Married to the withdrawn Count, she bore him a son (?) and took numerous lovers. Her maid was from the Orient and apparently taught her various sexual skills. Certainly it was known that di Fattori often visited the courtesans in Venice, not only to have sex with them, but to learn their techniques.

Nino gazed at the model in *Danae with a Nurse*: her knowing look, the easy way she exposed her nudity, one arm lying on a pillow, her left hand between her legs. She had certainly been beautiful, but there was no resemblance to Seraphina. Her descendant had been slender and dark-haired, without any of the pulsing eroticism of the countess.

Turning back to the notebook, Nino continued to read.

She was accused of witchcraft, but escaped punishment, various powerful men coming to her aid. (She also took one of her maids to court for theft, insisting that the woman be banished from Venice.) When her husband lost money on a fleet of ships which sank with his property, the Contessa applied to Pietro Aretino for help.

Nino looked at Aretino's portrait: a fat, greedy-looking man, with cunning eyes.

Not long after there is a record of the Contessa taking Angelico Vespucci as a lover, circa 1554. (Rumour has it she bore him a son, but this is not proven. Check the facts on this.) Their affair became the talk of Venice, the Contessa sharing her favours with Aretino and Vespucci at the same time. During one magnificent party, the trio put on an exhibition for their visitors, the sexual antics all but visible behind a transparent veil. On another occasion, gondolas were hired to cruise the Grand Canal, the couples in them making love in full sight. From the doorways and balconies people watched, throwing money to the most adventurous lovers.

In revenge the Contessa's husband took a courtesan lover from the Jewish Quarter. (Check name on this? Rena? Caterina? Nothing definite about this. Seems she came to work as a servant and was hired as a courtesan.) Some sources say she was an older woman, some say no more than a child. Certainly she had come from Milan. The count and Vespucci shared her favours.

171

Suddenly the phone rang beside Nino and a familiar voice came down the line.

'I've just got back to London. How are you getting on?' Johnny Ravenscourt asked, the dogs barking in the background.

'Pretty good.'

'You all right for money?'

'Yes, fine, thanks,' Nino answered, glancing at the papers in front of him. 'I'm just reading about the Contessa di Fattori. Personally I'm surprised her husband didn't kill her.'

'There *was* a theory at the time that he hired Angelico Vespucci to murder her—'

'Hired him? Why would he need to pay someone as rich as Vespucci?'

'He wouldn't. I imagine The Skin Hunter would have done it in the name of friendship . . . I suppose you've seen the website? The one that's just gone up on Vespucci? *angelicovespucci.1555.com*.' He laughed, but the sound was strained. 'Whoever put it up certainly knows a lot about him.'

'Anything you didn't already know?'

'No!' Johnny replied shortly. 'I'm the bloody expert! I've spent years on Vespucci and now some upstart thinks he can set up a website and steal my thunder. Bastard.'

Amused, Nino tried to mollify him. 'Should I look at it?'

'Suit yourself,' Johnny said, his tone sulky. 'To be honest, I emailed the site, but no one's come back to me yet. They're on to the Titian though. They know the portrait's turned up.'

Leaning back in his seat, Nino listened. His doubts about Johnny Ravenscourt were not lessened by the news of the website. Perhaps he had set it up himself, pretending there were other interested parties, other suspects. What *was* surprising was that the site announced the re-emergence of the Vespucci portrait – but then again, hadn't Johnny Ravenscourt been one of the first to know about it? Hadn't Seraphina told him? Certainly none of the dealers – Jobo Kido, Farina Ahmadi or Triumph Jones – would have deliberately made the news public.

Mistrustful, Nino chose his next words with care. 'So the portrait's common knowledge now?'

'It's on the net, so everyone will know.'

'Give me the website address again, will you?' Nino asked, jotting it down then returning to his previous theme. 'The Contessa di Fattori was an exhibitionist.'

'The Contessa was a one-off. After she died, the family became reserved, kept away from society. They were ashamed of her life *and* her death. But Seraphina admired her beauty.' He changed tack. 'Have you spoken to her husband lately?'

'Yeah, I talked to Tom Morgan yesterday. He's not been arrested. The police have questioned him again, but they let him go.'

'The Italian police couldn't find a dog in a tin can,' Johnny replied dismissively.

'Have they got any other suspects?'

'Not that I know of.'

Nino rifled through the pages in front of him until he found the piece of paper he was looking for. 'You made a note of a name – hang on, it's here somewhere – yes, that's it. Someone called Sir Harold Greyly, in Norfolk.'

'What about him?'

'Did you talk to him?'

'I was going to, but he was travelling overseas every time I got in touch. In the end, I moved on.'

It was a lie, and Nino sensed it. 'You wanted to talk to him about Claudia Moroni. Why?'

'I can't remember.'

'But it must have been important. Claudia was one of Vespucci's victims.'

'Like I say, I can't remember.'

In the background Nino could just catch a faint noise. A ping from Johnny Ravenscourt's computer to say that he had an email.

'I have to go, I've got a message!' he said, obviously excited. 'It's from the website. Somebody's finally answered me.'

With that, Johnny Ravenscourt clicked off the phone.

Thoughtful, Nino went back to his notes. Unable to concentrate, he turned to the computer and brought up the Vespucci website. On the last page, under CONTACTS, it read WEBSITE CREATED BY JEX. Jex, Nino thought, frowning as he made a note of the name.

He turned back to the paper on Vespucci. Johnny Ravenscourt had been lying, not in what he had said but in what he *hadn't* said. If Nino wasn't mistaken he had deliberately ignited his interest, then encouraged it by feigning indifference. Ravenscourt might act like a dolt, but Nino suspected that he was more devious than he appeared.

Reaching for the notes, Nino checked the name he had noticed earlier – Sir Harold Greyly, Courtford Hall, Little Havensham, Norfolk.

The address which would change his life.

28

New York

The body count was now up to three. Three women, all killed in the same way Vespucci's victims had met their end. The new Skin Hunter was active, inspired by the legend Triumph Jones had created. Had he never set his plan in action he could simply have bought the Titian portrait for himself. That would – *should* – have been enough for any dealer. His peers would have admired and envied him, his nickname gaining a platinum lustre. The prestige of owning a Titian should have been sufficient for even a mammoth ego.

But not for Triumph.

The same ambition which had cost him his marriage would now cost him his peace of mind. Sleep had deserted him, the lure of his business turned off. Even the pleasure of dining out had somehow become little more than a chilly formality. His friends might still gather about him, still engage him in conversation and gossip, but Triumph's mind never stayed with them for long. Instead it fixed on the names of the murdered women. It threw up images of their corpses, not seen but imagined in every terrible detail.

It seemed that every few days there was a report in the paper of another murder. In Venice, London, Tokyo. Perhaps only a ghost could travel so easily and so unnoticed? But this was no ghost, no legend that he had callously drawn up. This was reality. A man was killing women. Inspired by the original Skin Hunter someone was seeking to emulate – God forbid, exceed – his murders. It was as though a lunatic was now recreating what Vespucci had done four centuries previously.

Triumph suspected the police were likely to have connected the killings already. The publicity had ensured intense activity, the media demanding answers. What would happen next was inevitable: the news of a woman being skinned would travel quickly from Tokyo and they would remember Sally Egan in London, then, after a while, Seraphina. The police were bound to make the connection because there were too many similarities for the killings *not* to have been committed by the same man. And although Triumph had not engaged in the act of killing, he was indirectly responsible for the murders. It had been *his* PR which had drawn a lunatic out. *His* ego which had brought The Skin Hunter back to life.

He was responsible – and he knew it.

It would not be his buying and selling, his collecting, his numerous coups in the art world by which he would be judged. Triumph Jones would be victorious in something

177

altogether more heinous. Only Gaspare Reni knew the truth – but that didn't matter to the American. He knew what he had done and every waking moment scorched him with guilt. Overwrought, he became obsessed, developing a fantasy, a means of absolution. He would find the Titian and destroy it. He would send it back to the water. Back into the dark, the deep.

He had no idea if such a deed would stop the killings, but in his confusion Triumph convinced himself that it would prove miraculous. That somehow, if he could destroy the means by which the killer had been inspired, he could also destroy the man.

Having decided on his next course of action, Triumph sent out another message, knowing it would travel around the knotted vines of the art world within hours. *Whoever brought him the painting would be rewarded.* The man who brought the Titian back would be publicly recompensed, while privately becoming his saviour.

It never occurred to him that he might be summoning up the Devil instead.

29

Norfolk

Only two weeks until Christmas. Nino drove into the village of Little Havensham, parking his car outside a butcher's shop. Suspended from a row of steel hooks outside were the carcasses of turkeys and geese, inviting early purchase and orders. Next door a traditional greengrocer piled up his window with baskets of clementines, avocados, oranges, lychees and lozenge-shaped packets of dates, the whole presentation surrounded by a kitsch frosting of artificial snow. Walking in, Nino took his place behind a man waiting to be served, then asked for directions to Courtford Hall. Thanking the shopkeeper for his assistance, he made his way back to the car, only to be stopped by an elderly woman carrying a shopping basket.

'I couldn't help overhearing – you were asking for Court-ford Hall, weren't you?'

He smiled. 'That's right.'

'Well, I use to live there. Until the 1990s, when I was widowed and had to move to a flat. One of those modern places by the end of the green.' She seemed keen to tell her story. 'My nephew took over – Sir Harold Greyly. I suppose it's him you want to see?'

Having learnt quickly that listening was more profitable than talking, and that even the most unlikely people had good information, Nino encouraged her.

'Yeah, I'd like to talk to him. Unfortunately I haven't got an appointment, because I've no phone number for him to call ahead. I'm just dropping by on the off-chance he'll see me.'

'I'm Hester Greyly,' the woman said, putting out her hand. Willing, he took it.

'I'm Nino Bergstrom.'

'Unusual name,' she said, gesturing to his hair. 'Your appearance is unusual too. So much white hair on a young man.' She hurried on. 'I married into the Greyly family, so I was easier to put out to grass. Does that sound bitter? It wasn't meant to. Are you curious about the house or the family?'

The lie was smooth. 'Actually I'm a location finder for the film industry. We're always looking for interesting places to use and I heard about the hall for an E. M. Forster movie. It might be just perfect, but it's long shot.'

'*The film industry?*' she said, her eyes alert. 'How exciting. Perhaps I could help you. I was thinking of calling at the hall myself . . .'

She let the words hang and Nino caught them.

'D'you want a lift? I can take you there. Your nephew could hardly refuse to talk to me if I was introduced by his aunt.' He smiled, knowing that she would be a willing companion. 'Of course I'd understand if you were busy—'

'Oh no, I'm not busy. Not busy at all.'

Nino followed the directions to Courtford Hall. When they arrived, Hester climbed out of the car and looked around her, sighing longingly. Mullioned windows, bearded with variegated ivy and winter-bitten honeysuckle, caught the last rays of daylight and two stone statues book-ended the double doors of the entrance, the wood worn in parts and studded with iron nails.

Grabbing hold of it, Hester began to rap with a knocker the size of a serving dish. But no one answered the door. Instead a man appeared round the side of the house. He was wearing gardening clothes, cords tucked into Wellingtons, but he had the bearing of a military man and someone well practised in manners.

'What a surprise!' he said, kissing his aunt on the cheek and beckoning for them both to come in. 'How good to see you. I'm only sorry Clare isn't here, but she's gone to London to do some shopping and stay with her sister. Christmas, hey – gets worse every year.' He turned to Nino. 'Welcome. And you are?'

'This is Nino Bergstrom,' Hester said enthusiastically. 'A new friend of mine. He's a location finder. Wants to have a look at the hall for a film, something by E. M. Forster.'

Harold Greyly was all smoothness.

'Really?' he said, turning to Nino. 'Perhaps you'd like to make an appointment. You could talk to Mrs Grant, the housekeeper, or my assistant. I'm sure we can arrange a date that would be convenient for both of us.'

Immediately Nino stopped him.

'Actually I just need a few minutes, Sir Harold. If it wouldn't be too much of an imposition, could we do it now?'

Having beckoned for his assistant to approach, Greyly waved him away and turned back to Nino. 'Fine, come on through.'

With the air of the practised host, Harold Greyly ushered them into a comfortable sitting, room where two springer spaniels lay in front of a log fire, the day's newspapers dumped unceremoniously on the sofa.

Moving them out of the way, Harold turned to his aunt. 'Glass of sherry?'

'Lovely,' she agreed.

'And you?' he asked Nino.

'I'm OK, thanks.'

After pouring the sherry, Harold stood in front of the fire, giving Nino the chance to study him. His frame was upright, trim around the waist, his shoulders wide, his whole body suggesting time spent at a gym. Nino guessed his age at around fifty. Harold Greyly had kept his wavy auburn hair and his skin was weathered and marked with old acne scars around the eyes. He looked well fed and well bred, a country Englishman at one with his august surroundings.

'Nino wanted to look around the hall, but he was also wondering about our family,' Hester said, as though they had been talking about it in detail.

Nino was getting the drift quickly: the old woman was a bit of a mischief-maker. Having been 'put out to grass' she was eager to get back to her old home, even temporarily, and desperate to know what was going on.

Nino picked up from where she left off. 'I heard that the hall was one of the grandest properties in Norfolk. And one of the oldest, isn't it?'

'The foundations date from the fourteen hundreds—'

'Thirteen eighty,' Hester said firmly. 'Then there were wings and additions in the fifteenth century and more in the eighteenth.' She dimpled up at Harold, annoyingly helpful. 'Isn't that right, dear?'

He smiled, but the gesture didn't reach his eyes. 'You know the family history, probably better than I do.'

'Oh, I wouldn't say that—'

He cut her off. 'Hester, don't be modest.'

'I'm just trying to help,' she said, leaning back in her seat and sipping the sherry. 'Please go on.'

'I can give you a quick tour of the house,' Harold offered. 'We get people coming here pretty often. You know the kind of thing: journalists, people who write those home style magazines. I don't mind – I'm grateful to own such a wonderful place.'

'But you *don't* own it, do you?' Hester intervened. 'We're all just guardians, looking after the house and the books for the next generation.'

'You know what I mean,' Harold replied shortly, raising his eyebrows and turning away.

Having noticed several photographs around the room, Nino changed tack.

'You were in the Army?'

'I was. Retired now.'

'Harold speaks several languages,' Hester said proudly. 'And he's travelled all round the world, haven't you? And he's so well read, which helps with us having such a marvellous library. You know, all your travelling used to worry me when you first came here – would you settle into being a country gentleman?' Her tone was all barbed sweetness. 'But you have. Hunting, shooting, fishing. He's especially good at hunting, aren't you, dear?' She didn't wait for him to answer. 'One of the best shots in the county, I'm told. And he's game for everything – deer, rabbits. Skins them quick as that!' She snapped her fingers. Harold interrupted the flow as he turned to Nino.

'Did you want to look around?'

'I'd love to, thanks.'

Leaving Hester to her sherry, Harold took Nino on a tour. It was something he had often done before, that much was obvious, his enthusiasm a mixture of pride and boredom. Apparently his son was to inherit after him, and the Greyly line would continue as it had done for generations before.

'A place like this takes a lot of money to keep up, but it's worth it,' he went on. 'I made plenty—'

'In the Army?'

184

'God no!' he laughed. 'When I came out I worked as a consultant, putting the right people together with the right people – you know the kind of thing. Contacts. That's how I got my OBE.' He pointed to a painting on the landing. 'That picture's a Van Dyck. Not a copy, an original.'

'Must be worth a lot of money.'

'It's not a problem. We're insured and alarmed up to the hilt. We have to be, with the library, the silver and the paintings,' Harold continued, just in case his visitor was not what he seemed. 'We've not had a break-in since the seventies.'

'It's amazing,' Nino said, looking around at the oak panelling and the carved ceiling above the stairwell. 'It might be exactly what the film company's looking for. Can I take some photographs?'

Flattered, Harold allowed him to capture a few shots of the hall and upper landing, culminating in the drawing room. Knowing that he couldn't keep up the pretence for much longer, Nino pointed to a framed photograph on a side table, a faded picture of a debutante in the 1940s.

'It that your mother?'

'Yes.'

'It's all very English, isn't it?' Nino remarked, smiling as he took another photograph. 'You can tell from my name I'm a bit of a half-breed myself. My mother was Italian, my father Swedish. I suppose Courtford Hall's never seen any foreign blood? No dilution of the English line?'

Following Nino, Harold watched as he took several more photographs in the hall, finally concentrating all his attention on the ancient front doors.

'Oh, I wouldn't say that. There's always a little slip-up here and there in the best of families.'

Pretending to line up a shot, Nino's voice was casual. 'Really? Some ancestor you hide away? Some old scandal?'

Pausing, Harold considered his reply.

'There was an incident a long time ago. My relative was very excitable. She chose to marry a foreigner. She eloped, thank God. Saved us a lot of gossip.'

'Didn't the family approve of her choice?'

'He was a Venetian merchant.' Harold's voice was pure scorn. 'Called Moroni. My relative was christened Catherine, but changed her name to Claudia. To fit into Italy better, I imagine. Claudia Moroni – it would hardly suit Norfolk, would it?'

The name slapped down between them, as unsettling as a firecracker, and Harold's voice suddenly took on an undercurrent of suspicion. 'I thought you were interested in the house?'

'I am, but it's good to hear about the family too.' Nino clicked away, avoiding Greyly's stare. 'So she married a Venetian in trade,' he went on, refusing to acknowledge the insult and taking it as a joke instead. 'That's bad. Did she have children?'

'A daughter.'

'Hardly a threat to your lot, is it?'

'I beg your pardon?'

Nino could sense the enmity coming off the man.

'I mean a daughter isn't the same as a son who could

186

claim some inheritance. Did your ancestor ever come back to England?'

'No. She died in Venice.' Harold replied curtly. 'What *exactly* has she got to do with a film location?'

Nino shrugged. 'Oh, nothing. I just get bored looking at houses. Sometimes I like to know about the people who lived in them. It makes the place come to life.' He paused after taking the last photograph. 'I think I've got what I need now.'

'Really? You do surprise me.'

The words caught Nino off guard. They were said with an unexpected malice Harold Greyly's expression cold.

'What *exactly* do you want, Mr Bergstrom?'

Nino didn't miss a beat.

'What do I want? What I got, Sir Harold. Some great shots of a great house.' He opened the front door and stepped out on to the steps. 'Will you say goodbye to your aunt for me, and thank her for her kindness? I'll be in touch.'

Venice, 1555

The rumours have swollen, gross and unconfined. Three nights ago a mob collected outside Vespucci's house. I counted over thirty men combined, carrying torches in the fog, their voices raised in a frenzy, their hands wrenching at the iron gates to gain admittance. But the gates held. Only later did Vespucci come to the window and look out. The candles illuminated his lean shape, the portrait of his murdered wife hanging on the wall behind him.

All Venice believes him guilty, for what other suspect is there?

At nine the wind picked up, frothing a sea so high it threatened to drown us all. Some spoke of wickedness, that God was meting out punishment where we would not. We had a killer in our number. Behind iron gates, Angelico Vespucci lived like an innocent. Whored, enjoyed the worst depravities. And kept his freedom. The priests spurred us to action: Vespucci was the reason for our suffering. The Skin Hunter was killing Venice herself.

The mob comes each night. They stand at Vespucci's gates, they chant the names of Larissa and Claudia, summoning up the dead

188

as though they believe the living cannot touch him. Vespucci has hired guards who patrol the railings and shadow the doors.

Later he stands at the balcony window, Aretino beside him. He stands like a martyr before God, demanding understanding, his lean hands pressed to his temples. Aretino might defend him, plead his innocence, Titian might suggest support, the portrait coming more and more to life as Vespucci moves closer and closer towards death.

All but a few of the old priests are refusing to come out at night. They fear the dark and the ghosts of drowned dogs, and although the poor body of Claudia Moroni was buried in a crypt on the Island of St Michael, the grave was desecrated and her corpse stolen. Two days later the body was returned. The undertakers had wrapped her in white silk, but when she came back she was flayed and bound in the darkest of crimson.

30

Bored, Gaspare stared at the television and then clicked it off. He had worked his way through all the books Nino had brought for him and dismissed the art magazines. His respiratory infection now under control, he was feeling more alert but aching to be home, back at the gallery. He knew that he would have to remain in hospital, but his enforced idleness had made him restless, keen for an update on Nino's progress.

Having heard nothing from him since the previous day, Gaspare had spent an uneasy night making notes, drawing up a list of possible suspects. He dismissed the idea of a re-appearance of the original Skin Hunter. The killer was no supernatural force, so who was he? Someone copying Vespucci? Someone with a past record of violence? Someone who was known to be obsessed by the Venetian?

Jotting down two names, Gaspare considered them – Tom Morgan and Johnny Ravenscourt. Then he added the name

Jobo Kido as an afterthought. Why not? The Japanese dealer was an oddity, his collection depraved. Could he have crossed over? Instead of collecting the memorabilia of killers, might he have started to collect his own? Harriet Forbes had been killed in Tokyo, where Jobo Kido lived. It was possible.

The door opened, interrupting his thoughts, and Nino walked in with a takeaway Italian meal. Putting it down on the bedside table, he split the food between the two of them and passed some to Gaspare.

Smiling, Gaspare looked at it. 'Rubber pasta.'

'But pasta nonetheless,' Nino said, taking a mouthful and then pulling Gaspare's notes towards him. 'What's this?'

'Suspects.'

He read the names, shaking his head at the last. 'Jobo Kido? Are you kidding?'

'The man's twisted,' Gaspare said firmly. 'Years ago I saw his private collection. He's fascinated by killers. Don't tell me that's not relevant. Kido would do anything to get that Titian painting. Which, in case you've forgotten, is still out there somewhere.'

'Unless the killer's got it,' Nino replied, pointing to the sheet of paper. 'You can add another one to that list of suspects – Sir Harold Greyly.' He wiped some tomato juice off his chin with a paper napkin. 'His name came up in Ravenscourt's notes and I went to see him yesterday. One of the Greyly ancestors was The Skin Hunter's second victim.'

Gaspare's eyebrows rose. 'Claudia Moroni?'

'Yeah,' Nino agreed, taking another mouthful.

'Did he tell you about her murder?'

'No. And he got very twitchy when I started asking questions.'

'But why suspect him of being involved with the current murders?'

'I dunno,' Nino replied, putting down his food and staring at the old man. 'Something about him. Something off-key. He's travelled a lot, was in the Army and then made a killing with his contacts, arrogant bastard. He's now inherited a country pile after turfing out his old aunt, and she seemed a bit miffed. She also said something about Harold being a keen hunter.'

'He lives in the country – most of them hunt.'

'She said he could skin anything.'

Gaspare paused, putting his fork down and pushing the food away from him. 'Before you arrived, I was just thinking about the killer. I mean, three women, in three different countries. Who could do that?'

Nino was still eating. 'How d'you mean?'

'He'd have to have funds. He's either rich enough not to need a job, or he's self-employed. If he had regular employment, he'd have to keep taking time off work.'

'Not necessarily,' Nino replied, finishing his food and throwing the containers in the bin. 'Sally Egan was killed at night. After work hours.'

'But the killer had already been to Venice and then went on to Japan. A plane ticket to Tokyo costs money—'

'I agree. But surely the more important question is: why

did he choose them? Before we wonder about his means, shouldn't we try and work out *why* he picked these particular victims? That's the key, Gaspare. The women *must* have something in common.'

'But if the killer's copying Vespucci, shouldn't we look at *his* victims first?'

'OK.' Thoughtful, Nino nodded. 'I've been reading Johnny Ravenscourt's notes – not finished them yet – and they list Larissa Vespucci, Claudia Moroni and the Contessa di Fattori. But a website dedicated to The Skin Hunter lists a woman called Lena Arranti as the penultimate victim.' Nino paused for effect. 'Somebody out there's been doing their research. This information isn't readily available. It took Ravenscourt decades to find it. And this website only went up forty-eight hours ago. Doesn't that strike you as odd? A website glorifying The Skin Hunter appears at the same time as his crimes are being reenacted?'

'You think the killer created it?'

'Yes,' Nino replied. 'Yes, I do. I think the man who made the website killed the women. Perhaps it all started with him getting curious about Vespucci, then he became obsessed. Then, when he heard about the painting turning up – thanks to Triumph Jones' PR stunt – he flipped. Took it as a sign and started his own tribute. He wants to copy Angelico Vespucci – he wants to be him, to have his power, his legend.'

'It makes no sense—'

'Not to us. But to a fanatic, it would. About five years ago I was working for a company who were making a film about

Jack the Ripper. One of the many. I remember that the director said it would make a fortune. Even if it was bad, it would bring in a profit, because everyone wanted to know about a killer. Especially killers who had never been caught. Glamorous murderers. And The Skin Hunter has a kind of sick glamour. He created havoc in his time. He terrorised the Republic of Venice and yet he got away with it. Vespucci disappeared, and a scapegoat took the blame.'

'I wish we knew who that was.'

Nino turned to Gaspare. 'You think it's important?'

'I think everything we find out about Vespucci's important. Did the victims have anything in common?'

'Vespucci killed Larissa because she was unfaithful, but Claudia Moroni was a respectable married woman.'

Nino thought back over his conversation with Harold Greyly, repeating his words.

"My relative was very excitable . . . She eloped, thank God. Saved us a lot of gossip." He glanced over at Gaspare. 'Perhaps she wasn't quite the innocent she appeared?'

'And the Contessa di Fattori was a whore.'

'Yes, everyone agrees on that. And the website said that Lena Arranti was a courtesan, working from the Jewish Quarter in Venice.' Nino paused. 'There *is* a link between the women – sex. Larissa Vespucci was an adulteress. Lena Arranti was a prostitute. The Contessa di Fattori was promiscuous. Perhaps there was some sexual secret about Claudia Moroni? Perhaps *that* was why her descendant said that her elopement saved them from scandal?' Nino got to

194

his feet. 'If the theme *is* sexual – if Vespucci set out to punish these women – is that why women are being killed now? Does our killer want to punish women too?' He walked to the door, then turned. 'I'm going back to the gallery to finish Ravenscourt's notes. Then I'll talk to him—'

Gaspare flinched. 'Don't be stupid! We've just agreed that Ravenscourt could be the killer—'

'And if he is,' Nino said simply, 'someone has to stop him.'

31

New York

The news had only been out for an hour when it came to Farina Ahmadi's ears. Good God! she thought, hurrying back to her gallery on 45th Street. Who had ever heard anything like it? A top dealer virtually advertising for help in finding a famous work of art. Why didn't Triumph just put a fucking sign up in Times Square? she thought angrily, slamming the door of the gallery behind her and moving into her office. Once there, she made a call on her mobile and stood by the window waiting for someone to answer.

'What the bloody hell are you playing at?' she snapped, infuriated to find herself talking to Triumph Jones' recorded message. Severing the connection, she then dialled Tokyo, knowing she would wake Jobo Kido in the middle of the night and hopefully catch him off guard.

'*What!!!*' a voice answered, and Farina smiled to herself. He *had* been asleep. Good.

'Jobo, it's Farina.'

'It's one in the morning. What d'you want?'

'Triumph's drumming up help to find the Titian.' She could hear the dealer take in a breath and could imagine him sitting up in bed, shocked out of sleep. 'You know what that means, don't you, Jobo? Every fucking lunatic will come out of the woodwork. And now everyone will know about the Titian portrait. I mean *everyone*.' Her voice plunged. 'Are you listening to me?'

'Every word,' Jobo said, getting to his feet, his wife grumbling as she turned over in bed. Walking downstairs, he made for the kitchen, closing the door behind him. 'You woke my wife—'

'*I woke your wife!*' Farina snapped. 'Jesus! You moron, this is more important than your wife's beauty sleep!'

'Farina, calm down,' Jobo said, tying the dressing-gown cord round his waist and getting himself some water. 'Why did he do it? It doesn't seem like Triumph to advertise something like that. He's crazy—'

'Oh, he's crazy like a snake!' she snorted. 'He wants that bloody painting so much he's going to stoop to any depths to get it. And you know what that means, don't you? We lose.'

'*We* lose?' Jobo repeated. 'Why exactly are you letting me in on this, Farina?'

'The Titian's out there, hanging its arse in the wind. We *have* to get hold of it before it disappears again. Or worse, Triumph gets it. He can't win, not this time.' She thought of his steely confidence and cringed. 'I refuse to let him add one more scalp to his belt – particularly *that* Titian. I want it. And

I know you want it. But the way I see it, our joining forces would double our chances. We could share it.'

'*Share it?*'

'Stop repeating everything I fucking say!' she roared. 'Think about it. If we keep quiet, then who's to know that we're sharing it? We have to act! Triumph's calling on all sorts – thieves, villains, and all the loser dealers out to make a buck. He'll be up to his knees in fakes within a week. And even if he does manage to flush out the Titian, he'll lose it when we offer a better deal.'

'*If* we hear of it.'

'Let it be known that we're willing to top his offer and we'll hear of it.' She paused, confident. 'Come on, Jobo, it's a good idea. You could have the Titian half the time and I could have it the other half. East meet West – it would be a cultural gesture.'

'It would be a two-fingered gesture to Triumph,' Jobo replied, amused. 'But I want the painting for my collection.'

'And I want the painting for my husband. So what? We both want it, but Triumph wants it more.' She paused, her tone softening. 'He's rich, but I'm richer. And you're no pauper, Jobo. Together we could match – and top – any amount Triumph can offer. Naturally we would have to draw up a contract.'

'But to share the painting—'

'It's your choice, Jobo,' she said succinctly. 'Go halves, or get sod all.'

32

It was nearly eleven at the Kensington gallery as Nino finished reading the last of Ravenscourt's notes. There was no mention of the scapegoat, the man who had been the alternative suspect to Vespucci. And although the notes were detailed, most of the information was now available on the internet site, the creator of which was uploading new data continuously. Facts which had been long suppressed were now emblazoned for the world to read about. Only an hour earlier another copy of the portrait had been added, but this time there was an engraving of Vespucci's house in the background.

Nino knew that the house had long since been destroyed, that no evidence of the piazza remained. A hotel had been built on the site instead, The Skin Hunter's legend buried under four floors of bedrooms and power showers. Looking back at Ravenscourt's notes, Nino came across a later entry for Lena Arranti, matching it to the website. The date was the same: 8 December 1555.

Thoughtfully he jotted down the names of the victims, placing the dates of their death next to them.

Larissa Vespucci	4 November, 1555
Claudia Moroni	26 November, 1555
Lena Arranti	8 December, 1555
Contessa di Fattori	1 January, 1556

Surprised, he stared at the dates, then reached for his own notes and compared them.

Seraphina Morgan	4 November
Sally Egan	26 November
Harriet Forbes	8 December

His heart raced. The killer *was* copying Angelico Vespucci, using his methods, *on the anniversaries of the Venetian murders*. There was only one date left unfilled – 1 January. On that day another woman would be killed and mutilated, another tribute offered up to The Skin Hunter. Someone would die. But who? And where?

It could be in London, Tokyo or Venice. It could be any woman, anywhere. And until Nino worked out *how* the women were connected, he had no way of finding the next victim.

Or saving her.

Suddenly the phone rang, an unfamiliar, friendly voice greeting him. 'Is that Nino Bergstrom?'

'Yes.'

'This is Jean Netherton. You left me a message and asked me to get in touch. It's about Sally. Sally Egan.'

Relieved, Nino nodded. 'Thanks for getting back to me. I'm investigating Sally's death—'

'Are you the police?'

'No, this is a private investigation.' He thought of Gaspare Reni. 'I can give you a name if you want to check me out.'

She hurried on. 'No, it's all right. I *want* you to look into Sally's death. The police don't seem to have anything and it's been two weeks since she died.' Her voice picked up. 'I rowed with her that night. I'll never forgive myself.'

'What did you argue about?'

'I used to help look after Sally's father when she had a night out. Dear God, she deserved a break, but she was drunk when she got home and I overreacted.' She paused, struggling with her conscience. 'Sally liked to have a good time.'

'Sorry to be blunt, but was she promiscuous?'

'Yes,' Jean agreed. 'She liked men, liked sex. Well, I don't know about that. Maybe she just wanted to feel loved. Poor Sally had no one but her dad and lately even he didn't recognise her.'

'Did she ever tell you she was being followed? That she'd had any strange visitors? Any odd phone calls?'

'No, nothing. She just got on with her life. Looking after her dad was hard work and she had a job at a care home in the daytime. I don't suppose it was what she expected with all her talent—'

'She was talented? How?'

'Sally could paint, Mr Bergstrom. I don't mean dabble – she could really paint. She'd wanted to go to art school when she was younger, but what with her dad being ill, and her being his only relative, she had to give it up.' Jean paused, remembering. 'She showed me a photograph once of a picture she'd done for someone. It was a copy of one of the Old Masters.'

'D'you remember which one?'

'No.'

'D'you remember the painting?'

'Oh yes,' Jean said eagerly. 'It was a portrait of a man. Not a good-looking man – big, rather puffy eyes, wearing black clothes. It was old-fashioned. You know what I mean. The original must have been done centuries ago. Sally told me she'd been commissioned by a London dealer.'

Nino kept his voice calm. 'You don't remember who the dealer was, do you?'

'No,' Jean said regretfully, then brightened. 'But I think I might still have the photograph of that painting. Sally was very angry one day, said she'd missed her chance and threw out all her drawings, everything she'd ever done, and all the photographs she'd taken of her work. I didn't tell her, but when she went to work I got them out of the bin.'

'*You kept them?*'

'Yes. I thought one day she might want them back ...' Her voice caught. 'She won't now though, will she?'

Nino paused before continuing. 'Can I see what you saved?'

'If it'll help find out who killed her, of course you can,' Jean said, giving Nino her address and arranging to meet him the following night. Then she paused, regretful. 'She had a big heart, did Sally. But there was never anyone there to stand her corner or help her out. Not even me in the end.'

33

The house was a semi-detached in the suburbs of London, the mistress of the house nervous but welcoming. Shown into the sitting room, Nino took a seat on the red Dralon sofa and accepted a cup of tea. With biscuits. He could tell that Jean Netherton was uneasy, staring at him and taking a seat as far away as she could. He couldn't work out if it was because of who he was, or what she was about to show him.

'Here they are,' she said, putting a box on the coffee table in front of Nino. 'All Sally's drawings and photos.' She paused, unable to resist the question any longer. 'Your hair – is it natural?'

Smiling, Nino shook his head. 'No, I was ill. I recovered, but my hair turned white.'

'Ah, I see,' she said, relieved. 'I suppose it must help you a lot in your business?'

'Sorry?'

'Well, you look tough. I suppose that's important for a detective. You look like a man who can handle himself. I

204

mean, no one would take you seriously if you were a wimp, would they?'

Smiling again, Nino pulled the box towards him, taking off the lid and beginning to rifle through the remnants of Sally Egan's talent. He was startled by her ability. The drawings were impressive, even her sketches clever, and when he came to an envelope containing photographs he could feel his hands shake with anticipation. Scattering them on the table, he looked along the row of images. Jean pointed to the last one.

'There it is!'

She didn't need to tell him – Angelico Vespucci's face was immediately recognisable. Picking up the photograph, Nino studied it intently.

'She was good,' he said at last. 'Titian wouldn't have been ashamed of that.'

'I told you Sally had talent.'

'And she did this for a London dealer?' he asked, turning over the photograph and trying to read some writing. It was faint, written in pencil, and it took him a moment to work it out. 'Something Ahmadi . . . The first name begins with F and I think it's an A.' He glanced at Jean. 'Ring any bells? Did Sally talk about a dealer called Ahmadi?'

Regretfully she shook her head. 'No. She just said it was a dealer in London.'

'Well, there won't be that many London dealers called Ahmadi.'

'Oh, now wait a minute!' Jean said, remembering something. 'Sally said the painting was going abroad, somewhere exotic. She did tell me . . .' Irritated, she sighed. 'It's no good, I can't remember.'

'D'you know *when* Sally painted this?'

'About three or four years ago. Long before I knew her.'

He pointed to the photograph. 'Can I take it?'

'Of course.'

'You've been a big help,' Nino said, smiling and slipping it into his pocket.

'D'you want to take the rest?'

He frowned, baffled. 'What?'

'Everything else. D'you want to take it?' Jean said, passing him the box. 'Please, take it. Look at what she did, how clever she was. I know you're only really interested in that photograph, but I want someone to see Sally for what she really was. She wasn't like they say in the papers – she was unlucky, that was all. Look at her work, Mr Bergstrom. Don't judge Sally Egan by what she was when she died, judge her for what she *could* have been. If you do, somehow her death won't be such a waste.'

It was nearly seven thirty when Nino returned to Kensington. Letting himself into the gallery by the back door, he turned off the alarm and checked the answerphone. There were three messages: two from Gaspare, one from the police. The last recorded voice asked him, with cold civility, if he would call the station and ask for Detective Steiner. At his earliest convenience.

So when the doorbell rang thirty minutes later the name

coming over the intercom was a familiar one – Detective William Steiner. Frowning, Nino buzzed him in, waiting for the policeman at the top of the stairs. Showing him an identity card, Steiner moved into the sitting room and Nino offered him a seat. He was slight in build with curly, dry hair, wearing a creased grey suit that didn't fit and scuffed brown shoes.

'I'd like to have a chat with you, Mr Bergstrom,' he said, his voice surprisingly guttural.

Wary, Nino regarded him.

'Can I have the number of your police station? I'd like to check that you *are* Detective Steiner,' he said, taking down a number and making the call. When Steiner's identity was verified, he shrugged. 'Sorry about that. I just wanted to be sure who I was talking to. You can never be too careful these days.'

Steiner was unemotional, unreadable. 'You work for Mr Jonathan Ravenscourt, I believe?'

'Yeah, I work for him.'

'Doing what?'

'I'm looking into something for him.'

'What?'

'The death of a friend of his, in Venice. A woman called Seraphina Morgan.' Nino paused. 'What's the problem?'

Steiner ignored the question. 'Aren't the Italian police dealing with the case?'

'They are. But Mr Ravenscourt wanted me to look into the matter too.'

'But you're . . .' There was a pause as Steiner flipped open

207

his notepad and checked his facts, 'a location finder for the film industry, I believe.'

'I was.'

'But now you're a detective? Rather a change of career, isn't it? Or did watching all the private eyes on screen inspire you?'

Keeping his patience, Nino answered him. 'I'm just helping Mr Ravenscourt out.'

'But he's hired you. He's paying you for this *help*?' Steiner pressed him. 'There's no point being evasive with me, Mr Bergstrom. I'm privy to all of Mr Ravenscourt's affairs and he hired you on the twenty-seventh of November, and paid you a retainer of five thousand pounds. Is that right?'

'Yes,' Nino said warily. 'What's the problem?'

'What did he want to find out?'

'Everything about Seraphina Morgan's death,' Nino repeated. 'She was a close friend of his in Venice. He was upset, wanted to find out why she'd been killed. Who had killed her.'

'And why would he think *you* could find this out?'

Feeling suddenly under threat, Nino wondered how much to tell, how much to withhold. He had to give the police something, but not too much. Nothing about the painting or Vespucci.

'I knew Seraphina slightly – we met once. Actually we had a mutual friend.'

'Mr Gaspare Reni.'

'Why are you bringing him into this?'

'Into what?' Steiner replied. 'You said you had a mutual friend. We know you've been staying with Mr Reni at his Kensington gallery; I was just coming to an obvious conclusion ... You seem very jumpy, Mr Bergstrom. Is there a reason for that?'

'What's all this about?' Nino asked, his voice calm again. 'You've obviously been checking up on me – why? Tell me. You owe me that.'

'Mr Ravenscourt's back in Venice. He contacted us from there, told us about you. He said he was afraid of you—'

'*What?*'

'That you'd forced him to give you money in return for information—'

'*Is this a joke?*' Nino asked, dumbfounded.

'He said that you had come to *him* about the death of Seraphina Morgan. That you knew things no one else did. Things no one *could* know – unless they'd been her killer. Mr Ravenscourt felt he had to leave London because he was afraid of what you might do. After all, if you'd killed once, you could kill again.'

Incredulous, Nino stared at the detective. 'He's lying! He hired me to—'

'Mr Ravenscourt also said you had stolen some papers from him.'

'He lent me those!'

Steiner was impervious. 'He said you were trying to "steal a march on his book". Apparently Mr Ravenscourt had been writing a book for some years and you had come along and stolen his ideas.'

'He's mad,' Nino replied. 'It's all rubbish – the man's lying. I've never killed anyone in my life. Jesus, look at my background! I've never even had a speeding ticket. What the hell is the bastard talking about?'

'You, Mr Bergstrom. He's talking about *you*.'

Nino's mind cleared in that instant. Ravenscourt was setting him up. Nino was to be the scapegoat this time. While the police were investigating him, Johnny Ravenscourt was free to do as he pleased. It was the twelfth of December – and the last murder committed by Vespucci had been on the first of January. The anniversary was coming up fast and the killer was still out there.

'Everything he said is fantasy,' Nino insisted. 'Get Ravenscourt here. Let him face me, then we'll see who's lying.'

'I'd really like to do that, Mr Bergstrom,' Steiner said evenly. 'But unfortunately Mr Ravenscourt seems to have disappeared.'

34

Tokyo

Jobo Kido waited until his wife was asleep, then crept into his study and locked the door. Turning on the computer, he went on to the internet, looking for angelicovespucci.1555. com. The site came up immediately and he pressed ENTER. Almost as soon as he had typed hello a reply came up.

Mr Kido, how are you today?

Jobo: How do you know me?

Answer: *Everyone knows everyone. Are you wondering about the painting?*

Jobo: You know I am.

Answer: *In time you'll see it. But not yet, Mr Kido. Perhaps you'd like to ask me another question?*

Jobo: You mentioned three women.

Answer: *Three dead women.*

Unnerved, Jobo pressed on.

Jobo: Are they connected?

Answer: *You've disappointed me. I was expecting more from you.*

Jobo: Don't sign off!

Answer: *Then make it worth my while to talk to you. I can't tell you how the women are connected – you have to find that out for yourself. If you do, I'll give you the painting.*

Hands sweating, Jobo stared at the screen. He could get the Titian! Sod Farina Ahmadi, he wasn't going to have to share it after all. He could have the portrait all to himself. Hang it next to his other exhibits, stare at it, enjoy it. Relish it. It was the culmination of all his hopes: the depiction of a maniac, painted by one of the Old Masters. It would be worth millions. And it would be his.

Giddy, Jobo calmed himself, thinking of the implications of this correspondence. If the man on the computer knew who he was, did he also know where he lived? The thought made his flesh creep. Jobo might argue with his wife constantly, but he had no wish to see anything happen to her. Or himself. He would have to be very clever. Somehow manage to get hold of the painting – and expose the killer at the same time.

The picture *would* be his, but safely.

He turned back to the computer.

Jobo: Are we talking about Vespucci's victims, or the recent killings?

Answer: *The recent murders. The new Skin Hunter.*

Jobo: There's a new Skin Hunter?

Answer: *What do you think this is all about, Mr Kido?*

Hesitating, Jobo wanted to ask the obvious question, but resisted. Perhaps the man wasn't the killer and would be offended by the presumption. He might sign off, never contact Jobo again. And take the Titian with him.

Jobo: Did the same man kill all three women?

Answer: *You know he did. He skinned them.*

Jobo: They were killed in three different countries. How did he do that?

Answer: *Use your imagination.*

Jobo: Is he as clever as The Skin Hunter?

There was a long pause, moments passing before the answer came up.

Answer: *He won't be caught. The Skin Hunter is never caught.*

Jobo: Do you know what happened to Angelico Vespucci?

Answer: *Yes. He became me.*

And with that, he logged off, breaking the connection, and Jobo was left staring at the empty screen.

35

London

It was twelve days to Christmas. Lights were strung across Regent Street and around Oxford Circus, shop windows dragging buyers into their clammy interiors. Thick with the scent of candles and perfume, the stores grew sticky under the plastic mistletoe, shoppers overheated as the temperature plunged outside. Snow was forecast, a breakdown at several set of lights holding up the traffic from Piccadilly to Park Lane.

Having been discharged from hospital, Gaspare was back at the Kensington gallery, struggling to remember the code as he turned off the alarm. For a moment he stood in the hallway looking upwards, thinking of the break-in, listening for the sound of footsteps. Then, annoyed at his own timidity, he walked into the sitting room and flicked on a solitary lamp. The old familiar shapes came back in all their dim glory: the painted ceiling, the suit of Japanese armour, the set of kettledrums he had bought in an auction. All so random, like disparate friends greeting him for a surprise party.

Walking over to the central table, Gaspare noticed a jumbled assortment of notes. Some were in Nino's hand-writing, others he presumed belonged to Johnny Ravenscourt. He knew that Nino hadn't shown them to the police, and touched them gingerly, as though they were contaminated, before gathering them together and putting them into a plastic bag.

Moments later, footsteps announced the arrival of Nino, Gaspare feigning horror as he entered the sitting room.

'Ah, the Devil is loose. The killer is at large! Please spare me, don't hurt me!'

Ignoring the comments, Nino stared at his old friend. 'You got back from the hospital all right then?'

'Well, when I heard of your predicament I thought you might never get out alive.' He patted Nino's shoulder affec-tionately. 'You didn't think I'd let the police keep you in there, did you?'

'I don't know how you got me out. Detective Steiner seemed very eager to keep hold of me.'

'The police had nothing concrete. The benefit of living a long time is that you make contacts over the years. None of us were born old; some of us had very influential positions in our prime. And even long-term friends have debts to pay back. Let's just say that I made a phone call.'

'And that was it?'

Gaspare shrugged. 'I'd love to say I had that much power,

but apparently the police were only trying to scare you. They didn't really believe what Johnny Ravenscourt said, but they'd lost touch with him – thought he was up to something – and put pressure on you to find out what it was.'

'Up to something?'

'Mr Ravenscourt's known to the Art Fraud department. He has a record for smuggling fakes,' Gaspare said, smiling. 'It was a long time ago, and he's not been active since, but it's still on record.' He paused. 'How much did you tell the police?'

Quickly Nino filled Gaspare in, pouring two glasses of brandy and passing one to the older man.

'Ravenscourt tried to land me in it – which makes him look even more suspicious. If he's copying Vespucci I reckon he picked me to be his scapegoat.'

'Or he was just stirring up trouble,' Gaspare offered, passing Nino a letter with his name on it. 'When I got home, this had arrived.'

Taking it, Nino read.

Dear Mr Bergstrom,

We met the other day and I would very much like to speak with you again – concerning Claudia Moroni. Perhaps you would like to call me on Tel. Norfolk 845 - 9851.

Kindest regards,

Hester Greyly (Mrs)

Gaspare was looking at Nino with curiosity. 'Anything interesting?'

'It's from Harold Greyly's aunt. Perhaps she wants to tell me something he wouldn't.'

'Or perhaps she's working with him to get you back to Norfolk?'

'She asked me to ring her. Not visit.'

Gaspare shrugged. 'So ring. But don't go back there.'

Half an hour later Nino finally managed to get an answer on Hester Greyly's phone. The receiver was picked up, but there was no greeting, just soft breathing down the line.

'Hello?' he said, concerned. 'Mrs Greyly?'

'Who's this?'

Nino hesitated, not recognising the man's voice. 'Mrs Greyly asked me to call her. Can I speak to her, please?'

'That's not possible.'

'Is she ill?' Nino asked, uneasy. 'I need to talk to her. She sent me a letter—'

There was a rusting sound on the phone and someone else spoke. This time Nino recognised the voice immediately – it was Harold Greyly.

'Who's calling?'

'Nino Bergstrom. Your aunt sent me a letter asking me to get in touch. Can I talk to her, please?'

'I'm sorry, Mr Bergstrom, that won't be possible,' he replied, bone cold. 'My aunt died this morning.'

Nino's mouth dried.

'She fell down the stairs and broke her neck. So I'm afraid that no one will be speaking to her. And frankly I have nothing to say to you anyway, so I'd be obliged if you didn't contact me or my family again.' His manner was all crisp efficiency. 'You came here under false pretences, Mr Bergstrom. I feel I should warn you that any further harassment will be reported to the police.'

After putting down the phone, Nino took a long drink of his brandy and turned to Gaspare. 'Hester Greyly died this morning.'

'That was convenient.'

'Her nephew said it was a fall . . .' Nino paused, thinking back. 'She was a nice lady. Old school. She had something to tell me, or show me. But you can bet that bastard's emptied out her house, made sure I'll never see anything I shouldn't. I reckon he knew that she'd got in touch with me and I don't believe she fell – I think Harold Greyly killed her.' Nino finished his brandy, his hand shaking as he put down the glass. 'I'm not sure he murdered the other women, but he certainly could have killed his aunt.'

'But that would break the pattern. Vespucci killed four *young* women—'

'I know. And he killed them on specific dates. The same dates as Seraphina, Sally Egan and Harriet Forbes were killed. There's only one anniversary left – the first of January.' He held the old man's gaze. 'You think someone on a killing spree wouldn't deviate from it? Maybe Harold Greyly was *forced* to act. Maybe Hester was about to give him away and he had to kill her.'

'Or maybe Greyly didn't kill the other women?'

'Maybe not. But he *could* have done,' Nino said quietly.

'Greyly's ex-Army, disciplined, unemotional. He hunts and kills for sport. He's very aware of his status in life. I doubt he'd let anyone take that away from him without a fight. And there's something else. When he told me his aunt was dead his voice was flat. No grief, not even a pretence of it. There was nothing. Jesus, he could have been telling me the time.'

Venice, December 1555

On 8 December a body was found suspended from one of the bridges which leads to the Jewish Quarter. I saw this, bore witness to it. The woman was hung by a rope slid under her arms, the end fastened to one of the iron lamps above. Her chest was stripped of skin, also her legs, a star of David hanging limply against the shredded flesh. She loomed out of the heavy mist suddenly. Shaken, a woman shielded her child's eyes, and an old man crossed himself. In the wind which has not left us, the body swung like a side of beef, and from her toes, blood the colour of cranberries dripped into the canal below.

I could hear the rope scrape against the iron lamp which held it; I could see the carcass, red-raw, waving like a bloodied flag. I heard some woman scream and footsteps running. I heard shouts coming from across the bridge, a tumult of activity, panic and distress.

She didn't mind them. Even when men caught hold of the rope and tried to pull her upwards, to swing her on to the bridge, even then. What little unmarked skin remained was white as a winter stoat; much more bloodied where the knife had done its work. I think she had been very young, this girl of Israel. Even before I knew for certain, there was something of the child about her.

Three women are now dead. Yet this time Angelico Vespucci does not cringe, nor skirt the crowd. This time he is silky, Aretino telling all who listen that he is innocent. He was caught up with business, Aretino says. They were discussing their next venture. Vespucci was not abroad that night. The killer is not him. Look, says Aretino, I have the proof you seek.

He thinks his brilliance fools; that no one knows that secretly he has long traded with Vespucci. No one suspects that paintings leave Titian's studio bound for courts abroad, where fees demanded double the artist's charge. For nearly a year Aretino has betrayed his comrade. Thrown in his lot with the merchant, shored up his wealth by robbing his oldest friend.

But now the Devil has him by the tail. Aretino is off to Titian's studio. Maybe he wants to study Vespucci's portrait. To flatter the genius he tricked into immortalising a killer. And still I watch and wait. My time has not yet come. I have to stay my hand, wait to see what next occurs. For all his talent and his eloquence, Aretino cannot shield the merchant forever. Vespucci's face is changing, growing slack with all the horrors he has seen. His hands shake with a tremor, his confidence a sham. Daily the kindness he once possessed gives way to a dank depravity; and the weather follows his mood.

An awful stillness has come upon the city. The cold has had some part in it, but there is more, an undercurrent as dangerous as the sea snakes who swim in the depths at our feet.

221

The name of the last victim was Lena Arranti. She came from Milan, arriving in Venice to work as a servant, her beauty taking her from the kitchens to the beds of famous men. On the day she died, it had been her birthday. She was fifteen years of age.

And Angelico Vespucci's lover.

BOOK FOUR

Painting done under pressure by artists without the necessary talent can only give rise to formlessness, as painting is a profession that requires peace of mind.

Titian (1485–1576)

36

Venice

Grabbing hold of Johnny Ravenscourt, Tom Morgan hustled him backwards into his apartment, slamming the door behind him. Caught off guard, Ravenscourt put up his hands to ward the American off.

'Calm down!'

'Don't tell me to calm down, you fag!' Tom replied, jabbing at the other man's shoulder. 'I want to talk to you. Seems like I'm not the only one either. Why did you leave London so suddenly?' He pulled at Ravenscourt's arm, navigating him towards an armchair and then pushing him into it. Although Ravenscourt was the bigger man, he was cowed by the show of aggression and began to blather.

'What is it? What is it?' he pleaded.

Tom stood over him. He had lost some weight, and his exclusive clothes were creased, unkempt. A day's growth of stubble and swollen eyes hinted at neglect, the smell of

225

cannabis strong on his hands. And his feet were bare again, bloodless in the cold.

'What d'you know about Seraphina's death?' he demanded.

'Nothing!'

'You hired someone to look into it. Which is odd, seeing as how I was interviewed by the *same* man, sent by Seraphina's family.' His voice took on a warning tone. 'I never liked you, *Johnny*. I always thought you were a bad influence on my wife—'

'I knew your wife long before you came into her life! I was her oldest friend.'

'You were an emotional *leech*,' Tom snapped. He was jumpy, jerky in his movements. 'I know you were always trying to turn her against me. You wanted me gone and Seraphina to yourself. And now she's dead – and I want to know why you're poking your fucking nose into my business.'

'Your business isn't doing too well,' Ravenscourt said snidely, straightening his jacket. 'Don't forget who helped you out when you needed it—'

'I never asked Seraphina to go to you! You were the last person I'd have asked for help.'

'But she *did* ask me, didn't she?' Ravenscourt countered. 'And I *did* help you, Tom Morgan. Helped you save your bloody skin. One word from me to your employers and they'd have tossed your drugged arse out of the window in an instant.'

'You want to watch what you say.'

But the steam had gone out of Tom Morgan and his anger

226

had given way to a craving for a joint. A smoke would calm him down, he told himself. Life had been hell lately. Who could blame him for wanting to settle his nerves? Hurriedly he moved over to a cabinet and rolled a joint. Lighting it and inhaling deeply soothed him in seconds, as he slid on to the window seat.

He could see the canal below, the lamplight stippling the water, a knot of mangy ducks paddling under the bridge. It was true: his business was in trouble, and the old apartment he had once shared with Seraphina would soon have to go on the market. All the past was leaving him, all the memories of his wife disappearing with the home they had once shared. All that remained of Seraphina was the photographs and the papers and the numerous articles about her death.

'I don't know why Seraphina loved you,' Ravenscourt said dismissively. 'She could have done so much better.'

Tom turned to him. 'What are you up to, you fat bastard? Why leave London in such a hurry? Are you on the run from the police?' He paused. 'I wouldn't put it past you, Seraphina said you had a colourful history.'

'I was bored in London. I just wanted to come back to Venice. It was a rush decision.'

'I bet,' Tom replied, inhaling again, then blowing the smoke slowly between his lips. 'I miss her. I miss my wife.'

'I miss her too.'

'I was her husband.'

'Yes, and I was her friend!' Ravenscourt snapped back. 'You didn't ... you didn't have anything to do with her death, did you?'

To his amazement, Tom laughed. 'Funny, I was just going to ask you the same thing ...' He stared out of the window. 'She was different when she came back from her trip to London. Something had happened – d'you know what?'

'No.'

'But she used to talk to you. Even more than she talked to me,' Tom continued. 'And you hung out together a lot in the days before she died. Why?'

'She was my friend—'

'No! That wasn't it. It know you, Ravenscourt – you don't rate friendship that highly. You were stalking her—'

'Rubbish! We went out for meals, we went shopping!'

'But Seraphina didn't want to see you!' Tom snapped back. 'She told me that. She said you were making her uneasy. Asking her questions about her trip, quizzing her. Why?'

'I don't believe she said any of that,' Ravenscourt insisted, pouting. 'We were very close. She needed me. She confided in me—'

'*What* did she confide?'

'That she was pregnant.'

Tom waved the words away with his hand. 'The whole family knew that.'

'But did the family know that you didn't want the baby? That you told Seraphina to get an abortion?'

The words struck home.

'What?'

'Seraphina told me all about it,' Ravenscourt went on. 'How she wanted to have the child, but you were against it—'

'But I wasn't! It was the other way round! I wanted the baby, she didn't.'

'I don't believe you,' Ravenscourt replied, but he was obviously shaken. 'Why would she lie about it? Seraphina never told lies, and certainly not about anything as important as that.' Pausing, he turned away from Tom, trying to collect his thoughts. 'She swore blind that you didn't want the child. She said it was a bad time, that you couldn't afford to support a family.'

'But there was money coming,' Tom replied. 'Soon we'd have been loaded, more cash than we'd ever dreamed of. There was a windfall on its way, Ravenscourt ... You didn't know that, did you?' He grinned unpleasantly. 'Seems Seraphina didn't tell you that much after all. Kept the real goodies to herself. We had it all planned out and soon I'd never need your help – or *anyone's* help – again. Fuck the business, we weren't going to need it. We were going to be rich.'

His throat constricting, Ravenscourt struggled to control himself.

'What are you talking about?'

'Come on! I know she told you—'

'About what?'

Inhaling, Tom sucked at the joint. His mind was floating, all fury and frustration gone. The peace wouldn't last, he knew that. But for a while he could linger, just above reality.

'*What are you talking about!*' Ravenscourt repeated, his bulk rising out of the chair, his heavy features flushed. 'What did Seraphina say?'

'Let me tell you a story,' Tom began, looking out of the window again. 'There was a girl called Seraphina. She came from an old Venetian family, who weren't quite as powerful as they had once been. Well, Seraphina met a handsome prince in the USA,' he spelt it out, taunting Ravenscourt – 'and they fell in love. He was rich, but – as with her family – it didn't last. So Seraphina was looking for an opportunity . . .'

'*Tell me!*'

'Listen to the fucking story!' Tom retorted. 'And lo and behold, a golden opportunity fell into her lap. Well, her hands anyway. By pure chance she found a painting worth millions.' He paused, grinding out his joint and tossing the stub out of the window. The ducks hurried towards it, then, disappointed, moved off again. 'What a lucky girl. She left it with a trustworthy old dealer, a man called Gaspare Reni, knowing it would be safe with him until we could figure a way to smuggle it to Venice. That's where you came in, Johnny.' He paused, but when there was no reply, he carried on. 'You had a history of smuggling and Seraphina relied on that. On being able to convince you to help her. You two being so close . . . She was getting it all planned, all organised. The day before she died she was about to bring you in on it. We'd have given you a cut of the proceeds, you know. After all, there'd have been plenty to go around.'

Ravenscourt was watching him with despair. Cheated, desperate despair. 'But she died before—'

'Yeah, Seraphina was killed before she could talk to you. Before we could get the Titian from London to Venice.' Tom paused, staring at Ravenscourt. 'Don't look at me like that.'

'Like what?' he croaked.

'Like you think *I* killed her.'

'Did you?'

'Before we got the painting? No, that wouldn't make sense,' Tom replied, moving over to the big man. 'Did you kill her?'

'*No!* I was in London when she died.'

'Oh, but that's not true, is it?' Tom said. 'I saw you in Venice the following day. You could easily have come back the night before ... Of course, I could get the police to check it out.'

Ravenscourt's natural guile came back into play.

'And bring more attention on yourself? I don't think so. Remember the husband's always the prime suspect.' Standing up, he moved to the door. 'I'm leaving now.'

'I would. It's beginning to get dark and it's easy to get lost in Venice.' Tom turned back to the window. 'Oh, and mind the fog, Johnny. They say it's going to be bad tonight.'

37

It wasn't going to be the usual kind of Christmas. It wasn't going to be any kind of Christmas because Harriet Forbes was dead and her family couldn't come to terms with her loss. There was to be no tree, no celebration dinner, no festive decoration of the house. Christmas cards would not be sent, presents not bought, because none of it mattered. Besides, there were no grandchildren to cater for – Harriet had never married and Louisa was not the maternal type.

Unable to cope with the despair in her parents' house, Louisa Forbes took action. Applying for compassionate leave from work, she waited until the police – working with the Japanese force – had inspected her sister's flat and then, painstakingly, she went through every item herself. The action calmed her, and when it was done she rang all of Harriet's business contacts and friends. Someone knew something – it was just a question of finding out who. One letter, one note, one book, one article of clothing, one word

– she didn't know what it would be, but *something* would lead her to Harriet's killer.

Louisa Forbes didn't believe that it had been a chance murder, a crime or killer peculiar to Tokyo. She didn't believe it because she had looked into the death of Sally Egan and the killings were too similar for chance. The man who had killed Sally Egan had killed her sister. That was all she had. It was all she needed.

So when Louisa was approached by Nino Bergstrom she was more than willing to listen. Together they walked to a nearby bar, and having chosen drinks and taken a seat, Louisa looked curiously at Nino.

'You're not connected to the police, are you?'

He shook his head. 'No, I'm working for someone privately.'

'Can I ask who?'

'Gaspare Reni.'

She shrugged. 'The name means nothing to me. Did he know Harriet?'

'No, but he thinks that the deaths of your sister and a friend of his might be connected.'

She was intelligent, obviously so, her intense grey eyes fixing on his.

'Do you know anything about Harriet's death? The Japanese police don't tell us a thing. They treat us like fools, make us feel bad just for asking questions. They won't even release her body.'

She paused, sipping at the wine Nino had bought her. He had been expecting someone emotional but she was resolutely still. He imagined that she would be a loyal friend, a good wife, and she had a quality he admired – a kind of grace. The bar was already full of workers going home, grabbing a pint before the 6.57 train.

'Can I talk to your parents?' Nino requested.

'They won't talk to you – they're in shock. If you want to talk, talk to me.'

Nodding, he leaned closer towards her and dropped his voice so that he wouldn't be overheard. 'Your sister had a flat in London, didn't she?'

'Yes.'

'I'd like to see it. Could you take me there?'

'Now?' She bent down and picked up her bag. 'All right, we'll go now.' Her voice was composed. 'It's OK, Mr Bergstrom, I can cope. I want to help. Let's get on with it, please.'

When they entered the Highgate flat it smelt like any place closed up in cold weather. It wasn't damp but chilly, uninviting. Louisa turned on the lights and checked the post.

'I should stop the mail. How d'you do that?' She answered her own question. 'Post Office, I suppose.' Her long fingers rifled through the envelopes, then she dropped the pile on to the hall table and walked into the sitting room.

Nino followed her, looking at a wall of photographs. Harriet Forbes had been a traveller, that much was obvious. There were prints of the Far East, New York and Milan, Post-it notes stuck next to them, with the dates written in red. And on the space over her computer was her timetable – seven countries to visit over twenty days.

'Did she always travel so much?'

Louisa nodded. 'Since her twenties. Harriet was the restless sort, never liked to be in the same place for long.'

'Did she get on with her employers?'

'They were always changing. She would take on a project to do PR for one company, then go on to something else. It was a movable feast; the beauty business launches new projects all the time.'

'What about her private life?'

'Harriet wasn't seeing anyone at the moment.'

'There was no ex-boyfriend who might bear a grudge? No one rejected?'

'No. The police asked me the same question, but there was no boyfriend.'

He could feel the hesitation in her voice, and pressed on. 'Was there someone?'

'Harriet was gay,' Louisa said simply. 'She didn't think I knew. I kept waiting for her to confide in me, but she didn't. She did have a partner a few years ago, but it broke up, amicably. They stayed friends.'

'D'you know her name?'

'I've forgotten it now, but I saw a Christmas card once. The message was very loving, very sweet ... Harriet seemed to be ashamed of being gay. At least she kept it a secret, so I imagine she wasn't comfortable with it. She used to cringe when Mum and Dad teased her about getting married and giving them kids.' She breathed in, holding on to herself. 'My sister's work took up more and more of her life, until there wasn't room for anyone.'

Nino was reading the spines on books arranged on rows of white painted shelving.

'Your sister certainly liked reading.' Surprised he pointed to one volume. 'Machiavelli's *The Prince* – that's quite a switch from promoting make-up.'

'Harriet was smart, much too smart for PR,' Louisa said, folding her slim arms, her face composed. 'She used to say that she'd make a killing, put away a load of money, and then do what she really wanted to do.'

'Which was?'

'Harriet wanted to be a journalist, in the arts.'

An alarm went off in Nino's brain.

'What branch of the arts?'

'Painting.' Putting her head on one side, Louisa studied him. 'What is it?'

'Nothing.'

'Please don't lie to me, Mr Bergstrom. I can handle anything you tell me.'

He nodded. 'All right. The first victim, Sally Egan, was a painter. A very gifted one.'

'And?'

'She was commissioned by a London dealer to paint a man called Angelico Vespucci.' He caught a flicker of recognition at the name. 'You've heard of him?'

'It rings a bell,' Louisa said, concentrating. 'A while back Harriet wrote a piece for an art magazine. She was so thrilled she'd been commissioned.' Moving over to her sister's filing cabinet, she pulled out the top drawer and flicked through

236

the papers. 'My sister said it was very difficult finding out the information, so she was disappointed when they only published it on the internet.'

'What was the magazine?'

'I can't remember,' Louisa replied, still searching through her dead sister's files. 'But Harriet was angry about it. Said that they didn't treat her seriously because she was a PR agent, and not someone trained in the history of art. I remember it well because it really upset her, and Harriet wasn't someone who often showed her feelings.' Finally she drew out a slim file marked VESPUCCI. 'Here it is,' she said, handing it over to Nino. 'It took her weeks to write – she was so proud of it.'

Flipping open the file, Nino was confronted with a photograph of a face he knew only too well, together with a thoroughly researched and well written article. Her sister was right, Harriet Forbes *had* been wasted in PR.

'Why did she want to write about Angelico Vespucci?'

Louisa shrugged. 'I don't know. She said something about him being painted by one of the Old Masters—'

'Titian.'

'Yes, Titian,' she agreed, 'but otherwise she didn't talk about it. Is it important that both Harriet and Sally Egan had a connection with Vespucci?' Her eyes fixed on Nino. 'Or should I put it another way – it *must* be important that both of them had a connection. But why?' She took the reproduction out of the file and studied it. 'Who *is* Angelico Vespucci?'

'He lived in Venice in the sixteenth century. He was a merchant.'

'And?' she said, pushing him. 'What else about him, Mr Bergstrom? You have to tell me, otherwise I'll just look it up on the internet and find out myself.'

'He was a murderer, known as The Skin Hunter.'

She took the words full force, her fingers touching her mouth for an instant, her eyes closing then reopening. A moment passed, then another.

Finally she spoke. 'How many women did he kill?'

'Four.'

'How many women – apart from Harriet and Sally Egan – have been killed now?'

'Three,' Nino replied, watching as she sat down. After getting her a glass of water from the kitchen, he handed it to her. Her breathing was rapid, but her control was impressive.

'Was this other victim . . . Did she have any connection to Vespucci?'

'Yes.'

'Was she mutilated?'

'Yes.'

She looked up, holding Nino's gaze. 'Someone's copying Vespucci, aren't they?'

'I think so.'

'And his name – The Skin Hunter. Does it mean what I think it does?'

'He flayed, or partially skinned, his victims.'

238

'Like Harriet.'

'Yes,' Nino agreed. 'I'm sorry—'

'Don't be! I want to know. I need to know what this is all about . . . Has anyone else connected the murders?'

He shook his head.

'Not that I know of. The victims were all killed in different countries. The Japanese police haven't connected Harriet's killer with Sally Egan. I'm surprised you did.'

'He skins women! How likely is it that there are two people doing that? Of course I made the connection,' she replied, looking back at him. 'You said Vespucci killed four women. So there's one left.'

'We can't be sure—'

'Of course we can! If the killer's copied the Venetian's actions so far, why would he stop until they're completed? If he's mad enough to start, he's mad enough to go on . . . Have you any idea who he is?'

Pausing, Nino studied her. He was prepared to confide, but he wasn't about to endanger her.

'No,' he said evenly, 'I don't know who the killer is.'

She nodded. 'But you are going to find him, aren't you?'

It was the first time he had been asked outright. Gaspare had needed help, but it was the sister of one of the victims who put the question directly. *You are going to find him, aren't you?* And it was only at that instant that Nino realised exactly what he had taken on.

38

New York

Sitting beside the statue of Hans Christian Andersen, Triumph watched the people moving around in front of him. He hated New York at Christmas time; loathed the continual drinks parties and openings, the relentless gaiety of it all. Weighed down by guilt and riddled with uncertainty, he was hardly sleeping, his usual immaculate appearance muted with exhaustion. Suddenly a child walked in front of him and stopped, staring, fascinated by the black man who was sitting, immobile, in front of the bronze. A moment later, the child's mother hustled him away as the first light snowfall drizzled down on Central Park.

It was three thirty in the afternoon, the light ready to dip down into the dark beginning of the evening. Triumph huddled further into his coat as a stooped man of around forty came over and took a seat next to him.

'Cold, isn't it?'

Triumph sighed. 'I'm here, let's get on with it. You said you had the Titian portrait of Vespucci.'

When there was no reply he turned, staring at the Cuban's grainy face, his eyes narrowed under the snowfall as he lit up. The match flared, ignited the end of his roll-up, and then he blew it out, letting it drop to the ground. Patiently, Triumph watched the performance, his hands pushed deep into his pockets.

'I haven't got the painting yet—'

Triumph stood up.

'But I can get it!' the man went on, jumping to his feet. 'I've got a good lead. I just need cash to get some more information.'

'I'm getting nothing here but a cold,' Triumph replied, walking off, the man following him.

'Fucking bastard!' he shouted. 'You need me! You need me!'

No, Triumph thought, I don't need you. Or the woman who stopped me outside the restaurant last night. I don't need the dealer from Sweden who called by the gallery, or the junkie who stumbled into my path when I was walking to my car.

The news that he was looking for the Titian had certainly spread; there wasn't a day that Triumph hadn't been approached, the police questioning the wisdom of his action in offering a reward. But every offer, suggestion or deal had been bogus, and when he was unexpectedly tapped on the shoulder, he jumped.

241

'Christ, Triumph!' Farina said, laughing. 'Your nerves are shot!'

She was wearing a ranch mink, the collar turned up, her hair hidden under a wide-brimmed hat. The snow which had seemed so out of place in the park flattered her, making a translucent backdrop. Smiling, she slid her arm through Triumph's. If she found him tense, she didn't allude to it. Instead she walked with him for several yards until she got down to the matter in hand.

'That was very naughty of you, Triumph, putting out a reward for the painting. You'll get every loser on earth coming out of the woodwork.'

He walked on, letting her talk.

'Of course, you *could* get lucky; someone might know about the Titian. And they might tell you.' She twinkled up at him. 'You'd tell me, wouldn't you?'

Tell you what? he thought. That I'm going to destroy it? No, I don't think I'll tell you that.

'Of course,' he lied.

'My husband could make it worth your while,' she continued, her gloved hand clinging to his arm. 'You know how much I want him to have this painting. I'm sure you and I could come to some arrangement.'

'An arrangement?'

'We're the biggest dealers in New York,' Farina went on blithely. 'We should get the goodies. We deserve them. No point letting other dealers – *lesser* dealers – have a go. You know how I admire you.'

242

'You do?' he asked, inwardly mocking her.

'I always have,' she replied, pausing when Triumph stopped walking.

'This *arrangement*,' he said. 'I never thought of that, Farina. Never realised you were so attracted to me. Never thought of you and me . . .'

She was so taken aback she couldn't speak. Surely this man, this African-American, wasn't suggesting an affair?

'To be honest, I've always admired you, Farina,' he said, putting out his hand and stroking her cheek. 'And now I'm wondering *exactly* what you would do for the Titian. How far would you go?'

He was staring at her so intently she flushed.

'What the hell—'

Gently he slid her hand out from the crook of his arm, patting her shoulder in a paternal gesture. 'Go home, my dear. You're a great dealer, but a lousy whore.'

Then he turned, walking into the falling snow.

Without looking back, he could imagine the expression on Farina Ahmadi's face – the outrage. She would seethe with humiliation. At having been regarded as a whore – and rejected as a woman. Of course Triumph knew he had made an implacable enemy, but he didn't need Farina any more. He was tired of the deals, the hustling. Tired of a world which dealt in beauty, and employed all kinds of ugliness.

Preoccupied, he walked on, letting the snow fall on him as he rounded a bend in the park. But he never anticipated what would happened next. Wasn't expecting the blow to the back of his head which sent him reeling against the side of the bridge over the pathway. Staggering backwards, he felt the blood pour from a scalp wound, but had no time to react. When he was struck again, his legs buckled. Caught off guard, the elegant Triumph Jones fell clumsily to the ground, the side of his head striking the stonework, his hands scrambling for purchase on the snowy ground.

And all the time he was thinking of the women, the three women who had died for a painting. The three deaths he had inadvertently caused. And wondering if his would be the fourth.

39

London

Picking up the post, Nino walked back upstairs into the sitting room. The cold was stinging, the old-fashioned gas fire hissing into the room, its blue flames spluttering as he opened the letter addressed to him. Surprised, he read the signature, then looked back to the beginning.

Dear Mr Bergstrom,

I thought I would send you a little note in case we didn't have the chance to meet up. Life is so strange, and one can never leave things to chance, or so I find.

You were asking about our family and I overheard you talking to Harold about our ancestor, Claudia Moroni. He was rather evasive, for reasons which will become obvious. My nephew is a snob and very defensive about the family reputation. Charlotte – later Claudia – did not elope, she was thrown out of the family. With her brother.

Signor Moroni married her, but theirs was not a love match. Claudia did not love her husband, but her brother. There had been gossip in Norfolk about the incest, so she had to be exiled, along with him. She was sent to Venice. I believe there is a painting of her and Matthew. People think it portrays her and her husband, but that's not true.

I'm sure you know what happened to her. Her death was terrible; as big a scandal as her life.

My nephew would do anything to prevent this information being dredged up again. But I think your enquiries were made for some other reason than simple curiosity. I hope I'm right, but I feel certain that you need to know about this.

Use the information wisely. It caused much suffering once and I would hate to think such unhappiness could happen again.

Kindest regards,

Hester Greyly (Mrs)

Nino read the letter twice, now certain that Hester Greyly had been murdered. Incest was taboo, as much in the twenty-first century as ever. A prominent family might ride out murder, even criminal links, but not incest. He could imagine Harold Greyly's fear of exposure. His status would plummet: he – and his family – would be censored, reviled. The news would make the red-top papers, smut for gossip, the local pub and shop pointing him out. A man as proud as Harold Greyly could never have handled the fallout. His golf club, his shooting colleagues and his powerful friends would drift away and Courtford Hall would become a mockery without the applause of the admiring.

The incest between brother and sister had to be hidden at all costs. And it had been, for centuries. Until, suddenly, someone emerged and started asking questions about the exiled Claudia ... Nino could imagine the shock, the blow to the ego. Men killed for small change – how easy would it be for Harold Greyly to justify the murder of his aunt to protect his family name?

Nino remembered Hester only too well, and the provocative baiting of her nephew. She could never have imagined the reaction to her teasing, her poke to the pompous ribs. Never believe that Harold Greyly would kill her to keep her quiet. And it had all been for nothing, Nino thought dully. Because, acting on some impulse, Hester had put the family history down on paper and posted it. Making sure that even if the words were never spoken, Nino would *read* the truth.

Claudia Moroni's love of her brother was the link between her and The Skin Hunter. Incest would have made her a target, her immorality only temporarily hidden under the guise of being a respectable merchant's wife. Somehow Vespucci had uncovered her weakness, a sin which would have damned her in the eyes of society and of God. The perfect victim.

But if the links were obvious between the women in the past, what of the women in the present? It was true that Sally Egan had been promiscuous, and that Harriet Forbes had been gay, but Seraphina? She was happily married, pregnant. Was her connection with Vespucci merely a familial one? Or because she had found the portrait?

Walking back to the table, Nino looked over his earlier notes. He had spent the previous hour tracking down London dealers called Ahmadi. There were four in total, in various districts. He had duly called them all, discovering that the first three dealt in Turkish, Islamic, Dutch and American art, but the fourth dealt in Italian Renaissance painting. Ms Farina Ahmadi.

Putting in a call to her, Nino was met with the supercilious tones of her male secretary.

'What is this concerning?'

'My name's Nino Bergstrom and it's a private matter.'

He was condescending, arrogant. 'I'm afraid I can't connect you to Ms Ahmadi without knowing who you are.'

'Perhaps you could tell her that unless she comes on the phone I'll make a call to the press about Angelico Vespucci,' Nino said calmly. 'I think that should get me through.'

Seconds later, Farina came on the phone.

'What is it? Want d'you want? I should tell you that I'm not used to being threatened.'

'Who threatened you?'

'You did, Mr Bergstrom!' she snapped. 'We don't do business this way.'

'What kind of a way *do* you do business, Ms Ahmadi?' he replied coolly. 'Or perhaps I should talk to Triumph Jones instead?'

'All right! What d'you want? You mentioned Angelico Vespucci. Is that supposed to mean something to me?'

'You, and quite a few others in the art world.'

'I've never heard of him.'

'Oh, you've heard of him. You commissioned a woman called Sally Egan to do a copy of his portrait. Ring any bells?'

'Who the hell are you?'

'Nino Bergstrom. I'm privately employed. Undertaking an investigation for Mr Gaspare Reni.'

She snorted. 'Hah! Investigating what?'

'The death of Seraphina Morgan, who used to be Seraphina di Fattori.'

There was a long silence, Nino waiting for a response that didn't come. Finally, he spoke again. 'She was murdered in Venice—'

'I know!'

'Oh, good. That'll save time. I suppose you've also heard that Sally Egan was killed? Well, I was wondering why you hired her to copy the Vespucci portrait?'

'I wanted it for an exhibition we were doing – Lost Old Master Portraits. Obviously, because they were *lost*, we had to get copies done.'

'And after the exhibition, what happened to the painting?'

Her voice was impatient. 'I don't know! It's probably in store somewhere.'

He took a shot in the dark.

'So the painting that's suddenly turned up in London might not be Titian after all. In fact, it could be your copy.' He paused. 'Don't say you haven't heard about the Titian re-emerging.'

'How d'you know about it?'

'I saw it.'

'*You saw it?*' She was breathless. 'Christ, have you got it?'

'No. It was stolen from Gaspare Reni. I don't know where it is now, but I know Triumph Jones is after it, and others.'

'Jobo Kido,' she said under her breath, Nino smiling to himself as she continued. 'The painting you saw – did Reni see it too? Because if he said it was genuine, it was. Reni's no mug – he knows his stuff.'

'But the copy was very good.'

'How would *you* know?'

'I saw a photograph,' Nino replied. 'It looked like a Titian to me—'

'*Not to an expert!*' she retorted, nettled. 'And, like I said, I don't know where it is now. It might be in storage, or we might have got rid of it. If the copy's what you wanted to know about, I can't help you. It was worthless.'

'It cost Sally Egan her life.'

She ignored the comment.

'I suppose Gaspare Reni wants you to get the Titian back for him?'

There was silence down the line.

'OK, Mr Bergstrom, whatever he's paying you, I'll double it. Work for me instead.'

'I think,' Nino replied smoothly, 'that there isn't enough money on earth to make that sound attractive.'

40

Ginza, Tokyo

Jobo Kido was shocked to hear about Triumph being mugged in Central Park. He made some trite comment about being in the wrong place at the wrong time, but he was anxious. What had possessed his old adversary? Triumph Jones' behaviour was totally out of character. He was taking ridiculous chances. He must have known that his reward would have drawn out every runner and gofer in the art world. Petty criminals, forgers and failed artists would leap at the chance of relieving Triumph of some of his wealth. Why invite such lunacy? And why, thought Jobo for the hundredth time, would he be walking in Central Park after dark?

Perhaps his rival had a death wish? His actions were certainly provocative, courting danger . . . Jobo looked over to the window. The heatwave had finally broken, the temperature falling, the rain at its curdling best . . . Was it all to do with the Titian? he wondered. After all, Triumph's change in behaviour had started after the Vespucci portrait had been found. Was there some connection? Some reckless impetus which was driving him?

Giving the computer a sidelong glance, Jobo wondered if the American had also been in touch with angelicoves-pucci.1555.com. Had Triumph been communicating with the site's creator too? Was that the reason for the sudden and brutal attack? Unnerved, he stared at the dead screen. Was he taking a terrible risk? Was he walking into something he might come to regret? Perhaps Triumph's mugging should act as a warning?

But as he thought it, Jobo knew he wouldn't – couldn't – stop. The contact had promised him the Titian. All he had to do was to discover how the victims were connected to Vespucci. After that, the painting would belong to him. Not Triumph Jones or Farina Ahmadi, not even Gaspare Reni. *He* would have it. The pride of his collection.

After all, Jobo consoled himself, high achievers always took risks. He had to prove that he was special enough to own the work. This was no time to be timid. He glanced back at the screen, swallowing drily. It was late – he should have left for home an hour ago. The walls seemed oppressive, the car park outside aggressively silent. Then, suddenly, he heard footsteps.

But the gallery was closed, he thought, panicked. It should be empty.

Hurriedly Jobo locked the doors, flicking the lamps off. The footsteps crunched on the gravel outside, near the window, as Jobo held his breath and pressed himself

252

against the wall. Reflected in the mirror opposite, he could see the outline of someone looking in, the dark shape hovering for a moment, then moving on.

Hardly breathing, Jobo waited. Immobile, he listened.

Then he heard the entrance door open and saw the handle of his office door rattling hard against the lock.

41

London, December

'I'm going to Tokyo to talk to Jobo Kido and see where Harriet Forbes was killed,' Nino said, waiting for Gaspare to protest.

But he just stared at him. 'You need money?'

'I've still got plenty left over from Ravenscourt, the bastard. He owes me.'

'No news from him?'

'Nothing. And the police haven't been in touch again. Much as I'd like it, I don't think anything's happened to Ravenscourt – I think he's just backed off.' Nino paused. 'Well, go on. Aren't you going to ask me?'

'About going to Japan? No, I know why you're going.' The dealer shrugged. 'I can't say don't go, Nino – you will anyway. But I can tell you to be careful.'

'I know it's a long shot, but what else can I do? Farina Ahmadi's a dead end, Triumph Jones is in hospital in New York—'

'What?'

'He was mugged yesterday,' Nino explained. 'But what did he expect, putting out a reward for the Titian? I don't know why he just didn't paint a target on his forehead – it would have been quicker.'

'Who mugged him?'

'Take your pick. It could have been anyone out of a cast of thousands. Or it could have been the killer.'

Gaspare frowned. 'In New York?'

'He's been in Venice and Tokyo already, why not New York? Triumph Jones was never going to find the portrait that way. He must have been desperate.'

'He was lucky he wasn't killed.'

'Maybe that's what he wanted. Apparently he expected the police to swallow some story about falling down a flight of stairs.' Nino changed the subject. 'I've only got two weeks left to find the last victim. Some woman's being stalked now. At this very moment she's being watched. Hand-picked to be murdered on the first of January ... I can't let him kill her.'

'But you don't know who she is.'

'Not yet.'

'Nino,' Gaspare said carefully, 'how can you possibly track her down?'

'I can't, unless I find out her connection to The Skin Hunter. There *is* one. Every victim has had some connection to Vespucci. This woman will be the same.'

'But—'

'Seraphina's relative knew him, and she found the portrait; Sally Egan copied it; Harriet Forbes wrote an article on The Skin Hunter.' Nino was emphatic. 'The next woman he picks will have a connection too. I just have to find it.'

'And you think you'll find it in Tokyo?'

'Maybe. Harriet Forbes was killed there. Jobo Kido lives and works there.'

'Yes, and he might be a suspect.'

Nino shook his head. 'No, I don't think so. He's too obvious, Gaspare. He'd be the first person everyone would suspect. It's not Kido. But he might know something. Or there might be something about the place where Harriet was killed. I have to go.'

'What you're trying to do is impossible. You can't prevent a death when you don't know who the victim is—'

'*She knows Vespucci*,' Nino snapped. 'She's heard of him, read about him, painted him or studied him. *But there is a link.* And I do have one clue to her identity.'

'What?'

'In the killer's eyes, she'll be immoral. Sexually reprehensible. Just like Vespucci's victims. And she'll also be young and good-looking, like the others.' He paused, catching Gaspare's expression. 'What is it?'

'You're chasing a phantom.'

'No, I'm not,' Nino corrected him. 'The killer admires Angelico Vespucci. He worships him, otherwise why would he want to *be* him? Why would he copy everything he did? The killer didn't just pick his victims out of thin air, he

256

chose them because of their link to Vespucci. It makes sense to him. A twisted logic. Like it's meant to be, a sign for him to pick that particular woman.'

Gaspare sighed.

'All right, say all of that's true. But how did he find out about them? How did he know about the copy of the portrait and the article? He could easily discover Seraphina's link to Vespucci. Her ancestor was his mistress, after all. But the other two – that's more difficult.'

'Not if you'd studied him for years,' Nino said, sitting down and leaning towards the old man. 'You're an art dealer, Gaspare. You've spent decades reading, researching details most people could never discover. Or even know how to find. Look at that Bellini portrait, what you uncovered about that.'

'But I read books that had been written on Bellini,' Gaspare replied practically. 'Where's the killer getting his information on Angelico Vespucci?'

'He was famous in his time. I know that all the evidence about him was supposed to have been destroyed and forgotten, but I don't believe that. He's part of Venetian folklore – whether people talk about him or not, he existed. *Somewhere* there will be records about Vespucci. There must be—'

'Because the killer keeps putting up information on the website?'

Nino nodded. 'Yeah. Every day there's something new. Which means that the killer's got a source. Maybe he's been collating his material for years while he was planning this,

257

making the whole scenario perfect. The way he kills, the women, the dates – he's not leaving anything to chance. It's an offering to his idol, The Skin Hunter. A perfect replica of his deeds, the ultimate accolade. And you know something else? The killer might be mad, but he's clever. He wants someone to come after him—'

'You're joking!'

'No, I'm not. He wants his audience. He's no fool. He knows someone will have worked out the dates, and knows that his next murder will be anticipated for the first of January. It'll add to the thrill for him. Give him that extra buzz to prove he can tip us all off – and still get away with murder.' Nino paused, thinking. 'I sent an email to the Vespucci website, but got no answer. I thought he'd reply, but he didn't take the bait. Maybe I wasn't right for him.'

Baffled, Gaspare stared at him. 'What *are* you talking about?'

'I'm not cultured. I'm from the film business, I'm not a member of the art world. I wouldn't be educated enough to appreciate Titian, or a genius like Angelico Vespucci.' Nino smiled wryly. 'Not in the killer's eyes, anyway. No, our man wants to impress the professionals. He wants to be their equal in status. As smart, as respected. Not just by emulating Vespucci, but by copying a man so powerful he was painted by Titian. He's a snob.'

Gaspare looked at Nino blankly. '*A snob?*'

'Yes, because not only is he impressed by Vespucci's violence, but because the Venetian was so powerful. He had influence, money, status. I doubt the killer would have copied Rosemary and Fred West. They'd have been considered vulgar, working class. This man admires the life of Vespucci. And that's why I think the killer is someone who's had to educate himself.'

Impressed, Gaspare listened. He had been surprised when Nino had offered to help him solve Seraphina's death, but as the weeks had passed the dealer had watched his progress with admiration. Fully recovered, Nino Bergstrom was no longer the sick man who had convalesced at his gallery. He was tough; the task had re-energised him, and his thinking was incisive. A man who had never investigated anything before, he was determined to succeed. Prepared to run any lead to ground, to talk to anyone. Even ready to go after a murderer.

'Why d'you think the killer's badly educated?'

'Not badly educated, *self*-educated,' Nino replied. 'He's meticulous, pedantic, obsessive – all traits of someone with a chip on their shoulder. He wants to be the equal of the dealers, because they impress him. But if he *was* their equal, it would never have occurred to him to seek their approval. He admires *and* fears them. He feels inferior, he hasn't the imagination to be an original, so he copies.' Nino paused, before adding: 'I think the killer's solitary, bookish. I'd be surprised if he was married, or had a family.'

'Violent men have families.'

'Yeah, but they're usually opportunistic killers, men who act spontaneously. Not men who plan murders. That takes

259

time, and skinning the victims takes time and space. You couldn't do that in a modern semi with kids running a round.'

'Thank God,' Gaspare said quietly. 'But what happens when it's over? After he kills the four women, what then?'

'He won't kill four women,' Nino replied. 'He won't succeed in copying Vespucci, because he'll be stopped. *I'll* stop him. And you know why? Because the killer's fixed his attention on the elite, the dealers. He's not looking in my direction. To him, I'm a no-account, an amateur, a hick. And *that's* my protection.'

Venice, 1555

It was nearing midday when the priest came by, trailing a wary look. He came with a notepad under his arm, pausing outside the studio of Titian. His manner was hesitant, his black robes sodden about the hem where he had crossed St Mark's. The rain had added to the sitting water, and now no one traversed the piazza and stayed dry.

He was still standing outside when the rain began again, his face baffled, with the look of someone pressed to a duty they dreaded. I felt little pity for him, for the Church has stayed remote, Venetians resenting its distance. It was meant to give succour, people said, but the victims were never mentioned in prayers, and the killer has kept the city clean of priests.

But now another rumour has sprung up. As the victims increase and Vespucci shirks from his guilt, Aretino comes forth to shield the beast again. He has put it abroad that there is another suspect. That The Skin Hunter is not, nor ever has been, Angelico Vespucci. We heard this news just after dawn, when the death of Lena Arranti was still fresh, the little Jewish girl cut down but still hanging in memory, forever hanging, from the rope which had held her corpse.

Her body has long gone, but men shudder when they walk under the lamp which held her, and someone has thrown flowers on the bridge, and ivy in remembrance. There was talk of her skin being found, but no one would say where. Or maybe no one knew. Finally one of the Doge's confidants pinned a paper to the doors of St Mark's proclaiming that her skin was found, and would be blessed and buried. The note satisfied no one, and later messages cursed Vespucci and foretold that Venice would be damned until his punishment came.

There was talk of hanging him by the same lamp which had held the Jewish girl. Of stripping off his flesh and laying it under the paw of the Lion of St Mark's. He became the Devil who had committed unspeakable acts and brought the city to its knees.

And this unwholesome man, this font of pus, has all of Aretino's great protection. While Titian continues the portrait which will become famous throughout the world, Aretino picks up his handful of shit and throws it in the face of all Venetians.

He says:

'There is another suspect. Another man has done these dreadful deeds.'

He will reveal this person to us all, in time.

'Look away from Vespucci!' he says. 'There is no villain there.'

And now I am watching as the priest knocks at the door of Titian's studio. I have heard rumours of what he is to say. Of words formed by Aretino, but spoken by this cleric. Words with which the artist's friend will rip out his heart and make a scapegoat of an innocent man. He will name this man, this son, this blood tie, offer him up to take Vespucci's place. He will do it to protect his interests, his wealth. Aretino, bribed into silence by so many in the past, will bribe another to quieten a tongue that otherwise will destroy him.

Titian is occupied. See, he paints. He lights more candles, turns the canvas to them to extend his working hours. The effigy of Vespucci grows on the easel. He is coming to life in snatches, like a hanged man grabbing at the air. In the background of the portrait is an object no one can decipher. No one but me.

For all the rouge redness of the colours, the ebony blackness of Vespucci's clothes, the majesty of sleeping Venice behind, for all of this, there is some intimation in the pigment. A way the artist hints at what he knows. A token accusation in the paint. Behind the sitter's bulbous eyes and venal mouth, behind Vespucci's sloping back, is a shape defying interpretation.

I saw the master paint this. This object, this limp spectacle, this mordant shape of nothingness. He caught me watching him, turned and held my gaze, then turned away. And I knew he understood the evil of the image, but was committed to its depiction, painting the dissolution of a man, a record of goodness soured.

It was to be a masterpiece. A history of depravity, a warning. That others might look upon it and repent. Or so I thought.

We did not know the scapegoat's name. Not then, that came soon after. It came like the wind across Venice, cold and relentless, driving the damage home. It came from Aretino's mouth into the ears of his friend. Words no man should suffer to hear.

I am leaving now, taking one last look at the portrait of Angelico Vespucci. He is sleek, clever and terrifying, and in the candlelight the shape behind him makes more than a little sense. Titian has painted a hide.

A skin, emptied of life.

42

Ginza, Tokyo

The gallery had become a kind of prison. It wasn't a place of business any more, but of dread. It had taken Jobo Kido almost an hour to leave the previous night. Whoever it was who had broken into the gallery had so unnerved him that he couldn't stop shaking when he thought of it. He had watched the handle of his office door rattling, wondering if the intruder would get to him. Knowing – *knowing* – that it was the killer. The person he had been communicating with over the internet.

And then the rattling of the door handle had stopped. There was nothing else. No knocking, no calling out. Just a horrible and prolonged silence. Still pressed against the office wall, Jobo had waited, finally hearing the footsteps moving off, and then a car engine starting up. It had taken him several moments to move, he had been so terrified, and then he groped his way towards his office chair and collapsed into it.

264

In the semi-darkness he had stared blankly ahead, hardly able to gather his thoughts. This wasn't some game over the internet. He had called up the killer as surely as sending him an invitation. Startled, Jobo had then thought of home and rang his wife, almost relieved to be shouted at. At least she was still alive. Questions as to the whereabouts of his son had been met with hostile accusations. Since when did he care about his son?

Pulling on his coat as his wife kept haranguing him, Jobo had made for his car, arriving home fifteen minutes later to be told that it was dangerous to drive while he was talking on his mobile. He could have laughed, but he didn't. And his insistence that his family should make sure they were safe – that the doors were locked and any approaches by strangers rejected – had only inflamed matters.

'What have you done?' his wife had asked, arms folded, fierce in a blue housecoat. 'What have you done?'

What had he done? It was a good question. One that had left him sleepless that night, and one that was still resounding in his head the following morning. *What had he done?* He had managed to endanger himself and his family. His plotting had been amateur in the face of a professional. Jobo Kido might collect the images of murderers and tingle at their crimes, but the reality was altogether different. And he had no stomach for it.

The Japanese lithographs were selling well, the exhibition a success, as he walked into the gallery and nodded to a collector he knew. At any other time Jobo would have cornered the man, worked on him until a sale was assured, but not this morning. This morning it was taking Jobo Kido every inch of his control to function.

So when his secretary arrived with the post, Jobo was agitated, impatient, his usual even temper suspended. Snatching the letters from her, he moved back to his desk, opening the first two and then tearing into a small package. His mind was preoccupied, his gaze constantly returning to the computer, the blank screen hostile. Ripping off the brown paper, Jobo lifted the lid of the narrow box.

Then he screamed.

He screamed and stepped back as the secretary hurried in.

'*Get out!*' he shouted to the anxious woman.

Then he turned back to his desk and looked into the box again.

The skin was folded neatly, a nipple placed centrally among the ghastly folds, the flesh darkening, almost mummified. He sobbed under his breath, pushing his fist into his mouth to stop himself. Then, taking hold of the paperknife he lifted the lid and dropped it back over the box, covering the object inside.

Heaving, he struggled to stop himself vomiting, his throat burning with bile. His breathing was short, urgent, so panicked that he soon felt light-headed and walked to the window to lean out. It was five minutes before Jobo Kido could breathe regularly again and moved to the intercom to buzz his secretary outside.

'Did you see who delivered the package?'

'It was the usual mailman, sir.'

'Thank you,' he replied, adding, 'Forgive me for my behaviour this morning. I'm a little unwell.'

'Can I get you anything, sir?'

'No, no, thank you,' Kido said, clicking off the intercom and glancing back at the package.

He wondered if he should look for a note, but realised he couldn't even touch the box, and certainly not its contents. Events had escalated from there simply being an intruder in his gallery: now the killer was including him in his work, drawing Jobo further and further in. What had started as a desire to get the Titian had turned into a folie à deux. Jobo Kido, respected art dealer, was being made complicit in murder.

The package was sitting on his desk, glowering at him. He felt like weeping, he was so afraid. And there was no one he could go to for help. Triumph Jones was still in hospital recovering, and Farina would relish a chance of getting the portrait off him. Dear God, Jobo thought impatiently, what *was* he talking about? This wasn't just the Titian, this was more. Much, much more. He might long for the portrait, but at *this* cost?

Still holding the paperknife, he jabbed at the box, then slid it along the desk, tipping it over the edge into the waste-paper basket. He then put the bin in his private washroom and locked the door. The idea of calling the police had already been dismissed. What ructions might be caused if

Jobo brought them in on it? What chance of getting the Titian? And worse, what if, by bringing the police in, he enraged the killer? It wasn't just about him any more, Jobo realised – it was about his family too. The murderer had taken him under his wing, had adopted him, and any betrayal now might cost him more than he could imagine.

For the rest of the morning the dealer avoided contact with anyone. He kept to his office, made a few half-hearted business calls, and repeatedly looked at the clock. Eleven thirty snaked into twelve noon and his secretary brought him a drink of tea. Jobo thanked her then slumped back into his stupor. He was insensible, transfixed, incapable of knowing what he should do. Incapable of action. Just waiting for what was going to come next.

So when a white-haired man walked into the gallery off the street and began to look at the exhibits, Jobo remained in his office, watching him. The man was obviously European. He looked tough. And young, even though his hair was white. . . . Who was he? Jobo wondered, his imagination flaring into life. It couldn't be. *Could it?*

He stared through a glass partition disguised from the gallery, a means by which he could watch his customers without being seen, assess their clothes and manner and judge if they looked prosperous enough to warrant his attention. But this man didn't look like an art lover, Jobo thought anxiously. He was Caucasian – maybe the killer was too? The first victim had been killed in Venice, the second in London, and even though the third had been murdered in Tokyo, she had been an English woman. So had *this* man been the person who had sent the disgusting package to him? The man who had terrorised him the other night? Was he the killer?

And if he was, why was he here?

There was a sudden knock on his door.

'Yes, what is it?'

'You have a visitor, sir,' the receptionist said, surprised by her employer's renewed unease. 'Mr Bergstrom.'

Bergstrom, Jobo thought. That was Swedish or Danish, wasn't it?

He stared at the girl. 'Yes?'

'Shall I show him in, sir?'

'No!' Jobo shouted, then dropped his voice. 'What does he want?'

'I don't know—'

'Then find out!' he snapped, watching her through the partition as she spoke to the white-haired man in the gallery outside.

A moment later she returned. 'He says he wants to talk to you about Angelico Vespucci, sir.'

The colour left Jobo's face. This was what he had been afraid of. The killer was here . . . Quickly ushering the receptionist out of the room, he made for the back exit, moving out on to the street beyond.

But the receptionist had spotted the dealer leaving and pointed him out to Nino.

'That's Mr Kido!' she said. Surprised, Nino followed him.

Jobo Kido had the advantage of knowing Ginza, as well as being able to track the unmistakable white head of his pursuer over the shorter Japanese crowd. Moving swiftly, the dealer cut through an arcade, several burdened shoppers standing back as he hurried, almost running, towards the exit. When he arrived there he paused, relieved. No giveaway head above the black-haired Japanese crowd. Perhaps he had lost him?

But he hadn't.

'Mr Kido.'

Startled, he jumped when someone tapped him on the shoulder. 'Who are you? What d'you want?'

'My name's Nino Bergstrom. I've come all the way from London to talk to you.'

He flinched. 'I've nothing to say!'

'Are you afraid of me?' Nino asked, surprised. 'I'm not going to harm you. I'm trying to find out who killed Harriet Forbes, that's all.'

Taking in a breath, Jobo smoothed down his jacket, feeling foolish and embarrassed. His usual urbanity had deserted him, left him sweaty and confused in front of this imposing stranger.

'Harriet Forbes? She was killed at the airport, wasn't she?'

'Could we talk back at your gallery?' Nino asked, dropping into step with the dealer.

Once or twice Jobo glanced at him, trying to judge if he was trustworthy or lying. Was he what he purported to be? Or was he the killer? Was he, Jobo, being duped? Reassured into dropping his guard? Once back at the gallery, he ignored the receptionist's baffled expression and ushered Nino into his office beyond. The room was dressed with Japanese prints, anodyne images without impact, the furniture a bloodless European blend of steel and leather.

'Miss Forbes' sister has asked me to look into Harriet's death,' Nino began, taking out a letter. 'She's written this for you, to prove that I'm her representative.'

Jobo took it gingerly, read it, and passed it back. Of course it could be genuine, the dealer thought, but then again, anyone could run off a letter on a computer. The thought of the computer made him clammy and he kept his eyes averted from the lifeless screen on his desk.

'I didn't know the victim.'

'I understand,' Nino replied, 'but you know of Angelico Vespucci?'

Jobo's voice was a croak in his throat. 'Who?'

'Can I speak openly?' Nino asked, surprised at Jobo's nervousness. 'I'm working for two people, investigating crimes which appear to be linked. You know Gaspare Reni?'

'The dealer?'

'Yes. He's a friend of mine and because of that I got involved with the death of Seraphina Morgan.' Nino paused. The air in the room was leaden. 'It all comes down to the portrait, Mr Kido. You know the one I mean – the Titian.'

Jobo tried to smile but couldn't manage it.

'Titian? This is news to me.'

'But it isn't, is it?' Nino countered. 'You've known about it since it surfaced. You, Triumph Jones and Farina Ahmadi

271

are all after it. Gaspare Reni had it, but it was stolen from him. And it's not been found since.' He leaned towards the dealer and Kido automatically leant back. 'Someone's copying The Skin Hunter. But you know that too, don't you?'

'I don't know what you're talking about!'

Nino paused.

'Yes, you do. The way you ran off like that proved it. You were spooked when I mentioned the name Vespucci to your receptionist. I dare say if I hadn't known this area of Tokyo as well as I do, I'd have lost you. Which makes me wonder *why* you were spooked. Did you think I was coming for you?' He studied the man's face. 'Have you been threatened?'

'You have no night to ask me questions like this! I'm a respectable art dealer—'

'With a not so respectable private gallery.'

Jobo paused, staring at Nino furiously. 'What I have in my personal collection is no business of yours —'

'You collect images of killers. That's means you'd be after the Vespucci portrait. As a dealer and as a collector. Any Titian would be a coup, but this one – Titian's portrait of The Skin Hunter? Now, that would be the prize of your collection.' He stared into the dealer's face, trying to read him. 'You *are* being threatened, aren't you?'

Glancing away, Jobo found himself torn between wanting to confide and wanting to have Nino thrown out. He knew that he couldn't keep denying his interest, just as he knew he needed help. The incident the other night had terrified him, and he hadn't dared to go online since. As for the package he had received earlier . . . He swallowed with effort.

No one could remain in suspended animation. He *had* to do something. Back off? No, he'd gone too far. There was only one course of action Jobo Kido *could* take – get help. And sitting in front of him was Nino Bergstrom, hopefully ready to offer some.

'How much do you know about the murders?' Nino asked.

'Which ones?'

Jobo had given himself away and Nino was quick to react. 'So you know about the recent murders? I mean, the other two, apart from the one in Tokyo.'

'I might . . . have read about them.'

'Where?'

'News travels,' Jobo stammered. 'It was on the internet. And I noticed the similarities. The women were skinned.'

'I don't suppose you noticed the website – angelicovespucci.1555.com?' Nino asked. 'I can see from your reaction that you did. Have you looked at it?'

Transfixed, Jobo nodded dumbly.

'I sent an email to the site,' Nino continued, 'but I got no reply.' He was watching the dealer. 'Of course the killer wouldn't want to talk to someone like me. He's aiming higher – for the top.' Jobo said nothing and Nino continued. 'Did you correspond with him?'

The reaction was startling. Leaning forward in his seat, Jobo was almost pleading. 'He answered me! He answered my questions!' He took out a handkerchief and wiped his hands. 'I wanted to draw him out, find out more about the Titian. But I never expected him to ...' He stopped talking, jerking his head towards the computer. 'He talks to me. Every time I go online, he responds.'

'And you thought you could manipulate him?'

'I was—'

'Stupid,' Nino said succinctly. 'You let him in, Mr Kido. He was looking for someone just like you. Exactly like you. In fact, you were probably his number one choice.'

'Oh God. Why?'

'Your private collection. He thinks you're soulmates.'

Jobo put the handkerchief to his mouth. 'That's not all.'

'Has he been in direct contact?'

'Someone was at the gallery the other night. We were closed and everyone had gone home. And then I heard someone outside and I saw them look in at the window.' He glanced over, almost as though he expected to see the man again. 'He was rattling the door handle. I thought he'd get in!'

'But he didn't?'

'No, he went away,' Jobo replied, getting to his feet. Going into the washroom, he returned a moment later with the package. He was holding it in a towel, so that his hands didn't come into direct contact with it. 'This arrived earlier today.' He put the box on the desk and stepped back from it.

Curious, Nino took off the lid and stared at the object inside.

'Was there a note?'

Jobo shook his head. 'I didn't look for one.'

Lifting the edge of the cloth on which the skin was lying, Nino glanced under it. Then he checked the lid. There was nothing written anywhere on the package.

'I need to see what he wrote on the site, Mr Kido. *Everything* he wrote to you.'

Then, suddenly, there was a suspicion in the dealer's eyes.

'I don't know who you are!' he snapped. 'I don't know who sent you—'

'I told you. Louisa Forbes and Gaspare Reni—'

'*So you say!*' Jobo cried, almost incoherent. 'But you could be lying.' He pointed to Nino's pocket. 'That letter could be a fake! It could all be fake. You might have been hired by Triumph Jones or Farina Ahmadi to find out what I know. *You* could be the man on the website—'

'But I'm not.'

'*So you say!*' the dealer repeated. He was beginning to panic. 'I don't know who you are!'

'So phone Gaspare Reni. You know him. He'll vouch for me,' Nino replied. 'It's not me you need to be afraid of, Mr Kido. I don't want the Titian. I want to help.'

Kido shook his head. 'No one can help me.'

'Show me what he wrote,' Nino said again.

'I can't—'

'Show me! I can't help unless I know what's been going on.'

Nodding, Jobo turned on the computer, feeding in the name of the site and watching as it came up on screen. A portrait of Angelico Vespucci flashed up, followed by the words *The Skin Hunter. A Tribute.*

'He's mad,' Jobo said, slumping into his seat.

'He's clever,' Nino replied. 'Now, go into the site. Get him online—'

'*Now?*'

'Yes, now.'

He watched as the dealer entered the forum, logging in. A moment later a message came up.

Hello, Mr Kido. How are you today?

Raising his eyebrows, Nino glanced at Jobo. 'Satisfied? If it was me, how could I be talking to you online?'

'You couldn't . . .' Jobo replied, relaxing slightly. 'So, what d'you want me to reply?'

'Tell him that you got the parcel—'

'I can't!'

'Tell him.'

'No,' Jobo repeated, pushing away from the computer. '*You* talk to him.'

Sighing, Nino turned to the computer and typed in:

I received the package.
Answer: *Did you like it?*
Nino: Was I supposed to like it?
Answer: *You appreciate beautiful things.*
Nino: Whose skin was it?

Answer: *You're very direct today. Not like yourself. I do hope our conversations aren't being shared. I asked you for secrecy, for your absolute discretion . . . Is this Mr Kido I'm talking to?*

Nino glanced over at Jobo. 'That's why *you* have to talk to him. If you don't he'll suss me out and that'll be the end of it. The end of your Titian and God knows what else.' He pointed at the computer. 'Get on it with. And make it sound convincing.'

Jobo: Sorry, I was just wanting to know more about what you were doing. I haven't told anyone anything.
Answer: *Good. Are you any closer to finding out the link between the women?*

Nino shook his head to direct the dealer's answer and Jobo typed the reply.

Jobo: No.
Answer: *You'll have to try harder. The link is there, you have all the information you need to find it.*
Jobo: Can't you give me a clue?

There was a long pause before the response came back.

Answer: *You have to prove that you're worthy of owning the Titian. The answer is there if you're clever enough.*

Confused, Nino tapped Jobo on the shoulder. 'What he's asking you to do?'

'Guess the link between the recent murders.'

'Why?'

'I don't know.'

'*Why?*' Nino repeated impatiently.

'If I solve the connection, he'll give me the Titian.'

Incredulous, Nino stared at the dealer. '*And you think he'll keep his word?* He's playing with you. He'll get you running around and then he'll pull the rug out from under your feet. The killer isn't going to give you the Titian. He's going to make a fool out of you, if you're lucky. If you're not, he might do something much worse.'

'*I want that portrait!*' Jobo said, nearly shouting.

'You'll never get it. He's got it and he's keeping it. Think about it: the killer's hardly going to give up the likeness of his hero, is he? It's a taster, that's all. It's to keep you on the hook. The man's killed on every anniversary of Vespucci's crimes. Three killings so far – you really want to see a fourth? We have to stop him.' Nino shook his head disbelievingly. 'What's the matter with you? Are you fucking crazy?'

Breathing heavily, Jobo stared at the screen, his thoughts clearing. What *was* he doing? How could he think of going on with it? Even if he got the Titian, how could he look at it with anything other than distaste, knowing that it had cost three lives?

Ashamed, he turned to Nino. 'What can I do?'

'Answer him. Get back on the computer and talk to him. Draw him out.'

Jobo: Are you still there?

Answer: *I'm always here. I thought you'd gone.*

Jobo: I've worked out some of it. The killings are on the same
    dates as Vespucci's murders.

Answer: *Very good.*

Jobo: So there's another one to come?

Answer: *You know there is. On the 1st of January.*

Anxious, Jobo turned to Nino again. 'What do I say now?'

'Ask him who the victim is.'

'He won't tell us that!' Jobo replied. 'He knows we'd stop
it if he told us.'

'Just keep him online. We have to get him to slip up, give
us something.' Nino pointed to the computer. 'Go on, ask
him the woman's name.'

Jobo: Who's the victim going to be?

Answer: *You're getting lazy, Mr Kido. You have to work for your*
    reward. I do. The fourth victim is already chosen.

Jobo: Is she in Tokyo?

Answer: *Maybe.*

Jobo: London?

Answer: *Or Venice?*

Jobo: What if I guess who she is?

Answer: *You don't want to do that, Mr Kido. If you guess I'd have*
    to kill you too.

And with that he cut the connection.

Badly shaken, Jobo wrenched out the lead from the back
of the computer. The light flicked off, the white noise was

279

silenced. The package was still on the desk in front of him. Nino gestured to it.

'Have you called the police about that?'

'No. I haven't told them anything.' He looked at Nino slyly. 'You want to call them? Get them to examine the skin? Take fingerprints off the door handle? Or maybe you know some computer buff who can trace the website, see if the killer's communicating with us from London or from around the corner?' He paused, shaking. 'How long does it take to do forensic tests?'

'Too long,' Nino replied. 'We only have a week left. And if we call in the police they'll impound everything, take possession of your computer – and our contact to the site will be broken. You think there's a hope in hell of finding the next victim if we do that?'

Jobo shook his head. 'No. So what *do* we do?'

'You keep in contact—'

'But—'

'Listen to me. Keep in contact online and tell me everything he says.'

'But how will you find out *who* he is?'

'I don't know, but the site might lead me to him. It's all I've got.' He stood up to leave. 'I'll stay in touch—'

Panicked, Jobo swivelled round in his seat. '*Where are you going!*'

'To find the next victim,' Nino replied, composed. 'Stop worrying. The killer isn't after you, Mr Kido. You might think he is, but it's not your skin he wants. He's scared you enough to keep quiet and he thinks that you're greedy enough to play along with him for the painting. Let him *keep* thinking that.'

'But he broke into the gallery!'

'And if he'd wanted to hurt you, he would have done. He's killed before and not got caught. It's easy for him.' Nino paused. 'He doesn't want to kill you. You're not a big part of his plan. You're a bit player. Vespucci's the hero, the women are the stars. You represent the art world, the elite he despises. He just wants to get one over on you to prove how clever he is.'

Jobo looked unconvinced. 'How d'you know what he's thinking? What if you're wrong?'

'I might be,' Nino admitted. 'But remember, my life's on the line too. You think you're under threat? Well, you're not going after him, *I am*.'

43

Venice

Tom Morgan was looking around the old apartment, where he and Seraphina had once lived, apartment for the last time. His argument with Johnny Ravenscourt had been enlightening. The Titian wasn't with him, and judging by his reaction, Ravenscourt had no inkling where it was. Frowning, Tom glanced around the rooms, his gaze coming to rest on the painting of Claudia Moroni and her brother. It had never been of any real interest to him. But now it was. Although he had agreed to sell the apartment with all fittings, fixtures and furniture, he was damned if he was going to leave it behind. His knowledge of the art world wasn't great – that had been his wife's forte – but an old oil painting had to be worth money. And Tom needed money.

Taking it down, he placed an old print over the empty space on the wall and took the painting out into the hallway of the flats as the burly figure of Ravenscourt loomed up from the floor below. He had a florid look about his jowls and was breathing heavily.

'You look fucked,' Tom said, watching him.

'I heard you were leaving,' Ravenscourt gasped. 'Where are you going?'

'Only to the other apartment. I've sold this one; I can't stay here.'

'You must have made a fortune.'

'Not as much as I'd have made with the Titian,' Tom replied, gripping the painting.

Recognising it, Ravenscourt blustered. 'You can't take that—'

'I can and I will,' Tom snapped. 'The buyer got a good deal on the sale. He won't miss one painting.'

'But *that* one?'

'What?' Tom asked, holding the picture at arm's length and looking at it. 'What's so great about this one?'

'It's Claudia Moroni.'

'And that's supposed to mean something?'

'Look,' Ravenscourt said, his tone mollifying. 'Let me buy it off you. I'll give you a good price.'

'I don't think so. The Italian currency's failing. *If* I was going to sell it, I'd want US dollars.'

Ravenscourt nodded. 'OK, OK.'

'I said *if* I was going to sell it,' Tom continued, staring at the painting intently. 'Because you wanting it so badly makes me wonder why. Perhaps it's valuable?'

'Only to me. It's important for my research.'

'Into Angelico Vespucci?' Tom countered, laughing. 'You sad fag, where's all that research got you? You could have had the Titian, but you fucked up. Killing Seraphina—'

'*I didn't kill your wife!*'

'Someone did. And you were in Venice. And you wanted the painting. I wouldn't put it past you to try and cut me out.'

'Maybe it was *you* who cut *me* out. You were in trouble, banking on getting the Titian,' Ravenscourt replied. 'Don't try and bluff me.'

They stared at each other, neither man giving way, neither believing what the other said.

'Anyway, why are you still in Venice?' Tom asked. 'You told Seraphina you were going to spend Christmas in London.'

'I had to leave London for a while.'

'Why?'

'I had some trouble. I needed to get the police off my back.'

'I suppose it wouldn't have anything to do with Nino Bergstrom being back in Venice, would it?' Tom could see Ravenscourt pale and laughed again. 'Coming after you, is he?'

'Have *you* spoken to him?'

'About what?'

'The Titian. About the plan you and Seraphina had.'

'No!' Tom replied, shrugging. 'I haven't seen Bergstrom for weeks. Anyway, why would I tell him what we were up to?'

'You wouldn't . . .' Ravenscourt replied, his thoughts running on. 'Bergstrom's a nosy sod. I tried to get rid of him in London, but he's cropped up again. I wonder why he's back in Venice?' His attention shifted back to his original topic. 'We were talking about the painting. I'll give you a good price for it – although, by rights, you should give it to me. Something to remember Seraphina by. I was her closest friend – she would have wanted me to have it.'

'She wouldn't have given a shit,' Tom replied. 'She used to laugh at you all the time, say what a sad case you were. She mocked your "intellectual pretensions" and all your Italian boys.' He could see the colour leaving Ravenscourt's face. 'Seraphina thought you were a pig—'

'She wasn't like that!'

'Oh, but she was. Seraphina was nothing like she appeared. So frankly, Johnny, *if* you killed her I wouldn't let it keep you up at night.'

He paused, then suddenly pushed the painting at Ravenscourt, the dealer's big hands grabbing it to stop it falling, then reached into Ravenscourt's back pocket and took out his wallet.

'Thanks,' he said, putting the wallet back after taking out a wodge of notes.

'You bastard!'

'What are you complaining about? You got the painting,' Tom said, guiding Ravenscourt out of the apartment and slamming the door behind both of them. Finally, he slid the keys through the letterbox and dusted his hands off.

'I'm glad to be leaving. Seraphina never liked this place. Said it was bad luck.'

'It certainly was for her.'

Shrugging, Tom moved past Ravenscourt. But halfway down the stairs, he hesitated and looked back at him. 'I don't buy it, you know.'

'What?'

'Your big dumb act. Like Seraphina, you're not what you seem to be. I don't know whether I should laugh at you, or be afraid of you.' He paused, as though he was considering his options, then walked on, whistling.

44

Apparently the di Fattori marriage had been a charade for over a decade. Or so the Contessa told Nino as they sat in the apartment overlooking the Grand Canal. The height of the room prevented any intimacy, the arched ceiling as impersonal as a church. And seated under all this grandeur was the sparse frame of Seraphina's mother, the Contessa di Fattori. When she spoke the impression of fragility continued, her voice as brittle as her appearance.

In the weeks since Nino had last seen her she had lost weight, the veins on her forehead pronounced under the skilful make-up, her tinted hair too dark for her pallor. Erect, she looked like a person who had been tied to her seat, rigid with unease.

'Thank you for coming,' she said in Italian, then slid effortlessly into English. 'I have matters of the utmost importance to discuss with you. And of course I ask for your complete confidence.'

Nino nodded. 'You have it.'

She went on without a pause. 'My husband and I are getting a divorce.'

'I'm sorry—'

'Please don't be. Seraphina's death was too much for us. They say people either grow closer in adversity or break apart. We did the latter.' Her lips closed firmly, as though she was relieved to have the words out of her system. 'I have something to show you, Mr Bergstrom.' Reaching over to the table beside her, she handed him a substantial envelope. 'My husband was of the opinion that family matters should remain within the family. I, however, do not agree. But then again, I married *into* the di Fattori line, so perhaps I don't have the same loyalty to the name. Or the dead.'

Opening the package, Nino was struck by the age of the paper, a heavyweight embossed vellum.

'What are these?'

'Those are jottings written by the infamous Melania, the Contessa di Fattori. Painted by Titian, the lover of Pietro Aretino, the Harlot of Venice. Do you know what the name Melania means?'

He shook his head. 'No.'

'*Dark*,' she said wistfully. 'And she was. Not in colouring — she had red hair – but Melania di Fattori had a dark heart. Of course you know of her death, her murder? Very like Seraphina's, wasn't it?' She paused, sighing, although there was barely a sound. 'I've been thinking a great deal. About my daughter, about what happened to her. And I was speaking to Gaspare Reni this morning – he told me about the Titian

288

portrait.' She put up her hands to prevent Nino interrupting. 'It was right that he did so. I couldn't go on in ignorance, Mr Bergstrom. It makes sense that there was some connection between Seraphina and Melania . . . What Gaspare told me made me decide to show you these.'

'You want me to read them?' Nino said, gesturing at the papers.

'Every word. They might help you.'

'Have you read them?'

'Read them first, Mr Bergstrom, then we'll talk again,' she replied. 'My husband would never have released this information, and I ask you to keep it secret. I only give it to you because it might be of use. Melania was an extraordinary woman. Immoral, without conscience.' She breathed in. Again, the action was hardly audible. A wraith in a silk dress. 'We disguise so much, lie to ourselves, hide so many secrets. Melania did that. So did my daughter.'

'What kind of secrets?'

'The baby she was carrying . . . it wasn't Tom Morgan's.'

The words were a body blow.

'Did he know?'

'No,' the Contessa said firmly. 'Seraphina only told me . . . and possibly Johnny Ravenscourt.'

The name resonated unpleasantly. 'I know Ravenscourt. He's not the father, surely?'

'I don't know who the father was,' the Contessa replied. 'It's amazing how easy it is once you start to talk. Hiding things becomes a habit. You tell a lie so long you believe it.

289

Every word is considered for its impact. How much do I say? To whom? I suppose all ancient families are the same. Do you think so, Mr Bergstrom?'

'Maybe.'

'Yes, maybe,' she agreed. 'It's like recovering from an anaesthetic. I feel I can breathe again. If I want to. If I *choose* to.' She paused, as though she was considering her options there and then. After a moment, she spoke again. 'Seraphina's dead. I want to know who killed her. I know why—'

Nino was taken aback. '*You know why?*'

'Angelico Vespucci killed his victims because they were immoral. Seraphina was immoral too.' Her head went up, her eyes fixed on her visitor. 'You think it pleases me to say this about my own daughter? No – but it is the truth nonetheless. All the time Seraphina was growing up I'd look at her and wonder why she behaved so recklessly. At nineteen she left Venice and travelled the world. I imagine she had many lovers. We had nothing in common, Mr Bergstrom. I married young and remained married, without taking a lover.' She looked around her, tensing as her gaze fell on a painting of a red-haired woman. Nino didn't have to ask who the sitter was. 'That's Melania. Seraphina inherited the worst of her ancestor's traits . . . I used to worry that something would happen to her, but when she came back to Venice and married Tom Morgan, she was content.' The Contessa paused, then continued in the same quiet, listless tone. 'I believed she'd changed. After all, they were in love. But Tom Morgan was lazy, let his business slide, took risks, took drugs.'

'Did Seraphina?'

'No, she said not. She had no interest in drugs, or in drinking. She didn't need it, she said, she was always full of life. *Too* full of life. To my amazement she continued her education, worked as a scientist, using her brain. She could separate her life into little containers, into pigeon-holes: career, family, husband, lovers.'

'So she was unfaithful to Tom Morgan?'

'After the first thrill of marriage wore off, Seraphina started looking around.' The Contessa caught Nino's gaze and held it. 'Venetians close ranks against outsiders, but people here knew her reputation. It was only when she became pregnant that I was hopeful. Maybe, at last, she'd settle down.'

'What about her husband? Did Tom Morgan have lovers?'

'Too lazy,' the Contessa said dismissively. 'He likes to get "high", to lounge about. He's no taste for seduction. To be honest, I imagine he would find it tiring.'

'But he knew about Seraphina's lovers?'

'Isn't the question "Did he care?"'

'Did he?'

'He cared for comfort, for money, for a soft life,' she replied. 'He cared for my daughter, but never enough. Do I think he killed her? He could have done . . .'

Nino took in a breath as she continued.

'But when I heard about the other deaths, the murders so like Seraphina's, then I doubted it. It would take planning, cunning and energy – not traits Tom Morgan possesses.'

Her gaze moved downwards to her hands. 'But then Gaspare told me about the Titian portrait and I started to think again. The painting would be worth a fortune. An easy way for a lazy man to get rich.'

'But Seraphina never told *you* about the portrait?'

'No. But then a wife tells a husband more than a woman tells her mother,' she replied perceptively. 'Seraphina could have told Tom Morgan. And he could have been tempted . . . And if he killed her, I want to know. I *have* to know.' She rose to her feet. 'Read the papers, Mr Bergstrom. Read what Melania di Fattori wrote. She knew The Skin Hunter. She was his lover. If you're hoping to find Vespucci's imitator, perhaps you should first learn more about the original.'

45

'I need your help,' Nino said, ringing Gaspare from Venice. 'The Contessa di Fattori has given me some information—'

'She said she was going to.'

'Why did you tell her what was going on?'

'The woman's lost her daughter, and her marriage has broken up. What reason was there to keep it a secret from her? She deserves to know. If she was still with her husband I wouldn't have told her, but the Contessa's smart, she can handle it.' Gaspare paused. 'So, what did you want me to do?'

'Time's running out. I've got to find the last victim. So I want you to trace every woman who's ever been connected to Angelico Vespucci—'

'What!'

'Go on the internet and see what's been done on The Skin Hunter. We know about the copy of the portrait, and the article. The last victim *has* to have a link.'

'It could be anything.'

'I know!' Nino snapped back. 'But what else have we got

to go on? I'll read the stuff I was given, and then talk to Tom Morgan again. Incidentally, Seraphina's baby wasn't his.'

'I don't believe it.'

'It's true. Her mother told me.' Nino sighed. 'Every time I turn round there's another corridor leading off to God knows where. Motives in motives, claims and counterclaims. No one's what they seem.' He was thinking aloud. 'Less than two weeks, Gaspare. That's all we've got. We have to discover the link to the victim. We *have* to.'

Finishing the call, Nino turned back to the papers the Contessa had given him, drawing them out of the envelope and laying them side by side. There were three pages of handwritten Italian, the writing baroque.

November 1555

He is harvesting and speaks of nothing else. As for Aretino, such a conscience there, he worships Titian like a god and yet thinks nothing of deceiving him. Last night I lay with him again, Angelico Vespucci coming later, when the boar had finished. He watches, like he watches his pet whores, sweats in his excitement, his body wheezing with the thrust of pleasure.

Aretino writes of me in his books, gives me another name, as though I cannot guess the subterfuge. Poor Aretino, so very foolish for a clever man. And yesterday, when the rain stopped for an hour come afternoon, I chose another whore for my Vespucci ...

Nino stopped reading, the words staring up at him from the page.

... a little Jewish girl, come from Milan a month ago. She is naive and compliant; I think maybe he will love her. As he did the merchant's wife.

Claudia Moroni was a whim of mine. A response to a rumour I had heard some months before. I courted her, came to her home, flattered her into a friendship, then brought her to Vespucci.

He loved her within hours. Not for her appearance, which was poor, but for her wickedness.

'God,' Nino said softly. Contessa di Fattori, the whore of Venice, the consort of a murderer, was also Vespucci's procuress.

I watched her plead with him to keep her silence, but he'd have none of it. She lies with her brother – and so Vespucci wants her.

He tells me that he feels her corruption on his skin, that it dries like mud against his fingers. He licks his lips as though he can taste her poison, and calls her to him, time after time.

She comes across St Mark's, the priest with her. Passes through the bronze archway leading to Vespucci's room.

The priest sits fingering his rosary outside. He pays no mind to me, and so I watch the merchant's wife pay for her sins to stay secret.

At first Vespucci thought to make me jealous. Thought I would bay at the moon for him. And so I took the writer as my lover ...

Frowning, Nino stared at the words, remembering the portrait of Melania in the palazzo.

Provoked, Vespucci now thinks to take me from Aretino, tells me such tales, but I'll have none of it. All lovers lie. Until, until ...

His wife was found last evening in the Lido, stripped of her skin. He said he keeps it for her, promising to dress her when they meet in Hell. I still thought him a liar. A spinner of tales to court me, a cruel narrator scratching for some alchemy to keep me to his bed. I rolled upon him, begged to be given facts ...

He told me, curled the words out with his tongue, spoke of how he peeled the skins away and hid them. He will not tell me where, he taunts me with it, speaks of adding more.

And now Claudia Moroni has been found. Vespucci promised to craft a garment for me, to fashion a chemise from her dead hide. Afraid, I left for the mainland.

I thought Vespucci would follow, but it wasn't him. Instead came Aretino, begging my return. He said it was a jest, a bed sport, a bragging to make a woman moan ...

I knew if I went back I would never leave again. I knew if I lay with Vespucci, felt his hands working my flesh, that he would work my soul.

*When I next saw him he was washing himself, and the
water that left his skin had blood in it.*

Shaken, Nino pushed the notes aside and stood up. Melania,
the Contessa di Fattori, had supplied Vespucci with his
whores. Seraphina's ancestor had colluded with a murderer.
Willingly.

December 1555

*The little Jewish girl I brought him has been found. Dead also
… Aretino came to see me, lay against me in my bed, snuffled
his girth against my back and pleaded Vespucci's innocence. He
tells me he is not what people say, and I should stand an ally
to him. And I, drowsy with guilt, open my legs to him.*

*The portrait all of Venice talks about is nearly complete.
Titian says nothing of it, only that it will be shown in the
church where Vespucci worships. He says, come the last Sunday
in December, the painting can be seen by any with the will to
view it.*

*What Titian thinks of his sitter is impossible to know. Cer-
tainly he turns away from me whenever I approach and people
have pinned papers to my door, condemning me.*

*'The Whore of Venice' I am called. Vespucci something
else. His title, which will not grace his portrait — is that of
Skin Hunter.*

I know I will not live to see this black year's end …

Melania, Contessa di Fattori, had been depraved. Her deviancy had kept her tied to a murderer, her sexuality condemning her.

Possibly that was where Seraphina had inherited her traits. It explained how it was possible for her to be an adulteress and pass off another man's child as her husband's. The young woman Nino had met in London weeks earlier had seemed uncomplicated, charming. Her death had been a shock. But now it was obvious why Seraphina had been the next victim. It wasn't simply because of her relationship to the Contessa di Fattori, but because of her own sexual history.

They were alike, even in the way they met their end. Seraphina had not anticipated hers, but Melania had had a chance to escape – and had chosen not to. The fourth, and last, of the Skin's Hunter's victims, she was murdered and mutilated on 1 January, 1556.

While Nino was considering what he had just read, his mobile rang. He recognised the voice of Seraphina's mother immediately.

'Have you read the papers, Mr Bergstrom?'

'Yes,' he said uncertainly. 'Have you?'

'Should I?'

'No, Contessa,' Nino lied. 'They're of no importance. No importance at all.'

46

Tokyo, Japan

Jobo Kido wasn't sure why, but the last three times he had gone online, there had been no response from the Vespucci website. Anxious, he had tried at different times of the day, with no success, until finally there was an answer.

Jobo: Where have you been?

Answer: *What makes you think I've been anywhere?*

Jobo: I couldn't get a response.

Answer: *I was angry with you. I don't think you were very polite last time we spoke.*

Jobo: I'm sorry.

Answer: *You should be. If you want the Titian you play by my rules, not your own. It makes me wonder if you've been talking to someone.*

Jobo: No, no one.

Answer: *Not even the man with the white hair?*

There was a long pause before Jobo answered gingerly.

Jobo: I don't know who you mean.
Answer: *Think very carefully, Mr Kido. Do you want the painting, or do you want to continue to lie to me and lose it? Who is the white-haired man?*

His hands suspended over the keyboard, Jobo hesitated. If he gave Nino away would he be endangering him? But if he didn't give him up, he would lose the Titian. He cursed inwardly. What was Nino Bergstrom to him? Until a few days ago, he had never met the man. Why should he give up such a prize to shield a comparative stranger?

All his life Jobo had been waiting to be at the top of his game. The Titian portrait would propel him into the artistic stratosphere, into that platinum orbit Triumph Jones and Farina Ahmadi inhabited. The portrait of Vespucci was his by rights.

Jobo: He's called Nino Bergstrom.
Answer: *What does he want?*
Jobo: To catch you before you kill again.
Answer: *Are you helping him?*
Jobo: No.
Answer: *Have you worked out the connection between the victims yet?*
Jobo: No, how can I? I don't know who the last victim is going to be.

Answer: *What if I were to give you her name? Would you tell Mr Bergstrom? Or would you warn the victim?*

Stunned, Jobo stared at the screen.

Answer: *If you did either, you'd lose the Titian. So how much do you want it? Enough to sacrifice one life? Two lives?*

Jobo: I'll buy the painting off you.

Answer: *It's not for sale. It has to be earned. I'll ask you again, Mr Kido. If I tell you the name of the next victim will you keep it a secret? Or will you let her die? If she dies, can you read about it later? Can you hear all the details and know you could have saved her? How much does the Titian really mean to you?*

Agonised, Jobo stared at the words on the screen. His previous doubts had been annulled, his guilt suspended. And with Nino no longer sitting alongside him, Jobo Kido's greed overrode his conscience.

Jobo: I want the Titian. I swear I won't tell anyone who the next victim is.

Answer: *Very good, Mr Kido. But if you're not going to save her, why do you need to know? Until tomorrow.*

On that note, the connection was severed.

47

England

He was watching her and thinking that he had chosen very well. She had an interest in his passion, a mutual connection, and she was young and attractive. Of course she was a whore, but she had to be or she wouldn't be suitable.

The man stared at the photographs he had put on his computer, tilting his head to one side, his gaze tracing the line of her throat. Flaying a body wasn't easy. At first he had presumed that it would be – merely a peeling away. But it hadn't been like that at all. He had had to cut the flesh away from the muscle underneath, and that had taken sharp knives, not your usual kitchen utensils. In the end he had gone to a medical suppliers on Wigmore Street and bought a set of scalpels which had made skinning so much easier. Concentrating, he had sliced into the skin, making a V shape. When he had done that, he had lifted the bloodied flap and, holding it, had continued slicing it away from the body.

It had been very neat.

He had always thought of himself as a non-violent man, so it had been difficult for him to come to terms with what he had to do. But he wanted everything to be perfect – he wanted the homage to be *exact* – so the murders had been copied in every detail. And what he didn't know in fact, he followed in instinct; imagining what Vespucci would do.

After the first killing he found the flaying stimulating, almost as though he had two victims, not one. Of course the corpse was blood-red when he had taken the skin away, but the hide was soft, supple. It rested in his hands, and after he had washed it, it took on a chamois leather, butter-soft quality. Sometimes he even draped it over his bare arms, feeling the dead skin resting on his own.

Sipping a mug of coffee, he relished his memories. He had first come across Angelico Vespucci at school. One of those chance findings in the library where he used to hide out to miss Games. Of course he had had to keep his studious side a secret – girls never went for nerds and his peers only admired the tough boys. It wouldn't do for him, considered very cool, to be revealed as an intellectual.

So instead he studied in secret and polished his glossy outer image until he became more and more removed from his lower middle-class upbringing. His parents might be proud of his brain, but that wasn't what interested him; he wanted to feel something. Feeling had always been difficult. Over the years he had observed his mother crying when the dog was put to sleep, and his father overcome with affection at Christmas, happy with booze and sentimentality. He had watched them with curiosity. What *was* all this feeling everyone talked about? It was in films, books, computer games – feelings, feelings, always fucking feelings But not for him. He didn't feel anything.

But while he didn't feel, he *could* mimic. He could replicate any emotion. As a copyist, he was second to none. And no one ever guessed. He left his childhood and slid into his teens without emotion. He attracted a girl and had sex with her, without emotion. He tried cutting himself with a knife, and felt nothing. Nothing he experienced, read or saw touched that hidden nub of feeling. If it was there at all.

But it *was* there. It was just a question of stimulating it. Of finding some trigger which would detonate him into life . . . His attention moved back to the girl's photographs, then he entered the Vespucci website he had created. His gaze fed off the image of the Italian, the tips of his fingers resting longingly against the screen, tracing the bulbous eyes.

It was easy to remember when he had first heard of The Skin Hunter. The name had jolted him, given him a shift in the stomach, something he had never experienced before. The image, and the legend of a long-dead man, had evoked a *feeling*. A reaction so intense it had been almost sexual. A stripping away of all the dullness, until a waxen world seemed suddenly stained glass.

At last he was responding, and everything he read about Angelico Vespucci spiked his emotions. He revelled in the Italian's murders and the details of the skinning, taking Vespucci's feelings as his own. Somehow a dead killer had managed to skip the centuries and waken the psyche of a disaffected man.

After that first rush of adrenalin, he was addicted. Angelico Vespucci's victims were not allotted sympathy: they had disappointed the merchant, deceived him, been less than he desired. Committing himself to research, he delved into the archives in Italy and London and on the web, and even visited Venice. His obsession growing, he fancied that Vespucci walked alongside him, taking them through the same dank, restricted alleyways he had once walked, the Italian throwing a shadow behind his own.

He fell in love. Not with Vespucci, but with his crimes. *He fell in love.* Emotion saturated him; he could imagine the smell of blood and the skin of the women, he could feel their flesh between his teeth and climaxed in his dreams.

Two years passed, by which time he considered himself the foremost authority on Angelico Vespucci. Let the fat queer Ravenscourt think he held the crown, he would prove to everyone that *he* was Vespucci's premier admirer and natural successor. So he pleaded for guidance, threw himself on every listening devil, and asked for a way to absorb the Italian. To relive the Italian. To become the Italian. The reply was simple. He was to copy The Skin Hunter, in every detail. He would kill on the same dates, choosing the same kinds of women and skinning them as his predecessor had done. But he had to choose victims who had some link to Vespucci.

It was harder than he imagined. Vespucci had been famous in his time, but the Venetians seemed to want to scrub him from the records, and Italian libraries had little history of their killer. Persistent, he shifted through libraries and papers, and if he discovered a connection with any woman, he took it as a sign that she was to be a victim.

His hatred for the normal world increased. While engaged in research he was patronised by scholars and dismissed by art dealers. His amateur questions provoked scorn in them, their learning waved like an Olympian torch to illuminate his own kindergarten efforts. In all the time he researched Angelico Vespucci he was shown no kindness from the art world. Instead he was made to feel inferior, a common, ill-educated tyro.

As his admiration for Vespucci grew, his loathing of the art world intensified – and an addendum to his original plan took form. He would emulate The Skin Hunter and belittle the art world at the same time. Give them the runaround. Humiliate them as they had humiliated him. But in order to damage his enemy, he knew he had first to get close.

Idly, he touched his victim's face on the computer screen, scanning all the images he had taken of her. She would be the fourth, the last of The Skin Hunter's victims. She would be a masterpiece . . .

Closing his eyes, he leaned back. Well-spoken, if despised, he had made himself the perfect straight man for some of the biggest egos in the art world. His abuse at the hands of Farina Ahmadi had amused him – yes, he *felt* it, his determination to see her thwarted a direct result of her foulmouthed hectoring.

And then there had been Triumph Jones. Charismatic, knowledgeable, unbeaten Triumph Jones . . . Driven by some instinct, he had travelled to New York. The art world was a predictable place. The dealers handled fortunes but paid their staff a pittance. So if some personable young man offers to work for even less, he is let in.

Of course he is not seen.

The dealers bob in their shiny bubble immune to the staff.

He is not heard either.

Who notices a pillar?

Who thinks a rug can understand?

In time he becomes indispensably invisible. Silently doing their bidding, without cluttering up their space.

It took him over a year to penetrate the vacuum around Triumph Jones. Twelve months of serving, dogsbodying, eating humble pie like a duke would eat swan. He learnt, because he read the dealer's impressive book collection; he researched, because he was trusted; and no one – *no one* – expected the diffident Englishman would want to scurry endlessly through the forgotten archives. By the time he left Triumph Jones, he had darned most of the holes in his impressive body of research on Angelico Vespucci.

And then fate – the pretty witch – took an interest. On returning to England he was looking for employment and found it working at a country house. A country house with an old library, and an even older connection to Angelico Vespucci. A family connection, a blood tie.

307

He was singing, even in his sleep.

When he moved on from Norfolk he was ready, and all the little tendrils he had laid twitched with the music of knowledge. Having impregnated the art world through the thin skin of its belly, he was privy to information on the street. The porters talked. The receptionists gossiped. He heard of the Titian surfacing but did not know who had it. Rumours flourished like mushrooms in muck, Triumph Jones laying a PR trail to whip up a frenzy, an orgasm of desire. And when the American had finished churning up the art world, he resurrected the legend. *When the portrait emerges, so will the man.*

It was genius, fucking genius, he thought. It sent a tingle up the spines from New York to London, London to Dubai, Dubai to Venice. *And it let him in.* What better time to copy the works of Vespucci? What better time to bring him back from death? He had an excuse now. He had permission. He had a ready audience. Superstition was potent; even the most stolid could not fail to wonder if some demon had been roused.

He slipped up once. Suddenly the trail of the painting dried up. He even thought he had lost it. But within a day he had picked up clues which led to Gaspare Reni. The dealer had been old, but feisty. And when he left the convent gallery he brought the Titian home and hung it in his cupboard. At night he opened the doors and stared at it. His knives were sharpened, his wits also. He watched Seraphina Morgan and thought of her ancestor, the Whore of Venice, and was obsessed.

308

His first victim was a revelation. That surprised him, as did the amount of blood which came from her when he punctured the skin. He had mutilated her in Venice in a rented cellar next to an abandoned warehouse, then put her in the hired launch and taken her over to St Michael at night. It seemed the right place – in with the dead. The work had been hard, taking a long time, exhausting him so much that once he drove a knife deep into her stomach, churning it around the organs in fury. When he pulled it out again, he was ashamed. The skin was spoilt.

He would not do that again.

48

Pushing aside one book, Nino reached for another, avoiding Gaspare's intense stare. Together they had worked through most of the dealer's extensive art history collection, the bulk of which covered the Italian Renaissance, and the time when Titian and Angelico Vespucci had been active. Nino had known from the start that it was a long shot, more than a little doubtful that he would come across some fact in among the academic theories. But he had hoped.

And had been disappointed.

Exasperated, he had then turned to the internet. The email he had sent to the chat room of the Vespucci site had been ignored, and Jobo Kido had not been in touch since they'd parted. Instinctively mistrusting the dealer, Nino's attention turned to Triumph Jones. But although he was out of hospital, the American had not been forthcoming when he'd called him earlier.

'Can't you think of anything that might help?'

'How would I know who the next victim is?' Triumph replied, his voice dropping at the end of the line. He sounded lethargic, wavering. 'Maybe there won't be another killing.'

'You believe that?'

'No . . .'

'So help me. Have you had any further contact about the Titian?'

'I think we both know the answer to that,' Triumph replied. 'The painting's gone to ground. If any dealer in the art world had it, I'd have heard. If anyone else has it, they're not telling me – even for a reward.'

'You don't think that your mugging was connected?'

'I think a man who's a big enough fool to walk in Central Park after dark deserves everything that's coming to him.' He sounded defeated. 'But, Mr Bergstrom, if you're asking me where I think the Titian is now, I think the killer has it.'

'But how could he keep it quiet?'

'Maybe it's in another country. Maybe it's in *your* country. Maybe someone destroyed it.'

'No, it's too valuable.'

'*Really?*' Triumph said, ringing off.

Moving back to the computer, Nino typed in the name Vespucci and then looked at the listings. He had investigated every entry several times before and learnt nothing he didn't already know. Flicking on the table lamp, he glanced over at Gaspare. The dealer was reading again, concentrating, his glasses magnifying his eyes.

'Gaspare?'

He looked up. 'Yes?'

'We have to go through this, step by step.'

'All right,' the old man said patiently.

'Seraphina had the painting, and she was related to the Contessa di Fattori.'

Exasperated, Gaspare slammed his book shut.

'Dear God, not again! We've gone through this a hundred times.'

'And we're missing something!' Nino retorted. 'Sally Egan did a copy of the Vespucci portrait—'

'Which no longer exists. Or so Farina Ahmadi says.'

'You think she's lying?'

'She's breathing,' Gaspare said, raising his eyebrows, 'so she could be lying.'

'Harriet Forbes wrote an article on Vespucci.'

'Did you read it?'

'Yeah, it was interesting.'

'For him or against him?'

'She's dead. What do you think?' Nino remarked wryly. 'So what other areas could there be?'

Taking off his glasses, Gaspare yawned. Then he straightened up in his seat, turning to Nino.

'History.'

'I've researched the time that Vespucci lived, but not found anything written about him that we haven't already seen. Nothing particular—'

'Did you look in Italy? The Italian universities have History departments. Maybe they'd have something extra on Vespucci?'

Nino shook his head. 'There's nothing online.'

'I don't mean on the internet! Let's do it the old-fashioned way,' Gaspare admonished him. 'Let's pick the brains of tutors, scholars, historians.' He reached for his address book and thumbed through the pages, throwing it down and picking up another from his desk drawer. Peering through his glasses, he made a clucking sound with his tongue and then waved the book in front of Nino. 'Professor Cesare Lombardo!'

'Who is?'

'About ninety,' Gaspare replied, pulling a face. 'But when I knew him he was the foremost authority on the Renaissance painters in Venice.'

'He's an art historian. Vespucci was a merchant—'

'*Who was painted by Titian.* If Lombardo's still alive, he'll be worth talking to.'

Reaching for the phone, Gaspare put in a call to Rome, his voice rising with impatience as he talked. Fluent in Italian, Nino could follow what he was saying – that the Professor had been moved into a nursing home. He was fit, if frail. Writing down the number, Gaspare dialled again.

Asking for Professor Lombardo, he was gentle when he was put through.

'How are you, sir?' he asked, his tone respectful. 'This is Gaspare, Gaspare Reni . . . Yes, I'm well . . . living in London. You sound good, very good . . .' He laughed, amused. 'Yes, we are both still alive. I need some help, Professor. I'm looking for information on a man who was painted by Titian

– his name was Angelico Vespucci. And it's your speciality, that period . . .' There was a pause, then more conversation, and Gaspare made notes. 'Yes, yes, I know all that. I was thinking of anything more in-depth about The Skin Hunter. Perhaps you know of someone with specialised knowledge? . . . I see, Mr Patrick Dewick. He had a special interest . . . And where is he? . . . A hospital in London? Most illuminating . . .' He glanced at Nino, his expression incredulous. 'And Jonathan Ravenscourt wanted to talk to him. Yes, I know of Mr Ravenscourt. Did he speak with Mr Dewick? Did you pass this information on to him? . . .'

Nino was holding his breath without knowing why.

' . . . No . . . As you say, Professor, there are people we confide in and people we mistrust . . . I thank you for your help . . . grazie. Grazie. Ciao.'

Replacing the phone in its cradle, Gaspare glanced at Nino. 'He gave me the name of a male nurse who works in Ealing – Patrick Dewick. Mean anything?'

'No, but Sally Egan was a care worker. They could have met that way. He lives in London, so did she.' Nino paused, trying to contain his excitement. 'But why would a nurse study Vespucci?'

'Patrick Dewick is a psychiatric nurse,' Gaspare replied. 'Why *wouldn't* he?'

BOOK FIVE

Venice, December 1555

*They found part of the skin at noon on Sunday, hanging outside
the church, fluttering like a bloodied flag in the east wind. The
priest cut it down and took it away, we do not know where. Some
say it is a new victim, but I hear the hide fits part of the portion
taken from Claudia Moroni.*

*But there is more. The scapegoat has been named, at last. The
suspect who will absolve Vespucci's guilt. I heard it spoken outside
the studio of Titian, saw how the crowd mumbled the name, then
fell hushed. Aretino came out to talk, his eyes lowered as though
he could not bear to be the carrier of such news.*

*He said my friend is innocent, and the man who has done these
deeds is Pomponio.*

Pomponio, son of Titian. *Pomponio, brother of Octavio. Pomponio, priest of the Catholic church, estranged from his father.
Pomponio, feckless, a wanton spendthrift, cut off from his family
as a waster. Pomponio, the braggart, the idle, but The Skin Hunter?*

*The rumour traversed Venice within the hour, Aretino visiting
his friend, pleading with Titian to listen to him. That it grieved
him to impart such news. That he was forced to speak to protect
an innocent man . . .*

*I watched him talk, puffed up with bile and cunning, Titian
motionless, without words. His hand gripped the paintbrush he
held, his eyes turning to the man he had counted as his dearest
friend.*

'Pomponio is my son . . .'

*Dropping his head, Aretino glanced down. I watched him. As
ever, he did not see me, but I saw him. Saw him nail the foolish
Pomponio to a scapegoat's cross.*

*All of Venice knew of the bad blood between the father and the
son, but he was Titian's child, for all his carelessness. For all his
idleness, his greed, for all his loathing of the priestly vestments that
he was made to wear, he was the artist's son. Less than his brother
in talent, no match for his father's genius, a reluctant and unsteady
priest.*

But still his father's son.

*And Aretino thought him worth the sacrifice. Throw Pomponio
to the mob, to let Vespucci be . . . I knew his reasoning: his callous-
ness would justify his claim. Pomponio was no credit to his father,
what loss so poor an heir? I could imagine how easy Aretino would
have come upon his plan, picking a powerless victim to shield his
own interests.*

*Nothing would be allowed to harm the merchant. Vespucci could
take us all to hell and Aretino would stand apologist for him. And
all to save exposure. To save the artist knowing of his deceit. To*

save a fall from grace as great as that of Icarus.

We are to consider Pomponio The Skin Hunter. A mediocre man, a reluctant priest, to set the mob talking. And thinking. Perhaps Titian had banished him because he suspected his son? Perhaps he was privy to horrors committed and exiled Pomponio to ensure his child's escape? Perhaps this mild and vapid man could kill and fool us by his calf-soft ways?

By choosing the artist's son Aretino picks himself a lamb. But the lamb was raised with lions. The lions of St Mark's. While Aretino holds his suspect high to take the coming arrows, he shows his unclothed hand. Ruthless and unloving, he miscalculates. Loyalty lies with blood, not friendship.

He has betrayed his friend, and Titian knows it. Knows not of the monetary thefts but of Aretino's wickedness of heart. While Titian hears the mob outside his gates, while I hear people calling for Pomponio, while Vespucci slides through the mire of his own making, Titian grieves. He grieves for his child, and in grieving might rear up like a lion to strike against those who would injure his own.

I know it. Only I.

The accusation will not stand. But Aretino has made it, and in doing so, has marked his own demise.

The city is tormented. Cloud, heavy with fog, disguises the buildings and hides the water's edge. There is even talk of snow.

And, in silence, we await another death.

49

Greenfield's Hospital, London

Patrick Dewick was pushing a teenager in a wheelchair, the boy talking to himself quietly as he trailed his hand along the wall. Dewick was in his fifties, his hair thin and buzz cut, a gold stud in his left ear. It struck an incongruous note, out of character with the rest of his appearance.

Walking over to him, Nino smiled a welcome.

'Patrick Dewick?'

'Yep.'

'Can I have a word?'

Wheeling the patient into the next ward, Dewick parked him by the nurses' station and then moved back into the passageway. Jerking his head for Nino to follow him, he led him into the parking bays at the back of the hospital. Once there, he lit up, inhaling and coughing vigorously.

'Are you enjoying that?'

He gave Nino a bleak look. 'So, what d'you want?'

'I was told—'

'I don't like that.'

'What?'

'Sentences that begin "*I was told*" – it's always trouble.' He winked, mocking him. 'Go on, I was just playing with you.'

'You're a nurse here?'

'For fifteen years.'

'Long time,' Nino said, glancing around. 'Hard work, I suppose?'

'Not to me. I like it here . . . So what's this all about?'

'I'm looking into something for a friend. He was talking to Professor Lombardo in Italy, who said that you were interested in Angelico Vespucci.'

Dewick's expression didn't change. After a moment's pause he nodded his head. 'Oh yes, I remember . . . God, that was a while ago.'

'What was?'

'I was doing some research for a patient.'

'For a patient?'

'Yeah, she was a very troubled woman. Really sick. She came from . . . I can't remember now, but I could look it up.' He inhaled again. 'She'd been a teacher, I think, some kind of tutor, and then she'd gone into history and was writing a book about the Italian Renaissance.' He said the word and laughed, rolling it on his tongue. 'I said I'd help her. We do that sort of thing – it keeps them quiet, and it breaks the monotony for us.'

'What was her name?'

Dewick blew out his cheeks. 'You've got me there. She came in after she'd had a breakdown. Pretty woman, very smart but scared.'

'What was she scared of?'

'Her family, the world, herself.' He shrugged. 'What are most people scared of? Everything ... Anyway, I did some looking up for her, and spoke to Professor Lombardo—'

'He speaks English?'

'Well, I don't speak Italian,' Dewick replied, laughing, 'and then I passed on what he told me to her. *Susan Coates!* That was her name. I knew I'd remember it.'

Nino made a mental note. 'What happened to her?'

'She was discharged and I haven't heard from her since. She was depressed, but you felt she could find her way round it. I think she had a good chance to get well, but who knows? You can never tell, you just hope for them.'

'And what about Vespucci?'

He stared at Nino, baffled. 'Who?'

'Angelico Vespucci, The Skin Hunter, the man you were researching for her. What d'you remember about him?'

'You are joking? I don't remember a bit of it. He was some nutter in the past, but it goes in one ear and out the other. I've got enough to cope with – I don't need to fill my head with any more crazy stuff.'

Disappointed, Nino turned to go, but Dewick called him back. 'You should have spoken to the volunteer—'

'What?'

'Now, he was a weirdo, that one,' Dewick continued. 'He

and Susan got very thick, and he cut me out – said he'd help her with her writing. He was in her room day in, day out. I told the Sister about it. Didn't like the guy—'

'Can you remember what he was called?'

'Eddie Ketch.'

'D'you know where he is now?'

Dewick shook his head. 'He was sacked, chucked out for behaving in "an unsuitable manner" with the female patients.'

Nino could feel his heart rate pick up. 'Would Personnel have a record?'

'I doubt it,' Dewick replied, almost apologetically. 'Ketch was a volunteer, like I said. They can be a bit half-hearted about checking up on volunteers – or they used to be. It was only when he starting acting odd that they chucked him out. Ketch might not even be his real name.'

Certain he was on to something, Nino pressed him. 'Why would you say that?'

'Because there was something funny about Ketch. I've got a bit of a sixth sense for it. And he was odd, unemotional. Not like any other volunteer I've ever met. He could pretend, could Ketch, but he didn't feel anything. I could see it in the way he talked to the patients. He was listening, but not caring. I asked him why he volunteered once and he said that he was "between careers". Stupid prick. *Between careers* – what kind of a comment was that?'

'What did he look like?'

'Late twenties. He'd be thirty-one, thirty-two now. Slim, good-looking in a whey-faced way. Very well-spoken, I remember that – he sounded posh.'

'Did he talk about his family, friends?'

'Nothing,' Dewick replied, shaking his head. 'He came here like a lost soul, but it was like he found something.'

'In the patients?'

'No, in what Susan Coates was working on. Some Italian killer. I don't know much about it, but Ketch was fascinated, asking her all sorts of questions. I thought it was just the usual – you know, people like murders and stuff, but Ketch was taking it seriously. Like he was going to give a bloody talk. Not that it was new to him—'

'How d'you mean?'

'It was obvious he'd heard about the killer before – he said so. He used to swap stories with Susan Coates. She knew more than he did and he drew her out. It was like she wanted to please him.' Dewick paused, thinking back. 'Strange thing was that women liked him, I remember that. It was unusual, you see – vulnerable female patients can be jumpy around men, but all the women liked Ketch. The men didn't – you'd be hard put to find any man with a good word to say for him, but women – they took to him, trusted him, which surprised me because frankly I wouldn't have trusted that fucker as far as I could have thrown him.'

Personnel had the file on Susan Coates, but were unable to tell Nino anything about her whereabouts. It was illegal to give out patient information, the woman said. Perhaps you should talk to her doctor? But the doctor was even less forthcoming. As Nino walked past Personnel Reception again he caught the eye of the clerk. Aware that he had hit a brick wall, she said nothing, but lifted Susan Coates' file up quickly to show him the word DECEASED printed across it.

'Thanks,' he mouthed, walking over. Dropping his voice so that he wouldn't be overheard, he said, 'You don't remember a volunteer called Eddie Ketch, do you? Good-looking, well-spoken—'

'He was fired,' she whispered back, looking around to check no one was listening. 'What about him?'

'D'you know where he is now?'

'No . . . But hang on a minute,' she said, moving into the storage backroom and returning with an old photograph. It was a picture of a group of people sitting outside a pub, obviously hospital staff. Jabbing her finger on the left-hand side, she glanced at Nino. 'That's Eddie Ketch.'

Ketch was in the background, the only person not holding a glass. He was standing full on to the camera, his expression composed, emotionless . . . Smiling gratefully, Nino took the photograph and walked out.

He had his man. He knew it, could feel it: some shudder of recognition. This was the killer. Eddie Ketch – or whatever he was called – knew about The Skin Hunter. Had been fascinated, had grown close to Susan Coates, even became intimate with his tutor. And women liked Ketch, they trusted him. He was a man women would relax with. A man women would find attractive. A man who could be anything for anyone. Composed enough to calculate. Composed enough to kill.

He had murdered three women so far. Three down, one to go. And Nino had no idea who, or where, she was.

50

Snow seemed to be falling around most of the northern half of the world. It stopped the traffic on the A1 and M5, it grounded the planes at Heathrow and Kennedy Airport, and stamped its feet over a million suburban homes in France. In Venice the fog returned, and the snow spread further afield, trailing continents in its smothering grip. Soon the city of Tokyo winced under ice showers. From the side of buildings icicles dangled like malignant Christmas decorations, the water from burst pipes freezing in mid-air, and in the quiet back room of a flat in London a man sat in front of a computer screen.

He had made his choice.

Picked his last victim.

Only nine days to go before he would kill her.

The thought intoxicated him, made him wonder if Angelico Vespucci had felt the same sense of expectation and arousal. If he had also planned the murder ahead of time. Chosen di Fattori and then waited for the inevitable conclusion. Did Vespucci revel in watching his victim live out her last days, knowing that he would be the one to end her life? Did he see fear in her eyes, or mock her ignorance?

He didn't know, but dismissed the rumours of Vespucci's madness. The Italian had been inspired, not insane. He did wonder about the skins though, had thought about them a great deal, because he loved the skins he had hunted. Surely Vespucci wouldn't have destroyed his own collection? Surely the hides were still out there somewhere? Hidden, as poignant as the desiccated mummies from the past. Perhaps they had been wrapped in cloth? Or placed in metal vessels? Maybe secreted under floorboards, maybe between bookshelves? Or in some chilly Italian vault no living person visited? Maybe.

But they were somewhere.

It was the only loose end, and having no guidance from Vespucci on the matter he didn't know what to do with *his* skins. He had followed the Venetian faithfully, but after every murder he was left with the question of what to do with the hide. Where to hide the trophy.

Getting to his feet, he walked over to the wardrobe and opened the doors, gazing in at the portrait of The Skin Hunter. His head tilted to one side, his thoughts sliding. When the last murder was completed, he would decide what to do with the painting *and* the skins. It would be *his* choice, *his* decision – something in which Vespucci would have no part. The realisation thrilled him, left him short of breath.

327

Perhaps he would – in the final analysis – outdo The Skin Hunter? Improve on his acts, even embellish them?

The thought was like cream on his tongue.

Moving back to the computer, he entered the chat room of the Vespucci website, expecting to find an entry from Jobo Kido. Of course there was one; the Japanese dealer was practically salivating at the thought of getting the Titian. He moved down the other entries, ignoring another approach from Johnny Ravenscourt, and fixing on the message from Nino Bergstrom.

He had always known who the white-haired man was; it had simply amused him to push Jobo Kido, to discover just how far he would go to get the portrait. Apparently Kido would betray anyone. Which was just what he had expected.

Although he had no intention of replying to Nino Bergstrom, he was interested to see a new message from him. But a flutter of rage went through him as he read it.

Nino: I've been following your website for some time. I'm also an admirer of Angelico Vespucci and his crimes. But he was mad, and I'm not. In fact, I'm responsible for the deaths of three women already, and will commit a fourth. On 1 January.

Answer: *You don't know what you're talking about!*

Nino: Of course I do. Your site's good, but the real thing's better.

He was incensed. Surely this Bergstrom man couldn't think *he* was going to take credit for the murders? Bergstrom was a joke, a Hollywood lapdog. What the hell would he know, or care, about Angelico Vespucci?

Answer: *You're lying.*

Nino: I'm Vespucci's true follower. You're just a copyist. Everyone knows that I killed those women.

Answer: *It wasn't you!*

Nino: Prove it.

The man paused, staring at the words on the screen, suddenly realising that he was being played. Bergstrom wanted to get him to confess.

Clever, but not clever enough ...

Slowly, he typed his reply.

Answer: *If you're the killer, who's the next victim?*

Nino: You know who it is.

Answer: *Tell me her name.*

Nino: On the internet? Are you kidding?

Answer: *You don't know.*

Nino: Oh, but I do. And I'm going to stop you, Mr Ketch. Is it Ketch?

The man jumped, startled by the words.

Nino: Or are you someone else now? Should I call you Mr Vespucci? After all, you've copied his work, it seems only right you should take his name too.

Answer: *You're crazy!*

Nino: So tell me your name. Who are you? Deny you're the killer of these women. At the moment it seems that the only crazy one is you.

Answer: *You don't know who I am. Where I am. Or who the next victim is. And if you're thinking of trying to trace this connection, don't bother, it's been rigged.*

Nino: All right, we'll try another tack. *Why* are you killing these women?

Answer: *Are you trying to understand me now? Trying to create a rapport? You can't see me, Mr Bergstrom, but I'm laughing.*

Nino: Maybe I can see you. I'm closer than you think.

Answer: *You're bluffing. If the police in the UK, Italy and Japan can't find me, what makes you think you can?*

Nino: I'm *supposed* to find you.

Answer: *I don't think so.*

Nino: I do. I'm not going to let you kill another woman.

Answer: *You've no choice. In fact, you've only got nine days left, Mr Bergstrom, nine days to run around trying to find a woman you have no hope of saving. She'll die. She has to . . . I hope you're a good loser.*

Nino: Why don't you stop? Stop now and save her. The authorities would look on that as co-operation, even a show of remorse.

There was a pause before the man replied.

Answer: *You think I should stop now? And ruin the whole plan?*

Nino: You made the plan, you can change it.

Answer: *You think the police would take it into consideration?*

Nino: Yes, I think they would. It would help you.

Answer: *And if I told them where the skins were? You think that would help too?*

Nino: Yes, I do. I think that if you stop now, you can redeem yourself.

Answer: *Redeem myself? Be forgiven?*

Nino: If you save this woman and stop the killing, yes. Let her have her life.

Answer: *But what if she doesn't deserve it?*

Nino: Who made you God?

Answer: *There was a vacancy.*

Nino: You don't have to do it. You don't have to kill this woman.

The man paused on the end of the connection, smiling, then typed:

But I want to.

51

Venice

It had been playing on Tom Morgan's mind how much Johnny Ravenscourt had wanted the painting from the old flat. For once sober as a magistrate, Tom realised that he might have missed a trick, and that the portrait had been worth more than he had at first thought. Admittedly, he had helped himself to a couple of thousand out of Ravenscourt's wallet, but the fat bastard hadn't protested, had even believed himself – unless Tom was imagining it – to have got off lightly.

Having sold the old flat, and now settled in the rented apartment he had shared with Seraphina, Tom had relaxed into a state that only people with money in the bank can enjoy. Able to indulge himself, he spent a couple of days in a fug of highest quality marijuana and drank several bottles of champagne, but his thoughts kept turning to Ravenscourt and he wondered what Seraphina would have done.

If only their plan had worked. They would have been

millionaires. Not just comfortable, fucking cushy ... The high-ceilinged apartment was cold and Tom shivered and turned up the heating, the pipes juddering as it stirred into life. His life had not turned out the way he had anticipated; his existence had improved with the money made from the property sale, but his lack of interest at work guaranteed another plunge in profits.

Perhaps he should leave Venice? The company was making allowances for his condition – as the widower of a murdered woman – but for how long? How long before his arse was pushed into action again? He wasn't made for work, Tom realised – not really. It was all too brutal, too coarse for him ... His mind went back to the painting and, irritated, he left the flat, making for the piazza where Ravenscourt lived.

The sight of its magnificence inflamed his self-pity further. What had a shit like Ravenscourt done to deserve such luxury? By rights, if everything had gone to plan, he and Seraphina should have been enjoying the proceeds from the Titian sale.

But instead Tom was being shown into the drawing room where Ravenscourt was sitting reading a magazine.

He looked up. 'Spent all the money already?'

'I was thinking,' Tom replied, helping himself to some wine and sitting down by the window. 'Why did you want that painting so much?'

'The Titian?'

'Nah, the other one. The one with the couple in it. Who painted it anyway?'

'Some minor artist.'

Looking around, Tom turned back to Ravenscourt. 'I don't see it. Where have you put it?'

'Being restored.'

He nodded, thoughtful. 'That's expensive, or so Seraphina's parents always used to say. They said it wasn't worth having any picture restored unless it was valuable.' He paused, but Ravenscourt was still flicking through his magazine, forcing him to continue. 'So, was it?'

'What?'

'Valuable.'

'So-so.'

'So-so to you or so-so to me?'

Ravenscourt laid the magazine down, his reading glasses swinging from a chain around his neck. 'What d'you want to know?'

'Who painted it?'

'A man called Barmantino, a good artist but not a great one. It was one of his earlier works. And it was in bad condition—'

'Looked OK to me.'

'Yes, but you don't know much about art, do you? That was Seraphina's strong suit.' Ravenscourt leaned back in his seat. In the room beyond a uniformed Italian boy no more than eighteen was arranging some flowers. 'What's the matter anyway? You were happy enough to sell it.'

'Yeah, and you were very keen to get it. Why?'

'I'm an art dealer. It's what I do.'

'So why hadn't you wanted it before? God knows, you'd seen it often enough.' Tom paused, walking around, his gaze travelling to the canal outside. 'Water, water everywhere . . . don't you get sick of it?'

'It's Venice.'

Tom ignored the comment.

'The company sent me here, you know. I wouldn't have chosen it.'

Taking an orange from the fruit bowl, Tom began to peel it. He did so with dexterity, keeping the peel intact then dropping it, unbroken, into a large Murano vase.

Exasperated, Ravenscourt stared at him. 'What d'you want, Morgan? You and I aren't friends, we have nothing in common—'

'Not since Seraphina died.'

'So why are you here?'

'I've been thinking . . . Seraphina was afraid of water.'

'I know.'

'She never walked near the edge of pathways or bridges. Seems like a strange way to die, being chucked in the Lido.' He paused, chewing a segment of orange. 'And mutilated like that. Like Vespucci's victims. It made me wonder about why it had all started up. The Titian portrait of Vespucci, then the skinning of Seraphina, then the other women being killed.'

'*Are you accusing me?*'

'Of the murders?' Tom shook his head. 'I thought you might have killed Seraphina, but not the others. Why would you? There was no money in it. Anyway, I can't imagine you getting involved in anything so *butch*.'

'So what are you suggesting?'

'I don't know really. You could say I'm just feeling my way around.' He winked, taunting Ravenscourt. 'But you were always obsessed by Angelico Vespucci. You used to talk to Seraphina about it.'

'She was born and raised in Venice, with artistic parents, and her ancestor was the Contessa di Fattori – it would have been unusual *not* to talk about him.'

'But Seraphina finding the Titian – that was incredible.'

'Paintings turn up in the most unlikely places, in all manner of ways,' Ravenscourt replied, unfazed. 'But she should never have left it with Gaspare Reni. God knows why she didn't bring it home—'

'You know why. We had to find a way to smuggle it back to Venice. She could hardly bring it back in her fucking hand luggage, could she? *You* were going to help us get it back – but then she got killed ... God knows where the Titian is now.'

Ravenscourt shrugged.

'Who knows? Everyone's looking for it, in Japan, New York, London, but it's disappeared—'

'D'you think the killer has it?'

Frowning, Ravenscourt turned in his seat to look over his shoulder. 'How would he get it?'

'Steal it off Gaspare Reni. Someone did. Why not the murderer?'

'But how did he know it was with Reni? There were only two people who knew that – Seraphina and you.'

Tom smiled at the lie.

'Don't count yourself out, Johnny – you knew too. You can deny it all you like, but I'll never believe my wife didn't tell you about the Titian—'

Bristling, Ravenscourt threw down his magazine. 'You can fling accusations around all *you* like, but it doesn't make them true.'

'When's it coming back?'

'*What?*'

'The Barmantino painting that's being restored. The one you bought off me.'

Standing up, Ravenscourt moved over to him.

'You're right there – *I bought it*. It's mine now. So what I do with it has nothing to do with you.'

52

Infuriated, Ravenscourt watched the American walk out, listened as he heard his footsteps echo down the stairs and on to the piazza beyond. Curious, he then moved to the window in time to see Tom Morgan crossing the bridge which connected the houses on one side of the canal with the other. When he was certain the American had gone, Ravenscourt dismissed the servant and then closed the drawing room doors.

Anger had taken its toll on him. Anger that he had been cheated out of the Titian when he had been so close. That Seraphina's death had occurred before she had included him in a plan which would have netted all three of them a fortune. Why hadn't she confided in him sooner? Ravenscourt asked himself, surprised that Seraphina had been so sly. But maybe it had taken a while to connect the plan, and she had been killed before she could approach him. Or maybe it had taken time for her to be persuaded.

Smuggling the Titian out of the country would have been relatively easy for Johnny Ravenscourt. He had contacts from the old days and could press anyone into committing a minor crime for a major reward. Seraphina's deception had surprised him, but then again, he had only Tom Morgan's account of what she had said. Seraphina could hardly speak for herself.

He had always suspected Tom Morgan. Maybe he had pressurised his wife against her will, knowing how easy it would be for her to get her old friend on board. Everyone knew that Johnny Ravenscourt was immoral, greedy. Everyone knew he liked to mix with a rough crowd, the criminal element adding a frisson to his sex life. There had been more than a few thieves invited into Johnny Ravenscourt's bed over the years.

But to have lost out on the Titian portrait of Angelico Vespucci, his obsession! It was almost too much to bear ... He thought of Tom Morgan, uncertain of the American's motives and curious as to why he had taken such a sudden interest in the Barmantino painting. God knows it had been hanging in the Morgan apartment the whole time they had lived there, and he never even remarked on it before. Except to say that Claudia Moroni had been a plain woman.

Of course Seraphina had always liked the picture. She thought Claudia Moroni had had a fascinating face, a look which almost prophesied her death. She had often commented that she would make sure to keep the painting in the family, and talked of moving it into the new flat. And she wasn't blind to the fact that it was also a pretty good investment ... Ravenscourt frowned. If Seraphina was alive now she wouldn't have approved of her husband selling the apartment, or the painting.

Restlessly, he fiddled with the beaded chain on his reading glasses, uncertain of what to do next. He wasn't intending to return to England for a while – the police would be only too interested in his re-appearance – but in Venice he had no way of discovering what was going on in London. He was out of the loop and afraid that he might suffer for it.

Taking a breath, Ravenscourt realised that there was only one course of action open to him, and put in a phone call.

Nino answered on the third ring. 'Hello?'

'It's Johnny Ravenscourt—'

'You bastard!'

'Hear me out!' he pleaded, his tone plaintive. 'I had to get the police off my back—'

'And on to mine?'

'They let you go,' Ravenscourt said dismissively. 'What are you complaining about? Gaspare pulled in an old favour and I retracted my statement. Besides, you must have done well out of this. And I haven't asked for my retainer back. Have you spent all of it?'

At the other end of the line Nino shook his head in disbelief, and lied. 'Yes. All of it.'

'Whatever did you do with it?'

'I went to Japan on a wild goose chase. Which pretty much sums up everything about you and your story.'

'You saw Jobo Kido in Japan?'

'I saw him, but I'm none the wiser,' Nino lied again, mistrusting Ravenscourt and determined that he would give him no information. 'What d'you want?'

'I want you to carry on working for me—'

'Like hell.'

'Mr Bergstrom, I'll pay you whatever you want. You can go to Japan, New York – wherever you like. I just need to know what's going on – and I can't do that stuck here in Venice.'

'Go on the internet.'

'I don't see why you're so defensive,' Ravenscourt replied, his tone honeyed. . . . 'You should snatch my hand off. I've money to burn, so why not relieve me of some of it? I brought you in on this—'

'No, you didn't. I got involved because of Gaspare Reni's friendship with Seraphina.'

'I was much closer to her!' Ravenscourt snapped. 'And I gave you all my notes on The Skin Hunter. I gave you a head start, and now I want some feedback. I want to know who killed Seraphina—'

'And you want to know where the Titian is.'

'I'm a dealer – what's wrong with that?' he replied, then softened his tone. 'I admit, I'd like the painting. But so would a number of other dealers – that doesn't make me a suspect.'

'It doesn't clear you either.'

'You can't believe that I killed Seraphina, or the other women!'

'I don't know who killed them.'

341

'But you're still trying to find out?'

Nino paused, deciding to string Ravenscourt along. The dealer was stuck in Venice, so he could tell him anything and he had no way of knowing if it was true or not. And besides, if he carried on talking to Johnny Ravenscourt, the dealer might let something slip.

'Have you seen Tom Morgan lately?'

Ravenscourt relaxed, sure that Nino was back on board. Sure that he could deceive him again. He was tired of the skittish Tom Morgan and wanted him corralled.

'Actually, I saw Morgan today ...' Ravenscourt began, thinking of all the American's vicious jibes and his nosy interest in the Barmantino. 'He was acting very strangely.'

'How?'

'Jumpy, on the defensive.'

'About what?'

'Well, I hate to be the one to say it,' the dealer paused, then took aim, 'but I think he might have something to do with his wife's death after all.'

53

Greenfield's Hospital, London

In between shifts, Patrick Dewick lit up a cigarette at the back of the hospital, drawing in the tobacco smoke and relishing the sensation. Then he started coughing, finally spitting out a gob of phlegm which landed in the puddle at his feet. Sniffing, he leaned against the wall and stared upwards into the sky. It was going to snow again. Bugger it, he would have a hell of a time getting home. The car was unreliable and whatever his wife had said, Patrick wasn't convinced that she had put in antifreeze. He should leave her to it, see how she liked it when the bloody car wouldn't start at the supermarket. It would be another matter then – she wouldn't forget the sodding antifreeze next time.

His thoughts drifted, suddenly alighting on Nino Bergstrom. It had been peculiar talking about Eddie Ketch after so long – the man had always left a sour taste in his mouth – but oddly enough, once reminded, he couldn't *stop* thinking about him. The upset with Susan Coates had been uppermost in his mind, but there had been something else about Ketch which eluded him.

Inhaling again, Patrick screwed up his eyes against the cigarette smoke and peered into the falling snow. Under the overhang of the porch leading to the car park, he was sheltered from the worst of it, snow landing morosely on the concrete at his feet. Nino Bergstrom had asked him about Ketch's family. And he'd said that he never talked about them. But that wasn't true, Patrick remembered – there had been one instance when Ketch had slipped up, and mentioned a woman. A beautiful woman.

But Patrick was damned if he could remember her name.

Ketch had been angry that day, unusually emotional. He had left the ward and slammed into the men's toilet, where Patrick had found him, his face flushed, his hands flat against the wall, repeating a woman's name over and over again. His attractive face had been distorted with rage, but as soon as he spotted Patrick, Ketch had controlled himself. A moment later he looked normal – so normal Patrick had wondered if he'd imagined the whole incident. But he knew he hadn't. And he knew Ketch's rage had been directed at a woman. A woman he had known well. A woman he had obviously cared about.

After finishing his cigarette, Patrick was just about to re-enter the hospital and go back to work, when he paused. On a whim, he phoned the number Nino had given him, leaving a message on the answerphone.

'Lo there. This is Patrick Dewick, at Greenfield's Hospital. We spoke the other day, about Eddie Ketch. Well, I just remembered something about him. He had a girlfriend, a woman he was keen on. I can't remember her name – but I will, and then I'll call you again. I just wondered if it was important, that's all. Cheers.'

Clicking off his mobile, Patrick ground out his cigarette stub under his foot and went back to work. He *would* remember the woman's name.

But before he had time to pass it on, Eddie Ketch would have caught up with him.

54

24 December

In New York, Triumph Jones was watching the television news, dumbstruck. Meanwhile, in London, Farina Ahmadi had been about to catch a plane for Turkey to meet up with her husband and sons, but was staring, incredulous, at her iPad. In Tokyo, Jobo Kido was hunched over his computer, ignoring his wife's phone calls and staring at the screen.

All three dealers were reacting to the new entry on the Vespucci site, an entry which had now become breaking news worldwide, the police caught off guard in the USA, Italy and Japan –

PRICELESS TITIAN PAINTING OF ANGELICO
VESPUCCI OFFERED AS REWARD FOR
IDENTITY OF SERIAL KILLER . . .

'Look at this!' Gaspare shouted, calling for Nino. 'God, you won't believe it.'

Staring at the TV screen, Nino blew out his cheeks. 'He's upped the bloody ante. The bastard thinks he's untouchable. You know what he's doing, don't you? He's got bored with just copying Vespucci – he wants to outdo him.'

'But he's putting the reward on his own head!' Gaspare replied, his tone baffled. 'Everyone will be after it.'

'Yeah, but he's got the Titian, so he figures that no one can find it.' Nino moved over to the computer and typed in angelicovespucci.1555.com. Immediately the press release came up, followed by a banner headline.

The last murder committed by Angelico Vespucci was on the 1st January 1556

Turning the computer towards Gaspare, he pointed to the screen. 'Look at that. He's advertising. He's tipping everyone off, telling them he's going to kill again. And *when* he's going to kill again. No one's going to miss this now. Not with that press release. It'll go worldwide.'

'And someone will connect the murders.'

'I'm amazed they haven't already,' Nino remarked. 'It was only because they were committed in different countries that the connection wasn't made before. But they'll join up the dots now.'

'It might help,' Gaspare said hopefully. 'It might put women on their guard.'

'Every woman on earth?' Nino queried. 'It might have worked if it had just been London but the murder could

347

take place anywhere. It could be Italy, Tokyo, London. It could be one of the places he's hit before, or somewhere new. The woman he's got in mind could be working, travelling, or asleep in bed. *She could be anyone.*' Exasperated, he ran his hands through his hair. 'One week to go, and I'm no nearer to knowing who she is. Someone must be able to tell me *something*.'

'Forget Vespucci for a moment,' Gaspare said calmly. 'Think of what else they have in common.'

'The victims were all young and white. They all had jobs.'

'Go on.'

'Go on?' Nino snapped. 'That's it! That's all I know.'

'So think about the ways they *differed*.'

'*What?*'

'Just do it!'

Nino closed his eyes to concentrate. 'Seraphina was married, and pregnant—'

'With a child that wasn't her husband's.'

'Yeah. Sally Egan was single, childless and promiscuous. Harriet Forbes was single, childless and gay.' He opened his eyes and turned to Gaspare, thinking aloud. 'What if our killer's judging them like Vespucci would have done?'

'Go on.'

'Then he'd see them as adulteress, whore, deviant.'

'What's missing?'

'Happily married?'

Gaspare shook his head impatiently. 'No, that wouldn't be immoral! He's copying the Italian, he thinks the victims are all whores, so what else would he consider immoral? Don't think about it as we do now, think about it as it was in the past. What would have been judged immoral then?'

Sitting down, Nino thought back over everything he'd discovered, then nodded.

'*She's a mistress.* A woman who sleeps with another woman's husband—'

'Yes, that would make sense!'

'Our next victim's a kept woman, Gaspare. Bought and paid for.' His excitement rose. 'She's young, she has a job, she's white, and she's someone's mistress. And unless I find her, she's only got seven days left to live.'

55

Norfolk, 25 December

It was uncharitably cold as Nino arrived in Norfolk and headed for Courtford Hall, parking the car outside the gates and walking up to the house. Ice crackled under his feet and the imposing front door was bleached with frost as he lifted the knocker and rapped loudly.

It was Christmas Day, but there was no sign of it – no festive wreath, no tree, no decorations or lights, and when a lamp went on inside it shone disconsolately through the glass bullseye in the door. Finally there was a shuffle of feet, then the sound of the bolt being drawn back, and suddenly Nino was face to face with Sir Harold Greyly.

'What?' he asked, his tone slurred, his usual composure giving way to the demeanour of a drunk. 'What d'you want?' He blinked, standing up straight and staring at Nino as he pointed to his head. 'I know you. You're the man with all that white hair. You came here before . . .' He was holding a glass in his hand, tilting it so that some of the whisky dripped on to the flagstone floor.

'Can I come in?'

'Sure, sure,' Greyly said, too drunk to remember their previous acrimony.

Nudging Nino's back, he pushed him towards the sitting room, a fire banked high in the grate, fruitwood logs smelling of summer. But the walls were bare of cards or any other ornament and several dirty plates lay by the fire. Sir Harold Greyly had eaten, obviously, but not cleared up, the same fork pressed into service for every meal.

'Happy Christmas. It *is* Christmas Day, isn't it?'

'Yeah, it's Christmas Day.'

'You got nowhere to go?' he asked, his speech haphazard as he gestured to the drinks cupboard. 'Fancy a tipple?'

Surprised, Nino shook his head. Was Harold Greyly really so drunk that he couldn't remember what had happened when they last met?

'Are you on your own?'

'All on my own,' Greyly snorted. 'Christmas and all on my own. My wife and I – we had a fight you see . . .'

'No staff here either?'

'I gave them Christmas off,' Greyly replied, smiling at his own largesse. 'I didn't need them anyway.'

He poured himself another drink and flopped into an armchair. At his feet, the springer spaniels shuffled about for room, finally curling up again closer to the fire. The wood crackled, sparks shooting up the chimney, the logs piled precariously high.

'My wife left me. Said she hated me . . . Up and went. Kids all grown up, so now there's no one left. 'Cept me,' Greyly droned on, narrowing his eyes at Nino. 'What did you come for?'

'Now?'

'Now, and back then. I know you've been here before, but I can't remember why.'

Sighing, he slopped some of the booze on to his shirt and brushed it away. Despite the fire, the temperature in the room was chill, due to a draught coming from under the doorway which led into another room. A draught which suggested an open door beyond. Wary, Nino glanced around him, his gaze coming to rest on the drinks trolley. There were five bottles of whisky, three empty – and beside them was another glass which had been used recently.

'You've had company?'

Greyly belched, patting his stomach, and pointed to a photograph of his wife and two sons. 'They've gone—'

'When?'

'A week ago.'

'Why did they go?'

'Apparently I'm a pig. Come from a long line of pigs. Pig family. Only I'm a titled pig . . . A swine with a gong . . .' Greyly replied insanely, slurring his words. But although he was drunk there was something else about him. Drugged? Nino wondered. Was he on drugs?

'Are you ill?'

'Pissed.'

352

'Apart from that,' Nino pressed him. 'Have you been ill?'

Galvanised, Greyly leant forward in his chair, staring at Nino. 'You came to the house with Hester – I remember now! She was a nosy old bat, but kind. She brought you here—'

'That's right.'

Greyly slumped back in his seat. 'Hester's dead now.'

'I know – she fell.'

To Nino's surprise, Greyly put his index finger to his lips, jerking his head towards the closed door.

Following has gaze, Nino glanced over. The draught still snaked from underneath. It was too cold, he realised – too cold for the temperature of a house. *Someone had left the back door open.* Someone who had left in a hurry. Someone who had watched him arrive and didn't want to be seen.

'Who's been here?'

'No one . . .' Harold replied, picking at the corner of his left eye.

By his feet the dogs snuffled and shifted around in their sleep, the room morose and unwelcoming as Greyly carried on drinking. Nino could feel the cold slithering around him. Silently, he moved towards the door.

But as he reached it, Greyly shook his head.

'*No!*'

Nino paused, turning back to him. 'Who's in there?'

'No one.'

'There are two used glasses, so you must have had company. You might *still* have company. Who is it?'

Teetering to his feet, Greyly grabbed Nino's arm. His expression was fearful – even his drunkenness couldn't disguise that.

'There's no one here. Sit down and have a drink with me.' His grip increased on Nino's arm. Even inebriated, he was very strong. 'Sit with me! I've no one else. Fuck them all! I've no one left and it's Christmas. I don't like fucking Christmas anyway, all that posturing about. All that lord of the manor stuff.' He burped acidly. 'My wife's wrecked everything, you know. All families have secrets – *all* families. But no, she couldn't live with it. Cow . . .' He dragged Nino away from the door, pushing him into the seat next to his. His condition was deteriorating rapidly, his attention wavering. It wasn't just alcohol – there was something else. 'You came to the house with Hester.'

'Yes, I did,' Nino agreed, leaning towards him. 'And she wrote a letter to me, about Claudia. Claudia Moroni.'

Greyly's eyes were half closed, the glass tilted, whisky dribbling on to the front of his trousers.

Taking the glass from him, Nino shook his shoulder. 'Listen to me! I want to talk about Claudia Moroni.'

'She's dead too . . .'

'I know,' Nino replied, 'but you remember her story, don't you? Hester wrote and told me about her. About what happened to Claudia, why she had to leave England.' He shook Greyly again, trying to regain his attention. 'She was an ancestor of yours, and she was killed in Venice.'

His eyes widened, fixed on Nino, suddenly alert. '*Venice?*'

'Yes, Venice. She was killed by Angelico Vespucci.'

Nino could see some semblance of coherence returning, but as it did so, he could feel a heightening of the draught coming from under the door, and he had the sudden and unpleasant sensation of someone having entered; someone who was now listening to their conversation.

'Did someone come to see you today?'

'I don't know.'

Nino dropped his voice to a whisper. 'Did someone come to see you?'

'No. No ...'

'Who was it?'

'No one,' Greyly blathered. 'There was no one ... no one ... There's no one left. No one ...' His voice slid off, his head sinking on to his chest as he passed out.

Uneasy, Nino stood up, looking around for anything he could use as a weapon. Picking up a poker from the grate, he moved silently towards the door and opened it, standing back in case anyone rushed out at him. But there was no one there, only the draught, coming stronger and stronger. Stealthily he passed through the library, moving into the kitchen beyond. The room was in semi-darkness, but there was enough light to see a door swinging open.

A door which led out into the yard beyond.

56

Rachel Pitt knew it wasn't ideal, that he would probably never leave his wife. All married men said they loved you. That one day, when the time was right, they would tell their wives about you. Of course there never was a right time. If they ever did pick a day then one of the children would be ill, or the wife would be having a bad time at work, and he *couldn't*, just couldn't tell her now. He would, in time. But not this time.

It wasn't as though Rachel hadn't set deadlines over the previous two years. *If he hasn't left his wife by June*, she swore, *I'll finish the relationship*. But June always slid into July, then tripped the light fantastic down to Christmas. Which she always spent alone. A few times she had gone home, but her mother was divorced and Rachel could hardly see herself confiding. The grim reality of her mother's life – of her hatred of men and her increasing isolation – served as a mirror to her own existence. Was this to be her lot? If her lover didn't leave his wife, would she find herself too old and too bitter to find someone else?

There was no escaping the fact that she loved Michael and found snatching moments with him more palatable than having another man a hundred per cent of the time. Rachel had chosen her life, and she was sticking to it because the chance to walk away had passed. He was too close to her now. Too much a part of her. Too entrenched in her life to consider amputation. Everything she did she made a note of to tell him when they spoke. Her words, her actions, her thoughts centred around this one man who would never be hers.

Rachel had often wondered if she was a masochist. If she was, in some perverse way, punishing herself for some subconscious fault. Her appeal was obvious, so why attach herself to a man already attached? But she had stuck with Michael, even after she found out he was married. She should have walked away then, but he was charming and he made her feel secure and happy, and he understood her the way no other man had understood her before.

He was a marvellous lover too, and she knew that also kept her tied to him. And if, sometimes, she was jealous of his wife, he would reassure her. They hadn't been sleeping together for years. She didn't know him, love him as Rachel did. They stayed together for the children . . . Oh, she knew all the clichés by rote.

The same hackneyed phrases came out year after year, and even when Rachel ceased to believe them, she pretended she did. After all, the relationship wasn't completely one-sided. Michael had helped her out financially many times over the previous five years, and paid most of her rent. And when she had left her job and gone back to study full-time, he had supported her. Not that he couldn't afford it. Being in banking he was rich enough to carry two women, even three. Even three . . . She wondered about that sometimes. If he could cheat on his wife, could he cheat on her? He travelled around the world – surely attractive women constantly crossed his path? Younger women, prettier women, women he hadn't known for five years and become used to. Women fresh and flirty, who never thought about wives or children.

But Rachel did. It haunted her, the fact of his family. She might be able to dismiss his wife or count her as a harridan, but his children were omnipresent, a constant reminder of what she was doing. If the affair was ever discovered, she could imagine the fallout. The trauma for the children. The break-up of the marriage . . . No, who was she kidding? It would make the marriage stronger. Everyone knew how expensive divorce was, how prohibitive it was to split up shared properties, funds, bank accounts. And children. Whatever Michael promised her, whatever he assured her, he would stay with his family if it came to a choice. Men might like to stray, but in the end the duvet at home always sucked them back in.

Glancing back at her work table, Rachel noticed the time – nine p.m. Another evening spent alone. Why? She could be anywhere. She was moving in different circles, had studied theatrical design and contemporary playwrights, and was newly employed in a small London theatre. Assistant Stage Manager – maybe fully fledged, in time. But how *much* time? Did she really want ambition to dictate the way she lived? Did she want to be hanging about in dingy theatre wings while she waited for Michael's texts, or his furtive, hurried phone calls?

And lately they had been so short-staffed at the theatre that Rachel had been asked to widen her scope. Already ASM, she was drafted in to help with the reading of all the plays submitted. She had never realised how many people wrote. Words, scenes, whole complete, fascinating existences captured on sheets of A4 paper. She had never realised how extraordinary some lives were, or could be. Some lives, even *her* life. If she had chosen differently.

The light was fading as she sat, fingering some papers and staring at the photograph of her lover. It was close to Christmas again. Close to the time when families came together, if only to fight. Close to the time when all the motorways, airports and shops would be blocked with activity and people getting busy for the holidays. But not her.

And she had only herself to blame.

So when the phone call came half an hour later to say that Michael would not be able to see her as arranged, Rachel was expecting it. Without rancour, she wished him a happy Christmas and rang off. For a while afterwards she stood looking around her, smiling bitterly at the decorations he would not see, the turkey he would not eat. The one she was going to have to put in the deep freeze for some other occasion he would dodge. Slamming the freezer door closed, Rachel walked into the bedroom and realised that nothing would make her spend another Christmas there. Not alone. Not again.

In less than an hour she had packed and hired a car, a small Renault she could easily drive. Rachel Pitt was going to take herself away for the holidays. Away from her lover, her mother, her phone, the television, internet and newspapers.

She needed time to think. And she needed to think alone.

Venice, 1555

Pomponio came to his father's house around midnight on the 26th of December. He came with his shoulders rounded, wearing priest's vestments, a hood over his head. It was raining heavily, so heavily the water skittled from the roofs and splattered into the bloated canals below. A moon, white and round as a milk penny, glowered in the icy sky.

The fog had been gone for several days. In its stead came a cold so punishing Venetians stayed in their homes, the sky crackling with stars, a comet flying low over the Doge's Palace. It was an omen, they said. After three months, after three killings, there was always talk of omens. Of death, of weather that had already taken many of the old.

The cold came like another plague, but no fever this time; this was a sickness which sank into the bone, smothered all heat from the blood, bled down the flesh, and crept out through a hundred doors laden with souls too young for St Michael.

Terrified, fleeing for his safety, Pomponio had returned to his father's house, to the place from which had exiled himself, scurrying like a poor rat in through the studio doors. I left them together, could not watch. I, who have watched so much, could not look upon this.

The previous night the mob had turned their footsteps away from Vespucci's house. Instead they came, quiet, respectful but accusing, and stood at Titian's gates. There were no shouts, no calls for blood: only a dreadful silence under that sickened moon.

They came as though beguiled, as though Aretino's accusation had made a truth of it. As though the feckless Pomponio could become a devil overnight. He, who could barely bait a cat, was suspected as the killer. The Skin Hunter of Venice, the man who had made cowards of us all.

And inside, Pomponio hid like a child behind a studio screen, his monk's shoes sodden with water, stained dark as blood.

He pleaded his innocence, which was what we knew. And those were the last words I heard as I left, making for a house on the Grand Canal. There I stood and watched the high barred windows of Aretino's home, and knew he suffered. Not as a kindly man, but as one seen in his true colours. As one judged brutal in his arrogance. Terrible in his cowardice. A man who thought it fair to sacrifice another's child, to barter an innocent for his own ends.

Titian has dismissed him. He has closed his doors to a man he once treasured, to a friend he once loved. His heart is shuttered against him. And the love he once bore for this most odious of men is curdled. In grace did Titian curse him. In defence of his son, he called the gods down on the writer's head. He held his hands, palms up, and asked if there was anything he had ever refused to give.

362

His purse, his home, his food, his name.

His name . . . On saying it, Titian seemed to pause, to count the wisdom of its loan. To wonder at his own naive and reckless trust.

And I had watched it all. Watched Aretino buckle like a lame donkey under its master's whip. I saw him realise that all the lies were recognised and others suspected . . . He recoiled from the painter's anger and lost his footing on the step, his bulk driving him backward to the floor. For a moment he had looked as though he thought a hand might be offered to help him. But none was.

Instead Titian turned and spoke no more.

I saw him broken, Pomponio following his father from the room. And struggling to his feet again was Aretino – cowed, humiliated, seen for the evil he was.

And this time he saw me. After so many years waiting, with so little power, so minute a chance of revenge, I faced him. I had been a nothing in his eyes, but I remained within the artist's grace while he was banished. And I, who had waited so long on the moment, thrilled to the sight of his defeat.

He lumbered to the door, turned, and took long stock of me, as though to threaten. Then he left and made for Vespucci's house. His power gone, the scapegoat failed, he went to the only person who would still receive him. As the doors closed behind Aretino, a cry went up from across the water. A woman's cry, hardly more than the screech of an owl.

All night I sat beside the window, watching. The sick moon, weary of staring, ambled behind a covering of cloud. On the black surface of the water which surrounded us, waves curled and unfurled themselves, lurching inanely at an angry tide.

I am afraid of water and that night its darkness shivered within me. I thought what horrors there might lie beneath, what wrecks and bones of desperate men, what secrets, purses, weapons and close weeds shuddered within the depths. I wondered how the water would press down, how the cold might seep into the lungs, how someone quick and living would soon slide into that murky hollow.

It was seven in the morning when the church bell rang. It rang like a call to arms, and wakened me. Leaving the house, I ran to the sound, knowing before I arrived what I would find there.

Beautiful still. She had once been as wild and savage as an animal, but now she was quiet. Slowly the Contessa di Fattori was hauled out of the winnowing tide. Her face was ruined, her eyes fixed, her body still perfect in its shape, but flayed. And around her wrist a ribbon had been tied, a label fluttering in a bitter breeze.

It was the first day of January, 1556. And it came in with the tide and the body of a woman murdered only a little while before, in the dying hours of the dying year.

She was unrecognisable and the only identity her killer had given her was on the label:

The Whore of Venice.

57

Norfolk

Rushing into the yard, Nino was just in time to see a man running down the driveway. Moments later he heard a car start up and watched as the headlights illuminated the lane and then disappeared into the darkness. So there *had* been someone in the house, someone who had managed to get Harold Greyly drunk or drugged, someone who had wanted him incapacitated. And there could be only one reason for that – the intruder had needed time. Time to search, without being interrupted. But what had he been looking for?

Back in the house, Nino checked on Harold. He was unconscious, snoring loudly, his legs splayed in front of him. Unrecognisable from the arrogant Army man Nino had first met. Walking over to the grate, he damped down the blaze with the water Greyly presumably used to mix his whisky, worried that the chimney night catch fire. Or maybe that was what the intruder had wanted. Intruder? Nino wondered. Or killer?

It was too much of a coincidence to believe this had been a mere break-in. This had been planned by someone who knew Harold Greyly and the house. Someone who had come for a specific reason: to search. Perhaps they had known exactly where to look, and hoped that by banking up the fire so recklessly there might be an accident after they had left. And there would have been if Nino hadn't turned up.

Instinct told him that the intruder hadn't found what he wanted. Otherwise he would have left as soon as Nino arrived so as not to risk discovery. If he'd got what he had come for why would he have stayed around, eavesdropping? Perhaps he had hoped that Nino, finding Harold Greyly drunk and insensible, would leave. One thing was certain: he hadn't expected him to stay. And when he did, there was only one option left to the intruder – to run.

Moving into the library beyond the sitting room, Nino flicked on the lights. The collection was remarkable: antiquarian tomes of notable value rubbing shoulders with copies of modern classics. Fingering an Ian Fleming first edition, he turned to an Agatha Christie, his gaze moving upwards from the lower bookshelves. Using the library steps, he climbed up to the top row of books, where a Boccaccio leant bullishly against a Shakespeare First Folio. Scanning the spines, Nino remembered what Hester Greyly had said about how the family had amassed an impressive number of books over the centuries, some of which were extraordinarily rare.

A noise from the sitting room made Nino freeze, then he

heard the unmistakable sound of Harold's snoring begin again and relaxed. Pushing the library steps to the other side of the room, he climbed up to look at the highest shelf and was surprised to see a collection of plays, written in Russian, Chinese and Italian. Taking a volume down, he glanced at the content, then replaced it, stretching for another book. But in doing so, he overreached and lost his footing on the steps. Slipping, he grabbed at the shelves to stop his fall. But instead of supporting him the top two shelves came away from the wall, falling on top of him.

Several books landed on his head and shoulders before he could scramble back to his feet. Relieved to see that the noise hadn't roused Harold Greyly in the sitting room, he returned to the library. Picking up the books and putting them on the library table, he rested the broken shelving against the wall and glanced up to look at the damage. There was a gap of about three feet by four feet, and it exposed an area of what appeared to be fresh plasterwork. Something wasn't right. Climbing back up the library steps, Nino's hand went out towards the plaster.

Immediately it gave way.

Instead of resisting his pressure, the plasterwork was little more than putty as Nino's hand pushed through into a cramped cavity behind. Scrambling around the aperture, his fingers closed over several thin volumes.

Surprised, he pulled out the first and saw the title:

Assassini Italiani Famosi

367

Then he read what followed.

Uno degli assassini Italiani piu malfamati era il commerciante venezian. Angelico Vespucci, ce e stato conosciuto come il cacciatore della pelle.

It was easy to translate: *One of the most infamous Italian murderers was the Venetian merchant, Angelico Vespucci, who became known as The Skin Hunter.*

Hurriedly, Nino flicked over the first page to look at the frontispiece. And there was an engraving of the Titian painting, Vespucci's bulbous eyes staring at him. Reaching up again, he felt around the back of the cavity, bringing down two other volumes. One was a bulky, well-worn book entitled:

Assassini, che mutilato le loro vittime. L'Italia, XV° secolo allo XVI° secolo.

'Murderers, who mutilated their victims. Italy, 15th century to the 16th century.'

But it was the last volume which chilled him. It was barely thirty pages in length, written in longhand, aged, weathered, the paper breaking up around the edges. Climbing down the library steps, Nino moved over to the table and took a seat, reading the following:

Le vittime del cacciatore della pelle erano la suoi moglie, Larissa Vespucci, Claudia Moroni, Lena Arranti e Melania, Contessa di Fattori

It was a list of Vespucci's victims. But that wasn't what jolted Nino, it was what he found *in among* the pages. Additional notes. Newly written, in a modern hand. A list of The Skin Hunter's victims together with the list of their modern-day counterparts.

Larissa Vespucci	Seraphina Morgan
Claudia Moroni	Sally Egan
Lena Arranti	Harriet Forbes
Melania di Fattori	Rac

He was just about the read the last name when he was struck from behind. The impact of the blow was so violent that it propelled him forward, his head striking the edge of the library table and knocking him unconscious.

58

The persistent ringing of his mobile brought Nino round as he scrabbled in his pocket to answer it.

'*What?*'

'Mr Bergstrom? This is Louisa Forbes, Harriet Forbes' sister . . . Are you OK?'

Nauseated, the blood pumping in his ears, Nino straightened up in his seat and looked around him. Books were scattered all over the floor, but he could see at once that the three volumes he had found were gone. And the name of the last victim had escaped him too. He had had it in his hand and lost it. All but the first letters: Rac.

'Mr Bergstrom?' Louisa asked again. 'Are you OK?'

'I'm fine,' he said, getting to his feet and locking the house doors front and back. He could see the sleeping figure of Harold Greyly in the sitting room and pulled the door closed so that he wouldn't be overheard. 'Why are you ringing?'

'I've found something,' she said. 'Look, I can talk to you another time. I shouldn't have rung – it's Christmas Day.'

'Believe me, nothing you could do could make it worse,' Nino replied, holding some kitchen towel to the wound at the back of his head. 'Why aren't you at home with your family?'

'I am,' she said quietly. 'I just sneaked out to call you. I've been going through my sister's belongings. I've gone through them repeatedly. To be honest, I don't want to. I don't want to let go of her . . .'

He could imagine her intelligent face, her determination to do something, anything, which would help.

'Harriet had a stack of papers, like everyone. Accounts, bills. No diaries, I'm afraid – nothing that easy. I checked all her friends and no one could tell me anything that might point to who killed her. Her work colleagues knew her and liked her, and there didn't seem to be anything unusual about her life. She hadn't made enemies.' She paused, dropping her voice so that she wouldn't be overheard. 'You know Harriet wrote that piece on Vespucci . . .'

'The magazine folded.'

'Yes, it did. But one of Harriet's old colleagues knew the proprietor and gave me his name. I phoned him and he remembered Harriet, said she had talent. He remembered the piece very well – "A very erudite article on a very macabre subject." He recalled my sister because he had wanted to use her again, but had lost her contact details. Poor Harriet, if only she'd known . . .'

'Go on.'

'I asked him if he'd talked to my sister about the Vespucci

article, and he said they'd chatted, because he was impressed by Harriet's research. He asked her which reference books she'd used and who her contacts were. Apparently Harriet told him that there had been a couple of people, a man and a woman, who'd helped with the research.'

Alert, Nino pushed her. 'Who were they?'

'He didn't remember the man's name. Harriet just said he'd been difficult and she'd never go to him again. But he *did* remember something about the woman. She was called Rachel.'

Rachel – *Rac.*

Nino took in a breath. 'Rachel what?'

'I don't know.' Louisa could tell it meant something. 'Is it important?'

'Yes, I think it is.'

'Apparently Rachel was involved in the theatre, but I don't know how. She could have worked there, or been an actor, or in management. Or even a financial backer. The publisher didn't know, but Harriet mentioned to him that this Rachel woman had been involved in a play about Vespucci.'

The words reverberated in Nino's head. So *that* was the contact. Not a relative. Not a painting. Not an article. This time it was theatre.

'She wanted to put on a play about Vespucci?' Nino shook his head. 'Jesus, which theatre?'

'He didn't know.'

'But he must have some idea!'

'No,' Louisa replied firmly. 'I pressed him, but he wasn't

being evasive – he really didn't know. He would have told me, I'm sure of it. He'd liked Harriet and wanted to help and he was shocked by her death . . . He's sent me an email with everything he remembers. I was going to send it on to you.'

'Do.'

'He also mentioned all the press coverage on Vespucci—'

'Yes, I saw something this morning,' Nino replied, dabbing at the back of his head, the wound still bleeding. 'I was hoping they might leave it alone until after Christmas.'

'What, a story like that?' She seemed bitter. 'You know the press – they couldn't resist it. My phone's been ringing off the hook. Apparently they want to know all the details of my sister's death. It's big news, Mr Bergstrom – young women skinned in different countries round the world. Some lunatic copying Angelico Vespucci's work.'

'And the website's stirring it all up, whipping everyone into a fever.'

Louisa paused, controlling herself. 'There's only a week left, isn't there?'

'Until the anniversary of the last victim? Yes.'

'You can catch him,' she said emphatically. 'I know you can.'

He wondered at her confidence. He had a first name and he knew the connection between the mysterious Rachel and Angelico Vespucci. But that was all. He had no surname, no theatre. No country even. She could be anywhere on earth.

'If only I knew where the theatre was—'

'It'll be in a capital city,' Louisa replied, thinking back. 'Harriet had been travelling – I didn't know why then, but she said she had something to find out in London or New York.'

She rushed on. 'Maybe *we* could contact this Rachel woman? Or put out a search for her? God knows, there's enough in the media to catch her interest. She must know about the killings and Vespucci now. So why hasn't she come forward?'

'Maybe she hasn't made the connection,' Nino replied. 'People write about the Boston Strangler and Jack the Ripper all the time – it doesn't mean that they expect someone to come after them—'

'But she must have read about someone *copying* Vespucci.'

'She may have done, but so what? They make films, plays, books about murderers constantly. There's an industry out there thriving on serial killers. Rachel won't be overly worried. She probably thinks she's just another person interested in the Italian. Killers don't go after everyone who reads about them, otherwise half the population would be wiped out.'

'You've got to find her,' Louisa went on, her agitation obvious. 'You *have* to find her.'

'I will. Unless—'

'He's already got to her?'

'Or she's somewhere remote.'

'*You think she's hiding?*'

'She could be,' Nino agreed. 'She *might* have taken fright. Or she might be spending the holidays away from home. Gone for a break somewhere quiet, away from people.'

'Perhaps . . .' Louise's voice was questioning, 'we should go to the police?'

'And tell them what? They'll know all about Vespucci now – the press have seen to that. And they must have made the connection between the murders. That last entry on the website made it clear what the killer was up to. He's even advertising his next performance on the first of January.'

'But—'

'I can't tell the police anything they don't already know.'

'Except what we know about the next victim.'

'And what *do* we know?' Nino countered. 'She's called Rachel, and she's involved in a play about Vespucci. That's all.' He sighed. 'The police have plenty of manpower, but they don't understand what this is all about. I do. I was in it from the start. I'm ahead of the police. I've been in contact with the killer—'

He could hear her take in a breath. '*You know who he is?*'

'I know who he *was*. Who he is *now*, I have to find out.'

'So do it,' Louisa said firmly. 'And find Rachel – before he does.'

375

59

After finishing his conversation with Louisa, Nino went back into the sitting room. Harold Greyly was still sleeping, his breathing drugged, his neck bent awkwardly over the back of his chair. Worried that he might choke if he vomited, Nino slid a cushion under his head and turned off all but a single lamp. As the room darkened, the dogs woke and followed him out into the back garden. Cautious, Nino glanced down the lane. It was empty. He locked the gate, walked back into the house with the spaniels, and bolted the front and back doors.

The freezing winter air had revived his senses, his head clearing as he helped himself to food from the fridge and checked his mobile. Hearing the message left by Patrick Dewick, he immediately rang him back – only to get his voicemail. Disappointed, Nino walked into the sitting room and stared at Harold Greyly. Obviously he wouldn't be waking any time soon, which gave Nino a welcome opportunity to search the house further. He might have lost the hidden books – and the killer's notes – but the question uppermost in his mind was *why* they had been hidden in Courtford Hall in the first place.

Someone had taken a great deal of trouble to conceal the books. Someone with intimate knowledge of the house. Someone with access and time to move the shelves, create their hiding place, and disguise it. No stranger could have pulled off such a coup. It would have taken time and effort. The work of an insider ... Nino frowned. Perhaps Hester had investigated Vespucci herself. Or had it been Harold Greyly? He wasn't the killer, that much was obvious now. He had been unconscious when Nino was attacked. So what was the connection? Simply the relationship between Claudia and The Skin Hunter? The hidden taboo in a respectable family's past? Or her terrible murder?

The blood was drying on his head. Nino could feel it crusting over and realised how it must look against the pure white of his hair, making him even more conspicuous. But what did that matter now? The killer knew who – and where – he was. In a remote place, with a drugged man, trying to understand *why* a murderer had chosen to hide his notes in a country house in Norfolk.

But why hadn't he killed him when he had the chance?

Was this his home? Was this where he had been hiding out? Was he a member of the Greyly family? If so, was that why Harold Greyly had been so much on the defensive? Moving over to the desk under the library window, Nino searched the drawers, finding nothing more than stationery and bills. The centre drawer opened without resistance.

Apparently there were no locks in Courtford Hall. Even feeling behind the desk, and beneath it, gave up no secrets.

If *he* was going to hide something, Nino asked himself, where would he put it? The room gazed back at him impassively as he searched, pulling the cushions off the seats to check that there was nothing hidden underneath and looking behind every painting. Curtains were shaken, linings examined, shutters opened and closed, window seats plundered, rugs lifted and shaken – but with no result. He drew a complete blank.

So perhaps there was a safe?

Moving back to the sitting room, Nino bent down towards the stupefied man and shook him awake. 'Have you got a safe?'

'Whaaat?'

'Where's the safe?'

Greyly's lips were furred with saliva. 'What safe?'

'You have a safe. Where is it?'

'No safe!' he slurred.

'All right, let's try another tack. Who came here today? There was someone here – I heard them. They left, then came back and attacked me.' Nino shook Harold violently. 'Wake up! I need you. Who came here today?'

He could see a shift in Greyly's expression, from slackness to unease.

'No one! I've told you. No one ... No one comes here any more ...'

Nino didn't believe him. Someone had been there. Someone Harold knew and feared.

'Was it a member of your family?'

'They've gone . . .'

'You said you'd sent the staff home for Christmas,' Nino persisted. 'Did one of them come back? Did they try and rob you?' He shook the man urgently. 'Wake up! I need your help – you let them in. There was no break-in, so you knew them. You opened the door to them, so you must have trusted them. If not now, once. *Who was it?*' He jerked Harold upright, holding him by the lapels of his jacket. 'Look at me! Concentrate. Tell me the names of your staff.'

'Let me sleep!'

'Tell me their names!'

'Let me sleep!'

'You can sleep after you've told me.'

Harold's eyes tried to focus, but failed, his voice a mumble. 'Mr and Mrs Harrison, the cook . . . the gardener, Len . . . Len Owen . . . All been with me for years . . . All bloody old, on their last legs.'

'Anyone else?'

'Edward.'

'Edward? Who's Edward?'

His head was rolling, his voice blurred.

'Edward Hillstone. My assistant . . .'

Letting go of him, Nino stepped back. The memory returned, sharp and clear. When he had first come to Courtford Hall, Harold had wanted him to make an appointment *with his assistant*. And that assistant had been Edward Hillstone. A diffident young man in the background.

379

Edward Hillstone. Eddie Hillstone. Eddie Ketch . . Dear God, Nino thought, was *he* the killer? Vespucci's impersonator? Had he found him? If so, Hillstone would have been ideally placed. The Greyly family had a connection with Angelico Vespucci: an ancestor murdered by the Venetian. At Courtford Hall the killer would have access to the library, would be able to read the books on Vespucci and hide his own notes where no one would find them. Harold Greyly wasn't interested in the collection – he would have left Hillstone to his own devices, left him to his research and plotting, to his immersion in the legend of The Skin Hunter.

Moving fast, Nino left the room, making for the upper floors. He found the master bedroom, guest rooms and bathrooms, then followed a narrow corridor which led to the servants' quarters in another wing. He was running, only pausing when he reached a door on the third floor. The only one locked. Kicking at the handle, he broke the lock and entered.

The bedroom was cramped and extended a long way, half of its floor space under the sloping eaves. All the available wall surface was covered with bookshelves and a copy of the Vespucci painting loomed above the narrow bed.

The room was Spartan, neat, without character apart from the books and portrait. In the wardrobe were a few pairs of jeans and some T-shirts, a couple of fleeces neatly folded. On the bedside table was a copy of *The Book Collector* and an alarm clock set to eight a.m. Nothing out of the ordinary. Nothing unlike a thousand other bedrooms occupied by single men.

Frowning, Nino glanced around, opening some of the books and shaking them to see if there were any loose pages. Nothing. He continued his search, looking behind the books and under the shelves. Again, nothing. Wondering if he was suspecting the wrong man, he turned back to the wardrobe and opened it again. A long mirror on the back of the door caught his attention, a tiny edge of paper poking out at the corner. Pulling the mirror off the door, Nino stared at the collage in front of him.

The photographs told him he was on to the right man. There were some of Edward Hillstone, others of a young woman – a slim woman, dressed casually. But in every one her face had been blacked out with a felt-tipped pen. He thought of Patrick Dewick's message. Was *this* the woman who had broken the killer's heart? Or was this the next victim? Was this Rachel?

One thing was certain: Edward Hillstone had picked his lair with skill. Courtford Hall was the perfect place from which to operate. It was remote, with a pompous employer unlikely to fraternise with the staff. Hillstone would have been a faultless employee – quiet, efficient, determined not to draw attention to himself. And all the time he was working as Harold Greyly's assistant, he would have had access to the prodigious and arcane library.

Had Hillstone already known about Claudia Moroni when he first came to Courtford Hall? Or did he find out later, when his fascination with Vespucci grew? For an experienced researcher, it wouldn't have been difficult to discover that

Claudia Moroni had once been a member of the Greyly family. And in researching Claudia, Edward would have researched the three other victims. Stoking up his obsession, probably enjoying the added frisson of living in a family who had experienced The Skin Hunter's deviation first hand.

Nino could feel his heart pulsing as he flung back the mattress on the bed, hoping to find another selection of photographs. But that would have been too obvious for Hillstone. Hurriedly, he looked around, then tapped the floorboards. Nothing loose. He walked to the window, pulled back the shutters – but there was nothing to be found. There were more photographs, Nino knew it – but where? Then another idea came to him and he moved over to the door. It had been repanelled and he levered apart the space between the original and the façade. *The photographs fell at his feet.* Some were of Venice, horribly familiar – the exact place where the body of Seraphina had been discovered. Other prints were of a woman he recognised as Sally Egan. Some had been taken through her kitchen window, others were snaps of her walking home, a solitary figure under the dismal street light. And then there were the photographs of her skinned body.

He had taken the shots from all angles, her flayed corpse laid out on a plastic sheet, her skin placed neatly beside her like a lover. Repelled, Nino hurried through the other photographs, hesitating when he came to a shot of the airport in Tokyo and another image, of Harriet Forbes, sitting alone at a café window. The last prints were of Greenfield's Hospital, where Eddie Ketch had worked. Only it wasn't Eddie Ketch any more, it was Edward Hillstone.

Moving over to the desk, Nino looked for a computer, but there wasn't one. Hillstone wasn't that stupid. He had taken the most incriminating evidence with him. He might have been rushed, but he had made sure he took the laptop and the notes. As for the photographs he had left behind, perhaps he thought he would be able to explain them away. Or maybe he didn't care any more. Maybe being recognised as the killer was what he wanted.

But Nino knew one thing: Edward Hillstone wasn't going to let himself be caught yet. Not until after the last murder. Then he might even give himself up, surrender to the notoriety which would be his by rights. When Rachel was dead – when he had mutilated and killed her – then he would stop. In the meantime he was deliberately raising the price on his head. Putting up the Titian as a reward for his capture. Tainting the world with his promise of the bloodletting to come.

Of course there was no sign of the Titian portrait. Edward Hillstone would hardly risk having that in his possession. The painting was somewhere else entirely. Glancing around the bedroom, Nino looked at the upheaval he had caused – the overturned bed, the photographs scattered over the floorboards – and then he leaned forward, taking a closer look.

His gaze fixed on one of the pictures in which the face of the young woman had been blacked out. But across her chest was written one word:

JEX

He recognised the name at once. It was the name used by the creator of the Vespucci website. But it wasn't the name that caught Nino's eye, it was the *background* of the photograph. The image was grainy, hard to make out, but he could decipher a few letters on what seemed to be a hoarding. The last word was THEATRE. The first word was half blocked by the woman's figure, only the first syllable visible – HA.

Nino held his breath. He was certain that the woman in the picture was Rachel, and that he was now looking at a part of the name of the very theatre where she worked. HA ... THEATRE. How many theatres had names which began with HA? Not that many. Nino's hopes lifted for the first time in days. He had a lead, a chance to find the last victim.

He had a week.

A week to save her.

A week to stop Hillstone.

60

Ginza, Tokyo, 27 December

That morning there had been a new entry on the website angelicovespucci.1555.com. It read:

Angelico Vespucci's triumph is close. Only five days left. Only one victim remains.

As he had done repeatedly over the previous nine days, Jobo Kido entered the chat room of the site, trying vainly to conjure up a reply.

Jobo: Why don't you respond?

There was no answer, just the taunting message, making the killer's intention clear to everyone who visited the site. And his work wasn't confined to the internet any longer. Newspapers, magazines and television had picked up on the story and were running with it. It made the police look foolish. There were so many officers in so many different countries, but they couldn't find one man.

The lack of forensic evidence didn't help. The killer had left some DNA, but he wasn't on file in Italy, USA, Japan or the UK. His blood group was O, the most common, and as he had had no sexual relations with the victims, there was no sperm. He had committed the murders, taken the skins, and – to all intents and purposes – disappeared.

In five days the last victim would be dead, and Jobo still hadn't worked out the connection which would ensure that the Titian became his ... The killer's silence chided him. Obviously his failure merited no communication. Jobo Kido had had his chance, and failed. He would never hang the Titian in his Rogues' Gallery, never use it make his gory collection respectable. Instead it would go to someone who didn't understand and appreciate it.

His only consolation was the agony of his rivals. Triumph Jones was melting like an ice cream in July, his composure soggy. As for the foul-mouthed Farina Ahmadi, she was sulking in Turkey, cheated out of her victory. She might have twisted and coiled herself into a variety of modes and moods, but all her machinations had got her precisely nowhere.

The killer had the Titian, and apparently he was keeping it ... Jobo wondered about that, feeling a momentary shiver of hope. What would happen when the murderer was caught? Who would get the painting then? The answer was unpalatable – it would be impounded as evidence. Locked away with DNA samples and carpet fibres.

Desperate, he turned back to the computer.

Jobo: Are you there?
Silence.
Jobo: Why don't you talk to me?

To his amazement, he finally got a response.

Answer: *Welcome, Mr Kido. Have you solved the puzzle yet?*
Jobo: I thought you'd gone.
Answer: *Gone where? I told you, I'm everywhere. So tell me, have you solved my little riddle? Have you made the connection?*
Jobo: How long have I got?
Answer: *I think that's a no, isn't it? What if I were to say that I'd give you as long as my last victim has to live? Solve the puzzle by the 1st January and the painting's yours.*
Jobo: Do I have your word on that?
Answer: *Don't be tiresome, Mr Kido. Solve it, or lose it.*

61

Edward Hillstone felt so powerful he had an erection. Every newspaper he had seen over the past two days had borne some reference to him. On the television news he was discussed, and there was even a debate about him on *Newsnight*. He'd enjoyed that, even laughed, which wasn't something that came easily to him.

As for Nino Bergstrom, his intervention had been aggravating. Hillstone had been so close to getting everything out of Courtford Hall, the sodden Harold Greyly letting him and then realising that his obedient minion wasn't quite what he had seemed. Hillstone hadn't been threatened by his employer's bluster. Harold Greyly might think of himself as an Army man, but he was an ice soldier. A little heat and he was finished ... Of course Hillstone knew that Nino Bergstrom would have found his room, and his belongings. And the photographs. In fact, he was relying on that, laying down a mosaic of clues which would develop into a shrine to his ingenuity.

Hillstone might admire, even worship, Angelico Vespucci,

but as time went by he had found ways to enhance his devotion. Simple imitation wasn't going to be enough – he was developing his own embellishments. Hillstone would never deny that the Italian had been his inspiration, but his appetite for violence had increased along with his desire for recognition. If he stuck to The Skin Hunter's brief, he would merely be regarded as a copycat, always playing second fiddle to the hero.

Hillstone didn't like the idea. Didn't like to think that the last four years of dedication and research would result in Vespucci becoming famous, and him overshadowed. An imitator, nothing more. He wanted his own stab at notoriety, his own turn on the media merry-go-round. The Venetian had prompted him to murder, but Edward Hillstone was expanding its possibilities.

Like what he would do with the skins.

Musing, he wondered if Nino Bergstrom would uncover their hiding place and realised that he had misjudged the man. Dismissed him as an amateur sleuth, easy to dupe. His attention had been too focused on the dealers, in an effort to impress the people he despised. But Bergstrom had surprised him, gradually slotting together the disparate pieces – like Jobo Kido and Harold Greyly. But he would never find the next victim. Nino Bergstrom had only four days left, and the unsuspecting Rachel Pitt was lined up, ready for the kill. It didn't worry him that his cache of photographs might have been found – it would only underline to whoever found it what they were up against.

Hillstone breathed in, imagining the sleek feel of her skin, the intricate peeling away from the red muscle underneath, the sticky blood flowing from all the nicked vessels as he took away her hide. He would do as he had done before, following Vespucci's lead. First he would rinse the skin and hang it over a basin, then let it dry until it was stiffened. Only then would he take it down and knead some flexibility back into it, gently working the skin until it became pliable and easy to fold.

He liked that part the best: the folding of the hide, the careful arranging of it. Then he would secrete it, along with the other three skins . . . Thoughtful, Hillstone remembered the package he had sent to Jobo Kido. That had been a sensational move but reckless in hindsight, as it had left his collection incomplete. He had, once or twice, even thought of asking Kido to return it, but suspected that the dealer had either handed it over to the police or destroyed it.

No, Hillstone thought dismissively, Kido would never have gone to the police, because that would have meant questions, interference, the whole story of the Titian exposed. And then the painting impounded, lost to the courts. Not that Hillstone was going to let Jobo Kido have the portrait. He was just playing with him, teasing him, drawing the dealer into a combat which had only one winner: Hillstone. But it amused him to think of the Japanese connoisseur's panicked outpourings in the chat room. He had been so frightened the night Hillstone had visited his gallery, pressing himself against the wall as he peered into the window. And later, almost wetting himself when Hillstone had rattled the door handle.

It had pleased him to see the aesthetic Jobo Kido squeal like a girl. So much for learning, for artistic excellence – so much for all his pompous posturing. He had been scared. Just like Triumph Jones ... Rolling his head to loosen his neck muscles, Hillstone thought of the American. Of the ease with which he had been fooled. Of how, nudged in the required direction, he had followed like a farm dog working sheep. And how glamorous those sheep had been – Jobo Kido, Farina Ahmadi. Brilliant and wealthy and respected. And manipulated.

Hillstone enjoyed that, loved knowing that in London, New York and Tokyo his victims were panicking, with no idea what they were doing. So much for education, money and power – they were all chasing the same thing, mistrusting each other, and outsmarted by an amateur.

But in four days it would all be over. Rachel Pitt would round off the victims, his imitation of Vespucci complete. After that, he would disappear. Emulate the Venetian utterly. Dissolve into thin air as he had done. No one – not even Hillstone – knew where Vespucci had gone. If he had lived, or been murdered. Or if he had died of natural causes, old and silent, at ninety. All his painstaking research had failed on two counts. He had failed to discover how Angelico Vespucci died, or where The Skin Hunter had hidden his trophies.

Hillstone reached for the photographs in front of him, his gaze idling over the woman's features for a moment before he gathered up his knives and scalpels and put the kettle on the hob. Rachel Pitt was curvaceous, sensual, attractive, he thought as he waited for the water to boil and then poured it over the metal instruments. He wanted them to be very clean, very sharp, so they wouldn't tear her flesh. They had to cut evenly, so he could make a perfect job of her skinning.

She *was* pretty, Hillstone thought again. Perhaps, if he was particularly dextrous, he could peel off her face in one piece. He had always had so much trouble before, could never avoid tearing the flesh of the cheek or nose. But this was to be his last act, and it would have to be immaculate. He would take his time. Prepare himself and relax, to avoid any shaking hands. Give himself time to set up the table and lamps. Time to get the plastic sheeting on the floor. Time for everything to be perfect.

It was such a pity. He would have liked to pick someone else, but Rachel Pitt was corrupt. She was the mistress of another woman's husband. Supported financially like so many other whores. Stealing another woman's man, another family's father. It was wrong, inexcusable, immoral – anyone could see that.

In fact, Edward Hillstone wondered how she could live with herself. Even if it wouldn't be for much longer.

BOOK SIX

Venice, 1556

Aretino keeps to his house. Takes the passage from the back entrance across his private bridge to enter the city. He puffs with exertion, for worry has made him even more gross; he sweats with the weight of his sins and sends presents to Titian's studio, pleading for forgiveness.

Pomponio is innocent, Aretino says, I was wrong. So misguided, so duped by the merchant.

And what of the merchant, Vespucci? Aretino fears no exposure now. His championing of the killer is done with; and he will tell anyone with a mind to hear that Vespucci is no more. The mob which bayed outside the merchant's house is told of a disappearance. Vespucci has cheated the judge, the prison, the rope. The Skin Hunter has gone, and taken his prizes with him.

I was wrong, says Aretino, deceived as we all were.

But Titian will have none of it. Pomponio, still smarting from the accusations, plans to leave, but not before he rails against his father for being the writer's dupe. It does no good for Titian to respond; each word is taken as a blow, one more sliver of malice driven into the priest's tight heart.

Titian has lost his son. Again. And his friend. His closest ally levered from his side by treachery.

Vespucci gone, they showed the portrait in the church, Titian ordering where it should be placed. They suspended the merchant's likeness as they would have hanged the man himself. I heard some talk that the artist was offering it for penance. For payment of Vespucci's sins. That Titian's genius might atone for all the winter's butchery. Yet the night after it was exhibited, a fire started in the vestry. It burned the rafters, tore through half the roof, and every pew was rendered black as an imp's hand.

Only the painting was untouched.

On Titian's orders a notice was hung up in St Mark's Square, saying the portrait would be destroyed. Someone sent news to Aretino, who came to beg for it. He mourns his loss of influence with the painter, he fears his loss of revenue from Titian, as once he feared exposure from the merchant.

But Vespucci will not speak against him. For Vespucci will not speak again . . . He has gone, disappeared, leaving no trace. There is no body. None has come up from the water, surfacing, bloated on a late tide. There is no carcass left flayed for the birds to peck at, no music coming across the water, no sounds of a hundred lurid couplings, no grumblings from misers, gluttons, deviants and their whores.

The fogs of Venice lifted when the portrait disappeared. When it was gone the winds dispersed, and clouds as wide as continents gave way to the sun's return.

They say we have our city back. The darkness has left us; gone with Vespucci and his likeness. Gone with the merchant and the merchant's image. Gone on some nether tide, out to the sea, to the slithering depths of all damnation. They say we are no longer bewitched.

Look how the Doge recovers, the ships coming back to land.

They say the coldest and most terrible of winters is passed; that God is back among us. Some even tell of flowers come to blossom, of fruit ripening out of season, and angels settling on the bell tower of St Mark's.

But Titian sees no angels, paints no flowers. He grieves. A lesser man would seek out some revenge, but his regret is contained, and swells like a boil in the heart. He walks Venice like a man without his shadow and a hollow grows inside him.

And I watch him. As I watch Aretino. I see what others see, but Venice is not delivered yet.

Aretino might have picked the merchant's grave and made him own it, but another waits. The water sits beneath us, its cold wet mouth yawning in the darkness, its gills moving with the tide. It waits for the bloated carcass of Aretino to fall, panicked and gasping, into the muddy hollow of its lair.

Under the water he will go. Down with the dead soldiers, dogs and devils. Down with Vespucci, caught up in all the green weeds of his lies. Down with the suicides, the lusty priests, the cripples and the damned. Down with all the other traitors.

But Aretino suspects nothing. He walks like a man who has rid

397

himself of a threat, and is now sure of forgiveness. For Titian loves him still. In time he would, against judgement and logic, allow Aretino to return. Against reason, and tempting destruction, he would let him in.

He would.

But I will not.

62

In Kensington, Nino Bergstrom was on his computer, looking for Rachel. Working his way through newspaper art pages and internet listings, he turned to the *Spotlight* magazine for actors. But there was only one Rachel who was white, young and pretty.

He rang her, but a man answered, apparently her husband. Without alarming anyone, Nino asked if she would be available for an interview, only to be told that Rachel was in hospital preparing for the birth of her second child, in two weeks' time.

Wrong Rachel.

Checking *Spotlight*, and the US version of the actors' magazine, he looked for any reference to productions about Vespucci being cast. Nothing. Then he turned to *The Stage* and searched that paper. Again, there was nothing referring to The Skin Hunter, Angelico Vespucci, or even plays set in Venice. In desperation, Nino trailed through every forthcoming play about murderers and their crimes – of which there were many.

It seemed that every town, city or state was putting on some play about a killer. But none of them were about Angelico Vespucci. The morning came and went, Gaspare made lunch and Nino kept working. At three, the dealer went to a hospital appointment and Nino returned to the archives in the London Central Library, looking back into the past. Perhaps something had been written before, and was being rewritten? Again, he drew a blank. He worked through every listing he could find about theatre staff in the UK and the USA, looking for Rachel. But Nino knew it was a long shot. The theatrical world was a movable feast – people came and went monthly, or changed their names, or moved into different areas. And he didn't know what the elusive Rachel actually did. Actor, manager, agent, painter, costume designer or stage doorman. His request to discover the names of angels – the backers who put up money for shows – was met with silence. Most wanted to remain anonymous.

December 28 had passed, December 29 was coming in, and still Nino had nothing to go on. At one point he even wondered if he was completely off target, if the victim had simply been photographed in front of a theatre without having any connection to it. Deflated, he then checked his last search – and *this* time there was a result: three theatres whose names began with HA.

HAMPTON THEATRE
HAILSTONE THEATRE
THE HAMLET THEATRE

The first was in Basingstoke, the second in Dorset and the third in Battersea.

Tapping out the name of The Hamlet Theatre, Nino entered their website. At the top of the home page was a list of reviews, all favourable and widespread in the press, some of the theatre's actors surprisingly well known.

Welcome!
We are a small company, but one of the most
innovative in the UK. Although we have only been in
existence for seven years, our play on W. H. Auden –
Salut, Salut – was a hit on Broadway in New York, and
in the West End, London.

At present we are working on several new ideas, one of
which might be an investigation into a charismatic, but
murderous, figure from the past.

A charismatic, but murderous, figure from the past ... Nino couldn't think of a better way to describe Angelico Vespucci. Checking the phone number, he rang the theatre and a young woman answered.

'Hello?'

'I was wondering if I could speak with ...' Nino glanced at the computer, 'Harvey Enright.'

'Who's speaking, please?'

'My name's Nino Bergstrom and I think I might want to invest in your theatre,' Nino lied, knowing it would get him put through. And it did.

Within an instant an affected English voice came over the line. 'Hello? Can I help you?'

'I'm thinking of becoming an angel,' Nino said, glancing repeatedly at his notes. 'I don't know much about any of this, forgive me. But I've come into some money and shares hardly seem the way to go at the moment.' He blundered on, wondering how convincing he sounded. 'I'd like to invest. Perhaps in your theatre. Well, your productions anyway. I'm very interested in new companies, and yours seems to be very ...'

'Thrusting.'

'Yes,' Nino replied, 'that's the word ... I know very little about the theatrical world. You see, I've been working in the film business for a long time, but want to change tack.' He checked his notes again. 'On your website you talk about a new production you might be undertaking, about a murderer from the past?'

'Yes,' Enright agreed. 'We have two plays in mind. The one we most want to pursue at the moment is about a woman who works in engineering and discovers a talent for invention.'

Nino grimaced. 'And the other one?'

'Well, it was a good idea, unique. But lately the character in question has been getting a lot of press.'

'Who was he?'

'A man called Angelico Vespucci,' Enright replied, and as Nino heard the name he let out a long, relieved breath. 'Unfortunately there have been some murders recently, copies of his crimes. You might have read about it?'

'Yes, I think I have. Fascinating character. Were you writing the play yourself?'

'No, I'm no wordsmith. Directing is my forte.'

'So who's writing the play?'

'Rachel—' he replied.

Nino was hardly breathing. 'Oh, *Rachel*! I know her, I think. Rachel Andrews? Came from Brighton originally?'

'No,' Enright replied. 'Rachel Pitt. She's from up north, Lake District. Smashing girl. Anyway, she's actually our Assistant Stage Manager, but she had this idea for a play. Apparently she's been working on it for a long time. Ran it past me, and frankly it sounded interesting . . . Would you like to come in and talk, Mr Bergstrom? We'd be delighted to chat to any angel, existing or prospective.'

Making a non-committal remark, Nino rang off. The name hummed in his head – Rachel Pitt, from up north, the Lake District. Rachel Pitt . . . Grabbing the London telephone directory, he found three people called R. Pitt. After phoning the first two – Ronald Pitt and Rita Pitt – he tried the last number.

This was it. This *had* to be Rachel Pitt. He had found her. Now he could warn her. He could prevent her death . . . The number rang. Again, and again. It rang out, then finally was answered.

Hi, this is Rachel. Sorry, there's no one here at the moment. If you want to leave me a message and number, feel free.

Distraught that she hadn't picked up, he left a message.

This is Nino Bergstrom. Please call me as soon as possible, it is urgent. Please, Ms Pitt, call me when you get this message.

Leaving his number, he put down the phone, and realised his hand was shaking.

63

Waking late, Rachel turned over in bed and opened her eyes. Where the hell was she? And then she remembered and stretched lazily. She had managed – by the sheer fluke of someone cancelling at the last minute – to rent a tiny cottage for Christmas and New Year, close to where her father had been born. It was in a village called Crook – a stone house hardly large enough for a hobbit, but cosy. '*El dar la bienvenida*,' Michael would have said, curling the Spanish vowels around his tongue ... She shook off the thought of him, unwilling to let him in. The cottage was hers, filled with provisions, wine and plenty of cut logs for the fire. She did have neighbours, but it seemed that on both sides they were away for the festivities, which left Rachel pretty much alone. Only this was a different type of aloneness. This was away from London and the flat and it smelt, looked, and even felt different. It felt hopeful.

Since arriving the previous day she had walked endlessly, enjoying the landscape – such a contrast from built-up Battersea. She had even spent a whole hour watching a farmer rounding up sheep, not noticing that the rain had started and her boots were waterlogged. A peace she hadn't felt for years came like a salutation to another life, a choice she had long denied herself now possible. Up in the hills, with the rain and the sound of drinkers leaving the village pub at eleven, bathing in a small enamel bath and drinking water that tasted of the mountains, Rachel experienced an epiphany which was long overdue.

She had forgotten the loneliness which had dogged her. Even on her own, she wasn't as bereft as sitting in her flat and waiting, endlessly waiting, for the phone to ring. It was a relief not to have to think up ways to amuse, seduce, or interest her lover. It was a release not to be terrorised by her silent phone, or urgent text messages. And slowly Rachel came to realise that loving Michael had become a form of penance.

How could she be anything other than an appendage to his life? While she made him the nucleus of her world, he had a wife and children, a career, a dozen social duties and membership of clubs. When he was with her, he loved her. But how much of his attention could she hold when he was elsewhere?

The answer was brutal. But it was only up in the hills of the Lake District, away from pylons and mobile-phone masts, trains, subways and sirens, that she could hear it. And as the days passed Rachel became dislocated from her previous life: her life with Michael. Instead her career slipped back into top gear, her attention moving back to the Hamlet Theatre. Amused, she lay back on the pillows, her hands behind her head, thinking of Angelico Vespucci.

It was a fabulous idea to write a play about him. She knew it, had always known it, but her ambition had waned as her neediness had grown. Ideas, words, images that would once have shimmered inside her had turned to ash and, incredulously, seeing her actions at arm's length, she did not know herself.

When she returned to Battersea, to the Hamlet Theatre, she would talk to Enright again, get him geed up about the play. She could do it, she could get him back on side. He was already hooked, she could see that. And besides, Rachel thought, there was plenty of interest in Vespucci now ... She rolled over on to her side, looking out of the tiny window down into the village below. Since she arrived she hadn't bought a paper or turned on the television. She had left her mobile behind, and there was no telephone in the cottage. But she could remember only too well reading about The Skin Hunter before she left London. It had been on the news and all over the internet, and the last piece she had read had been sent from the killer – some lunatic taunting the police to find him before he killed again.

Yawning, Rachel pulled the duvet over her and closed her eyes. Soon it would be New Year, and she had already decided on her resolution. She would end the affair, slough it off her body like dead skin, and return to the theatre. There she would hustle and bargain and push until Enright agreed to put on her play. He liked it. He was just nervous about her being a newcomer. So what? Rachel thought confidently. There had to be a beginning for everyone.

She relaxed into the pillows, sliding into sleep. Outside the last of the daylight slunk down into the lifeless trees, the hills snow-tipped and quiet, no cars about, no sounds. Only the drinkers inside the pub, calling last orders at the ringing of the bell.

64

30 December

As he walked up the front steps to the block of flats in Battersea, Nino could see a family watching television in a front room, and rang the ground-floor buzzer. He heard someone curse and an Indian man opened the door and stared at him.

'What is it?'

'I'm looking for Rachel Pitt,' Nino explained. 'She lives upstairs.'

'So?' the man asked as his wife moved into the hall behind him.

Pushing him aside, she smiled at Nino. 'Can I help you?'

'Rachel Pitt lives upstairs, doesn't she? I need to talk to her – it's urgent.'

'Such a lovely girl, so very kind. Is it bad news?' the woman asked as her husband walked back into the front room.

'Someone in her family's been taken ill,' Nino lied. 'I can't get her on the phone and she's not answering her bell.'

'Oh, she went away. She's on holiday until New Year—'

'Until New Year?' Nino repeated sharply. 'D'you know where's she gone?'

She put up her hands for a moment, calling for her husband. 'Daruka! Daruka!'

He came back into the hall, his expression impatient. 'What is it?'

'Do you remember where Rachel said she was going on holiday? This gentleman needs to contact her; someone in the family is ill.'

Shaking his head, he moved closer. 'She did tell me, but I can't . . . the mountains somewhere.'

'The mountains?' Nino repeated. 'In this country?'

'Yes, yes, in England.'

'The Peak District?' Nino offered.

'No. That is not it.' He turned to his wife again, speaking Hindi', then turned back to Nino. 'Up north—'

'The Lake District?'

'Yes!' he agreed, nodding. 'That's it. She's gone to the Lake District.'

'D'you know *where* in the Lakes?'

'No. She said it was a village. That's all.'

As her husband moved back into the house the Indian woman looked at Nino sympathetically. 'I'm so sorry we can't help you more.'

Frustrated, he hesitated on the doorstep. To have come so far and hit another dead end. Rachel Pitt was up in the Lake District, but where? It was a big place, with God knows how many villages. It would take him days to check them all out. Days he didn't have.

Changing tack, he asked, 'D'you know where her family live?'

'She only has a mother, and she never talks about her. Not lately, anyway.' The woman paused, suddenly suspicious. 'I thought you said it was someone in her family who was ill?'

'It's a cousin. He lives abroad,' Nino said, hurrying on. 'Look, I have to find Rachel. It's important. You have no idea how important.' Scribbling his name on a piece of paper he gave it to the woman. 'Please, help me. I *have* to find her.'

She looked at him, concerned. 'Is she in trouble?'

'No,' he replied. 'Worse. She's in danger.'

65

His glasses pushed up on his balding head, Gaspare was relaxing in the sitting room, listening to Rachmaninov. No matter how many times he heard the piece, he was moved by it, temporarily taken away from his anxieties, suspended between D flat and middle C. So when he noticed a sound break through the music, he was surprised and went downstairs.

Someone was knocking on the back door. He could see a large figure outlined against the glass and hesitated, remembering his previous heroics.

'Mr Reni! Mr Reni!' the voice shouted.

Cautious, Gaspare approached the door. 'Who is it?'

'Jonathan Ravenscourt.'

Keeping the chain on, Gaspare opened the door a couple of inches. 'What d'you want?'

Ravenscourt was flustered and dishevelled. 'Can I come in?'

'I don't think so. I don't know you.'

'You know *of* me—'

'Yes, and I don't like what I hear,' Gaspare replied, his tone sharp. 'You got a friend of mine in trouble with the police – I had to dig him out of it.'

'I retracted my statement!' Ravenscourt said, pushing at the door. 'Look, I'm not going to hurt you, I've never hurt anyone in my life. Not physically anyway. What I did to Nino Bergstrom was wrong, but I've sorted it out with the police now and I want to help him out. For God's sake, let me in! On come on, Mr Reni, I ask you – do I look like a maniac?'

Relenting, Gaspare took off the safety chain and Ravenscourt moved into the kitchen and took off his cashmere coat. His trousers and shoes were spattered with mud.

'I came to ask you something,' he said, 'something about the Titian—'

'Not that bloody painting again,' Gaspare said dismissively. 'I wish I'd never set eyes on the thing. It's been nothing but trouble—'

'Of course you know all about it.'

'Everything.'

'About there being another murder?'

'Yes, and Nino's on a wild goose chase, trying to find the last victim. The police can't find the killer, so God knows why he thinks he can.' He looked at Ravenscourt's dirtied clothes. 'What happened to you?'

'It's raining.'

'Mud?'

'*What?*'

'You look like you've been rolling in mud.' Gaspare tilted his head to one side. 'I don't want to offend you, Mr Ravenscourt, but I don't believe a word of what you're telling me. I don't think you're trying to make up for what you did to Nino. I think,' he paused, wily to a fault, 'that you're trying to find out what's going on. If we know anything. And if the Titian's been found—'

'Am I that transparent?'

'You're a dealer. I'm a dealer. So yes, to me you're *that* transparent,' Gaspare replied, as he moved away and began to prepare some coffee.

His instinct told him not to throw Johnny Ravenscourt out. He had every right to suspect him – and his motives. But there had to be a reason why Ravenscourt had come back to London. And Gaspare wanted to know what it was.

Passing him a cup of coffee, Gaspare poured himself another and took a seat at the kitchen table. Surprised, Ravenscourt followed his lead, loading two spoonfuls of sugar into the coffee and stirring it idly.

'So the police aren't after you any more?'

'I've satisfied them.'

'Lucky boy,' Gaspare said drily, regarding Ravenscourt over the rim of his cup. 'Did someone attack you?' He gestured to his clothes. 'You can't have got that dirty walking in the rain.'

'I fell over,' Ravenscourt replied shortly.

'Fell or pushed?'

He smiled, sighing. 'I had a ridiculous idea ... er ...

414

I thought that if I went back to where the Titian was originally found . . .' He shrugged, embarrassed. 'I'm not light-footed and I fell over on the shingle—'

'You went back to where Seraphina found the Titian? What for?'

'I don't know,' Ravenscourt admitted. 'Returning to the scene of the crime – something like that. Maybe I wanted to play amateur sleuth. Maybe I wanted to see what she saw. Be where she'd been. We were very close. Seraphina confided everything to me . . .' His voice trailed off. 'Didn't it ever strike you as odd that she was so conveniently there? Just when the Titian washed up?' He sighed, frowning at the mud on his trousers. 'If only someone else had found it, she'd still be alive. If only it had been some other person, some other woman.'

Thoughtful, Gaspare stared at him. 'It was just a fluke that Seraphina found it—'

'A fluke that killed her. A fluke that took away my best friend,' Ravenscourt replied pettishly, sipping his coffee. 'Have you seen the papers today? Angelico Vespucci's becoming the *piatta del giorno*.' Gaspare smiled at the remark, but said nothing and let Ravenscourt continue. 'You know, I made a very interesting purchase lately. I bought a portrait of Claudia Moroni—'

'The second victim?'

Ravenscourt nodded. 'Yes, it's of her and her brother. A testimony to their incest – quite sensational. I've had several dealers already asking to buy it. Anything connected to

415

Vespucci is much sought after. I expect a call from Jobo Kido any time now.' He pursed his lips. 'Have you seen the Vespucci website today?'

'No. Why?'

'The killer's crowing again. Such an ego! If they catch him no doubt he'll make another fortune—'

Gaspare wasn't giving anything away. He and Nino might know the identity of the killer, but he wasn't about to tell Johnny Ravenscourt. He didn't trust him. Suspected he was, in some way, complicit. Did he know who the killer was? Or was he trying to find out if anyone else did?

'What d'you mean, *another fortune*?'

'Well, the killer has the Titian, hasn't he?' Ravenscourt continued. 'Put it up as a reward for his capture. It's very *Mission Impossible*. I imagine they'll make a film of it – *The Skin Hunter II*. I mean, Vespucci was the original, but the new man's modern, available for interview. If he pleads not guilty it will go to court, all the revolting details will come out—'

'And you'll be able to sell your book.'

'Yes, I've been talking to an agent already,' Ravenscourt agreed, moving on. 'But of course there has to be a good ending. In the book – and in life.'

'Meaning?'

'That there are only two days left. Today and tomorrow.' He paused, holding Gaspare's gaze. 'Two days before he kills the last victim. Now, be honest, Mr Reni, what are the chances of Nino Bergstrom finding the last victim in two days? No one knows who she is. And even if he *did* find her, how could he stop the murder?'

Ravenscourt stood up, rinsed out his coffee cup and put on his coat. His heavy face was pink from the kitchen warmth, the mud drying on his trousers and shoes.

Turning round in his seat, Gaspare looked up at him, puzzled. 'You said you wanted to help. How?'

'I've found the skins, Mr Reni—'

The words had all the force of a bullet.

'You've done *what*?'

'I told you, I bought the painting of Claudia Moroni. It looked very dirty and heavy when I got it home. Being an oil painting, I was surprised to find there was a wooden back nailed on to the canvas. As you know, they normally only do that with panel paintings. When I removed it there were four folded skins inside. Dried up, quite brown, like wrinkled old apples . . .' Stunned, Gaspare watched him as he rubbed his hands together. 'Each was labelled: Larissa Vespucci, Claudia Moroni, Lena Arranti and Melania, Contessa di Fattori. They were tied with ribbon into tight little bundles – so tiny for human skins. I bought the painting on a whim – I never realised that it hid The Skin Hunter's victims.' He drew on his gloves languidly. 'It was very lucky – and I wondered if they might not make a useful bargaining tool.'

Gaspare was scarcely breathing. 'For what?'

'I was the first person to research Angelico Vespucci. I spent years on it. Only to be cheated by some murderer and

417

any halfwit with a computer who calls themselves an expert. *I* am the expert on Angelico Vespucci!' His high voice dropped, cunning replacing outrage. 'I want to know who killed my friend, who murdered Seraphina   But I also want to profit from the situation.'

Contemptuous, Gaspare stared at him. 'Are you in your right mind? What kind of person would suggest—'

Ravenscourt put up his hands to stop him continuing.

'Don't lecture me, I've no morals – you'd be wasting your breath. I'm merely offering assistance for Mr Bergstrom, something which might come in useful. The killer's obsessed by Vespucci – don't tell me he wouldn't long to get hold of the skins of his victims. Who knows, he might put them with his own collection and make a real show of it.' Ravenscourt walked to the door and paused. 'Bergstrom has two days to save the last woman – he might need something to bargain with, a way to make the killer stay his hand.'

'And in return?'

'My inclusion in the whole fanfare which will follow – as the paramount expert on The Skin Hunter. I want involvement in press interviews, TV, books – and the money all that will bring.'

'You'd make money from corpses?'

'Why not? The dead don't need it.'

Gaspare was so shocked that it took him a moment to reply.

'And what if Nino fails? If he doesn't find the victim and

418

stop the murder?' His voice was barely audible. 'Or worse, what if *Nino*'s killed and the murderer escapes?'

'Then I keep the skins,' Ravenscourt said, opening the door. 'Come on, Mr Reni, you know as well as I do that no one can afford to be sentimental in business.'

66

Only an hour after Nino had talked to Rachel Pitt's neighbours, his mobile rang.

'Hello?'

A small, embarrassed voice came down the line. 'I'm Vicky, a friend of Rachel's . . . I just picked up your message. Look, I know I shouldn't have listened to her calls, but Rachel's got some secret man stashed away and I wanted to find out who he was, so I listened to her answerphone. But he didn't leave a message – you did. And you don't sound like a boy-friend. You sounded really worried, and I had to ring you back—'

Nino interrupted the flow. 'Are you in Rachel's flat now?'

'Yeah, I come to water the plants. She does mine and I do hers when she's away—'

'D'you know where she is?'

'A place called Crook, up in the South Lakes. It's a hamlet between Windermere and Kendal. Her dad came from there originally, and she said she was going back for—'

'Have you got her mobile number?'

'Nah, she left the phone here. Would you believe it?' Vicky replied, obviously amazed. 'It's on the table in the bedroom.'

'What about the Lakes? D'you have a telephone number up there?'

'Nothing, sorry. What's it all about? Is she in trouble?'

He skirted the question. 'If Rachel rings you, give her my message and number. Tell her to call me. Fast—'

'What are you going to do?'

'Go up to Crook and find her,' Nino replied, about to ring off.

She caught him just in time.

'Hey, Mr Bergstrom! Do me a favour when you talk to Rachel, will you? Don't tell I listened to her messages. I mean, she might think I'm nosy or something.'

Walking to his car, Nino checked his phone and returned a message from Gaspare. The old man took a while to answer; Nino could picture him making his way downstairs from the sitting room to the telephone in the hall. It was no good telling him to get an extension or a hands-free phone – Gaspare liked things just the way they were.

'Hello!' He was out of breath, Nino could hear it.

'Why don't you get another phone?'

'I like this one,' the dealer replied, smiling to himself. 'You got my message then? That bastard Johnny Ravenscourt was here this afternoon—'

Nino stopped walking. 'What the hell did he want?'

'To deal. He's found the skins of Vespucci's victims.'

421

'God Almighty . . . where?'

'In the back of the painting of Claudia Moroni, in a panel. They were dried up, folded into parcels, and labelled.' Gaspare paused. 'This is deep water, Nino. You should get the police on your side.'

'And then what? They'd haul me in, interview me, and before I knew it another day would have passed.' He shook his head. 'I've done what I can – I've left an anonymous message, giving them the name of Edward Hillstone.'

'If he's still using that name.'

'It's the best I can do . . .' Nino hurried on. 'I've found out where Rachel went. She's up in the Lake District. I'm going—'

'It'll take hours to get there!' Gaspare replied, anxious and trying to warn him off. 'You've done enough. Let someone else take over.'

'I can't,' Nino replied, arriving at his car and getting into the driver's seat. 'Don't worry about me—'

'Don't be stupid! How can I *not* worry about you? I should never have let you get involved in the first place. I know why you wanted to – but stop thinking you owe me. You don't. The only thing you owe me is your safety, your life.'

Turning on the engine, Nino tried to reassure him. 'Relax. Eddie Hillstone kills women, not men.'

'Perhaps he'd make an exception for you. He's fixed on his purpose. He won't let anything, or anyone, stop him now. How can he? He's all over the internet, the news. He'll have changed his name again. He's been Eddie Ketch and Edward Hillstone – by now he could be someone else entirely.'

'I can find him—'

Gaspare doubted it.

'Can you? He's clever. Remember, he's been plotting this for a long time . . . You don't know what you're up against. He has to kill this last time, to prove himself. *He has to*, because he's been advertising the killing. Getting the media revved up and the police looking like fools. He's running on adrenalin and the whole world's watching. How can he let *anyone* steal his thunder?' Gaspare's voice wavered. 'Please stop. While you still can—'

'I can't let him kill her.'

'*Kill who?*' Gaspare countered, his tone desperate. 'Rachel Pitt is a stranger. I'm sorry for her, believe me. I don't want her to die. But I don't want you to die either. Don't risk your life for someone you don't even know. She's not your responsibility—'

'If not mine, whose?'

67

Leaving London in the rush-hour traffic, it took Nino over five hours to drive to the South Lakes, and another half an hour to find Crook. It had started to snow as he entered the road to the hamlet and the cottages were in darkness, the only light coming from the pub. Parking, Nino got out of the car and stretched, moving towards the pub entrance. It said CLOSED but he could hear voices inside and walked in. A couple of men were seated round a fireplace, the landlord leaning against the bar and smiling a welcome.

'Hello. You're new round here.'

'I've just driven up from London,' Nino said, nodding to the customers who were looking at him curiously. 'Could I get a drink?'

'Beer?'

'It's cold outside – make it a brandy,' Nino replied, turning to the nearest man. 'I don't suppose you get many strangers around here?'

'Not many, no. Less around this time of year. You come up to see someone?'

'Rachel Pitt,' Nino replied, glancing back at the landlord. 'She's taken a cottage here.'

The landlord looked at his customers then back at Nino. 'She expecting you?'

'It's a surprise,' he lied. 'We had a quarrel and I've come up here to make up. It was my fault – but you know women, she wouldn't let me explain. She just ran off.' Nino could see that he had the men's sympathy and carried on. 'She left without even giving me the address or the phone number.'

'She's just across the road, lad,' the landlord said, moving around the bar and walking to the window. He pointed to a small cottage with two worn steps up to the door. 'That's where your girl's staying. No lights on though. Might be better to wait till morning, in case she doesn't let you in. You can stay here – I've guest rooms upstairs—'

'You didn't let that other bloke stay,' one of his customers said, laughing.

The landlord shrugged. 'I didn't take to him.' Nino frowned. 'What was the matter with him?'

'I dunno. Just sent him to the next village.' He raised his eyebrows. 'So, you want a room or not?'

So Hillstone was here already, was he? Nino thought. Outside, watching, waiting. For a moment he was afraid that he might strike early, the attack brought forward. But then he realised Hillstone wouldn't deviate from the plan he had made; from his homage to Vespucci. The last killing was set for the first of January. Not an instant before.

The room in question turned out to be larger than expected,

425

but cold. Nino locked the door behind him and moved to the window. Across the road he could see the cottage where Rachel was staying, and he rubbed his forehead, realising how tired he was. Kicking off his shoes, he lay down on the bed, pulling a rug over him and checking the time. It was 11.30 p.m. and he needed to sleep. He would just rest for an hour or so, he told himself – just a couple of hours.

Having checked up on her, Nino knew that Rachel was safe, only yards away from him, and he could relax a little. Tomorrow was 31 December. He had found her in time. Nothing would happen to her until 1 January. Which could, of course, be just a moment after midnight on the thirty-first. But not before. Edward Hillstone was trailing the event, like a movie blockbuster, building up the tension until the final moments. But he wouldn't strike early – that would ruin the climax.

So for now Nino could relax a little. Just a little. In the morning he would talk to Rachel, explain what was happening and get her to safety. Whatever Eddie Hillstone said, whatever he bragged on his website, he wasn't going to get her. He wasn't going to emulate The Skin Hunter. He was going to fail and the world was going to see what a craven bastard he really was. Taking in a slow breath, Nino imagined Eddie Hillstone in jail, reading the headlines which mocked his failure. No fanfare for him, no misplaced glamour of the serial killer. He had failed, fallen short. Lost out to a sixteenth-century Venetian.

His eyes closed, his body heavy with exhaustion, his breathing slowing down, Nino slid into sleep.

68

Edward Hillstone was finding the whole experience even more thrilling than he had hoped. To see Nino Bergstrom up in the Lakes, watching over Rachel Pitt like a guardian angel, was a revelation. What on earth was he doing? Bergstrom didn't even know the woman. If he had been a sentimental man, it would have been touching. But then again, Edward wasn't a sentimental man, and he decided that Nino was not so much interested in saving the victim as catching the killer.

Shifting his position, Edward looked down on the village from inside his parked vehicle, a nondescript white van with no markings. Even more nondescript under the first falling of snow. He clapped his hands to warm them, then drank some stewed tea from his thermos flask. He had to admit that he not been expecting his victim to run off to the Lakes. That had been an unexpected development, especially as he had worked out precisely how he would break into her Battersea flat.

But Edward liked to think of himself as adaptable. Reaching for his laptop he went online. The BBC news was talking about him, but not as its top story. Fuck it, Edward thought. Come January the first they'd have him on top. He'd be front-page news then all right.

He sighed, entered his website and typed an update:

Tomorrow is 31st of December – which leaves one day to go until the last victim is killed on the 1st January.

Beneath this, a timer counted down to that glorious day.

In a way it would be sad when it was all over, Edward thought, trying to conjure up some feeling of regret. But he couldn't manage it. His feelings extended only to Vespucci and killing, nothing else. And even that was waning a little . . . He stretched his arms in the cramped van, and stared out into the village beyond. Movement, Edward thought. There he was – the hero, Mr Bergstrom. As if he would let that white-headed bastard steal his thunder. *He* was the hero. *He* was The Skin Hunter. Bergstrom was just an amateur.

But a persistent amateur, Edward thought, watching as Nino walked across the narrow road towards the cottage where Rachel was staying. He looked anxious, knocking at the door and waiting, waiting for an answer. Of course, Edward thought, he could have killed her already. Had thought about it – for a nanosecond – the previous night. The idea of Nino Bergstrom running up to the Lakes just to

428

find a body was enticing. But not *that* enticing. No meddler was going to upset Edward's plan. The death was planned for the first of January.

Not a moment before.

69

31 December

'Just a minute! Just a minute!' Rachel called out, running down the stairs a little after eight o'clock in the morning. Opening the front door of the cottage she looked dishevelled – and surprised. 'Oh, hi . . .'

'Rachel Pitt . . . ?'

She nodded.

Can I come in?'

Pausing, she looked Nino up and down. 'Who are you?'

'Can we talk inside, please? It's very important.'

She let him in, walking into the tiny sitting room and stoking up the fire. The snow had made the temperatures plunge and although she was warmly dressed she had also wrapped a scarf around her neck. It was dark red, fringed, making her skin translucent, her hands in mittens. Unlike Seraphina, she was tall and athletic, with striking good looks.

As her visitor sat down she watched him, standing by the fireplace to put distance between them.

'Who are you?'

'Nino Bergstrom. You don't know me, but I'm here to help you.'

'*Help me?*' she repeated. 'I don't need help.'

'You do,' Nino replied, keeping his voice calm. 'I've been trying to find you for days. Your friend Vicky told me where you were—'

She looked blank, almost irritated. 'I'm sorry, I don't know what you're talking about.'

'I don't want to scare you—'

Her eyes widened. 'But you are.'

'Just hear me out, please. You know about the murders that have been happening lately? The man who's imitating Angelico Vespucci?'

Now she was listening.

'I've written a play about him.'

'I know. That's why I'm here. There have been three murders, and all the women killed had some connection to Vespucci.' He could see her turn pale, and hurried on. 'One was connected by a relative, another by copying Vespucci's portrait, another by writing an article about The Skin Hunter—'

'*What?*' she said hoarsely.

'And you've written a play about him.'

Incredulous, she snapped.

'So what? I can't be the only person on earth who's done that. There must be dozens of people writing about Vespucci, especially now. I don't see why you had to come up here and frighten the hell out of me—'

'It's you that he's picked.'

The words shook her.

'How d'you know that?'

'I'm sorry—'

'You're wrong!' she replied, but her voice caught on the words.

'I wish I was. But I'm not. He's after you.'

'Really?' she said, trying to compose herself. 'Have you got any evidence?'

'I've seen photographs of you in his possession. I've seen your name on a list.'

She flinched. *'What?'*

'I've been after this man for weeks. Police in Italy, Japan and London are after him too, but every time he's got away. I've only just found out who he is—'

'So catch him!'

'I'm trying to,' Nino assured her. 'He's got a website about Vespucci and he's trailing the next killing on the first of January.'

He could see her grip the mantelpiece. 'Jesus . . . why are you telling me all this?'

'I have to warn you.'

She was fighting panic. 'But it's the thirty-first now!'

'That's why I'm here. I'm going to stop him. I swear, he won't get to you . . .'

Bewildered, she turned away. The fire was crackling – she could feel its warmth – but it was making no impact on the cold inside her.

432

' . . . I think you know him.'

Turning, she stared at Nino. '*What?*'

'Have you any enemies? Someone you had an argument with? A man you rejected?'

'But you said he was coming after me because of Vespucci—'

'He is. But he must know of you, or what you were doing, because your play hasn't been performed yet.' Nino paused, then continued. 'I was thinking about it all the time I was driving up here last night. The killer could have found out about the first victim's connection through a relative – that would be easy. He could have found out about the portrait copy. It was for an exhibition, after all. Likewise, the article. That was published on the internet. But your play? Hardly anyone knows about that – apart from the people at the theatre.'

She shook her head. 'Not even them. Only Enright knows about it there, and he's no killer.'

'You must have told someone else,' Nino persisted. 'Think, Rachel. Who did you talk to?'

'Michael, the man in my life . . .' She trailed off, thinking of her lover. 'No, it wouldn't be him. I've known him for years. Not him.'

'So, who else? What about friends? You must have told a friend about it?'

'Not really. I was superstitious. I thought it was bad luck to talk about the play until it was going to be performed. So I kept quiet about it.' She shivered, rubbing her mittened hands together. Her nails were bloodless.

'How long have you been working on it?'

'I had the idea about four years ago. I heard about Angelico Vespucci and thought it would be a good subject.'

'Where did you hear about him?'

She was getting agitated, her mind wandering. Fear, cold and encroaching, was making its presence felt.

'I . . . I . . . don't remember . . . maybe at . . . I can't remember!'

'Take your time.'

'I don't have much of that, do I?' she snapped back, her eyes filling. 'D'you know why I came up here for the holidays? To get away from London, to get away and clear my head. I made a resolution to end my relationship and move on. Make a new life. And now you've come here and told me I don't have a bloody life left—'

'You do,' Nino assured her, 'if you help me. Come on, Rachel, think. When and where did you first hear about Angelico Vespucci?'

She tossed back her head and focused. 'I went to university, where I read English. I learned Italian when I worked in Rome for a while. I was a nanny . . . Then I came back to London and entered the theatre. The Hamlet Theatre . . .' She was getting desperate. 'I can't remember! I can't remember how I heard about The Skin Hunter—'

'A book?'

'No.'

'A film?'

'No!'

'Did you hear about him at a party? At a dinner?' Nino pressed her. 'On a holiday?'

'A holiday . . .'

'What about a holiday?'

'Wait a minute,' she said, glancing away and forcing herself to remember. 'I took a trip five years ago. It was when I was in Italy, and it was a cultural tour of Venice. Some passengers had dropped out and the tickets were really cheap, so I said we'd go.'

'Who's we?'

'I took the kids I was nanny for. They weren't babies, and I thought it would do them good. Actually, to be honest, I had second thoughts about it as soon as I'd got the tickets. I thought it was going to be a lousy trip, hauling the kids along. But it was a mixed group, and there were some people of my own age. I suppose they grabbed the chance, like I did.'

'Were they Italian?'

'Most of them,' she sighed, trying to remember. 'We didn't get close. I was busy with the kids and it was only two days. But there was a group of Italian girls who were flirting all the time and an Englishman who was very reserved.'

Nino heard the word *Englishman*.

'Did you get on with him?'

'No, not really. He asked me out and I said no. He was pissed off about it, but he wasn't my type.' She paused, remembering. 'Oh God . . .'

'What?'

' . . . I remember now. We'd been talking. That's how it started. It was him that told me about The Skin Hunter. We

435

chatted, then one of the kids was sick and I had to leave . . .'
She turned to Nino, ashen. 'Oh God, was it *him*?'

'What did he look like?'

'Tall, attractive, well-spoken, easy to talk to. All the girls were trying to get his attention . . . *Was it him?*'

'Maybe. Can you remember anything else?'

She hesitated, then nodded. 'I asked what his name was and he said Jex. I remembered it because I'd never heard it before and I thought he was making it up.'

Jex. The name of the creator of the Vespucci website. Jex. Aka Edward Ketch. Aka Edward Hillstone . . .

Badly shaken, Rachel held Nino's gaze. 'Who is he?'

'His name's Edward Hillstone.'

She nodded, holding on. 'So you know who he is – but you don't know *where* he is?'

'No.'

'I want to go home,' Rachel said suddenly. 'I want to go back to London. It's where my flat is, where my things are. If I'm going to die, I want to die there.'

'You're not going to die—'

'How d'you know? You said there had been three other murders. You didn't save those women, so what makes you think you're going save me?' She paused, clenching her fists, losing control. 'What do I do? *Oh, Jesus, what do I do?*'

'I'll stay with you—'

She brushed him off.

'I don't want *you*! I want Michael. I want the man I love. I want him.' Panic was making her frantic. 'Get out!'

'I'm not leaving you,' Nino said firmly. 'If you want to go back home, fine, I'll go back to London with you. But you can't be on your own—'

'I won't be alone! I'll call Michael . . .'

She trailed off. Who was she kidding? He would be busy, or out. *Leave a message, I'll call back.* He'd be with his wife and kids. He'd not be there for her, even if she was going to die. *Not available. Sorry* . . . Slowly she looked at Nino. He was a stranger, but he was trying to save her. He had driven all the way from London to the Lakes to help . . . Jesus, what the hell was she thinking?

'I'm sorry,' she said at last. 'Sorry for what I said.'

He nodded. 'D'you still want to go home?'

'Yes.'

'OK, go and pack – I'll drive you back.'

'I hired a car,' she said, frowning. 'I can't just leave it here.'

He didn't like to say that the car was the least of her worries.

'I'll sort that out for you. Just get yourself ready and we'll leave.'

Making for the stairs, Rachel turned and looked back at him.

'Why does he want to kill me?'

'He's copying Angelico Vespucci. You have a connection because of the play you've written.'

'*That's it?*' she asked, incredulous. 'That's *all* there is to it? I don't believe you.' She shook her head. 'There must be another reason he picked me.'

A moment shimmered between them.

'The Skin Hunter killed women he thought were immoral. His imitator is doing the same.'

It took her a moment to process the words. To remember Michael. To remember that she was a man's mistress. To realise why she had been singled out for murder.

'Oh,' she said, turning away. 'I see.'

Snow made the journey slow and hazardous. At times the motorway traffic slowed down to thirty miles an hour, the landscape a blurred furring of white. In the passenger seat beside Nino, her bag on the back seat behind them, Rachel sat motionless. The seat belt was fastened across her chest, an inky band against the red of her jacket, her hair tied back, the scarlet scarf still around her neck. She looked like Christmas, all rosy warmth, all wool and softness, and yet her skin was icy. Deathly cold.

At times she would speak, but most of the journey she was silent, staring ahead. Sitting beside her, Nino wanted to talk, to say something to distract her but there was a terrible distance between them. She was longing for another man, afraid of her future, of the death prophesied on the internet – the death she now knew as her own. And meanwhile Nino was trying desperately to convince himself that he would save her.

Without knowing if, or how, he could.

70

Gaspare glanced back at the newspaper and reread the small piece at the bottom of the third column on page five. He had got a message from Nino to say that he had found Rachel and was returning to the capital with her. He wasn't going to tell Nino what he had just seen. In fact, he had almost overlooked it, but the name had caught his attention.

It read:

> Mr Patrick Dewick, 59, a psychiatric nurse at Green-field's Hospital, Ealing, was found murdered yesterday. He had been missing for several days and his body was found in woodland, partially buried. He leaves a widow and two sons.

Gaspare threw down the paper. Patrick Dewick, the man who had put Nino on to Eddie Ketch, was dead.

Nino was wrong – the killer *did* kill men. He must have realised that Dewick had tipped Nino off and murdered him to prevent him saying any more. Gaspare shivered, unnerved.

If the killer had been watching Rachel Pitt, he must have seen Nino up in the Lakes. Must have known that he was going to try and stop him. And that was the last thing he wanted.

Gaspare glanced over at the clock – twelve thirty already. The morning gone, the afternoon hot on its heels. Only thirty-six hours until the New Year – the first of January that everyone was waiting for . . . He sat down at the table, watching the traffic outside. Kensington Church Street was busy, the Christmas lights due to come on when the daylight faded, the statue of Christ alone and forgotten in His urban shrine.

Thinking of Seraphina, Gaspare remembered. She was back in his sitting room again, her coat and feet wet from scrabbling in the shingle, handing him the Titian painting. Then later, afraid, asking him to destroy it. And then he remembered the news from Venice, recording her death. She had been the first.

God only knew who would be the last.

71

The flat was chilly because the heating had been switched off, and although there had been no snow in London it had been raining heavily. At the doorway, Rachel hesitated, Nino walking in before her and looking around. Reassured, she had followed him but now stood, aimless, in the sitting room. Her hands were restless, moving from her face to her hair, her gaze moving round the room as though she hardly knew the place.

'D'you want me to get the police?'

'No!' she said shortly. 'I want you to be here. I trust you. You catch him, OK? You catch him. You can – I know you can. I don't want the police.'

'Are you sure?'

'What would they do? Take me to the station and interview me, then let me go . . . then what? Don't tell me they'll be able to stop the killer. Don't say they'll be able to protect me – they didn't protect the other girls. *You* found me. They didn't.' She started pacing, five steps one way, five steps the other. 'Even if the police kept me in overnight, he'd still get me when I came out. And he'd be mad then, because I'd messed up his plan.' Still pacing, her voice was staccato. 'No, I want to be here. I want *you* to stay with me . . . When he comes, you can stop him.'

Nino touched her shoulder. For a moment she looked as though she might cry, then rallied.

'I'm OK,' she reassured him. 'I'm OK . . .'

'Good. I'm going to look round the flat, check the windows and doors. Get to know the place.'

He didn't add that he was worried about the layout. The flat was old and on two floors – ground floor and basement – with a landing in between. A landing with a window. Beginning in the basement, Nino checked that the front door was locked and bolted and saw – to his relief – that the windows were barred. No chance of anyone getting in there.

On the landing Nino checked the window and glanced out into a small communal garden beyond, where the back gate swung in a sulky breeze. Hurrying outside, he locked the gate, then turned, looking *into* the flat. There was a clear view into the sitting room from all sides. The killer would have been able to watch Rachel for some time, would have seen her in the kitchen and also in the sitting room. Had he watched her talking on the phone? Or working on her computer? Nino paused, looking around. Yes, there it was – the computer on a work table under the far window. The killer would have seen Rachel there, her back to him, not knowing she was being hand-picked for a kill.

Thoughtful, Nino returned to the flat, bolting the door after him. The first floor was the next to get his scrutiny – Rachel's bedroom and a guest room opposite. He tried the windows of the guest room, relieved that they had been painted over and were resistant to opening, then walked into the master bedroom. It was untidy, but the windows were closed and locked. Likewise the bathroom. To all intents and purposes – unless the killer had a key – he couldn't get in.

Returning to the kitchen, he found Rachel making tea. In silence, she passed him a mug and a cheese sandwich.

'Sorry, it was all I had.'

Looks good. Thanks. Aren't you eating?

'No, no appetite . . . Are all the doors locked?'

'Yes.'

'And the windows?'

'Yes.'

'It's going so fast.'

'What is?'

'The time.' She glanced at her watch. 'It's two o'clock now. Before long it will be dark again, day over. Year over . . . Jesus, what a mess . . . Will he come tomorrow? Tomorrow's the first . . . But he could come just after midnight, couldn't he? He could – it would be the first then, wouldn't it?' She bit down on her lip, fighting panic. 'All those people in Piccadilly Square celebrating, counting down the seconds to the New Year . . .' She was shaking uncontrollably. *'He's going to kill me, isn't he?'*

Nino shook his head.

'No. He's not going to kill you, Rachel. You're going to have a long, happy life. You're going to see in at least another fifty New Years. And one day, when you're old, you'll tell your grandchildren all about it. They won't believe you, of course, but you'll tell them anyway. It's not the end, Rachel.'

She stared at him intently. 'You can't be sure of that.'

'Oh yes I can,' Nino replied. 'In fact, I've never been so sure of anything in my life.'

72

The traffic was the one thing Edward Hillstone hadn't made allowances for. For the first hour it had been easy to follow Bergstrom's car. Enjoyable, in fact. The van was anonymous, with nothing to give it away – he could have followed Bergstrom for days without drawing suspicion to himself. But then some idiot had pulled out without signalling, making him swerve on to the hard shoulder. It had taken Edward almost four minutes to get back onto the road, four minutes in which he had lost track of Bergstrom and Rachel Pitt.

He suspected that they were going to Bergstrom's temporary home at the Kensington gallery, or Rachel's flat in Battersea, Bergstrom playing the hero and making it easy for Edward to fall into his trap. He smiled at the idea, at Bergstrom's arrogance. Either place would suit him, Edward thought. Both places were familiar to him. After all, he had stolen the Titian from Gaspare Reni's gallery, and he knew Rachel's flat almost as well as his own. But it still irked him that he had lost contact with them, and he felt a sullen annoyance as he drove the remaining hours alone.

It wasn't the way it was supposed to be.

But then again, everything else had gone so smoothly, it was just a blip. Tonight was the real climax. Let Rachel Pitt think she might have another full day to live. Let her long to see another morning, afternoon and evening. Let her enough think she had twenty-four hours, another one thousand, four hundred and forty minutes – when, in reality, what she had was a second.

On the last chime of Big Ben, when TV, radio and internet connections everywhere welcomed the New Year, he would kill her.

And after that, he would be famous.

73

11.20 p.m.

Standing outside Rachel's flat, Edward savoured the murder to come. He would kill her, then take her back to his home in Spitalfields. There he would make an announcement of her death on the website, proclaim his success – The Skin Hunter brought back to life. A 21st-century Vespucci to be celebrated. Anonymous, but triumphant . . . Edward breathed in to steady himself. After he had killed Rachel Pitt, he would take his time, relish the New Year's Day spent removing her skin from her body. Then he would take photographs – of the flayed Rachel, and the skin of Rachel. Two Rachels for the price of one. The images would be over the internet in seconds, the world seeing what he had achieved. From continent to continent he would be famous. And feared.

It wasn't difficult to image the reactions of the dealers. Jobo Kido would despair, realising he was never going to get the Titian; Farina Ahmadi would burn at being outclassed; and Triumph Jones – not so Triumphant now – would slip into a guilty old age. Bested. Beaten. All his machinations coming to nothing. And the pompous dealers who had belittled Edward Hillstone in the past would be seen for what they were – fools.

His journey was almost over, Edward thought, looking back. He had been dedicated – no one could deny that. From his first interest in Angelico Vespucci to his growing obsession, he had never veered from his route. Even if it had taken him off-course occasionally. Poor Susan Coates. Clever, but quite mad. It had been worth volunteering at Greenfield's Hospital just to talk to her. What she knew about Vespucci was second to none. Edward had even begun to like her – before he was moved on. And then he remembered Sir Harold Greyly. So rich, so lazy, so full of his own importance that he had jumped at the chance of help.

Put the library in order, he had demanded, passing it over to the amiable, well-spoken Edward.

Greyly had been stupid too – not like his aunt. Hester Greyly was anything but stupid. She had been Edward's first real deviation. But he had *had* to stop her talking to Nino Bergstrom about Claudia Moroni. The old woman might well have said something which could lead to him. Her death had been inevitable and had succeeded in throwing Bergstrom off his scent – at least for a while. Until Bergstrom had revisited Courtford Hall to talk to Harold Greyly. The squire was out of it by then. Edward's anonymous letter to his wife explaining how their family was going to be exposed in the media had done the trick. The taboo of incest and the red tops had beached the marriage and, once alone, Harold Greyly turned a hobby into a career. Within a month he was sodden with booze.

Edward leaned against the wall, staring at Rachel's flat. Angelico Vespucci might have had some limited reputation in Venice, but he, Edward Hillstone, would go global.

It was so close now. So very close . . . When he had finally got back to London, Edward had shaved, taken a shower and changed his clothes, then eaten a light meal, but drunk no wine. After a short sleep, a little music had filled the rest of the time and it was ten p.m. when he finally left Spital-fields in search of Rachel Pitt. He had checked out the Kensington gallery first, but the place had been deserted and in darkness, not even the old man around. When he looked in the window, Edward could see the red light flick-ering on the alarm. No one was there, which meant that Bergstrom had taken Rachel to her place.

Of course he could have hidden her somewhere else, but Edward didn't think so. Not for a minute. He was getting to know his pursuer now, even getting to admire him a little. And he suspected Nino of having an ego – a desire to win. Having found himself drawn into the whole business by accident, Bergstrom wasn't a man to shy from a challenge. He had been ill, Edward knew – as always, he had done his research. Perhaps Bergstrom was trying to prove something, especially to himself? A man who had been weakened and made vulnerable would want his power back.

Edward Hillstone did not underestimate Nino Bergstrom. Not any more.

Suddenly a light came on and Edward checked the time – 11.44 p.m. It was in the sitting room in the basement of the flat, a small side lamp on the computer table. So Rachel Pitt had thought she was safe, had she? Had locked her doors and windows and drawn her blinds. He knew there were no police in there, but Bergstrom was there, maybe. Likely, in fact.

Smiling, Edward watched as Rachel sat down in front of the computer. She had obviously just bathed – she had a thick bathrobe on and a towel wrapped round her hair, her head and shoulders silhouetted against the queasy glow of the computer screen. Excited, Edward wriggled his fingers, feeling the itch in his palms. There were only a few minutes to go and he was hot with arousal . . . He leaned forward, peering through the blind. It blocked out some of his view, but he could see Rachel's silhouette, imagine how she would scream when he grabbed her, how the knife would slide into her neck and severe the jugular vein. How the blood would run over his gloves and how she would jerk uncontrollably. They all did that.

In that instant another thought occurred to Edward. Perhaps Bergstrom hadn't told Rachel Pitt that she was a victim. Perhaps he hadn't wanted to scare her. Perhaps he was now hiding somewhere. Waiting for the killer to make his move . . . Uneasy, Edward looked around. But there was no sign of Bergstrom. And then he spotted something through the wrought iron gate which led to the street – *Bergstrom's car*. It was a little way off, but he recognised it immediately and could just make out the familiar, unmistakable white head of hair. Bergstrom! Where the hell was he going?

Edward didn't hesitate. Wherever he was going, Nino Bergstrom wasn't in the flat with Rachel Pitt. This was his chance . . . Noiselessly, he ran down the alleyway between the houses, jumped the gate, and then paused by the back door. Like so many other people, Rachel had hidden a second key in case she locked herself out. It had taken Edward a while to find, but in the end he had discovered it tucked in among the dying plants in the window box. He had then copied it, so she would never know.

It was the copy he slid in the back door now, turning the lock, pushing it slightly ajar. Silently he walked in. He could hear faint music, and see the light from the computer coming through the partly opened door of the sitting room.

His breath caught in his throat as he reached into his pocket and brought out the hunting knife. It felt familiar and heavy in his hand as he gripped it and moved further into the room. For one second he relished the thought of the kill – then he rushed her. He rushed towards the computer and the seated figure, lunging at Rachel, the impact throwing her off the seat and on to the floor.

The last thing Edward Hillstone expected was the punch to his throat, his head exploding as he struggled for breath. Gasping, he rolled over, crawling on all fours, wrenching at his collar in an effort to breathe. The first kick hit him full in the ribs, sending him backwards, the second landed in his solar plexus, rendering him helpless. Caught by surprise, winded, struggling for air, Edward Hillstone stared up at his attacker in disbelief.

In the struggle the head towel had come off – and instead of Rachel Pitt standing there, it was Nino Bergstrom.

74

Securely tied to a chair, Edward Hillstone was still gasping for breath, trying to form his words, spittle drooling from the left side of his mouth. Nino had taken off the towelling robe and was standing in his jeans and shirt, facing the killer. Despite Hillstone's temporary dishevelment, it was obvious why he had been so successful. He was personable, almost refined, a man who could have easily blended into the art world or worked at a country gentleman's retreat.

The knife that he had dropped was now on the sideboard, out of reach, and Nino had phoned the police. Watching him, Edward shook his head to try to clear his thoughts, his hands working against the rope which held him.

'Where is she?'

'In my car.'

He nodded, almost amused. 'It was a wig?'

'Rachel works in a theatre,' Nino replied. 'It was easy for her to get hold of a prop. I knew you'd be fooled by the white hair – it's what everyone notices. You were no different.' He checked the rope, winding some more around

Hillstone's neck before finally knotting it at the back of the chair. 'If you struggle, you'll strangle yourself. If I were you, I'd keep still and plead insanity.'

Reaching into Edward's pocket, he took out his keys and wallet, checking the address on his driver's licence. Then he walked over to the window, waiting. Only minutes later a police car pulled up outside.

And as the police entered by the front, Nino left by the back.

454

75

'Make your way to the gallery now,' Nino said, leaning down to talk to Rachel in the driver's seat. 'Gaspare's expecting you.'

'Where are you going?'

He ignored the question, tapping the top of the car. 'Go on, go now. I'll be over later.'

Waiting until he saw the car disappear down the street, Nino hailed a cab, arriving outside Edward Hillstone's home twenty minutes later. It was one of the Georgian silk merchant's houses, narrow, on four storeys, its paintwork freshly done. Glancing up, Nino looked for any lights turned on, but there were none and he opened the door, moving into an unlit hallway. The walls were painted dark green, the cornice picked out in gold, the effect luxurious and oppressive at the same time.

First he checked the front room, which was empty and well furnished. Next he moved into a snug, again empty, and then went further into a modernised, galley-style kitchen. Everything was lavish, the fridge stocked with food, wine in a pantry beyond. But what caught Nino's eye was a woman's handbag on the table. He wondered fleetingly if it had belonged to one of Edward Hillstone's victims, but his attention was distracted when he turned and spotted a slatted wooden door beside the main exit.

Opening it, Nino flicked on the light. At once he could see a number of stone steps leading down to a cellar beyond. Wary, he moved downwards, turning on another light as he reached the bottom of the stairs. The space surprised him: it extended to half the length of the house. At the far end was a sink, a table in the centre, and beside it what looked like an operating trolley. But this – unlike the house – was decrepit, the surgical instruments well used and filthy.

Everywhere was the sight of fresh, and dried, blood. Gore caked the scalpels and the plastic sheeting on the floor and across the table. The smell was there too, the stink of blood catching on the back of Nino's throat as he moved further into the private slaughterhouse of Edward Hillstone. Unnerved, he glanced around, spotting a pair of surgical gloves thrown on the floor, used and bloodied; a waste bin piled high with swabs; and patches of torn clothing, stained with faecal matter. Along the sides of the table were grooves like those on a morgue slab, where the blood could run and be filtered into a bucket at the end. And the bucket was still there, the blood congealed, dark red, turning to brown.

Fighting a gag reflex, Nino moved away, catching sight of an imposing, ebonised cupboard. It was like a kitchen cupboard, but locked, without door handles. Using one of the knives from the table, he levered the lock open. And there, inside an old cupboard lined with floral wallpaper from the 1950s, was Titian's portrait of Angelico Vespucci.

Nino was about to reach for it but stopped when he heard a sound overhead. Flicking off the main light, he hurried to the bottom of the cellar steps and turned off that light too. In the darkness he could hear someone moving around, ascending the stairs from the hallway to the first landing. Pressing himself further under the steps, Nino listened in the dark. Could Edward Hillstone have escaped? And if it wasn't Hillstone, *did he have an accomplice*?

Were there two killers? Did one kill and the other mutilate the bodies? Stepping on to the bottom stair, Nino moved upwards. After every step he took, he paused, listening, before taking another one. He could see a faint glow at the top of the steps coming from under the cellar door. Someone had turned on the hall light . . . Silently, Nino continued to climb, finally reaching the top of the steps and moving out into the hall.

He glanced towards the front door, but it was still bolted. Then he looked into the kitchen, staring at the table. The handbag had gone.

Gripping the banister rail, Nino mounted the stairs. He still had the knife he had picked up in the cellar, and was holding it in his hand, ready to strike. But no one jumped him. No one came out from any of the upstairs rooms. No one confronted him on the landing. It was only when he reached the top of the staircase that he saw a light coming from a bedroom at the end of the corridor.

Tightening his grip on the knife, Nino walked towards the room, reaching the door and slamming it backwards against the wall.

He had wanted to startle the intruder.

But she wasn't startled at all.

Seraphina Morgan, formerly Seraphina di Fattori, looked into the mirror and smiled at him.

76

'Eddie's been caught,' she said simply. 'But then you know that, don't you?'

Transfixed, Nino stared at her. 'You're dead. You were murdered in Venice—'

'*Was I?*' she replied, swivelling round in her seat, lush and bronzed. 'I don't think so.'

He remembered her coming to Gaspare's studio with the painting. Remembered the old man's grief at her murder. Remembered his own dedication to find out who had killed her.

'*What the hell is going on?*'

'Have you found the Titian?' she asked, ignoring his question. 'I heard you downstairs, so I suppose you have.'

'What are you doing?' he asked, approaching her. 'What are you playing at? Why would you let everyone think you were dead? Why would you *do* that?' He paused, trying to gather his thoughts. 'Were you working with him? With Hillstone?' She said nothing and Nino continued. '*You planned all this?*'

'The night we met you seemed very unsure of yourself. I put that down to your having been so ill. I must say, I never thought it would be you that caught us.' She put down the hairbrush in her hand, smiling. 'You're trying to work it out, aren't you? Thinking really hard ... I can see that in your face.'

'So why don't you explain it? Or shall we just wait for the police to come and you can talk to them?'

'But then you'd never find out the truth, because I'd hardly tell them, would I?' she countered. 'Shall I start? I met Edward Hillstone a few years ago—'

'On the Italy trip?'

'Yes!' she said happily. 'The same trip that Rachel Pitt was on. I know you've found out about that – you must have done. Anyway, where was I? They do this in films, don't they, Mr Bergstrom? Always confess at the end, tell the audience how it was done. You would know, you being in the movie industry—'

'So how *did* you do it?'

'Eddie and I had a fling. He wanted me more than I wanted him, and he was obsessed with Angelico Vespucci. It turned him on to think that I was a descendant of one of The Skin Hunter's victims. He's a very good lover, you know. But then men that don't really feel too much always are. They can lose themselves in the moment. A very cold fish, is Eddie. It's what makes him so attractive.'

'He's a killer.'

'Not then – that came later, although he was always fan-

460

tasising about killing women. He'd talk about it in bed, describe what he'd do, how he'd mutilate them. I thought it was just sex talk . . .' Her tone was light. 'We met up quite often and he talked more and more about Vespucci, and then something strange happened.'

'Go on.'

'My family are into the arts. Well, you know that from Gaspare Reni. I knew about the art world, and I heard the gossip—'

'But you're a scientist—'

'With a wide circle of friends,' she said mockingly. 'Offspring of the rich and well-connected. They hear things and someone heard about the Titian painting re-emerging. You can't keep that kind of thing a secret in art circles, Mr Bergstrom. It's a business that feeds off gossip.'

'So?'

'I heard about Triumph Jones being involved and about his being in London when I was. In fact, I was going to talk to him about the Titian, but when I arrived at his hotel they said he was out. That was bad manners.' Her tone was curt, offended. 'I knew he was there, so when he left, I followed him. He has a sly reputation, does Mr Jones. His actions had piqued my interest. I followed him in a taxi and he got out on Grosvenor Bridge, with a parcel. About the right shape and size for a painting . . . You are following all this, aren't you?'

'Every word.'

'He was looking around to see that no one was watching. He didn't see me, obviously, and then he threw it into the river!' She shook her head, incredulous. 'It came up on the bank pretty quickly and I picked it up . . . I don't know if he saw me . . . I looked at it and knew what it was . . . Then of course I asked myself, what should I do?' She put her head on one side. 'It was the portrait of Angelico Vespucci. The rumours had been right, but I'd never expected to be the one who found it.'

'So why did you come to Gaspare Reni's gallery?'

'I needed somewhere to hide it in London. With someone respectable. I knew the old man would never destroy it, but he *would* look after it until I worked out how to get it home.'

'But you were so frightened that night,' Nino said, remembering. 'You were afraid of the painting when Gaspare told you the story about Vespucci.'

'Just acting,' she replied deftly. 'I knew the story already. How could I *not* know? I just wanted to make it all look believable. And it did. When I left the gallery I contacted Eddie. He was hardly able to talk he was so excited, and when I told him about the rumour Triumph Jones had set in motion he went frantic. "When the portrait emerges, so will the man." She smiled, cold eyes. 'That was his excuse to kill. That's what set Eddie off.'

'And you didn't stop him?'

'Why should I? I wanted the Titian. But more than that, I wanted out. Wanted to leave my old life, leave my husband in particular – the lazy American oaf. But how could I? It

462

was the painting that gave me the idea . . . *I could die.* Without actually dying.'

Incredulous, Nino stared at her. He was trying to match this Seraphina with the young woman he had first met in the Kensington gallery, but could find no trace of the original.

'You let everyone think you'd been murdered. Your family, your husband—'

'Oh, don't waste your pity on Tom,' she countered. 'When he knew there was a Titian in the mix he was more than willing to go along with it. For a while I even let him think I was going to work with him. And Johnny Ravenscourt. He'd been involved in smuggling so it seemed logical to suggest we could hire him and split the proceeds.'

Nino nodded. 'I get it . . . Then you plan your own death, so you don't have to share with anyone. Except Hillstone.'

'But I didn't mind sharing with Eddie – he was doing most of the work, after all. It was everyone *else* I wanted to get away from.'

'So the woman who was found murdered, the woman everyone thought was you – who was she?'

Her expression was composed, with an undercurrent of triumph.

'A suicide. I'm a scientist, I work at the hospital in Venice. I knew someone who'd help me out and turn a blind eye to what was going on in the morgue one night. You can bribe pretty much everyone if you offer them enough. He identified me by the necklace 'I' was wearing. A sentimental present he had given to me when we first married.' She shrugged again. 'We took her body—'

'And Hillstone mutilated it?'

'Well, I didn't!' she replied, angered for the first time. 'Killing was *his* dream, not mine. And besides, I never really believed he'd go through with it. People say all kinds of things—'

'Not usually about killing people.'

She shrugged.

'Maybe not.'

'So then what happened?' Nino pushed her. 'You'd disappeared, so you were out of the picture.'

'And Eddie stole the Titian from Gaspare Reni's gallery—'

'He attacked an old man in the process.'

'He didn't kill him,' she responded. 'It could have been worse.'

He was finding it difficult to look at her. 'Then Hillstone hid the painting here?'

She nodded. 'Yes, in this house, which he bought in the name of William Jex. Eddie loves to change his name. In the past he'd had to, to keep one step ahead, but he enjoys it too. And of course it made him a lot harder to track.' She took in a slow breath, as though she was tired. 'You found him though. That was clever. Maybe I should have thrown my lot in with you, Mr Bergstrom?'

He ignored the remark.

'You haven't explained the most important part – why Hillstone started killing.'

'I told you, he'd always wanted to imitate Vespucci. When Triumph Jones put out that bloody painting, he had carte blanche,' she said thoughtfully. 'He said The Skin Hunter went for whores, so he'd have no shortage of victims. Then we came up with the idea of a link.'

'A link between the women and Vespucci?'

She nodded.

'It was inspired, wasn't it? I remembered Rachel Pitt on that Italy trip, how she'd been talking to Eddie about The Skin Hunter. She even made a throwaway comment that she'd like to write a play about him. That set us thinking, I can tell you. Then we started looking for other women who had some connection to Vespucci ... Eddie was red hot on that – he'd worked in Greyly's library and had already found out about Claudia Moroni.' She paused, her tone peevish. 'I can't believe my husband sold that painting to Johnny Ravenscourt! And now Johnny's gloating, talking about it on the internet ... I liked that picture.'

'Any particular reason why?'

'You mean the incest between Claudia Moroni and her brother?'

'Nothing else?'

Seraphina paused, alert. Her intelligence was tipping her off, her cunning suspecting something more. 'What else?'

'Should there be something else?'

'There is, isn't there? *Tell me!*'

'You never examined the picture, did you?' Nino said.

'What a shame, Seraphina. You missed out there. Angelico Vespucci hid his trophies *behind the panel on the back*.'

The shock almost winded her. '*What?*'

'The skins were in your possession all the time you lived in that apartment with Tom Morgan. You lived with the picture, looked at the painting every day – and never knew what it held.' He taunted her. 'Just think what Eddie Hillstone would have made of that—'

'*Shut up!*' The colour had left her face. 'I don't believe it! Ravenscourt's not put it up on his website. He hasn't said a thing about it.'

'Of course he hasn't. He'll wait until Hillstone comes to trial and then make a killing with the publicity. To have hides from The Skin Hunter's victims – it'll make him famous. And to think you were sleeping under them, night after night, without even knowing—'

'*Stop it!*'

'Oh, don't take it badly, Seraphina. You can't win every time,' Nino continued, provoking her. 'Anyway, you haven't finished your story. I know you want to tell me what you did. I know you want to brag. So go on, tell me – who found out about Sally Egan?'

She paused, but couldn't resist.

'Eddie did . . . But *I* found out about Harriet Forbes.'

'You knew he was going to kill those women, and you didn't tell the police?'

She shrugged.

'You didn't think to warn them? What had Sally Egan, Harriet Forbes and Rachel Pitt done to you?'

466

'You saved Rachel Pitt!'

'*But the other two are dead.* And you could have saved them.' He stared at her. 'Why, Seraphina?'

'Why what?'

'Why did you do it?'

'Why d'you think?'

'It was all about sex, wasn't it? The ultimate kick for you and Hillstone?' He paused. 'But I don't understand why he punished the others but didn't judge you.'

She smiled slyly. 'Because I was clever – and he loved me.'

'Did you come up with the idea of your own murder?'

'You don't think Eddie did, do you?'

Nino smiled. 'It was a clever move. By thinking you were the first victim it made the legend all the more real. Vespucci *had* killed your ancestor, so of course his imitator would kill you.' He was trying to weigh her up, his voice wary. 'But if you knew Hillstone had been caught, why did you come back here? Why not make a run for it?'

'And go where? I'm dead, remember.' Her voice shifted, taking on a gentler tone, suddenly vulnerable. 'I was confused. I wanted to stay here to clear my name, to give my side of the story. Eddie Hillstone made me do these terrible things—'

'No, he didn't. You *chose* to do them,' Nino insisted, knowing where she was leading.

'*But I didn't think he'd kill them!* I never really thought he'd kill them . . . When he murdered Sally Egan, I was so afraid, I didn't dare say anything. If he could do that to them, he could do it to me.'

467

She was sliding into another performance. Snaking towards an escape route.

'You're lying,' Nino replied. 'You took a dead girl and mutilated her—'

'Not me!'

'*You organised it!* You're as guilty as Hillstone. You knew when he carved up her body, when he mutilated her face to pass her corpse off as yours, that he was capable of anything. You relied on that. You could play him along, let him get his fantasies out of his system. After all, what did it matter to you? You'd got rid of a husband you despised and had a Titian you could sell for six million, at least.' He paused. 'You have no defence—'

She thought otherwise.

'*He forced me to go along with him*! I lied! It was *his* idea to fake my death, it was Eddie all along.' Her voice wavered. 'Not me – I had to do what he said. *I had to.*'

'I don't believe you—'

Irritated, she dropped the vulnerable act and went on the defensive.

'It doesn't matter what you think. In the end, it's Edward Hillstone's word against mine. And who d'you think people will believe? My family will be so glad to get me back, they won't ask too many questions—'

'Maybe not, but the police will.'

'There's no proof I colluded with Eddie,' she went on, her tone confident. 'I made sure of that. Nothing in writing, nothing anyone saw or could have overheard. We were lovers once, that's true, but he used my feelings for him and turned them against me.' She swivelled round in her seat, her dark eyes holding his stare, her voice plaintive again. '*Eddie Hillstone used me.*'

'No.'

'Yes.'

'It won't work, Seraphina. No one will believe you. You'll be jailed. Locked up, just like you should be.'

'Will I?' she said, standing.

He saw her rise and took a moment to react. She was very erect, her head high, her back straight. So straight that it made her pregnancy even more obvious, the swelling of a baby growing fast.

'Of course ... Your husband told me you were pregnant.'

'But it's not his,' she said, touching her stomach. 'It's Eddie Hillstone's. You see, he raped me ... But I want to keep the baby. That why I did what I did, Mr Bergstrom. I had to do everything he asked to save my child. *That's* why I had to go along with him.' She paused, her tone helpless, faking desperation. 'You can't punish me. I'm as much a victim as the other women.'

77

Edward Hillstone was arrested and charged with two counts of murder and one of attempted murder. He was also charged with the mutilation of a corpse, fraud and theft. After the investigations had continued for another three days he was charged with the murders of Hester Greyly and Patrick Dewick. The lawyer for Seraphina Watson – Seraphina di Fattori as she was be known from then onwards – put forward a charge for the rape and abduction of his client.

In all the newspaper articles, and on television, Seraphina di Fattori made a perfect witness. Vulnerable, articulate – and pregnant. With all the power of her family's name and the help of a respected team of lawyers, she was assured that she would never spend a day in prison. After all, she had done nothing. Had she?

And Eddie Hillstone stayed quiet. He never spoke out against the charges, or offered details or excuses. And he never turned against Seraphina. Instead he allowed her to become the Joan of Arc of all martyrs, watching from his cell, his computer banned, his medication monitored. A social psychopath was the verdict of the psychiatrist. A man without empathy or feelings, but inherently responsible for his crimes; a man knowing the difference between right and wrong. A man capable of planning, and waiting.

All Eddie Hillstone wanted to know was if the Titian had been found. And where, and who now had it. It seemed that, in the end, his murders were secondary to his greed. But to Nino he seemed *too* composed, oddly admiring of the man who had caught him, even asking Nino to visit him in prison.

Curious, Nino agreed, watching as Edward Hillstone entered, flanked by two guards. After they seated the prisoner, the men stepped back and stood by the wall as Nino faced Hillstone across the table.

'How are you?'

Surprised, Nino smiled. 'I think I was supposed to ask you that . . . You wanted to see me?'

'Yes,' he said, leaning slightly forward. 'What are they saying about me in the papers? The bastards won't let me see any, or watch television, and the internet's off limits.' He smiled – the first time Nino had ever seen him smile. The effect was unexpectedly warming. 'What are they saying about me?'

'That you're a murderer.'

'Who's got the most publicity?'

'What?'

'Me, or Angelico Vespucci?'

'I think you win by a short head.'

471

Hillstone leaned back in his seat, nodding. 'Liar . . . I didn't finish the last murder. I failed.'

'You killed four people. Equalled his score.'

'I killed two *men*, and two women. Vespucci killed four women.' He shook his head, as though they were talking about the football.

'What did you do with the skins?'

'I sent half of one to Jobo Kido in Tokyo,' Hillstone admitted, then shook his head. 'The rest . . . it may be better you don't know. I'll tell you something, though – I underestimated you, that was my mistake. I knew I could fool the art world and the police. If I kept the murders in different countries, I knew it would keep them all guessing. Knew I'd have time to finish before they'd even worked out what the hell I was doing . . . But I never made allowances for you.' He put the tips of his fingers together, pressing them until the skin was white. 'They won't tell me who got the Titian.'

'The police,' Nino replied. 'They got it from your old house when I let them in.' He paused. 'It's been impounded as evidence.

'Pity,' Hillstone said simply, sighing.

'Why didn't you give her up?'

'Who?'

'Seraphina. Why didn't you turn on her?' Nino asked. 'She's turned on you, letting you take all the blame, saying you forced her into it. Pretending to be a victim. Even saying you raped her.' Hillstone was listening but said nothing,

472

forcing Nino to continue. 'Why let her off? She's guilty – you know that and so do I.'

'Do I?'

'Yes, you do,' Nino replied, frowning. 'You shouldn't take all the punishment.'

'I'm the guilty party.'

'You're both guilty.'

Hillstone's expression shifted momentarily. From resignation to – fleetingly – amusement.

'Seraphina's as responsible as you are,' Nino continued. 'She worked with you, she organised things for you. She found Rachel Pitt. She picked out victims for you ... How *can* you let her get away with it?'

'You think she will?' Hillstone asked. 'You think she's *that* smart?' Rising to his feet, he shuffled over the guards. 'I'm done,' he said simply.

And he didn't look back.

78

It was 17 January, cold with a wind chill, when Nino called in at The Hamlet Theatre, asking for Rachel Pitt. After a few moments she came out to see him. She was smiling, her hair tied up haphazardly, her nails painted dark red.

'Hi.'

'Hi you,' he said, returning the smile. 'How goes it?'

'Good.'

She had thanked him repeatedly, until he was embarrassed and the word was worn thin. A couple of times they had even talked about that last night, Rachel remembering the wig she'd borrowed. The bad wig which had saved her life.

'But it wasn't really the wig, was it? It was you.'

It took her ten days to stop flinching when people passed her on the street, eleven days to stop checking behind the bathroom door, and it would probably take more than a lifetime to stop remembering.

'I finished with Michael,' she said, smiling and pulling a face. 'Ouch.'

'How does it feel?'

'My heart? Shattered. My self-esteem? Triumphant.'

Smiling, Nino consoled her. 'Hearts recover.'

'Do they?'

A moment shimmered between them. It caught them out, unexpected but not unwelcome.

'Perhaps we could go for a drink sometime?' Nino asked tentatively.

'Perhaps we could. But you know what they say, don't you?'

'No, what *do* they say?'

'Never date a hero.'

'That's fine,' Nino replied, smiling. 'It was getting to be a burden anyway.'

In New York, Triumph Jones heard the news of the Titian being impounded as evidence. It would be held by the Art Squad of the British police until the trial of Edward Hillstone was over. After that, other arrangements would be made. Triumph Jones wasn't interested, because he never wanted to see the Titian again. It had cost four lives, ruined a dozen others, and his devotion to the noble art of painting seemed suddenly absurd. That any picture could be valued above a life was madness. Even a Titian. Even *that* Titian.

Since the murders Triumph Jones had aged. To everyone's surprise, the mugging had not been connected to Edward Hillstone. If anything, it was considered that he'd brought it on himself by publishing the Reward announcement. Whatever had possessed him? Triumph thought. How deluded had he been to think he could retrieve the Titian by inviting every criminal to try and cheat him? But he had been desperate. And men who are desperate and floundering will try anything to lessen their guilt.

He had been responsible for four deaths. And he would die knowing it.

The alarm went off again at two thirty, and again Jobo Kido rose from his bed and drove to his offices to turn it off. When he had done so, he paused by his desk, looking at the computer and thinking of the exchanges he had had with a murderer.

The thought horrified and thrilled him at the same time. To think that he, Jobo Kido, had been involved with a serial killer. A man who had threatened him, come to his door, sent the vile package through the mail. Terrifying and unbelievable as it was, it *had* happened. And it had changed the Japanese dealer.

He would never admit to anyone, least of all his wife and son, that he was exhilarated to have been – indirectly – a part of Edward Hillstone's crimes. It thrilled him to think of it; made him believe that he had a better insight into his exhibits. That when he visited his private collection and looked at Jeffrey Dahmer or Son of Sam he was just a little closer to understanding them. Not *too* close, but close enough to satisfy his ego, while keeping him safe.

Of course the unfilled gap on the wall annoyed him. By rights the Titian should have been hanging there. But the

Titian was never going to be his now, so instead Jobo had hung another exhibit. It was crudely framed, because he hadn't wanted to risk asking a professional to undertake the job, but it was adequate. A frame was a frame, after all. It was what was *inside* that mattered.

Jobo paused, thinking of his new exhibit. A piece of skin. Part of the hide of a murdered woman. The piece which had been sent through the mail weeks earlier . . . At first he had intended to destroy it, but he couldn't bring himself to commit such a violation. So he displayed it instead. Without a label, obviously. No point bringing the police down on his head. It was Jobo's *private* pleasure. A reminder of his dabbling with a lunatic. A concrete image of an insane mind.

Or, to put it another way, a gift from Edward Hillstone to an admirer.

Having lost any chance of getting hold of the infamous Titian, Farina Ahmadi feigned total indifference. It was a weak portrait anyway, she said imperiously – in appalling condition. Not one of Titian's finest works. And besides, who wanted the image of a serial killer hanging on their gallery wall?

The whole matter had been fucking disgusting, she told everyone. It had made her despair of the art world and the people who populated it. And besides, everyone knew that the Alim Collection would never dream of exhibiting such a painting.

She told her husband the same.

He told her she was a fool and that he was seeing another woman.

The following day Farina filed for a massive divorce settlement.

And a week later Sally Egan's copy of the Vespucci portrait was sold at auction for an undisclosed sum.

Triumphant, Farina made a bid for the Alim Collection.

The fight is ongoing.

The only person who really triumphed was Johnny Ravenscourt. His profile escalated. He was – as he had hoped – featured on television, radio and the press as the leading expert on Vespucci. For once, his picaresque background was an advantage as he regaled the world with stories of Angelico Vespucci, The Skin Hunter. He then exhibited the portrait of Claudia Moroni and her brother, making a gargantuan profit out of their incestuous relationship. And her tragic death.

However, it was the discovery of the victims' skins which propelled Johnny Ravenscourt into global notoriety. Lacking any morals, he exhibited them wherever they were requested – for a formidable fee. His fortune, which had always been impressive, swelled with the blood money of Vespucci's victims, the macabre, beribboned skins displayed like Bulgari jewels.

People in numerous countries around the globe came to gawp at the flayed hides and read the stories of the murdered women. Larissa Vespucci, Claudia Moroni, Lena Arranti and the Contessa di Fattori became household names, their lives and deaths the subject of numerous programmes and articles. A film was mooted as Hollywood took up their cause, tying together the connection between The Skin Hunter and Edward Hillstone. And in the middle of all this interest, money and fame, was the burly figure of Johnny Ravenscourt.

He flourished. Lived as sumptuously as Vespucci had once done. Had no end of boys at his bidding, and the grudging respect of the art world. His smuggling days were no longer regarded as a disgrace, but as cavalier roistering, and the police watched with disbelief as their one-time irritant shimmered in the glow of public opprobrium.

And then, one morning, Johnny Ravenscourt was found dead. Apparently he had suffered a massive heart attack. But oddly, at his mansion on Eaton Square, the phone line had been cut and the burglar alarm turned off. Despite his fabulous wealth and possessions, nothing had been stolen. Silver, paintings, antiquarian books, jewellery, wine and cigars were untouched. A solid silver chess set, a Bechstein piano, a Russian malachite table and a Louis XIV commode were ignored. The Rolls-Royce, Mercedes and Bentley cars remained in the garage. There was no damage.

The day before Ravenscourt's death the skins of Vespucci's victims had been put on a boat to be shipped over to the USA for a controversial exhibition in New York. Later it was discovered that at the very time Johnny Ravenscourt had died the ship had been hit by freak weather and had sunk in the middle of the Atlantic. The crew was saved.

The hides of The Skin Hunter's victims were lost forever.

79

Edward Hillstone, aged 34, of Spitalfields, London, committed suicide in Wormwood Scrubs Prison on 14 January. He had been charged on numerous counts and had pleaded not guilty to all of them, forcing a jury trial. Although Hillstone had not been considered a suicide threat, he had hanged himself in the early hours.

He left no suicide note, just a brief letter to Nino Bergstrom.

It read:

I couldn't leave without giving you the answer you most wanted. I was The Skin Hunter, and you asked where I hid the skins. You know they weren't in the Spitalfields house, and I wouldn't have put them with the Titian. So I leave you with a puzzle, Mr Bergstrom.

You're clever, you beat me. Now solve this.

The skins are where they should be.

Regards,

Edward Hillstone

'The skins are where they should be . . .' Puzzled, Nino read the letter to Gaspare for the third time, both of them weighing the words.

'Where should skins be?'

Gaspare shrugged. 'Does he mean it literally? Like the skin on an animal?'

'Or on fruit?'

'Or on milk?'

Nino raised his eyebrows. '*On milk?*'

'So you make some better suggestions,' Gaspare retorted. 'I'm doing my best.'

'"*They are where they should be.*"' Nino repeated the words. 'A skin should be on a body. But the skins were taken off the women's bodies. So does he mean that they're in a grave, perhaps?'

Gaspare shook his head. 'Nah, that would be too difficult. There are millions of graves – where would you look? Italy? Japan? London?'

'Skins . . . where should they be?'

'Hillstone wants you to find them,' Gaspare said. 'That much is obvious. So the clue must be solvable.'

They sat in silence, both preoccupied with their own thoughts. At times Nino would think he had the solution, then slump back in his seat, disappointed. A wind blew up outside, making peevish darts at the gallery windows, a car alarm going off just after six. Another hour droned on, then, suddenly, he rose to his feet.

Surprised, Gaspare looked at him. 'What is it?'

'I think I've solved it,' Nino replied, grabbing his coat and running out.

On the street, he phoned the police in charge of the Hillstone case and told them what he suspected. He knew they would listen to him and follow it up, contacting their colleagues abroad. All he had to do now was to wait. Just wait, for an hour. Give them enough time ... Impatiently Nino paced, checking his watch every other minute, Gaspare watching from the gallery window above. The day lengthened, wind tossing up rubbish, a splatter of cold rain making gloomy haloes round the street lamps.

The minutes sulked along until, finally, the time had come. His hand shaking, Nino took out his mobile. Looking up a number he hadn't used for a while, he phoned Venice, a maid answering at the di Fattori residence. After asking to speak to Seraphina, he waited for her to come on the phone.

'If you want to tell me that Eddie's dead, I know already.'

'You've got them, haven't you?'

'What are you talking about?' she asked, her tone wary. 'Got what?'

'The skins. The skins of the women Edward Hillstone killed. He told me—'

'Liar!'

'You said there was no evidence. That no one had seen or heard anything. That you could explain everything by saying Hillstone had you in fear of your life. But you can't explain everything.' Nino paused, hearing a commotion on the other end of the line, the sound of footsteps and raised voices. 'Hear that? That's the police, Seraphina. They've come for the skins. And they'll find them, won't they? Like Hillstone said, they're *where they're supposed to be*. And that's with you.'

He could hear her drop the phone and took in a breath. Like all killers, Seraphina had kept trophies. She hadn't been able to resist. And it would be the skins that would damn her.

A normal woman – or a woman under threat, as Seraphina di Fattori claimed to be – would never keep such mementos.

Edward Hillstone was dead. But he had got his revenge.

Venice, 1556

I came to Venice from Rome. One of seven children and damaged at that. It was the year I was ten and was put upon a boat for Venice. They told us the Republic was like Heaven, that children cried to be admitted and food was plentiful. They said, I remember, that no one minded a twisted foot. That I would be welcomed, treasured for my difference.

I was not treasured. The boat was thrown about in the sea and made me sick, I leaned over the side and vomited, my face looking back at me from water as dark as a burnt candle stub. I am afraid of water, always have been. They took us to the quayside, pulled us up, pummelled and pinched, and people came to view us in the heat. I was still sick from the boat and stood like a goat, whining and trying to hide my deformity.

He was passing on the street and turned to the bargaining voices of the people, of those wanting little servants to pet and bully. I would not be chosen; I was not pretty, nor quick. I feared my house would be a poor place, my owner quick in temper. And I could not

485

even speak when I was taken by the arm, and stumbled clumsily.

Come with me, he said. Come on, come with me.

He was tall, with a beard and a coaxing voice, and he walked at my pace without making me a laughing stock for limping. When we came to his home he unlocked a garden gate and guided me in. Lemons were hanging heavy from trees, oranges ripe in terracotta pots, a cat sunning itself by an open door.

Come with me, he said again.

I believed it then. That Venice was a Heaven children cried to enter. Mute, I looked around me, at paintings high as trees, at faces real as those I had just passed. On easels and against walls, canvases reeking of oil paint and linseed threw up scenarios of living things that were not living. He had depicted dogs, fur that was trembling to be stroked, water that would trick a river's flow, and women so beautiful they prompted tears.

From that day on I was the master's servant. I grew with Titian, had no talent to be honed, but served him as a child his father. Without a family, he loaned his to me. And so I grew to love him as I grew in age. I kept his studio, made his food, washed his clothes. Although there were many other servants, I let no one close. For Titian had rescued me. Had saved my life. No harm, I swore, would ever come to him. No injury. My life, no less, was forfeit should it serve him.

And so I watched. And so I learned. People do not see cripples. Or if they do, they think them idiots. I was no fool. And so I saw my master triumph. The Doge was his friend, kings admired him, Venice held him up as a cross before battle. And yet for all of this, he let the writer in.

486

It was a solemn day when Aretino came to Venice. Puffed up with reputation, eager to triumph, seeing in Titian a brilliance and a fullness of heart to massage dry. But Titian grew to love this ravenous dog. He loved the beast. He made excuses, feted him, advanced this corpulent bag of pus until his name did rival Titian's own.

And he never once suspected what I knew.

It was last Thursday that Aretino came to Titian's home and begged for entrance. As I well knew, my master would eventually relent. And so he did, letting this murderer, this traitor, this mountebank, enter his life again. And to what end? To what dank scandal? What unrivalled disgrace?

I made them supper, watched them eat. The pig wheezed and snuffled about his food, laughed, told stories, sought to beguile again. And Titian, watching like a chicken does a fox, was mesmerised by him. They ate. I served them. They drank. I poured the wine. Outside the sea waited for its next drowning.

And I waited too.

Aretino was talking of some dancer, some new whore, and paused, his sharp eyes startled. His hands, those bloodied hands, clutched for his throat as though some bone was stuck there. Titian turned, reached for his friend, but Aretino was already falling, dead before he found the floor. He never saw me tamper with his food. He never saw me pass a plate to him unlike my master's own.

A single heartbeat took him from this world. May demons take him to the next.

The news went round Venice that Pietro Aretino was dead. Choked on his food. Died for his gluttony. A hundred victims revelled at his

487

passing. Freed from his vicious pen, loosened from his lies and calumnies, out of reach of his thefts and plots and killings, the city is at peace. The Dog of Venice joins the Whore, and the Merchant also. The triumvirate of evil is now done.

And so he ends. And so the story ends.

Outside the sea is still, the moon red as a watermelon in the heated night. Fogs that have plagued us for months melt in the warm air while torches flicker on the canals and on the tide. Venice sleeps on, the sweet sea curled like a blanket around her. The church bells sleep also, as do the water rats. Behind locked doors, couples turn to each other and cling; somewhere a mother holds a child against her heart; and as the hours turn through the beating of the night, a clock chimes in the breaking dawn. The baker has now woken, and the priest rises and bows his head towards the cross.

And in his studio, Titian works on.

Epilogue

The Titian portrait of Angelico Vespucci was held by the UK police Art Squad at a secret location. It was kept with a number of another valuable retrieved works of art at a destination known to only a half-dozen select members of the police force. Hidden in a high-security building in the countryside, heavily alarmed and patrolled by dogs, impenetrable and secluded. Even the nearby villages had no idea of its whereabouts, or its purpose. Yet, on 4 November – on the anniversary of Larissa Vespucci's murder, the Titian's portrait of *The Skin Hunter* disappeared.

No one has ever recovered the painting of Angelico Vespucci.

But in Venice the rumour still holds.

When the portrait emerges, so will the man.

And they wait.

Bibliography

Titian – Ian G. Kennedy (Taschen)
Titian – Cecilia Gibellini (ed) (Rizzoli Art Classics)
Venetian Painting – John Steer (Thames and Hudson)
The World of Titian – Jay Williams (Time Life)

Bellini, Giorgione, Titian and the Renaissance of Venetian
   Painting. Exhibition at the National Gallery of Art,
   Washington

Read on for an exclusive extract from Alex Connor's internationally bestselling conspiracy thriller:

THE REMBRANDT SECRET

The first victim was forced to swallow stones.

The second was whipped to death.

The third was stabbed in the heart.

Inspired by real events, *The Rembrandt Secret* combines mystery and murder with the hidden truth behind one of the world's most famous artists.

1

His body was bent over, his head submerged in the confines of the basin, his knees buckled, trousers pulled down. Blood seeped from between his buttocks, intensive bruising around the top of his fleshy thighs. On the floor beside his puffy right knee lay the toilet brush, its handle bloodied. A series of small nicks covered his lower back and the skin of his scrotum was mottled with burn marks. Although his head was submerged, the back of his neck showed the imprint of fingers; his wrists bound together with the same gilt wire often used to hang paintings.

It had taken him a long time to die. As he fought, he had struggled, his wrists jerking against the wire as it cut deep into his flesh, down to the wrist bone in places. Repeatedly his head had been dipped into the filled basin, then pulled out, then submerged again. When the water finally began to enter his lungs, his body had reacted, foam spittle gathering at the corners of his mouth. Much later it would rise from the corpse to make a white death froth. Against the push of water, his eyes had widened, the pupils turning from clear orbs to opal discs as he stared blindly at the bottom of the basin.

The killer had made sure that the death of Stefan van der Helde would horrify not only the people who found him, but also his business associates and his cohorts. In sodomising him they had exposed Van der Helde's hidden homosexuality, humiliating him and bringing down one of the top players in the art world. But there was more to it than that: a reason why no one would ever forget the death of Stefan van der Helde. When his body underwent post-mortem examination the pathologist found stones in his stomach. Apparently, over a period of hours, he had been forced to swallow pebbles, one after the other, each one larger than the last, until they threatened to choke him. Even when his oesophagus reacted and went into spasm, he was forced to keep swallowing, his gullet bruised and torn in places by the stones.

They found twenty pebbles in Stefan van der Helde's stomach. They found the water that drowned him – and the twenty stones. The pathologist didn't know what it meant. Neither did the police. No one knew the meaning of the stones. By the time they did, the world would have plunged into recession; the auction houses losing fortunes on collapsing sales; and dealers forced into ruin as bad debts were called in and old favours demanded repayment. As the year ground into an unsteady and claustrophobic spring, the global art world was in a depression no one had foreseen or prepared for.

And from behind elegant façades and glossy reputations crept the venal underbelly of the art world. In a matter of months the financial collapse of the market was underscored by a moral malignancy that left no one unscathed. And four people dead.

It was, some said, a culling.

2

London.
The present day.

Tucked tight in the central kernel of the capital, in amongst the crochet of streets off the thoroughfare of Piccadilly, lies Albemarle Street. Every building is dissimilar. In shop fronts gilded with fashion logos, porters in funereal suits open doors for tourists and the wives of Russian oligarchs alike. Other shops have been there for over a hundred years; a dusty sprinkling of snobbery courts the passer-by with windows cradling bespoke shoes or hand-rolled cigars. And dotted among the By Royal Appointment signs and robin's-egg blue Tiffany boxes nestles the Zeigler Gallery.

It had first opened in 1845, but attracted no notice. After that, it had changed hands several times, closing during the Second World War. Left abandoned, its walls denuded of paintings, the building had sat out the fighting alone, the flat above remaining empty. The rates had been too high, the landlord too greedy. At the height of the war there had been a suspicious fire in the gallery. Some said it had been caused by a tramp, sneaking in and falling asleep with a lighted cigarette in his hand. But neither the tramp nor his cigarette – not even a stub – had ever been found. Yet soon afterwards there *had* been a real fatality: a soldier killed whilst on leave, his body left in the back of the gallery, hidden among the empty packing crates. The soldier – who had worn no dog tag and carried no identification – had never been named and the murder was never solved. But the death of the unknown soldier had cast a pall over the building and the gallery had acquired a ghost. Or so rumour had gone.

Then, in 1947, the gallery had been reopened by a Polish man called Korsawaki. He had come from Warsaw – where he had been forced to leave behind a fortune and a family – to try to make his name in London. In his home city he had been a dealer of some note, but in the austere years directly after the war he made little headway in London. Forced into selling cheap prints, he was soon grubbing around for any means to pay the rent and, by the time 1949 came around, Korsawaki had left. A couple of other dealers followed, with little success, and the gallery gained a reputation for being jinxed. Left deserted as its neighbours flourished, it had one brief spell in the sunshine as a café. But soon the clink of dishes and the pulse of conversation ended, and the doors were closed and bolted once again.

And so they stayed, until one bitingly cold morning in 1963 when a young man had paused on Albemarle Street and seen the FOR SALE sign in the window. Curious, Owen Zeigler had leaned forward, peering in, but all he had been able to make out was a deserted interior with a staircase on one side and a skylight at the end of the room. He tried the door handle, but it was locked. Then he had stepped back – almost into the path of an oncoming car – to stare upwards at the flat above. The windows had given nothing away, but Owen had felt drawn to the place for some reason that escaped him. Intrigued, he tried the door again without success, and then noted the name and address of the estate agent.

That afternoon he had visited Messrs Lyton and Goldthorne, asking for details on the gallery. They – spotting a potential customer for a property which had proved virtually impossible to shift – encouraged his interest. In fact, Mr Lyton had taken Owen to the gallery within the hour, pushing open the door and waving his prospective customer in. A little probing told Mr Lyton that Owen had family backing and that his father was a dealer in the East End.

What Owen *didn't* tell the agent was that Neville Zeigler dealt not in fine art, but in a variety of 'collectables'; a Jew who had come to London before the war; a Jew who had learnt the business the hard way; a Jew clever enough to develop an eye for the marketable and, later, the valuable. And over the years Neville had instilled in his only child a terrifying ambition. He would take Owen to Bond Street and Cork Street and show him the galleries and tell his son

– no, *insist* – that one day there would be a Zeigler Gallery within this cluster of culture and money. With a ferocity which might have daunted a lesser child, Owen learned to develop his natural appreciation into a skill. Neville's long hours of labour in the East End afforded Owen a university place – and the son repaid the father well.

When Owen Zeigler finally entered the bull ring of the art world, he was clever, adept and confident. He could pass as an upper class scholar, a natural inheritor of a cultural career. With his innate ability and his further education, his progress was seamless. But what people didn't know was the other side to Owen Zeigler, the side inherited from his Jewish father, along with Neville's shrewd, invaluable business acumen.

Encouraged by the widowed Neville, who knew the fortunes to be made in the art world, Owen was told to keep quiet about his background and 'get climbing'.

'You've a foot in both camps,' Neville told him. 'You know about culture, and you're street-savvy too. Use it. And remember – there's plenty of room at the top.'

Of course Mr Lyton didn't know any of this, but was impressed when Owen returned a day later having uncovered the gallery's erratic history – which he used as a bargaining tool. In short, by the time two weeks were up, Owen Zeigler had become the new gallery owner. And by the time three weeks were up, the interior had been painted, the flat above was furnished, and there was a new sign outside: after an uncomplicated delivery, the Zeigler Gallery had been born.

In that same bitter winter, Owen held an opening to which his neighbours came to gawp and to criticise, a few to predict disaster. But the dealers from Dover Street and Bond Street realised within minutes of walking through the door that they had a serious new rival. The market at that time was swamped with French art, and the Impressionists, the gauzy country scenes, were becoming commonplace – almost boring – by their very repetition. So Owen had chosen another speciality – Dutch art. Not the thundering names of Rembrandt or Vermeer, in which he could not afford to trade, but the smaller followers, and the still-life painters.

There had been only twenty paintings exhibited on that cold winter day in 1963, but by the end of the month eighteen had been sold. Owen Zeigler's career had been launched. Not perhaps as a grand, ocean-gobbling liner, but as a swift, clever little lighter that could ride the waves of the art market and survive . . .

And all this, Owen Zeigler's son, Marshall, remembered, looking at his father in disbelief.

'Where did all the money *go*?' Marshall asked

Owen put his head in his hands. Now in his seventies, he looked no more than sixty-five. Years of careful grooming, and long walks in London parks, had kept him lean, and his hair, although grey, was thick and well cut. In front of him was the desk he had used since the first day he had begun business at the gallery. A desk on which many a cheque had been written, and across which had passed many a handshake. Above it hung a Dutch painting by Jan Steen. Valuable, as were all the pictures in the gallery, the insurance rising regularly over the years to accommodate and protect Owen's success. The burglar alarms, red lights flickering outside like out-of-season Christmas bunting, all connected to nearby police stations.

Still staring at his father, Marshall thought back to his childhood. His first ten years had been spent in the flat above the gallery, but as his father had prospered the family had been moved out of London to a country house, Thurstons. During the week, Owen had lived in the flat, spending his weekends in the Georgian stereotype of up-market success. But when Marshall's mother had died, Owen had returned frequently to Albemarle Street, leaving his son in the care of a nanny, and later the rigid arms of public school.

'Where did the money go?' Marshall repeated.

His father made a movement, almost a shrug, but the action dropped off, half-made. 'I have to do something . . . I have to.'

For the first time Marshall noticed that his father's hair was thinning slightly at the crown. Even his expert barber hadn't managed to disguise it, he thought, knowing that it would embarrass his father if he knew. Then he noticed the raised veins in his hands, the liver spots puddling the tanned skin. His father was getting old, Marshall realised, unaccountably moved. All Owen's little vanities were becoming noticeable, obvious ... Marshall glanced away, thinking of the telephone call which had brought him back to London, his father asking him to return from his work in Holland.

'I need to talk to you,' Owen had said, his voice shivering on the edge of panic. 'If you could just come home.'

He had done so at once, because his father had never been possessive or demanding. Marshall might have longed for more closeness as a child, might have grieved alone for the loss of his mother, but in his teens he realised that his father's affection had never been withheld. Just neutralised. Having lost his wife so unexpectedly in a plane crash, Owen had spent the next decade in waiting, almost as though some other plane – real or ephemeral – might bring her back. As though, if he refused to accept her passing, she would one day arrive at some spiritual terminal. Where he would be waiting by the gate to bring her home.

But she never did come back, and Marshall watched as his father finally faced the truth, ten years after her death. He watched the grief, sitting with his father in the country house, staring into country fires or country views. He listened to old memories that had never been his, memories from before his birth, and realised that inside some men there is one space for one woman. And if that woman is lost, the space is never filled again. With a father so bereft, Marshall absorbed his own grief alone, and by the time Owen invited him to talk about his mother's death, she had been parted with. As beautiful, but out of time, as his grandfather's old French paintings.

His thoughts coming back to the present, Marshall prompted, 'You said the money had gone.'

'All gone,' Owen said, nodding.

'How?'

'Debts.'

'Debts?' Marshall was shaken. His father had never intimated that money was tight. 'You never said you were struggling. The last show was a success—'

Still seated, Owen turned his face upwards to his son, fixing his gaze. 'I've been cheated.'

I've been cheated . . . The words seemed to swell in the gallery, skim along the picture rails, slide across the red silk on the walls, and then slither up the staircase into the dark beyond. A creeping sense of unease swept over Marshall, the same feeling he had had as a boy sleeping in the flat above, remembering the old story of the building. And listening for the ghost of the unknown soldier. The young man who came out at night, who walked around the gallery below, then crept up the stairs in the darkness.

'Who cheated you?'

'I should never have believed him.'

'Who? Who are you talking about?'

'Manners.'

Manners. The name fell like a corn thresher, slicing the air between the two men. Tobar Manners, one of his father's

503

oldest friends and a fellow dealer. Tobar Manners, with his small pink hands and dandelion hair. Tobar Manners, quick, clever, mercurial, always so charming to his father, but another man to Marshall. Indeed, it was Manners who had told Marshall about the murdered soldier, taking delight in frightening a child with stories of a ghost and then laughing, insisting he was only teasing, but knowing that he had planted a poisonous thought. Many disturbed nights of his childhood Marshall put down to Tobar Manners. Many times, waking at a sudden noise, he blamed his unease on his father's changeling friend.

'What did he do?'

Owen shook his head.

'Dad, what did he do?'

'I've been in debt for some time,' Owen said slowly, the words crisp, as though he could keep back his panic by the control of his delivery. 'Business has been bad. The collectors aren't investing, and the auctions have been hit too. A couple of galleries have even closed down.' He paused, grabbed at a breath. 'In the last few years, I overbought. I came across some good paintings and thought I'd have no problem selling them. But then there was the credit crunch. Not many people buy at these times . . .'

'But the big collectors?'

'Are holding back.'

'All of them?'

'No, but not enough are investing to stop me going under.'

'Christ!' Marshall sat down next to his father. 'What about the house?'

'Remortgaged.'

'The paintings,' Marshall said, feeling some panic himself, 'sell what you've got. You might make a loss, but you'd raise some money.'

'Not enough,' Owen replied quietly, his hands clenched together. 'I didn't want to tell you how bad it was. I thought I could get out of it, I thought if . . . I sold the Rembrandt . . .'

Slowly, Marshall lifted his head, staring at his father. The painting had been in the family since 1964, when Owen had bought it in Germany. At first he had believed it to be painted by Ferdinand Bol, a pupil of Rembrandt's, but after numerous tests and some intensive research, it had proved to be genuine. It had been the first spectacular triumph of his father's career. A seal on his talent as a dealer. Marshall could remember hearing the story repeated by his father, and by Owen's mentor, Samuel Hemmings. *Watch your back now*, Samuel had warned him, *now you have enemies*.

'Did you sell the Rembrandt?'

'I took it to Tobar Manners . . .'

'And?'

'He said it wasn't genuine. That it was by Ferdinand Bol, as we had originally thought—'

'But it *was* genuine!'

'It's all in the attribution, Marshall,' his father said shortly. 'There's no cut and dried proof—'

'Samuel Hemmings backed your opinion,' Marshall interrupted. 'Surely his name carries enough weight?'

'Samuel is a controversial historian, you know that. What he says is accepted by some people and vigorously denied by others.'

'Usually when there's money involved.'

At once, Owen flared up, his unruffled urbanity overshadowed by hostility.

'I know what you think of the business, Marshall! There's nothing you can say about it I haven't heard before. You made your choice to have nothing to do with the gallery or the art world. Fine, that was your choice, but it's my life, and despise it all you will, it's my passion.'

The argument was worn thin between them. Owen might be committed to art dealing, but Marshall wasn't blinded to the realities of the trade. And trade it was. A hard, tight little trade where a pocket of honest men traded with a legion of those without scruples. Dealers who had inherited galleries, working cheek by jowl with titans who had bought their way in. Deals brokered between old-school traders and the hustlers who drafted in dummy bidders to up the price on a gallery's painting at auction. Not that all of the auction houses were blameless; the process of *burning* was well known. If a painting didn't reach its reserve, it was supposedly sold, but instead it was *burned*, put away for years until the market had either forgotten about it, or presumed it had been put back on sale again by a private buyer. That way no famous name was seen to lose its kudos and market value. Because market value was imperative. For every Cézanne that scorched through its reserve and set a new benchmark, a dozen other Cézannes in museums and private collections rose in value. Over the sixties, seventies and eighties the art market had inflated the value of Van Gogh to such an extent that one purchaser had to put his painting in store for twelve years for insurance reasons. Art was being priced out of the galleries and off the walls into the steel tombs of bank vaults.

Sighing, Marshall realised that this was no time to resurrect the old argument and moderated his tone. 'So Manners said it wasn't a Rembrandt?'

Owen nodded. 'He said it was by one of Rembrandt's pupils. Besides, there was no signature on the painting—'

'There's no signature on many of Rembrandt's paintings!' Marshall snapped. 'That never stopped them being attributed to him. And God knows there are enough paintings *with* his signature that people doubt are genuine.'

'Tobar was sure mine wasn't genuine. When I asked him to buy it, he was told that it was by Ferdinand Bol. He had it looked at twice, thoroughly investigated.'

'By whom?'

'By specialists!' Owen barked, hurrying on. 'Tobar was so sorry. He said that he would give me as much as he could, but nothing like I would have got for a genuine Rembrandt … Jesus, I *trusted him*. I've known Tobar for years, I had no reason *not* to trust him.'

Unbidden, images curled in front of Marshall. Images of Christmases, of private views, of visits to the gallery – and in every image was Tobar Manners. Always there. Sometimes alone, sometimes in a group. Manners and Samuel Hemmings, and other friends of his father's, talking, laughing, swapping stories about dealers or customers. Gossip flirting from one glass to another; snippets of information traded over caviar and canapés; cankers of venom floating into greedy ears.

'What did he do?' Marshall asked finally.

'He bought the painting off me.'

'And?'

'I just heard,' Owen said blindly, 'I just heard about it. The sale in New York. Someone showed me the catalogue, and there is – was – my painting. The same one Tobar had bought from me as a Ferdinand Bol. Only it wasn't. It was in the catalogue as a Rembrandt. *It had been sold as a Rembrandt.*' His words were staccato, gunning his story out. 'Tobar Manners gave me a fraction of its value! He cheated me!'

Shaken, Marshall stared at his father. 'Have you talked to him? Confronted him—'

'He said it wasn't his fault!' Owen replied, his voice raised, anger making bright spots of colour on his cheeks. 'He said he had sold it on to someone as a Ferdinand Bol, and they had cheated *him!*'

'You don't believe him, do you?'

'Of *course* I don't believe him!' Owen hurled back, getting to his feet and walking over to the window.

To his amazement, Marshall could see that his father was shaking, his elegant body trembling, his hands clenching and unclenching obsessively.

'It made a fortune at the auction,' Owen went on. 'Broke all records for an early Rembrandt. *My painting made a fortune.* A fortune I could have saved the business with. A fortune that was *mine*! Jesus Christ,' he said desperately, 'I'm finished.'

Sensing his father's despair, Marshall tried to calm him. 'Look, you can sell your stock – everything you've got. There are thousands of pounds hanging on these walls, you can raise money that way.'

'Not enough.'

'It must be!' his son replied, feeling a sinking dread. 'Call your collectors, auction what you've got. Ring your contacts. There must be some way to get money—'

'It won't be *enough*!' Owen snapped, control gone. 'I have debts you don't know about. Debts to many people, some of whom are pressuring me now. I can't afford the upkeep on this gallery. I kept thinking that things would improve, and then times got tough for everyone. People still bought, but much less over these last months. I can't shift the stock, Marshall, I can't raise money. There was only the Rembrandt left. It was always in the background, like a safety net. I knew that would raise enough to pay off the debts and get me straight again. But Manners . . .'

He stopped talking, his anger drying up, and an eerie

calm came over him before he spoke again. 'He won't admit it, but he *did* cheat me. He lied to me, knowing I was in trouble, he lied to me ... How many times did that man come to my home? How many times over the years did I help him out? Lend him money to tide him over when he was struggling?'

Owen was no longer talking to his son, just staring at the desk in front of him. 'I'd only been here for a few weeks when Tobar Manners introduced himself. Your mother never really took to him, but I always thought that that was because he could be spiteful about people, and she never liked gossips. And when your mother died, Tobar was very kind ...'

He was a leech, Marshall wanted to say. My mother saw it, and so did I, even as a child. And he wasn't smart, nothing like as talented as you. So how did he manage to dupe you? You could run rings around him once. You laughed at him with Samuel Hemmings. Not unkindly, more indulgent. But you let him in, too often and too close. God, why were you so stupid with the most treacherous of men?

'I've got a bit of money put away. You can have that.'

'No, I can't take anything from you,' Owen replied, then smiled sweetly, as though the offer momentarily obliterated the seriousness of his situation.

'What will you do?'

'Manage, somehow.' He was trying to fight panic, to press a lid on the scalding tide of his own despair. 'I'll talk to the

510

accountant and the bank again.'

'Will they help?'

'I don't know. Maybe . . .' he replied, back in control again. The father, not the panicking man. 'Don't worry about me. I was just so shocked by what's happened. I shouldn't really have troubled you, got you worried. I'll find a way round this.'

Unconvinced, Marshall looked around the gallery. 'You need a change. You should get out of here for a while, Dad. It'll help you think. I could come and stay with you at Thurstons for a bit. I don't need to get back to Amsterdam straight away.'

'It might . . .'

'It would do you good.' Marshall pressed him. 'We can talk if you want, or you can just relax.'

Owen nodded but averted his gaze. He was embarrassed to be seen as a failure by his son. Embarrassed and ashamed that he had panicked, crying like a child. After all, what could Marshall do? He hadn't the money to rescue him, and couldn't have guessed at the full plunging extent of the debts . . . He had never been a gambler, Owen thought, he should have known. Should never had fallen into the trap of over-buying, then relying on a friend to get him out of trouble – even a friend he had helped, a person who owed him a debt of honour. The shock of his imminent ruin fizzed inside Owen's head, along with the queasy realisation of his own stupidity. He knew that the painting was genuine. He had looked at it for years, treasured it, admired it, petted it

511

like a favourite child. It had never been a follower's work. It had been painted by the Master's hand. And he had sold it short. Confused and panicked, he had listened to a cheat and been treated as a fool.

'You need to get away from here,' Marshall said, breaking into his father's reverie.

'It's jinxed.'

'What?'

'The gallery,' Owen said softly. 'When I bought it, I knew about the rumours. Nothing succeeded here for long. People came and went. Perhaps there *is* a ghost . . .'

'Bullshit.'

To Marshall's surprise, his father laughed. 'I wish I was like you, Marshall. I really do.'

'I always wished I was more like you,' his son said honestly, touching his father on the shoulder. 'We could go to Thurstons tonight—'

'I can't,' Owen cut in hurriedly. 'I can't just run away.'

'But if you got away you'd clear your head.'

Owen sighed. 'There are things to do. I have to see to a few things here before I can leave.'

'All right,' Marshall agreed finally. 'Then let me stay here and help.'

'No,' Owen replied, straining to smile. 'I should never have got you involved. It's not your worry, I just panicked, that's all. You're right, Marshall, there *is* a lot of stock; perhaps I can raise enough to pay back some people.'

'What about asking the bank for a temporary loan? Just to tide you over?'

Mirthlessly, Owen laughed. 'They didn't seem to think I was a good bet.'

'Then let me go and talk to *my* bank.'

'No,' Owen said, almost harshly. 'Leave it be, Marshall. Just talking to you has helped. I'll go through the stock tomorrow and draw up some figures. There are some people I can talk to . . .' He trailed off, looking around him. 'The Rembrandt would have sorted all this out, paid back all my debts. It sold for a *fortune*, did I tell you that?'

Surprised, Marshall nodded. 'Yes, Dad, you told me.'

'Manners cheated me.'

'So why don't we confront him together?'

His face set, Owen shrugged his shoulders. An odd gesture, resigned and feckless at the same time. 'What's done is done. I know this business, I made enough money out of it myself—'

'Not by cheating people.'

'No,' Owen agreed. 'And not by cheating friends.' He paused, then straightened up, smoothed his hair, his urbane charm restored. 'It might not be hopeless.'

'Are you sure that there's nothing I can do?'

'Nothing,' Owen said calmly. 'You go to Thurstons and I'll come at the weekend.'

Marshall nodded. 'I've some business to see to first, but I'll come back and we'll go together. OK?'

'OK, OK.'

513

Relieved, Marshall touched his father's arm. 'When you get away from here you'll feel different, I promise. It will all be different by the weekend.'

MEMORY OF BONES

Alex Connor

A ruthless collector in New York.
A scandalous son of the Ortega family.
A killer hired by the most dangerous man in London.

They've nothing in common, except the skull of Goya: one of art's most coveted lost artefacts.

And the fight to gain ownership of it . . . whatever the cost.

Quercus
www.quercusbooks.co.uk

ALSO AVAILABLE

LEGACY OF BLOOD

Alex Connor

The competition is raging.
The conspiracy is emerging.
The body count is rising.

A Hogarth artefact – as mysterious as it is priceless – is being flown
to London. Many collectors would kill to have it in their possession.

As will the figure who wants to keep its secret hidden . . .

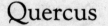

Quercus
www.quercusbooks.co.uk